The Aesthetics of Resistance
Volume 1

THE AESTHETICS OF RESISTANCE

Volume I

PETER WEISS

Translated by Joachim Neugroschel • With a foreword by Fredric Jameson & a glossary by Robert Cohen

DUKE UNIVERSITY PRESS *Durham and London 2005*

The publication of this work was supported
by a grant from the Goethe-Institut.

Printed in the United States of America on acid-free paper ♾
Typeset by Tseng Information Systems in Trump Mediaeval.
Library of Congress Cataloging in Publication data appear
on the last printed page of this book.
The Aesthetics of Resistance, volume 1, was originally
published as *Die Ästhetik des Widerstands*, volume 1
(Frankfurt: Suhrkamp Verlag, 1975).

Contents

Foreword: A Monument to Radical Instants

Fredric Jameson

The Aesthetics of Resistance, Peter Weiss's three-volume historical novel about the struggles of the German Communist anti-Hitlerian networks from 1937 to the end of World War II, marks a powerful intervention in German historiography, or more precisely into the sense of history and the construction of the past in which Germans and leftists of the last decade of the Cold War still lived: an intervention felt in both the German West and the German East (it was published in both countries) and cutting across, while acknowledging, the sterile polemics about Stalinism still current in that period. Posthumously (Weiss died six months after the publication of the final volume in 1981), it now has a significant role to play in the historicity a united Germany must construct in order to incorporate the experience of the German Democratic Republic—a problem distantly comparable to the intellectual and historiographic appropriation of the complex and varied life world of the conquered South after the American Civil War. The new Germany is necessarily in search of a new vision of its own past, at the very moment when History, which will not stop for that effort of Hegelian *Er-innerung* and reconstruction of collective identity, is about to absorb Germany and its neighbors into some new and larger, transnational unity (at the same time that it threatens to annul even the autonomy of that new unity into the even larger networks of an all-subsuming late capitalist globalization).

But this is not merely a local German agenda: such dilemmas also confront the Left in general in the world today; and the modification of Germany's sense of its own radicalisms and revolutionary impulses must necessarily contribute to the reconstruction of a worldwide left vision of its vocation and its possibilities in a seemingly post-revolutionary world situation in which capitalism and the ever-expanding penetration of the free market are commonly felt to be henceforth unchallenged. But the failure of the reconstruction of the former DDR means that some future German radicalism will emerge in unexpected forms from those conquered provinces, and emerge without warning, like all great revolutionary moments, very much according to Benjamin's messianic figures: "Every second of time is the strait gate through which Messiah may enter."[1] Thus here too the messianic preparation for a rebirth of the Left in Germany, and out of its older revolutionary traditions, stands as an allegory for the Left in general: Stalin, the cultures and strategies of Soviet Communism, the Leninist dimension itself, will never be reborn, nor is such a rebirth even desirable for revolutionary impulses (such as those depicted in Peter Weiss's novel) which deplored, feared, and loathed so many of the things associated with the old Soviet Union; but it will only be out of an unflinching contemplation of the past, an *acknowledgment* of it (to use Stanley Cavell's keyword), that the radical Novum of some new political and revolutionary movement can surge, unrecognizable, and seemingly without warning. But this contemplation is not required in order to "learn from the past and avoid its mistakes"—a silly notion at best; nor either to "make amends" and confess the guilt of the Stalinist period—for guilt is both a paralyzing impulse and a task in which, if properly considered, virtually everyone in the world might well be involved. Rather, just as in the familiar dialectic of the Communist period (reflected over and over again in the endless discussions and debates throughout *The Aesthetics of Resistance*), for which the defense of the Soviet Union was both impossible and unavoidable, so now the idea of the Soviet period, the memory of that immense historical experience, brooks no detour, even though there can be no reassuring way of "coming to terms with it." Such a confrontation with the past must also necessarily include the resistance to it and the disgust with which (West) German readers today greet the older political literature of the West German Gruppe 47 pre-unification writers,[2] as well as that which postmodern readers in general bring to the now dead past of the interwar years and of World War II—a boredom sometimes mingled with curious stabs of nostalgia, and strengthened by consumerist habits for which the outmoded and the old-fashioned are somehow more intolerable than the palpable shoddiness of much of what is truly contemporary. There is no right way of dealing with the past—forgetfulness is no more therapeutic than a mesmerization by persistent trauma; but history is not made up of passing fashions which you are free to discard or replace. Still, the afterlife of Peter Weiss's novel can be explained by the historically modified role it is called upon to play in this new post–Cold War period, so different from the still feverishly political situation of the early German 1980s. This is the excuse (along with the unfamiliarity of the work to readers outside Germany or Sweden) for adding a contemporary confrontation with this text to the already voluminous critical work on Peter Weiss.[3]

Yet the active intervention in the past, the return to the only too familiar dilemmas of a worldwide left politics in the Hitler era—but this time beyond the sterile alternative of apologia or strident anti-Communism—this is not the only vocation of this "novel," nor the only intellectual context in which its originality and power can be felt. The unavoidable references that have already been made to memory, collective and individual alike, remind us that for good or ill the last few years have known a feverish preoccupation with historical memory (and also autobiography), with mourning and melancholia, and finally with the Holocaust itself.[4] *The Aesthetics of Resistance* commemorates political failure and defeat, but scarcely overlooks the physical suffering and martyrdom that accompanied such defeat; and to this also it wishes to provide, not a monument of some sort (the question of monuments is also one of the burning issues of our period), but rather a machine for reliving that sheerly corporeal agony. This is not a testimony, either,[5] that witnesses might piously record and preserve: but rather an immediacy of the body and the anguished mind which we are ourselves called upon to retraverse by way of reading. It is a peculiarly juxtaposed set of materials: sparsely selected yet vivid landscapes along with interiors and rooms which have a different function; the visual lessons of many paintings; and finally the sheer suffering of bodies whose primary sexuality (chastely absent from these pages) is replaced by pain. Peter Weiss has his contribution to make to current theories of the body as well as to the varied figural or intellectual, or sometimes wordless or impossible, modes of approaching something like the Holocaust. Yet, this is not a book about the Holocaust, I think, although a place is made for that within it. Still, it would be enough to remember the critiques addressed to his Auschwitz play, *The Investigation*—that in it Jews were assimilated unacceptably to the other victims, most notably to Communists; that the event was thereby stripped of its uniquely Jewish meaning[6]—a reproach which can be prolonged to the *Aesthetics* as well (despite Peter Weiss's own half-Jewish origins)—to realize that the work cannot be claimed for Holocaust literature and the Holocaust tradition. But it certainly remains central to all the themes and theoretical questions raised by the debate over that literature, from that of the impossibility of representation all the way to that of the uses of memory.

The reconstruction of the past and of some future Left; the commemoration of the suffering of the dead—to these projects must be added another, already registered in the title: yet *The Aesthetics of Resistance* is not so much a contribution to aesthetic theory as rather the working out of an aesthetic pedagogy. For this is also a *Bildungsroman*, in which a young German worker learns a politics of resistance in the vicissitudes of history, but also appropriates a whole aesthetic culture, which is meant to complete that first and political education and which may in many ways even precede it and prepare the cultural (and dare one even say, in keeping with the German context, "spiritual" [*geistig*]) receptivity for those more pragmatic lessons and dilemmas. Famously, it is with a visit to the Pergamum altar by three schoolfriends that the novel begins: the first form of physical suffering in these pages is that of tortured statuary—the agony of the Titans crushed by the Olympians; the first political lesson is a mythological and aesthetic, an imaginary one—the vision of defeat, the triumph of the Olympian rulers over the rebellious demigods. The first step in this aesthetic pedagogy, in this aesthetic formation of the subject, is thus one of "a massacre impenetrable to the thought of liberation":[7] a seemingly frustrating and paralyzing first step.

Yet this is a proletarian *Bildungsroman*, a pedagogy of the subaltern: and it is worth remembering that, of the hundreds of characters who people this vast novel, only three are fictional: the unnamed narrator and his parents. All the rest are real historical figures on whom Weiss did voluminous research. Nor should we forget that these three central fictive characters are only objects of autobiographical identification in a severely mediated way: for Peter Weiss was a bourgeois and his father a business manager. It would be abusive to suppose that the novelist was free to transpose his own experiences effortlessly into those of a fictive youth, who just happened to be a working-class subject growing up in a working-class neighborhood. The debates that have swirled around Proust's fictional description of heterosexual love from a supposedly homosexual standpoint[8] ought to find their resonance and their analogy here, if we assume that this representation is also simply the description of an already existing experiential state of things or state of mind.

But the pedagogical framework, if it means anything at all, means that we have to do here not with a state of things but with an emergence and the modification of all such previous "states": this is a self-fashioning, a construction of subjectivity, in which the subject attempts to master and reappropriate even those blows from outside which might ordinarily be thought to be beyond his control. He is to do this through art and culture, and, collectively, with his fellows and a few teachers (Brecht as well as the psychiatrist Hodann), to construct a new education for himself and for them. Politically and theoretically, of course, this pedagogical framework takes a philosophical position, which is recognizably that of certain new or oppositional Marxisms which have asserted the indispensability of consciousness and culture over against the reductions by a mainstream of praxis to the economistic and the narrowly political-ideological.

Yet this is not merely a philosophical or an intellectual position: it has its symbolic working-through in the concrete process of reading itself. For whatever the value of such pedagogical demonstrations for a properly working-class or subaltern public itself (and it may be safely assumed that today the afterlife of *The Aesthetics of Resistance* is more secure in the former East Germany than in the old Bundesländer)—and whatever the implications for a socialist state in these new proposals for an *Erbe* and a new cultural tradition, and in particular for the hotly debated question of the appropriation or not of the bourgeois artistic tradition, not to speak of the precapitalist ones—it must also be remembered that we—the new current readership—are ourselves mainly middle-class people, formed under capitalism. Peter Weiss's personal effort of an imaginative self-projection into the *Bildung*-situation of a working-class protagonist from the 1930s is thus itself an allegory of our own possibilities of imaginative sympathy as readers of this text: it is his mediation that can alone make our own reading possible; even though one also wishes to reassert Sartre's famous insistence on the incomparable richness imposed on texts and narratives which cannot avoid addressing two distinct publics, two distinct readerships.[9]

Yet to all these programs must be added a final one, a formal project this time, quite different in its problems and obstacles from any which have been mentioned thus far. For this is also a historical novel, and it must somehow confront and solve in new ways all the dilemmas which the newly emergent genre of the historical novel has had to grapple with at least since its first codification by Sir Walter Scott. Yet despite this respectable generic cover, apologists for the work have been remarkably defensive. Thus it has become conventional to begin discussion of *The Aesthetics of Resistance* by acknowledging its formal peculiarities: Manfred Haiduk calls it a "Monstruum"; Robert Cohen suggests that, of the three volumes, only the last is really a novel; and so on.[10] Formal innovations no doubt always make for problems and difficulties in reading: but it can happen, more rarely, that the formal innovation lies far more centrally in the demand for a new reading practice. This was the case with the *nouveau roman*,[11] whose experiments with what is called "real time" in the media will be suggestive here; and it is also and preeminently the case with Peter Weiss, even though the innovation his book proposes is utterly different in meaning and spirit from theirs.

On completing his violin concerto, Schoenberg is said to have exclaimed, "Now they will have to invent a completely different way of playing the violin." But I believe that a true avant-garde is characterized not merely by a modification in the way a work is constructed or executed, but also by a program of changes for its reception (it is true that the performing of an already written musical score lies somewhere in between these poles, which are often thought of as active and passive). New kinds of perception, new forms of listening attention, are explicitly demanded, along with the new material or content, the new formal structures, of the "text" in question. These programs then allegorically project the vision of a new community organized around them, so that while the essentially collective production of a given avant-garde is necessary in order to mark a given aesthetic moment as such, it is not sufficient. In this spirit, the *nouveau roman*, whose collective character as a "school" is in any case relatively dubious, is at best a borderline case.

Peter Weiss, to be sure, reflected throughout his life and work on the possibility of an avant-garde, both artistic and political; but one may say, following the Deleuze of the film books (for whom political films are defined as such precisely by the absence of community and praxis), that that work, relatively solitary in its emergence, even though it is marked by collaboration and collective performance, mourns the loss of the possibility of an avant-garde more than it manages to reinstate one.[12] Comparable in that perhaps only to the expressionist group COBRA, his essentially late modernism attempts to repeat one of the earlier, now classical forms of the modern, but where the great majority of this production finds its coordinates in the "great moderns"—non-avant-gardists, writers of a solitary book of the world,[13] like Joyce or Mallarmé—Weiss still thinks in terms of movements, like surrealism and experimental film. In that, it is worth underscoring the analogies between Weiss and another immense yet unclassifiable figure of the postwar, who also tried to "reconcile" art and politics, Marx and Freud, sexual revolution and social revolution. Pier Paolo Pasolini was if anything even more of a loner than Peter Weiss, projecting his vision of the collectivity back into the myths and rituals of premodern villages and tribes, as supremely in the *Medea* (1970), with its cannibalism and magic, and its lament for the modern "desacralization" of the world (the centaur teacher Chiron first appearing as centaur, then in modern dress clothes on two legs—because we moderns have lost the framework in which we believe in centaurs). But I want to underscore a more basic analogy between Pasolini and Weiss—both otherwise incomparable, and Weiss virtually without any national tradition of his own—contemporaneous with the Beats, but here too without any genuine similarities, nor can I think of any other figures to compare them with. What they shared formally, besides the themes I have mentioned, is that crude hacking simplicity of the pedagogue who initiates forms, who feels no particular respect for a series of formal exercises or innovations, but chops into the medium in order to convey a point which would be unsophisticated and programmatic in the form of a philosophical position[14]—as for example—the juxtaposition of Marat and Sade themselves, or the thesis on magic I have just alluded to in Pasolini's *Medea*. Add to this the reliance on preexisting texts—most often documents, in the case of Weiss, rather than myths or the tales of the *Decameron* or *The Arabian Nights*, in that of Pasolini.

I have indulged this comparison in order to position Weiss in the postwar period, in a framework a little wider than the merely German one. The politics of both figures would merit attention, but for our purposes it suffices that alongside the reinvention of a kind of avant-garde art, both were passionately nostalgic for a vanguard politics as well, and both keenly attentive to the sexual liberation of the 1960s and 1970s. Pasolini's work is however drenched in sexuality from the very beginning, in contrast to the relative chastity of *The Aesthetics of Resistance* (which would have to be juxtaposed to the sexual themes of the earlier works, along with the emblematic figure of Sade himself).

Yet in Pasolini, as with COBRA, a preoccupation with history takes the form of the archaic and the mythic, and expresses the conviction that collective life can only be glimpsed, let alone recaptured, by a return to pre-capitalist societies, from the astonishing rituals of Medea's tribal society all the way up to Boccaccio or *The Arabian Nights*. Contemporary works, such as *Theorema* (1968), are framed politically—the factory owner's gift of the factory—but in programmatic or utopian ways; even the early images of Roman low life and Pasolini's favorite *Lumpen* exclude the perspective of a historical interpretation and causal analysis of the recent past.

Weiss is thus alone, among the late modern writers (not to speak of overtly postmodern ones) to confront the dilemmas of the historical novel as a form; and this in so uncompromising a fashion as to demand a thoroughgoing (and, as has been seen with the critics, often a so perplexing) revision of conventional narrative and representational techniques. This is not to ignore the moments of narrative bravura of an older modernist style: as, for example, the great cross-cutting montage at the end of volume 1, in which the show trials and the execution of Bukharin alternate in dramatic Sartrean fashion with Hitler's *Anschluss* of Austria and the feverish discussion of the foreign militants on the rapidly deteriorating Republican front of the Spanish Civil War (253–68/288–304). Nor must we forget Brecht's flight from Sweden at the end of volume 2, during which, "collapsing on the gangplank, between the German embassy building, on the left, and the German freighters flying the swastika, on the right, he had to be virtually carried on board" (2:331): all this preceded by an extraordinary comic sequence in which, visited by the Swedish secret police, who examine his library, Brecht celebrates their departure by pelting them with Edgar Wallace and Agatha Christie paperbacks from a second-story window. Yet such narrative set-pieces are inevitably affairs of beginnings and endings, whose unique tempos call forth the architectonic as such, the grand arabesque which is construction fully as much as decoration.

Otherwise this ostensible story of the teeming and dramatic events of the onset of World War II is conveyed by way of endless conversations and debates about political positions and strategy, housed in a strangely abstract space, whose very lyrical openings—onto the orange groves of Valencia, for example—at once turn into historical and economic disquisitions on the region and its agricultural characteristics. This is decidedly not the kind of vivid representation of the experience of history we have been trained to expect from fiction: with signal exceptions—the rather painterly account of the Bremen uprising of 1919, not to speak of the grisly step-by-step description of the executions of the last of the resistance network in Plötzensee, about which one could to be sure argue that such corporeal vividness is achieved primarily by way of its contrast with the time of discussions and debates, a time of waiting and of enforced passivity, in which history can only arrive in the form of news and rumor—historical events are here for the most part mediated, and "represented" at best second-hand, by way of a weighing of the conflicting evidence and a sifting of detail. Still, and particularly since the *nouveau roman* has been fleetingly evoked above, it is worth registering a similarity between the passage of historical time in this novel by Peter Weiss and the scoring and registering of reading time I have elsewhere described for a (nonhistorical) novel by Claude Simon[15] (a novelist to be sure equally obsessed with history, but in a far more experiential way, and through deep memory and repetition). In *Les Corps conducteurs* a narrative apparatus is constructed in such a way that the time of reading has been dissociated into two distinct registers: on the one hand the time of the individual sentences and words, the microscopic fragmented perceptions we receive one after the other, up very close, in proximate vision and magnified reception; and the time of the pages and of the book itself, which slowly runs out, irreversibly and surely, irrespective of the minute content of the present of the words themselves. The clock is ticking, one wants to say, or better still, the meter is running: the page numbers are still changing, piling up, no matter how intolerably paralyzed or suspended we seem to be in an endless reading present. So in Weiss also: the time of history continues, despite these endlessly suspended arguments and exchanges out of time. Spain is slowly and irrevocably lost; the German armies inexorably colonize Europe; the war itself at length draws to a close—despite the agonized fixation of the characters upon their positions and perplexities, their ideological clashes, and their interrogation of the demands of the concrete situation itself, an interrogation which must remain abstract and a matter of thinking and argument, however urgent and particular the dilemma, which is in any case bound to be overtaken by events and transformed into a new and utterly different one. What can account for such a radical and seemingly perverse choice of narrative strategies, whose massive preponderance throughout these nine hundred pages goes well beyond any reasonable intention to bring out and articulate the ideological and philosophical issues at stake in the war itself?

To be sure, *Marat/Sade* is there to remind us, if need be, of the dichotomous nature of Peter Weiss's conceptual imagination: everywhere in his work, forces and positions are defined by way of oppositions, from which the great political divergences of the Comintern and antifascist periods can scarcely be expected to be exempt. One imagines serious historians attempting to be even-handed, and to do justice even to the reasonings and motivations of those on the "wrong" side (here primarily the Stalinists and the orthodox party members, since, as in Malraux, the fascists and the Nazis are rigorously excluded from this cast of characters). Still, the discourse of the historians is fatally monological, as Bakhtin might have said; and any empathetic reconstruction of Stalinism is bound to be a set-up, in which the foreknowledge of historical failure and revelation to come cannot but influence the drift and the outcome. Nor is Weiss above the fray himself: as has been said, the pedagogical focus secures an option for cultural politics which will be incorporated in the doomed yet larger than life figure of Willi Münzenberg—supreme genius of Communist agitation and world propaganda in the Poular Front period, hunted pariah in the first years of the war, when his body will be found hung from a tree in a French forest during the exodus. Hodann, the Reichian psychiatrist, who insists on the place of sexuality and the transformation of daily life in the midst of any committed politics, offers a realist and approachable analogue in the personal experience of the narrator. Yet even these passionate commitments (which are unmistakably those of Peter Weiss himself) cannot be expressed, let alone validated, without an argument with the opposite side; they have to emerge in struggle with persuasive adversaries, who sensibly and reasonably insist that the revolution must first be defended and secured against a frightening array of dangers and enemies, before the luxury of full personal and social liberation can be indulged. Finally, neither side wins these ideological battles; but each needs the other to achieve full expression and historical representation.

We may enumerate some of these oppositions, which are related but not identical. Clearly the great schism and opposition between German Social Democracy and the Communist movement (inside and outside Germany) will be a central preoccupation: in a scene on a bench in Paris during the 1930s, the narrator's father takes the position of disillusioned Socialists, while Herbert Wehner argues a Communist one (the narrator must himself reenact the argument with his father as he draws closer to the party). In Spain, to be sure, it is anarchism which becomes Communism's ideological adversary, and whose leaders and spokespersons are one by one physically eliminated.

Yet in a work whose palpable aesthetic preoccupations have not yet sufficiently been outlined, there will also be artistic oppositions, which are argued out fully as much in aesthetic as in political terms: most obviously that between modernism and realism, in an immense movement in which the deciphering of the utopian and social impulses at work in modern art will be matched by a faithfulness to the most neglected monuments of a genuine social or socialist realism. We will return to this, the narrator's aesthetic education, in more detail later on.

Yet this opposition inevitably generates that other one of which we have already spoken, which is related but not the same: the Münzenberg position on cultural politics, as it confronts the more military or sheerly political, resolutely non-aesthetic, strategies of others in the Communist movement. Hodann is then there to secure the modulation of this theme into the Reichian one of sexual politics as over against the conventional Left.

Finally, in a very different register there is the opposition of the father to the mother: the first a locus of historical working-class memory (the Bremen uprising), now withdrawn from current struggles; the mother sinking into a visionary and nightmarish schizophrenia, into a stubborn silence and mutism, born of the trauma of the collective agony and displacement by the Nazi armies and finally by the rumors of the death camps themselves; the father obsessed by the "machine" of this society. Both are thus locked in the past, but in active and passive registers respectively; the one brooding over the failures of praxis, the other immobilized by intense and vivid physical suffering relived over and over again. The narrator will unite these two registers, but overcome them in some new and future-oriented way, offering the promise—if not yet the image or representation—of the possibility of productively combining agency and mourning. Yet to all these we must finally add that opposition in which we ourselves share as readers: namely, that between bourgeois and proletarian experience, in which the whole notion of subalternity necessarily appears; the lack of access to this or that mainstream culture, the way in which mainstream (or bourgeois) culture is marked as belonging to others, and to some inaccessible upper-class or privileged elite, the sheer physical obstacles, finally, to the acquisition of culture by working people who have no leisure for its acquisition, or even for the acquisition of its preconditions. All of this is given to us in the account of the narrator's *Bildung*, and in the harsher reactions of his family and fellows to an alien culture whose overt ideologies are often either privatized or aestheticized, if not openly those committed to oppression or repression—as at the very outset the glorification of the conquering Olympians in the Pergamum altar. This is an issue which, as we shall see, will lead to a hermeneutic deciphering far more complex than anything deployed in an exclusively bourgeois context.

It would flatten out the specificity of all these issues and oppositions to resume them under the great antithesis of politics and art, which is nonetheless inscribed in its fashion in the very title of the work, and which is certainly one of the fundamental themes under which this work was composed. Yet it is always worth remembering Adorno's remark—it being understood that in the twentieth century art itself is bound up with the problem of the avant-garde—that people today cannot imagine the degree to which, before the break of Stalin's socialist realism in the early 1930s, the two avant-gardes were absolutely linked, and the fortunes of avant-garde art were never felt to be dissociated from those of vanguard politics (something Perry Anderson also points out for artistic modernity in a famous essay).[16] For us, or at least until very recently, when it is vanguard politics that has seemed to vanish, it was the other way round; and the various Western traditions have all seemed to insist on the way in which vanguard art—mostly conceived as modernist poetry—finds its precondition in an absolute separation from the political or from "social issues." But Peter Weiss was one of the rare late-modern artists who refused this separation; and who tried, virtually by fiat and by an effort of the will, to put the two vanguards back together (as early as *Marat/Sade*), his originality having been the sense that dilemmas and contradictions relate fully as much as they separate, and that to impose the problem of the two avant-gardes is also at least partially to overcome it.

But we have not yet replaced these forms and materials within the problematic of the historical novel as such, whose dilemmas—duly registered at the birth of this form of genre, and belatedly codified by Lukács in his *Historical Novel*[17]—can only be intensified in modernity with its demographic increase in technological innovations. Even the "traditional" historical novel, however, was inscribed at the center of two irresolvable oppositions or contradictions, which only palliatives (like Lukács's "average hero" or observer) could weaken in such a way as to allow the novel to be written in the first place.

The first of these axes, unsurprisingly, is the opposition between the individual and the collective, or, better still, that between individual or existential experience and that dimension of collective reality inscribed in institutions, as what Sartre calls the practico-inert, in economics and the market as well, which finally and necessarily transcends all individual categories.[18] It is important to disjoin this problem from the act of witnessing as such,[19] even though the same impossibilities reign in that more restricted and specialized form of experience as well: for who has ever seen the depression, or the market system, or the nation-state? who has ever seen war as such?—something not to be restricted to the witnessing of a battle (even though Stendhal famously, and very early in the career of the historical novel as a form, inscribed even that impossibility in his historical narrative of the "experience" of the battle of Waterloo).[20] One is tempted to suggest that this is something of a spatial dilemma, with its temporal analogy in the individual biological life span equally out of synchrony with the great waves and rhythms of properly historical change.

Yet in modern history there have been rare moments in which the antithesis between the existential and the collective seems to have been transcended, if not overcome. These are not battle scenes, although for the bourgeois reader the battle offers their most accessible analogy, other versions being ideologically subsumed under the stereotype of mob violence (even though it might also be added that for Americans World War II has sometimes seemed to offer a "moral equivalent"). The strong moment, however, clearly remains the experience of revolution, with its lower-order forms in the general strike and the mass rally or demonstration. Were we speaking ontologically here, I would want to argue that precisely in such moments the isolated being of the individual subject is heightened and dissolved, lifted up and transfigured, into a kind of collective being of a fleeting or ephemeral type, which nonetheless left political theory has always attempted to re-create in the concept and to prolong in new institutional arrangements (the "construction" of socialism as a temporal process, for example, rather than the actual institutions of some achieved socialism). Certainly Peter Weiss was fascinated by such moments, as the father's narratives of the Bremen uprising testifies (1:86–87/1:100–106), and as the two emblematic novels also show, on which the narrator meditates at some length: Kafka's *Castle* and the less well-known *Barricades in Wedding* by Klaus Neukrantz, a proletarian work from the 1920s which tells the story of an ill-fated Berlin uprising. These two works—for the bourgeois reader clearly of unequal value—dramatize the classic philosophical opposition between the making and what is made in the realm of history: reified structure from the outside, the dynamic historical process of struggle and collective resistance from the inside.

But they also problematize any contemporary effort to reinvent the great collective scenes through which a Scott or a Manzoni, and later on a Victor Hugo or a Flaubert, attempted to dramatize history and make it visible to the individual reader/witness. Such scenes, rare and precious enough in literary history, and generally (as has been observed above) subsumed under this or that ideology of the mob famously codified by LeBon and Freud, wager their stakes on the possibility of a kind of collective narration, one which is not exactly impersonal or omniscient, but rather somehow extrapolated from extinct or nonexistent grammatical and verbal categories such as the dual: a kind of "man" or "on" (to appropriate Heidegger in his German and French versions, English having no equivalent) which, far from being the realm of the inauthentic, would offer a glimpse of the truly collective itself as it is momentarily revealed to be the demiurge of what we call history.

But demography and globalization mean that today this fiction of a truly collective narrative—or at least of a truly collective narrative moment—can no longer be sustained: it would be the worst sort of allegory to imply that this or that local street fight can truly stand in for the collective process (or if you prefer, can in the present situation convince us that genuine revolution is still conceivable, let alone possible). It is therefore not on the level of a linguistic innovation or a language experiment that Peter Weiss can resolve the formal problem of collective representation: the opposition between the isolated individual and collective history will certainly be inscribed here, over and over again, in the physical separation and loneliness of the individual militants and in the great collective forces at work beyond them, in Moscow or Berlin. But it is the form of the work as a whole that tries to convey the dilemma (and thereby negatively to offer its very representation).

The formal contradictions of the historical novel can, however, also be registered in a different way, in the opposition between power and its effects: but this is already a system which implies a frame, an extreme situation, such as war or revolution, since normally the locus of power is less visible and more difficult to anthropomorphize. Kings and queens, presidents, leaders, and bosses continue to exist in peacetime, but their real control over events, and above all their relationship to the functioning of a given social system itself, with its inequities and uneven privileges, its chances and its sacrifices, is less plausible, and certainly harder to dramatize. Even Hegel's concept of the "world-historical individual" is an intermittent one, its appearance dependent on the capacities for change inherent in a given moment of the system itself. Still, the aporias of such peacetime representations of power persist over into the crisis situations themselves, when these are interrogated with sufficient formal intensity.

If we look, indeed, more closely at the existential reality of decision-making, or of what is today loosely called power, it becomes evident that it is a diminished or impoverished situation which at its outer limit resolves into a room or a communications center with banks of telephones and the entrance and exit of innumerable messenger-bureaucrats. The dictator, at the center of this web, experiences very little in immediacy; everything is mediated to him (for example, it is said that in his early years of power, Stalin depended on his first wife, still a student, to tell him what was going on in the outside world and what his subjects were thinking and saying).[21] Far from being a full center on the order of Hobbes's sovereign, made up of innumerable little human beings, let alone Borges's aleph or Dante's ingathered Book, the center of power is existentially empty, and the attempt to represent it must at best fall back on conjectural psychology: as witness the innumerable debates about Hitler's real motives or intentions—debates which either move in the direction of psychosis or childhood trauma or, on the other hand (as most memorably in A. J. P. Taylor),[22] decide to reduce this figure to a conventional German statesman, with fully rational plans, projects, and war aims. Thus, for Lukács, the "world-historical individual" must never be the protagonist of the historical novel, but only viewed from afar, by the average or mediocre witness (that such a figure can on the other hand be the center of historical drama, for Lukács, is explained by the fact that in that case it is we, the spectators, who are the witnesses, and who continue to observe the world-historical gestures and utterances from outside).

It was the originality of Solzhenitsyn to have grasped this, in *The First Circle*, and in a memorable scene to have given us an unaccustomed portrait of the dictator in his solitude:

> And he was only a little old man with a desiccated double chin which was never shown in his portraits, a mouth permeated with the smell of Turkish leaf tobacco, and fat fingers which left their traces on books. He had not been feeling too well yesterday or today. Even in the warm air he felt a chill on his back and shoulders, and he had covered himself with a brown camel's-hair shawl.
>
> He was in no hurry to go anywhere, and he leafed with satisfaction through a small book in a brown binding. He looked at the photographs with interest and here and there read the text, which he knew almost by heart, then went on turning the pages. The little book was all the more convenient because it could fit into an overcoat pocket. It could accompany people everywhere in their lives. It contained two hundred and fifty pages, but it was printed in large stout type so that even a person who was old or only partly literate could read it without strain. Its title was stamped on the binding in gold: *Iosif Vissarionovich Stalin: A Short Biography*.
>
> The elemental honest words of this book acted on the human heart with serene inevitability. His strategic genius. His wise foresight. His powerful will. His iron will. From 1918 on he had for all practical purposes become Lenin's deputy. (Yes, yes, that was the way it had been.) The Commander of the Revolution found at the front a rout, confusion; Stalin's instructions were the basis for Frunze's plan of operations. (True, true.) It was our great good fortune that in the difficult days of the Great War of the Fatherland we were led by a wise and experienced leader—the Great Stalin. (Indeed, the people were fortu-

> nate.) All know the crushing might of Stalin's logic, the crystal clarity of his mind. (Without false modesty, it was all true.) His love for the people. His sensitivity to others. His surprising modesty. (Modesty—yes, that was very true.)[23]

Here, then, the final form of this approach to the center brings us up short against a play of mirrors, and reality oscillates between its own reflections in some final static movement. It is as though Stalin himself became the reader in search for the ultimate representation; as though the emptiness of his own consciousness, his own *pour-soi* (an emptiness shared by all other human reality), incited him as well to substitute his own image for the missing self. The ultimate book within the book thus proves to be a children's biography, in which Stalin has turned into his own stereotype, power feebly and toothlessly attempting to find its own delectation in all that can be represented of itself. This extraordinary moment marks a kind of climax in the approach of the historical novel as a form toward its own limits and the impossibility of its representational aesthetic. After this the classical historical novel is at an end, and its world-historical individual must become an antihero.

This is the sense in which the most thoroughgoing and productive recodification of the larger form has been the new genre of the Great Dictator novel, most widely practiced in Latin America. But here what comes to the surface is the profound ambivalence of the figure, who fascinates at the same time that he repels. But it is a constitutive ambivalence which now reflects the geopolitical structure of the forms of power available for representation in the Latin American countries. For here the great dictator is still a monster, but one whose very inhumanity is required by the nature of the situation of sovereignty itself, that is to say, by the equally monstrous and overpowering presence of that force such a dictator can alone resist: namely, the United States.[24] Whence the mixture of admiration and loathing that these figures call up in the reader. From a structural point of view, however, this is the equivalent of saying that this particular center of power is ultimately not really the center, since its very power is ultimately not really the center, since its very power is reactive, and the true center lies elsewhere, to the North, remaining itself unrepresented.

We must thus appreciate in this light and context the wisdom of Malraux's choice, in his novel of the Spanish Civil War, *L'Espoir*, not to represent the enemy and not even to show fascist figures and protagonists as such, since the reader can have no real access to the Otherness of their evil, and thus at best risks a kind of mesmerized external fascination.

Camus's decision, in *La Peste*, to dramatize the occupation in terms of disease is clearly a more doubtful matter. This is also, as we have said, the case with *The Aesthetics of Resistance*, whose immense cast of (real, historical) characters remains limited to the Left, or to the various lefts within the antifascist movements.

Still, if the pole of power can finally not be represented, why should the same be true for the other pole of ordinary people, the subjects of power and the recipients of its effects? Why should some genuinely historical representation of daily life in a given crisis not be achievable? I think that this perfectly proper question also takes us to the heart of what is unsatisfactory in Lukács's more general notion of "typicality." But let me anticipate, and jump rapidly ahead in time to our own period, in order, by way of a form I have discussed in some detail elsewhere,[25] to show a kind of final formal outcome and a structural dilemma already implicitly in the earliest version of the historical genre.

For what "nostalgia film" shows us is that at the same time that history, the historicity of the various distinct historical pasts and periods, degenerates into visual images of itself—styles, pop music, appliances, clothing, hairdos, the furnishings of a given era—so also does the "knowledge" of historical events and the contents of historicity become degraded into the stereotypes of the simplified history manuals taught in the schools (or later on recycled through various television "instant replays"). This means that what we now take to be "typical" of a given historical period—its ideological preoccupations and struggles, characteristic events, the very kinds of people who populate its social space—are little more than stereotypes drawn from just such childhood reading as we found Stalin absorbed in. This is why "nostalgia films" fail to solve the older as well as the newer problems of historical representation (that they necessarily deal with historical materials is, however, constitutive of the "genre," if it may be called that). There is no novelty in the invention; we never encounter the contingent or the unexpected in such representations; and in that sense they fail to offer one of the basic pleasures of narrative form as such. And this is because we already know their content: their characters and events are always-already examples of a preexistent historical knowledge (or pseudo-knowledge). They must necessarily come before us as already familiar, since their validation as such depends on precisely such recognition by the spectator that, yes, that was what was happening in that particular period (the Roaring Twenties or the Great Depression)—I acknowledge that I recognize those "types" of characters, those "types" of events.

And this is the deeper reason why, at the pole of collective representation (as opposed to that of power or the state), the classic genre of the historical novel also confronts a fundamental dilemma: it must (insofar as it is also a novel) offer a narrative of individual lives and stories. But insofar as these stories are those of really individualized (that is to say, privatized) characters, there opens up here a realm of complete arbitrariness where the novelist's imagination reigns supreme. Yet this is to say that those private stories can be stories about anything: they are completely disengaged from their putative historical context; they could just as well furnish a contemporary novel as anything set in the past (once one removes the historical trappings, the costumes, the spatial layout, and the like). But insofar as those stories purport to entertain organic or constitutive links with a genuine historical situation, their motivation and their content will always reflect just that precooked stereotypical knowledge of a given past we have found to operate so close to the surface in postmodernity. "Typicality" in this sense is an unholy synthesis between a narrative particular and a conceptual (historiographic) universal; the latter tends fatally to transform the former into sheer example, thereby divesting it of its narrative immediacy.

Contemporary historical fiction will be authentic only if it confronts these contradictions and formal dilemmas in some energetic fashion that originates a formally innovative (if only provisional) solution. *The Aesthetics of Resistance* will never serve as a model for future historical representation; but nothing can do that anyway. Yet its structural novelties (so often, as has been seen, perceived as awkwardnesses or formal flaws or transgressions) can only be appreciated and evaluated in that light.

Peter Weiss's "solution" to these dilemmas—which is to say his intensified articulation of them—takes the form of a depersonalized collective voice which I will call a dialogical agon. It is a concept I want to model on that of a depersonalized individual subject whose forms one finds throughout contemporary literature, committed as it is to the theory and practice of a radically depersonalized consciousness beyond all individual identity and subjectivity: the famous "decentered subject" or "consciousness without the me" (Blanchot), sometimes illicitly celebrated in a rhetoric of the "death of the subject" or as an ideal schizophrenia (Deleuze), and to be found in all those enigmatic third persons of modern literature, more mysterious, as has so often been remarked, than any of its first-person characters, inasmuch as we can see and observe them, but must ourselves be confined to looking out through the gaze of this narrative one, which then takes on something of the unknowability of Kant's noumenal subject, always adding "the I to all its acts of consciousness," while itself remaining unknowable and inaccessible. Yet these approaches to some anonymous individual subjectivity, which has become depersonalized and inaccessible, owing to the movement of history, and about which it is never clear whether modern philosophy's varied efforts to do away with its illusions of subjectivity simply replicate the tendencies in late capitalist society or on the other hand propose energetic reactions to it, remain locked in the "philosophy of consciousness." They are so many descriptions of the monad, which variously attack Descartes or enlist new interpretations of him with a view toward undermining his subjectivist and idealist heritage. Nor is it surprising that this should be so: one does not break out of monadic isolation by the simple act of taking thought; one does not produce collective forms and experiences by fiat.

In any case, and for the very same reasons, we find it difficult to think the collective except as modeled on the individual: the much-decried slogan of "collective consciousness" remains in place, however much we wish to analyze collective dynamics in a fashion rigorously distinct from those of the individual. Greek choruses, depersonalized historical narrative, "subjects of history," myths and archetypes, banal allegorical "representatives" of group forces—such are the traps and failures which lie in wait for any narrative commitment to collectivity (nor are their traces absent from this novel either).

This is why it seems desirable to resurrect the program of a poststructuralist onslaught on individual consciousness—itself finally yet another avatar of an old individualist bourgeois subjectivity—and in particular to attempt to transfer its essential themes—decentering, depersonalizing, the notion that "identity" is an object for consciousness rather than its "subject," the materiality of a language which now "speaks us" rather than the other way around, the objectification of intention, the analytic dissolution of subjectivity into so many layers of stereotypes and of the inauthentic voices of a public sphere saturated with transpersonal information and images—to the new collective program.

Peter Weiss's conversations and debates—which take up so enormous a part of this three-volume novel—mark just such a new formal innovation; and if we read them as the interference of extraneous types of discourse—political commentary, philosophical argument, historical information; if we see the various interlocutors simply as so many mouthpieces for the author, or for the various ideological positions he means to represent—then we have let a constitutive tension go out of the reading, and it slackens into mere retrieval. Yet a new text cannot really impose its new form of reading on us (as Plato says, when its father is gone, it cannot reply; it merely offers mute silence to our questions and conjectures); the reader must somehow restore the impossible aesthetic imperative of this experiment in collectivity and must grasp every moment of the irresolvable conflicts as a movement of absolutes. This is to say that in these obsessive rehearsals of the past—mistakes, missed opportunities, necessary crimes, or accidental miscalculations—and in the anxiety-laden, fearful, and hopeful prognoses of the future that accompany them in the form of strategies and tactics, assessments and the helplessness of sheer lack of knowledge or information, throughout these exchanges in which language itself seems discredited by the facts of the past and the unpredictability of the future, the reader must at every point reconstitute a present.

I observed above that one of the temporal peculiarities of the text lay in an irreversible movement of history beyond the sterile opposition of fixed antitheses that never seemed to get off the mark: now we must add to that temporality the other related one, that history never exists in a past that preceded the current dilemmas or in a future in which they would be once and for all surmounted: it exists as sheer present in the heated disagreements of what may otherwise seem contingent circumstances and a merely particular content. Thus what is intolerable in these conversations is their very truth, aesthetic as well as historical: an eternity of debate and discord, a perpetual present of ideological passion and politicized consciousness. The reader is being trained to live within that present, already a modification of the traditional temporality of the novel and its readerly expectations. It will be interesting therefore to see how Peter Weiss can end his narrative (which began conventionally enough with the biological youth of his protagonist). History ends it to be sure but in some other, external way, which we know, but which is outside the text—as it is outside of and external to the characters and their debates about it.

Yet in another sense, such narrative resolution—or the illusion of such an impossible narrative resolution, as that generally presides over what is called fiction—has itself been drawn within the text, within the very content of the debates and arguments among its characters. For it is what is called *unity*, and all these verbal and ideological struggles turn on it in one way or another: since unity—or unification—is necessarily the most burning issue in all political theory which aims at action or praxis, rather than at simple rules for power or the analysis of power's mode of functioning in the status quo. It is this concentration on collective action (whether on the Right, as with Carl Schmitt or Hobbes, or on the Left, as with

Machiavelli or Lenin) which distinguishes the new science of politics that emerged in this century from the traditional bourgeois political philosophy into which it seems once more in the process of disappearing without a trace. And it is clear enough that its premise or fundamental starting point must be the question of unification—of which here the debates between Socialists and Communists offer only one empirical "example" and dramatization: for the end or aim can only emerge in the process of action itself; but action cannot begin until a unified agency is constituted: Gramsci's meditations on the "historic bloc," Laclau and Mouffe's theorization of a kind of momentary hegemonic constellation—so many diverse contemporary reflections on the unavoidable first step or principle of unity itself.

So it is that the urgency of the dialogical, about which I've argued elsewhere that it has to be conflictual and antagonistic, is fueled by a passion for a unity that can never come into being. Yet Bakhtin's supreme example was in any case Dostoyevsky, whose fevered debates between irreconcilable *Weltanschauungen* surely offer the model of a narrative pitched on this level beyond individual or the monadic. We have to invent a way of reading this text and in particular these endless dialogues as though politics had taken the place of Dostoyevsky's metaphysical passions, and as though each of these interlocutors had become a kind of vehicle for the absolute on the order of Dostoyevsky's figures.

But there is a dialectic at work in the raw materials themselves: such a radical formal modification in the role of dialogue and in the way in which conversation advances narrative events cannot leave the rest of the novelistic apparatus intact. If here conversation as such tends to become an event in its own right, and a unique historical event at that—some mixture of feverish waiting and frustration, of rationalization and hope—we would expect the other conventional features of the traditional novel to be modified accordingly. This is preeminently the case with space itself, whose new role in Peter Weiss we must now characterize.

The nature of this space will naturally enough be determined by the nature of the event—the ideological debate-discussion—that it houses and of which it then stands as a kind of abstract container. This space has already been alluded to metaphorically; it is none other than the room itself which for the most part bounds the events of this novel: where the room is replaced—the museum island in which the initial viewing and discussion of the Pergamum frieze is conducted, the park bench in Paris on which the narrator's father explores future political possibilities with Herbert

Wehner—these relatively more open, or at least opening, spaces mark a move toward the larger world, which will be identified in a moment.

Otherwise the room itself becomes a kind of absolute here: and that its essential form is abstract and utterly denuded is underscored for us in the opening section of the novel, where the kitchen takes on the traditional role of the place in which working-class families talk, assess situations, and make their decisions. Yet in this opening section (in which the narrator prepares to leave for Spain and the civil war) an even more fundamental process of stripping away and of abstraction down to an almost geometrical figure of extension is imitated, as it were, by the emptiness of the narrator's apartment, from which the parents have already left in flight to Czechoslovakia, taking all their furniture and belongings with them. Indeed, this moment of empty waiting, in anxiety and impatience in which one life is finished and another has yet to begin, proves to be an even more revealing form, an even more receptive vessel for the specific potentialities of the novel's categories of experience: for in this last night in Hitlerian Germany, the narrator dreams of an abolition of the room as such—the moldering corpse of his father (in reality still alive) shatters the floorboards, and the dreamer is allowed to float in oneiric suspension, like some of Chagall's flying figures, across the nightscape of Berlin. We will return to the significance of the oneiric in Peter Weiss later on: suffice it to say that if the sheerly dialogical agon is the strong form or category of experience here (with the abstract room as its correlative space of possibility), then there is a sense in which the oneiric is its other term, its opposite and its complement.

It may then be asked whether the oneiric in its turn has any specific spatial vehicle or vessel that is characteristic of its narrative operations, or whether in fact it is not precisely characterized by the utter absence of any such spatial container, being the radical opening up of all space. Yet there is such an alternate space within Peter Weiss's production in general, and that is painting as such, or at least painting as he conceived and practiced it. It would be a mistake to characterize these large figurative and nightmarish works as surrealist inasmuch as Peter Weiss, coming out of the German expressionist tradition, was for a long time suspicious of the French movement and only began to appreciate it after the war, at a time when he had virtually completed his work as a painter: still, the Max Ernst–style collages which he constructed later on are certainly in that second modernist tradition, at the same time that they offer a second mode of representation of the oneiric which is much closer to the collages of documentary raw materials which make up most of the plays as such (and whose research certainly underpins *The Aesthetics of Resistance*, even if it is not visible there). Peter Weiss himself associated the first figurative painting with Kafka, but we will see later on that this seemingly conventional reference has an unexpected specificity which tends to remove it from the stereotypically nightmarish.

This is obviously not the place to speak of Peter Weiss's considerable achievement as a visual artist: yet one further feature does demand mention in this particular context. It is the fact that he painted or drew virtually every room he dwelt in over the course of his life (and most of these representations have been preserved). The portrait of the room thus becomes a virtual genre in the framework of a work whose originality was, among other things, to have modified any number of traditional genres in idiosyncratic and profoundly meaningful ways. To memorialize your daily life in the form of the room is certainly to say something significant about that daily life; as I have suggested above, it is to produce a new category—and this Novum greatly outweighs the more conventional suggestion of an autobiographical sketch or note *pour mémoire*. Not to amass materials in view of some future account of a life, then, so much as to underscore some new conception of a life as the story of a movement from room to room; and this is precisely the conception—heightened by historical crisis and the convulsions of war—that we find in *The Aesthetics of Resistance*.

Once the new spatial category is set in place, its empty or abstract frame begins to evolve and to submit to all kinds of variations and developments in its content. It is as though the movement of the novel across space and through history offered some secondary and as it were philosophical advantage: to permit the interrogation of the category of the room from a variety of perspectives, to draw out its possibilities and dramatize the limits which not only inhere in it but also stand as its content. If indeed we follow Deleuze in thinking that a filmmaker or a painter also produces concepts as the philosopher does, yet in the distinctive and different nonconceptual form of their own media,[26] then indeed this series of rooms can be thought to be philosophical in its implications as well. The narrator himself directly reflects on these possibilities at the moment of leaving the last space he might have called "his": "Ownership molded the attitude that was taken toward things [in the bourgeois novel and its descriptions], while for us, to whom the living room never belonged and for whom the place of residence was a matter of chance, the only elements that carried weight were absence, deficiency, lack of property" (1:116/1:133–34; the whole passage is of the greatest interest).

So the very nature of the room will be modified in clandestinity: or better still, a deeper feature of the room not normally accessible to legal or bourgeois or peacetime perception will in the new crisis situation be brought out. One thinks, for example, of Rosner's room in Stockholm (2:176): the gnome-like militant becomes virtually a prisoner in a back room sealed off from the official "apartment" of his hosts (an illegal, he must avoid any notice by the Swedish authorities). Yet in this room (to which we will return) paradoxically his political task is the diffusion of information to Communist movements all over the world—his clandestine journal is the recipient and the source of worldwide knowledge in strict correlation and inversion to his own lack of mobility.

When one thinks of clandestinity in Nazi Germany itself, however, the figure of imprisonment becomes even more intense. Thus the spaces

through which Bischoff arrives back in Germany from Sweden: she spends three days and nights in the hold of the ship, and this new spatial modulation of room-like concealment has an unexpected result, a strange new ontological enhancement of her perception: "She perceived the whole ship, distinguished the directions of the footsteps, and whether a door had been opened or shut, when something was scraped or dragged, she recognized the movement of the lever of the mechanical telegraph, and adjusted to every maneuver of the ship itself. She rose through the ship, became it herself, heard its pulse and its shuddering in her ear, in her fingertips, her skin was at one with the vibrating metal plates" (3:73). This is in a sense an aesthetic apologia for the novel as a whole: how can one claim a generalized aesthetic interest for a work thus imprisoned in sensory privation as well as in the enforced lack of knowledge imposed by clandestinity? Yet in such a situation the signals from the outside become magnified, and their receivers undergo an unusual training in the decipherment of signs along with the apprehension of dangers. This is the perceptual world of *The Aesthetics of Resistance*; and we will have to see to what degree this simultaneous impoverishment and heightened sensibility figures in the larger picture of *Bildung* and proletarian cultural formation the novel means to propose.

Yet the final form of the room will clearly enough be the cell itself, and in this instance the death cell, from which the only spatial opening out is onto that covered inner courtyard in which the prisoners are hanged or guillotined: the novel itself wishes to be a different kind of opening in which their resistance and suffering finds memorialization and an active potential for energizing posterity.

These enclosed spaces, however, have their own specific dialectic: a

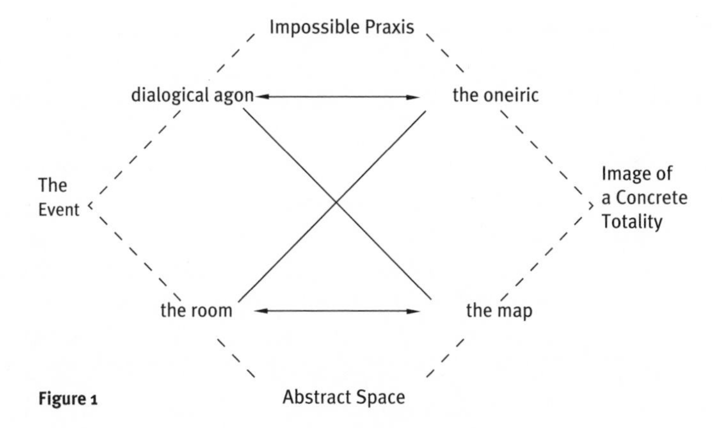

Figure 1

perception and a groping reading of the outside of them can themselves—a kind of blind cognitive mapping—only be organized by and projected onto some larger grid; just as the very movement of the clandestines from one room to another demands advanced planning and spatial foresight. The other pole of the closed room therefore turns out to be the urban map: mapped by foot by the clandestines as they move through Berlin (1:86–87/1:87–88), as they remember the topology of Bremen (1:89/1:97), or are treated exceptionally to an outside tour of Stockholm, like Bischoff during her provisional imprisonment (2:78–87). The narrator is able to juxtapose larger pieces of geographical space in his movement from Spain to Paris and then on to Sweden; but it is essentially the underground figure of Bischoff whom we accompany across the urban grid as such, returning with her first to Bremen and then to Berlin itself in wartime in the third volume of the novel (3:64, 158). We therefore confront a veritable system, which may be represented as shown in figure 1.

But we must not leave the matter of space without recording a further potentiality, and it is a rare moment of aesthetic flowering in the midst of the paralysis of collective action and the asphyxia of existential experience. We are in a room again, it is Rosner's, and one of the rare moments in which, besides the visits of the narrator (whose clandestine task it is to deliver information and remove copy from this frustrating "communications center"), two other important militants—Stahlmann and Arndt/Funk—join him for a truly conspiratorial discussion on the fate of the underground in Germany and the possibilities of action, at a time when the first rumor about the Holocaust and the fate of the Jews is beginning to emerge from the continent: "This room, three and a half meters long and two meters wide, as high as a shaft, with dusk gradually darkening the green lampshades (the shutters could no longer be opened)—this tomb was the headquarters of the Party in the underground, a provisional headquarters, only for a few hours, to be struck again as the various participants scatter to their own individual 'tombs'" (3:114). As the impossible conversation disintegrates without agreement or prospects, each of the three drifts off into his own private musings, Stahlmann to his experiences at Angkor Wat (to which a long chapter has already been dedicated), Arndt to his hobby of gardening, and Rosner losing himself in the Italian opera still quietly murmuring over the radio: "So, as I moved through the dawn to the train station, I took with me the picture of the three comrades, from out of their other existences, the unshakable spokesman of the Comintern paying homage to the art of song, the grim party organizer caring for his fragrant and decorative flowers, the man of war surrendering himself to a stone dancer on a frieze" (3:127). Nor should we forget the aesthetic fulfillment of the narrator as well, the would-be future writer, who has himself transformed this frustrating argument and fetid airspace for once into an aesthetic image—the very image of imaging itself.

Still, in the midst of these abstractions, characters remain and continue strongly to exist: that they are historical, and bear the names of real people, is no more relevant to their poetic or novelistic representation than the provenance of the names in Dante's *Commedia*. But no less relevant either: both works (Dante's being in a certain sense one of the models for this one) are prophetic investigations of History, which nonetheless rely on narrative techniques not greatly differing from what one finds in ordinary fiction. Yet as in Dante as well, these are not merely historical figures, who are present in the work on account of the purely empirical fact of their having existed in real history. Both works develop on the premise that empirical history also vehiculates transcendent meanings: and the characters thus somehow embody those meanings in what I hesitate (owing either to the frequency or infrequency of the uses of this term) to call allegorical. In *The Aesthetics of Resistance*, which also wishes to chart the *Bildung* of the proletarian student, militant, and author-to-be, they all have a function, which I want to outline briefly with respect to three of these supporting figures or characters.

Hodann begins the work and ends it: he summons the narrator to Spain to work in his clinic at the front, and the work closes, not so much with his death in Norway in 1946, after his break with the Party, as with his great speech at the end of the war, calling for unity once again and projecting a new kind of cultural politics (3:258), for which the term Cultural Revolution is perhaps not misplaced. For it is an essentially cultural politics that Hodann "represents" in this novel: behind him the dead figure of Münzenberg looms, the only truly world-historical figure celebrated in this novel, whose achievements in the enlargement of merely political propaganda to a Popular Front program of culture and the unification of left intellectuals and writers generally are nonetheless philosophically more restricted than what Hodann's program embodies.

As a doctor and a psychiatrist, Hodann allows the fundamental concern with healing to be introduced into the twin dynamics of civil war and class struggle. Following Reich, he insists on the ideologically baleful effects of sexual repression and the necessity to link political commitment with sexual liberation. More modestly, in the context of the Spanish Civil War, he underscores again and again the constitutive relationship between political melancholy—the crippling discouragement of the losers with their embattled positions both in Spain and in the larger international situation—and sexual deprivation. (Not coincidentally, the political work of the war's end and of the new postwar situation also begins with the soldiers: the German prisoners of war in Sweden will become the first new space in which a properly German radical political reeducation must begin [3:254, 262].)

Sexuality as a constitutive part of culture or of a revolution in consciousness: just as the narrower elements of the Party disregard and postpone genuine cultural questions, so in a context of left Puritanism generally (the revolutionaries themselves did not have the benefit of an already achieved cultural revolution), this emphasis on sexuality is even more scandalous and threatens a significant break: Stahlmann "brought along the magazine *La Voz de la Sanidad*, which had published an article by Hodann on sexual problems of soldiers in the war. Such a discussion, he said, was petty bourgeois; in a liberation struggle, such as was being waged in Spain, sexual needs had to be put last, and in a time like this it was not part of a physician's duties to deal with private matters" (1:228/1:260). But what Stahlmann calls private matters (*die Privatsphäre*) are in fact public ones, or such is the argument of Hodann himself. It is a discussion framed by anxieties and arguments around Stalin's trials, as well as around the execution of the POUM leaders: and in particular by an impassioned denunciation of what we would today call the sexism and patriarchal prejudices of the politburo itself, by a woman militant, Marcauer, who will later also be arrested (1:275/1:293).

Hodann is also to be sure a father figure for the narrator, who cannot be said to have had bad fathers, only insufficient ones; his own illness and chronic fatigue reinscribe the body in the form of political weakness and strategic lucidity ("pessimism of the intellect"): "Although Hodann staked everything on the bringing into reality of that democracy whose seeds had been laid in the German underground, he was also a seer, and an adept of human weaknesses and confusions, and it was this that suddenly brought him up short" (3:256)—not a fit of coughing, however, but a sobering sense of the postwar political program of the Party members returning from the East, and its continuity with the mistakes of the past he had so often denounced. The Hodann figure thus sets in place a profound materiality or physicality of culture at the same time as a premonition of the impossible dilemmas of this postwar left future (which is now our own past).

I have said that the framework of Peter Weiss's novel excludes fascism and the Nazi "point of view": now I must correct this assertion by identifying a major figure who had her moment of sympathy with the Nazi mass movement: for the task of an intelligent and thoroughgoing cultural-political strategy will be to seek to grasp the mass appeal of fascism with a view toward reappropriating its energies and its utopian impulse. But the Swedish writer Karin Boye also sets in place another dimension of sexual politics with the fact of lesbian desire, at that time irreconcilable with left politics and unthinkable in its context. Her suicide, in 1942, then poses yet a different kind of scandal for the political movement: namely, that of an overdetermination by political discouragement and the then impossible world situation, as well as by sexual misery and by personal guilt. This overdetermination itself poses a dilemma for the narrow political psychology of the time, whose horizons the novel can itself not transcend:

> It may be the case [Hodann said] that some people are dominated by the idea of an unbridgeable gap between art and political life, while for others art is precisely inseparable from politics. Maybe these were only different conceptions of the same basic matter, and those who thought that she did not fail on account of the pressure of external realities on art, but rather because of the damaged and diminished power to bring art, that is, autonomous thought, to bear on and to change a seemingly unshakable external reality itself—those people had perhaps thereby only made themselves a life preserver, in order to stay on the surface, whereas Boye could not stop herself from diving as deep as possible. (3:48)

Is this only to say that unlike Hodann, who constitutes a whole program for the future and for politics, whatever its immediate fate in the postwar period and the Communist movement as such, Boye is laid in place as an unresolvable contradiction, on some future agenda? To be sure, Peter Weiss's own program overtly calls for some new unification of art and politics, as has been said above; but the status of such a program or cultural politics within the work of art itself can equally well be served by failure as by success. To have shown the antagonism between these practices and axiological domains, to have articulated that tension in the form of a contradiction, this is also in some sense to solve it artistically: one recalls Hegel's doctrine about limits (he's thinking of Kant's rationally unknowable noumena and the alleged limits of Reason), that whoever traces a boundary line is already beyond it and has already begun to incorporate it. Here too, under certain circumstances, difference can unify or relate fully as much as sheer identification.

All of which is to neglect Karin Boye's art itself, which is equally reappropriated by the process of *Bildung* of the novel: her *Kallocain* is a kind of *1984* to be sure, or perhaps less anachronistically a kind of *We*, a political dystopia. But it is one of the rare modern dystopias to have been based on the Nazi rather than the Communist movement. This work (less well known outside Sweden) clearly marks the psychic liquidation of her 1930s fascination with Nazism (the search for a lost father, as Hodann diagnoses it [3:41]). The novel is a science-fictional depiction of a scientist who invents a truth serum in order to help the Absolute state abolish truth altogether. Yet this is a leap ahead into nightmare, which confronts Boye with a vision of a post-ideological conflict between two instances of state terror. As with the schizophrenic nightmares of the narrator's own mother, there is here set in place yet another vision of the future, along with another distinct discourse or mode of representation of such a future: the question of culture cannot be properly raised unless we mention both things, both dimensions—the form or language of the vision and its content. In any case, this ending, along with Boye's art, can provoke the same stupid and realistic, unavoidable questions that Hodann's therapies aroused: are such cultural productions energizing now, in the midst of crisis and struggle? where is the place for the negative in an embattled political culture?

These are questions then equally appropriate in the case of our final figure, Brecht himself, whose relationships to his own doubts and discouragements were notoriously far more tactical and Machiavellian than for either of the other figures. There is no doubt for many of us some great historical and literary satisfaction in this lengthy encounter with Brecht (whom Peter Weiss himself can only have glimpsed from afar during the former's brief stay in Sweden); whatever the accuracy of the portrayal, this is the section of the novel that comes the closest to the traditional pleasures afforded by the historical novel as a genre. The portrait has been described as a hostile one: besides Brecht's evasiveness about the Moscow trials, the presence of the various women is underscored, along with the rumors about them; and the narrator's own fictive role as a helper makes it clear enough how Brecht, to adopt a naïve American idiom, "uses people." Meanwhile, we have already observed his well-known physical cowardice and his disgrace at the end of volume 2, on his flight out of a Sweden now menaced by Nazi armies. No one would want to minimize these defects of character, for they are in fact precisely what fascinate us about Brecht and indeed, to be a little more provocative about it, what endear the personage to us. The Brecht we are shown here is not, however, the object of a satiric portrait but rather the space of literary and theatrical production itself. Peter Weiss uses this pretext to write or at least to imagine a project conceived by Brecht himself but never realized: an opportunistic project no doubt, for as an attempt to get his works performed in exile, Brecht always planned new works on the basis of national traditions (some were completed: *Herr Puntila* for Finland, for example; some left unfinished, as with *Der Brotladen* for the United States). The Swedish stay suggested a revolutionary episode from what we cannot too hastily call Sweden's middle ages (since alone of all the European countries Sweden never knew feudalism): rather a kind of first bourgeois uprising against the nobility in 1434, led by the serendipitously named Engelbrekt. The resultant sketch often sounds more like a Peter Weiss play than a Brecht one: tableaux, static speeches of ideological position, a seeming absence of those intricate and paradoxical exchanges in which Brecht inverts folk wisdom and common sense, cynically reifying the resultant maxim in a song placard or silent-filmic over-title. Yet even for Brecht himself we can draw some aesthetic consequences from the results (while Brecht's questions to his collective research staff are often more Brechtian than the narrator's summary of what in any case never gets written).

But it takes us some time to get to Engelbrekt himself: for a whole prehistory of the Swedish political situation, going back some eighty years, must first be set in place: the story of the struggle against the Danes for the accession to the throne of the Infanta Margareta. This is all sketched out in the style of the medieval theater, with levels for the classes, pageants, and the like: but it seems to me that its lesson for us is the drive of Peter

Weiss—in that compulsive archival scouring of the past for suggestive details and empirical inspiration which he shared with Brecht himself—to begin before the beginning, ever to seek out the sources of the seeds of time in the prehistory of their own flourishing germination. It is this impulse generally, then, which accounts for what seem to be lengthy historical essays and factual narratives interpolated throughout the novel: the history of the coast of Valencia, for example, stretching all the way back to the Phoenicians (and not coincidentally to the builders of the Pergamum altar); the history of Swedish Social Democracy in modern times (including the brief contact of one of its founders with Lenin as he passed through on his way to Petersburg and October [2:277]); the story of Angkor Wat. These seeming digressions in another ("non-fictive") type of discourse will find their deeper justification in Peter Weiss's conception of the aesthetic and of *Bildung* when we get to it: suffice it to say now that they mark a refusal of the distinction between form and content which is also a refusal of that between art and its non-artistic or historical pretexts. The material of the work of art has its own semi-autonomous history: but that history is itself part of the material, and one must seek it out just as one must appreciate the physical and chemical properties of the stone—quartz or granite, marble or porphyry—which makes up the building or the statue. This is an appreciation that must be achieved through knowledge itself: a knowledge which in this situation is not distinct from the aesthetic that henceforth includes it.

Yet Engelbrekt's appearance—surging suddenly out of nowhere when history demands him (2:214)—presents the work-to-be with the formal problem of the revolutionary break with the past, which can thus no longer be incorporated except as what is repudiated. Is the preliminary work then useless and a waste of precious time? In any case it has been frequently broken off, not only by Brecht's own illnesses but also by the heavy mood and confusions with which the collaborators receive the news, first of the German invasion of Poland, and then, in the East, the Soviet one (yet another cross-cutting section). Perhaps not altogether labor lost, however, and it is at least partly clear that what has been laid in place here is a conception of the work of art as a process fully satisfying in itself, and a collective process at that. Such a view of the work as process has surfaced any number of times in the modern period, from Valéry to *Tel quel*: but the collective constitution of the process has less often (which is a polite way of saying hardly at all) been added to the formulation, save in the various avant-gardes, most notably among the surrealists. The name Brecht is thus relatively unique in signifying not an individual artist but a group, thereby incarnating not only what is necessarily and implicitly collective about any theatrical production, but also what is central for any Marxian view of production and praxis. (It is not inappropriate at this point to mention the unmarked collaboration, from *Marat/Sade* on, in all his works, between Peter Weiss and his spouse, Gunilla Palmstierna-Weiss.)

Still, the unfinished play is as valuable for its formal dilemmas as for its achieved historical glimpses. The dramatization of revolution is the foremost of these, for not only is its temporal structure problematic, as we have seen; its "representational" system must also raise doubts and problems from any left perspective, insofar as Engelbrekt's moment is that of sharp popular unrest, and his very essence as "world-historical figure" consists in the hopes invested in him by a collectivity which cannot itself really be represented on stage (2:222). As with all left works (see above) Engelbrekt's political problem is the achievement of unity between the various dissatisfied classes who have very different agendas; his downfall and assassination are the result of a situation in which he has been able to serve the interests of one party (the great nobles), who now no longer need him and can throw him aside: a vanishing mediator, who embodies the truth of a revolutionary and a populist rhetoric that was little more than an ideological mask for the more privileged component of this "popular front." Here is then the central formal problem, which is also a political one: what Brecht and his co-workers took for a genuinely revolutionary moment turns out to have been a mere bourgeois revolution. There has been a good deal of interesting debate over whether a so-called bourgeois revolution is really a revolution at all in the Marxian sense; nor does the term particularly matter, provided we separate the two kinds of historical events sharply from each other. In that case, the first or bourgeois variety, with its necessary end in failure, can be the object of various kinds of representations, from Marx's ironic-satiric one in *The Eighteenth Brumaire of Louis Bonaparte* to Michelet's tragic narrative of the Great Revolution. The question would then be whether a socialist or proletarian revolution can be represented at all, since it precisely aims at challenging the political as well as the aesthetic sense of "representation" itself.

It is thus extraordinarily telling that Brecht's greatest moment of enthusiasm for this material comes at the moment when Engelbrekt, in order to threaten the royal city of Stockholm, finds himself obliged to dig a considerable canal in order to reinforce the siege. "The building of the canal, Brecht opined, would almost be worth an entire play in its own right. Here we could separate the principle of collective work from the power of egotism and profit. . . . A dragging and a hauling, a slave labor, yet voluntarily performed, as meaningful as after a triumphant revolution" (2:250). (This is, after all, the epic moment of Magnitogorsk, the Dnieper hydroelectric project, and the White Sea–Baltic Canal.) So the representation of production itself is at length laid in place, an impossible representation no doubt, as so many socialist realist novels testify, and yet here—in *The Aesthetics of Resistance*—inscribed as what cannot be represented, yet as the necessary and absent center of all work and value.

Such labor is first and foremost physical, to be sure, and the current theoretical celebration of the individual body as the very locus of materialism rarely enough includes labor alongside its privileged themes of desire and suffering. It may seem paradoxical to discuss suffering, trauma, and the body alongside Weiss's oneiric discourse, and yet the latter is the dialectical complement of the former, just as it constitutes a strange reversal and fulfillment of that "caverned" perception we attributed to the figures in the room or the cell, those "overwakened" senses that the condemned Heilmann evokes again on the eve of his death and in the content of a long final letter precisely devoted to dreaming: "There would be much to say about the abyss into which each of us has sunk, about the stone we taste and which seems through the outer efforts of our consciousness to have become as porous as dough in which our fingers can plunge and penetrate and yet our hands feel its hardness, so confusing is this new feeling" (3:211).

The Aesthetics of Resistance thus in fundamental ways calls out precisely for this "theory of dreaming" which Heilmann only tentatively elaborates on the eve of his execution, and which draws its ultimate poignancy from the fact that he will never dream again, "will never again fall asleep" (3:216). The lifelong significance of the oneiric for Peter Weiss himself can be documented by the paintings as well as the extensive role of dream protocols in his earlier fiction, all this theoretically reinforced by that appreciation for Jung that he derived from his youthful frequentation of Hermann Hesse (we may also suppose a certain distance from that side of Freud intent precisely on the analytic destruction of the "charm" and fascination of the dream experience). Yet we may at the same time detect a certain tension in Peter Weiss's relationship to this material, a refusal to abandon himself to the facile mythographies of a Jung or to the equally facile "automatic writing" of the surrealists either.

It is this tension—rather than any final conceptual "position" on dreams—which we must retrace in *The Aesthetics of Resistance*. "In the dream, I am a body that refuses to learn Thought" (3:214). At the same time, the dream is that space of infinite possibility before the world itself, as the youthful comrades once speculated in their discussions of Rimbaud or Hölderlin:

> We spoke about seeing in dreams. Asked ourselves how within such absolute darkness this intensity of colors could develop inside us. They are produced by our knowledge of light. Knowledge sees. Illumination stimuli are no longer present, but only remembered. We observed that the dream contained these earliest images, sharp and exact in every detail. Then in an immense variety reflections superimposed themselves on each other, ordered intuitively as they belonged to specific groups of experiences, they cluster together, or rather they swim, they float around the various emotional centers, they search each other out as sperm to the egg, lead to continuous insemination, each cell of feeling seems to be receptive, releasing ever newer apparitions generated by the ever changing thrusts, similarities and identities never occur, can owing to the perpetual flow itself never take place, yet always related images in this or that region, according to the goal-oriented intensity of the impulse toward its basic form, and sometimes it can even happen that the original image itself suddenly emerges, everything that concealed it washed away in a flash. (3:211)

In this earliest version of a kind of youthful "interpretation of dreams," then, the immense and demiurgic, generative productivity of the dream is somehow challenged by the real object of desire and the impatience of the Freudian "wish" that imperiously seeks fulfillment. But now Heilmann wonders about a different problem, a different tension, namely, "why we do not in dreams experience the suffering of which we are observers" (3:215). He juxtaposes with the oneiric that different and wakeful, yet equally intense, imagination with which he relives in sympathy that pathway of experiences, humiliation and pain, which his comrade Libertas must have traversed on her way to a neighboring cell. This is a different mode of image perception, in which the visionary suffers as much from his own helplessness and paralysis to change her destiny as from Libertas's own suffering.

I think that it is here that we must position the mother's schizophrenic hallucinations, which alongside the executions constitute the other affective pole of volume 3. Here clearly Peter Weiss faced a technical problem: how to incorporate the experience of Eastern Europe and the Nazi concentration—and then death—camps in a narrative whose trajectory takes us from Berlin in 1937 to Spain, and after Spain to Paris and Sweden, only to reinfiltrate wartime Germany (Bremen and Berlin) in the person of the clandestine Bischoff at the same time that the narrator is able to piece together at a distance the executions of his old comrades on the Plötzensee. The (relatively awkward) solution lies in the flight of the parents from Czechoslovakia in the first days of the war: they are only able to make their way across Poland in the throes of the blitzkrieg, accompanying the exodus of populations in flight, including considerable groups of Polish Jews and passing near the significant railroad crossing of Oswiecim on an immense detour through White Russia and Lithuania, until they reach Riga, the Swedish consulate, and safety. Even this laborious journey is interrupted, however, when the mother, separated from her husband, identifies herself as Jewish and follows the refugees on their own path, huddling together with them in an act of wordless solidarity:

> She felt the thick warmth, she belonged to these sweating bodies, seized one of the feverish hands and gripped its fingers together, and as the hands reached to grasp each other, she pressed her face against a moist cheek. Arms, breasts, hips, straggly beards, a crowd made out of limbs, beating hearts, hoarse breathing, that she was in their midst gave her strength. The foul air was a blossoming for her, she breathed it in deep, she lived within this organism, never would she wish to emerge from out of this closed space, separation would be her own destruction, her downfall. (3:12)

And so it proves: her rescue precipitates her into a psychic withdrawal and a silence from which she never reemerges (only breaking it once, when she has been present at a discussion of the first rumors of the actual death camps themselves [3:134]). Thematically, this solidarity stands in dialectical opposition to the father's paranoid fantasies about machinery, and in particular about the universal war machine itself: it is an opposition which completes the image of the death camps in their two dimensions—the Eichmann-organized functioning of the logistics, the suffering of the victims. Yet two other features of the mother's fate seem more significant.

For one thing, the mother's sympathy and solidarity, like Heilmann's impossible attempt to imagine and to feel in the place of his beloved, are failures: she has, according to Boye, who becomes close to her in the final months, "passed beyond the limits of our power to imagine" (3:25). In her last moment of speech she tells of the grave in which she lay with the still warm and twitching bodies of the dead and dying (3:128): yet her unspoken and unspeakable hallucinations show that even solidarity as extreme as this cannot come to terms with the absolute of other people's physical suffering. This is not however, at least on my view, a portrait of trauma, even though the narrator associates the mother with Dürer's great image of Melancholia, the angel paralyzed in silence and an almost catatonic inaction and incapacity to produce or create (3:136–137).

It is no doubt this association which prompts Hodann to suggest the other path of artistic expression: this is one of the moments in which the narrator's vocation comes to the surface in the form of that future conditional which will dominate the last pages of the novel itself ("someday it would be possible to describe what my mother experienced . . ." [3:139]). For it is on that level of linguistic re-creation that the real problem of trauma (or what Shoshana Felman would call "testimony") is to be located: in the failures of language and the impossibility of expression—this, rather than the failure of sheer imagination, is the real problem of the relationship with the past, which is not so much that of reliving it as that of doing something with it:

> Our incapacity to follow my mother was not conditioned by anything metaphysical or mystical, it was just that as yet we possessed no register for what transcended the ordinary, our helplessness was merely provisional, had not our whole development proved that concrete judgments were gradually constructed first out of dawning approximations and groping experiments . . . I thought that what now came upon us could be expressed only with some new language. But Hodann replied that for our purposes there would never be another language than the one known to everybody, and that what was to be expressed, in order to make it incomprehensible would have to be transmitted by way of the same old used-up words. (3:139–40)

The relationship of all these materials to each other can now be suggested by the diagram in figure 2.

And thus at length we come to the ultimate theme, the most important and central one, of pedagogy. In reality, with what has been termed above "the narrative resolution of trauma" we had already arrived there. For if the new cultural revolution, the new proletarian pedagogy, as it is the novel's vocation to describe and to embody it, is a kind of aesthetic education, it is also very much an effacement of subalternity and a transcendence of the trauma of historical defeat, class oppression, alienated labor, and the paralyzing humiliations of ignorance. The great works—

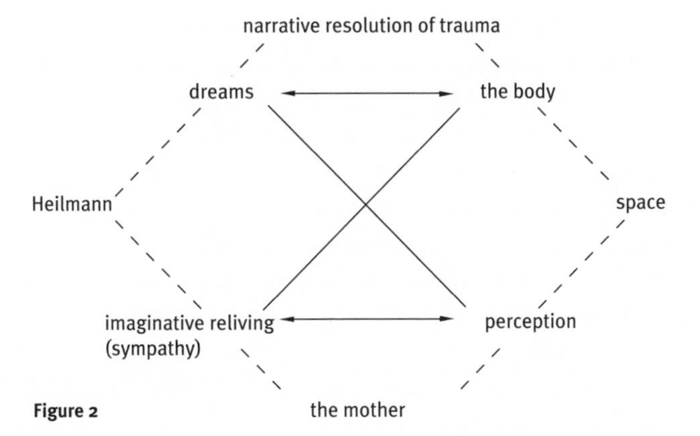

Figure 2

those "monuments to radical instants"—are no doubt memorials of pain and suffering: the butchering of the Titans in the Pergamum frieze, the starvation, debility, and cannibalism of the survivors on Géricault's raft, the mute screams of *Guernica* as well, along with the minute daily fears and anxieties of Kafka's characters; but the question is, rather, how to draw energy from such endless images of horror, how to enhance praxis and production by the spectacle of this charnel house, the "nightmare of history"?

The famous opening sequence on the Pergamum altar remains the fullest statement of this aesthetic, which it may be useful initially to frame in the reduced terms of a "critical method," supplementing it with other set pieces from the later pages—on Picasso, but also on Menzel and Koehler—and with the equally monumental discussion of Géricault in the next volume (significantly enough, volume 3 contains none of these aesthetic exhibits or readings).

The proliferation of themes and digressions around the Pergamum frieze makes it clear that any simple opposition between form and content needs to make way for a far more complex movement of multiple reversals and inversions. So it is, for example, that in the midst of the slow agony of the Spanish Republic, the narrator and Hodann, amid the orange groves of the landscape, begin to speak about "events that had occurred along this coast two millennia earlier" (1:282/1:321). The classical world of the Pergamum altar is now discovered to have had its outpost here in Valencia, and a history of the Spanish peasantry and that Spanish agricultural labor whose story will at length find its climax in the civil war reveals its immemorial continuities with the public work of art contemplated in the first pages. An emphasis on violence and death, on the failure of a thousand mortal generations to overcome their misery, is enough to secure this view of history from the idealistic illusions otherwise almost always implicit or explicit in theses about cultural continuities over time. But this materialism is also reinforced by the sharp mental reversal administered by such a view: we do not normally connect the Spanish Civil War with the classical past, and, even more fundamentally, we do not often see the history of oppressed classes as a continuity: continuities are always on the side of "culture," that is to say, on the side of the modes of living of the dominant classes. To invert these ideological priorities is thus not necessarily to revive an idealist conception of history, so much as to administer a materialist shock to just such categories and stereotypes. Thus Walter Benjamin recommends a dual procedure: "For the materialist dialectician discontinuity must be the regulative idea of the tradition of the ruling classes (essentially the bourgeoisie), continuity that of the oppressed classes (the proletariat)."[27] The figure of Heracles, whose mythic travels afford a different kind of link between the eastern and western shores of the Mediterranean, will be discussed in a moment.

In fact, it is precisely the idea of the methodological reversal which will provide the key to so many bewildering twists and turns in Peter Weiss's aesthetic analyses here: nor, given the agon-organized structure of his dialectical thought generally, should there be any surprise in the way in which the sympathetic contemplation of a given aesthetic position suddenly and without warning generates the emergence of a not always predictable opposite.

Yet the first moves are logical enough: the bloody triumph of the Olympians over the giants is a celebration and a warning, and transposes and expresses the power of the Attalid dynasty that commissioned the frieze. And just as this translation of human rulers into divine ones effaces history with a vision of the sheer eternity of power, so also the sculptors must make of the frieze itself a superhuman artifact, from which all traces of production have been removed: stylistic perfection, then, here also serves the ideology of the masters. Yet this shift of attention toward the production of the work reminds us that class struggle can also be identified there, in the pulling and hauling of unskilled labor under the direction of the builders and master sculptors. Nor is the monitory effect of the frieze some merely "historical" one, which present-day viewers can abstract in the name of pure aesthetic reception: "We heard the thuds of the clubs, the shrilling whistles, the moans, the splashing of blood. We looked back at a prehistoric past, and for an instant the prospect of the future likewise filled up with a massacre impenetrable to the thought of liberation" (1:9/1:14). But this reactivation of historical memory opens an access to the Alexandrian period generally, and in particular to Pergamum's own failed revolution, the uprising of Aristonicus (1:41/1:49), and even, ironically, all the way back up to the nineteenth century and the ideological reasons for the newly united German Empire to "buy" the newly excavated altar and transport it to Berlin (1:43/1:51). These seemingly extraneous historical footnotes are not only part and parcel of our reinterpretations: "And after a lengthy silence, Heilmann said that works like those stemming from Pergamum had to be constantly reinterpreted until a reversal was gained and the earth-born awoke from darkness and slavery to show themselves in their true appearance" (1:44/1:53). More than that, I think we have to conclude that, for such analyses from below, the split between form and content, between the intrinsic and the extrinsic, the aesthetic and its context, has not yet taken place. It is only for the bourgeois spectator or reader that it exists, only there that at best it has to be struggled against and overcome. It is the structure of bourgeois daily life and subjectivity, and the collective division of labor and privileges of power which tacitly underpin that structure, which exclude the social unity of the work of art as something that can no longer be perceived or conceived, that escape bourgeois categories of perception and reception, let alone analysis. A true "aesthetics" of resistance therefore will not seek to "correct" bourgeois aesthetics or to resolve its antinomies and dilemmas: it will rather search out that other social position from which those dilemmas do not emerge in the first place. The difficulties under which that other, proletarian aesthetic education labors, however, are of a different kind: not the philosophical or conceptual antinomies of form and content, but rather those of subalternity: fatigue after work, lack of access to knowledge and information, repudiation of the aesthetic as class privilege, underdevelopment, finally, of a stubborn will to appropriate the achievements of the dominant class—aesthetic as well as scientific and technological—in the interests of building a new social order. In the present instance one may say that the very existence of the project of a proletarian aesthetic education is a sign that this will already exists.

This is also to say that from the standpoint of suffering and defeat aesthetic experience is not devalued but rather able to emerge with a new kind of unity, transcendent as well as immanent: the problem of suffering adds urgency to the purely formal side of art, that is to say to the dilemmas of representation and the sign systems deployed, and otherwise so refractory to this ultimate mute and inexpressible experience. The nature of class subordination meanwhile, by revealing the solidarity between the "extrinsic" situation of the classes in the historical context and the "intrinsic" labor presupposed by the work of art itself, volatilizes the old (bourgeois) critical problems, endlessly and unproductively turning around the sticking point of some "specificity," some unique poeticity or literariness, of the aesthetic object itself. The commitment to suffering in the novel itself can thus be grasped not as some morbid fascination and intention of memorializing this past and these dead; but rather as the keeping open of a historical perspective—very precisely that of subordination and resistance—which enables praxis as such. Contemporary discussions of melancholy and mourning, which begin with the latter's paralysis in muteness and inaction (as with the narrator's mother), are only gradually moving toward an understanding of the ways in which such experience (politically termed "the experience of defeat") can also constitute an energizing precondition for action. At the very least, and to reverse the argument, Peter Weiss's novel can only be adequately read and grasped if this perspective is conceivable.

Now there is very little time to rehearse the other aesthetic demonstrations contained in this novel: one would want to single out the extraordinary concentration which replaces Géricault's *Raft of the Medusa* in the position it deserves, between Dante and the Isenheim crucifixion, by restoring a situation of truly subaltern French colonization—the African destination as a sop thrown by the English to the losers of Waterloo—to the derisory and gratuitous conditions underlying the catastrophe (2:7–34). In *Guernica*, on the other hand, it is the bizarre presence of a winged Pegasus in Picasso's earliest sketches, which allows us to reidentify the utopian moment of this bleakly archetypal work (1:294/1:332–36). The juxtaposition of Menzel's great factory painting with Koehler's *Strike* (1868—the first North American socialist realism!) allows the reader to identify the inescapable links between the painter's inevitable class position and his technical and representational capacities (1:310–15/1:352–60). The reading, finally, of Kafka's *Castle* as a proletarian novel (1:157/1:179) itself powerfully reverses canonical stereotypes and offers a new way into this nightmarish magic realism, whose gestural strangeness is the result of the paralysis of a disempowered and subaltern population.

There remains the question of the figure of Heracles, a leitmotif which runs from the absence of the legendary figure from the Pergamum fragments to its reemergence on the very last page of the novel. Heracles, I believe, is meant to figure a heroic temptation by the symbolic or the mythic: the hero, the "world-historical individual," destined to fulfill the hopes of a whole people: none of the real historical figures is a hero in this sense (even though the agony of Lenin's final illness is characterized as a "shirt of Nessus"). Is Heracles, then, meant to figure the illicit longing for positive heroes, or, worse yet, for charismatic leaders? Is he not also a locus for the old dilemmas of a ruling-class leadership in underclass political movements? For after all, on the frieze itself, his empty place stands among the Olympians rather than the Titans; while in an extraordinarily tortuous speculation, Heilmann attempts to reread the mythic labors as a covert form of resistance and of encouragement to the lower classes (1:14–20/1:23–25). I think we must see Heracles as an allegorical rather than a symbolic motif: that is, a place-marker for problems of representation, rather than an inscription of ideological content. Scherpe has characterized this function admirably: "Missing from the fragments preserved of the frieze is its most important symbol: the lion's paw of Heracles—according to the novel's symbolism the final and perfect historical act of liberation of the oppressed. The novel's last sentence cannot be in the historical indicative. . . . Peter Weiss' *Aesthetics of Resistance* wishes to be an indication, a sign of this historical work of liberation that has not yet become history. The empty space in the frieze, at the spot where the lion's paw of Heracles would hang, designates precisely something absent, unrealized. Literature cannot and should not fill this space by way of compensation, but rather render its contours sharp and visible."[28]

One final bourgeois opposition is displaced and cancelled by the perspective of *The Aesthetics of Resistance*: it is that between critic and writer. For the narrator's aesthetic education, the pedagogical training in the appropriation of a different class culture, is also the preparation for his vocation as a writer whose observation of history as a witness is also at one and the same time an intervention in it. The circularity of such narrative forms—the *Bildungsroman* which ends up in its own production—is familiar; the conclusion of this one in the future conditional is not. Anticipations of the failure of postwar hopes—the Cold War, the loss of unity in the revival of the Socialist-Communist split, the Stalinization of the East—are somehow destabilized by a tense which robs them of their sheer empiricity and allows something like an alternate future perfect to rise alongside them. Here factual history, seemingly as unshakable as being itself, is transformed—to use Habermas's glorious expression—into an unfinished project: what seemed over and done with is thus opened up for a new beginning, a new continuation. This is surely the ultimate and fundamental lesson of Peter Weiss's novel, a lesson about the productive uses of a past and a history that is not simply represented or commemorated but also reappropriated by some new future of our own present:

Again and again, when I would try to convey something of the time that ended with May 1945, its consequences would impose themselves on me. Across the experiences already soaked with death, there would superimpose itself a future colored shrilly, and once again filled with torture, destruction, and murder. It would again and again seem as though all earlier hopes would be brought to nothing by lost or forgotten intentions. And even if it did not turn out as we hoped, nothing would be changed about those hopes themselves. The hopes would remain. Utopia would be necessary. Even later on those hopes would flame up again countless times, smothered by the superior enemy and ever newly reawakened. And the realm of hopes would become greater than it was in our time, and would be extended to all the continents of the globe. The poorly repressed discontent would grow and the drive to contradict and to resist would not be lamed. Just as the past was unchangeable, so those hopes would remain unchangeable, and they—which we once, when young, burningly experienced—would be honored by our rememoration of them. (3:274–275)

Notes

1. Walter Benjamin, "Theses on the Philosophy of History," in *Illuminations*, trans. H. Zohn (New York: Schocken, 1969), 264.
2. See the by now notorious Friedenspreis speech of Martin Walser, reprinted in *Erfahrungen beim Verfassen einer Sonntagsrede* (Frankfurt: Suhrkamp, 1998).
3. I have drawn heavily here on the indispensable work of Robert Cohen, the annotator for this volume; see *Understanding Peter Weiss* (Columbia: University of South Carolina Press, 1993), which includes extensive bibliographical references, including his other works in this area.
4. See Dominick LaCapra, *History and Memory after Auschwitz* (Ithaca: Cornell University Press, 1998) for extensive bibliographical information.
5. See Shoshona Felman and Dori Laub, *Testimony: Crises of Witnessing in Literature, Psychoanalysis, and History* (New York: Routledge, 1991).
6. See James E. Young, *Writing and Rewriting the Holocaust* (Bloomington: Indiana University Press, 1988); and for a more balanced general study of the matter, Robert Cohen, "The Political Aesthetics of Holocaust Literature," *History and Memory* 10, 2 (1998): 43–67.
7. References will henceforth be given in the text, with citations from the three-volume East German edition of *Die Ästhetik des Widerstands* published by Henschelverlag, Kunst und Gesellschaft (Berlin, 1987); and, for the first volume, to the translation by Joachim Neugroschel published in this book. In the case of volume 1, the English reference will be given first; thus the present reference is 1:9/1:14. Translations from the last two volumes are my own.

8. On Proust, see Jean-Paul Sartre, "Présentation des *Temps modernes*," in vol. 2 of *Situations* (Paris: Gallimard, 1948), 20–22. And see also, on Weiss's denial of any autobiographical elements, Klaus R. Scherpe, "Reading the *Aesthetics of Resistance*: Ten Working Theses," *New German Critique* 30 (fall 1983). Scherpe's collection, edited with Karl-Heinz Götze, *Die "Aesthetik des Widerstands" lesen* (Berlin: Argument, 1981), is still very useful.
9. Sartre, "Qu'est-ce que la littérature?" in *Situations*, 2:143–50.
10. "A difficult book. Critic Heinrich Vormweg called *The Aesthetics of Resistance* monstrous . . ." (Cohen, *Understanding Peter Weiss*, 160). "Ein unbequemes Buch . . ." (Manfred Haiduk, "Nachwort," *Die Aesthetik des Widerstands*, 3:278). "This uncooperative work . . ." (Scherpe, "Reading the *Aesthetics of Resistance*," 100).
11. See below, n. 18.
12. Gilles Deleuze, *Cinéma* (Paris: Minuit, 1985), 2:281–91. Deleuze thus takes a quite different position from that of Jean-Luc Nancy, whose *Inoperative Community*, trans. Peter Connor et al. (Minneapolis: University of Minnesota Press, 1991), argues for the impossibility of *any* group solidarity after the end of the regimes of actually existing socialism.
13. See the work of Franco Moretti: *The Modern Epic: The World-System from Goethe to García Márquez*, trans. Quintin Hoare (London: Verso, 1998).
14. "For that very reason he has to start immediately, and whatever the circumstances, without further scruples about beginning, means, or End, proceed to action." G. W. F. Hegel, *Phenomenology of Spirit*, trans. A. V. Miller (Oxford: Oxford University Press, 1977), 240.
15. See Fredric Jameson, *Postmodernism, or, The Cultural Logic of Late Capitalism* (Durham: Duke University Press, 1991), chap. 5.
16. T. W. Adorno, *Aesthetische Theorie* (Frankfurt: Suhrkamp, 1970), 376–77; and Perry Anderson, "Modernity and Revolution," *New Left Review*, no. 144 (March/April 1984): 96–113.
17. Georg Lukács, *The Historical Novel*, trans. Hannah and Stanley Mitchell (Lincoln: University of Nebraska Press, 1983).
18. Jean-Paul Sartre, *Critique of Dialectical Reason*, vol. 1, trans. A. Sheridan-Smith (London: Verso, 1976).
19. See n. 5 above.
20. *The Charterhouse of Parma*, chap. 3.
21. N. S. Khrushchev, *Khrushchev Remembers*, trans. Strobe Talbott (Boston: Little, Brown, 1970), 42–44.
22. A. J. P. Taylor, *Origins of the Second World War* (London: Hamilton, 1961).
23. Alexander Solzhenitsyn, *The First Circle*, trans. Thomas P. Whitney (New York: Harper and Row, 1968), 86–87.
24. I am indebted to Carlos Blanco Aguinaga for this insight.
25. Fredric Jameson, *The Cultural Turn* (London: Verso, 1998), 7–8, 82.
26. Gilles Deleuze, *Cinéma*, vol. 1 (Paris: Minuit, 1983).
27. Walter Benjamin, *Gesammelte Schriften* (Frankfurt: Suhrkamp, 1982), 5:459–60.
28. Scherpe, "Reading the *Aesthetics of Resistance*," 105.

ALL around us the bodies rose out of the stone, crowded into groups, intertwined, or shattered into fragments, hinting at their shapes with a torso, a propped-up arm, a burst hip, a scabbed shard, always in warlike gestures, dodging, rebounding, attacking, shielding themselves, stretched high or crooked, some of them snuffed out, but with a freestanding, forward-pressing foot, a twisted back, the contour of a calf harnessed into a single common motion. A gigantic wrestling, emerging from the gray wall, recalling a perfection, sinking back into formlessness. A hand, stretching from the rough ground, ready to clutch, attached to the shoulder across empty surface, a barked face, with yawning cracks, a wide-open mouth, blankly gaping eyes, the face surrounded by the flowing locks of the beard, the tempestuous folds of a garment, everything close to its weathered end and close to its origin. Every detail preserving its expression, brittle fragments from which the whole could be gleaned, rough stumps next to polished smoothness, enlivened by the play of muscles and sinews, tautly harnessed chargers, rounded shields, erect spears, a head split into a raw oval, outspread wings, a triumphantly raised arm, a leaping heel circled by a fluttering tunic, a clenched fist on a now absent sword, shaggy hounds, their jaws clamped into loins and necks, a falling man, his finger stub aiming at the eye of the beast hanging over him, a charging lion protecting a female warrior, his paw swinging back to strike, hands endowed with bird claws, horns looming from weighty brows, scaly legs coiling, a brood of serpents everywhere, with strangleholds around bellies and throats, darting their tongues, baring sharp teeth, bashing into naked chests. These only just created, already dying faces, these tremendous and dismembered hands, these wide-sweeping pinions drowning in the blunt rock, this stony gaze, these lips torn open for a shriek, this striding, stamping, these blows of heavy weapons, this rolling of armored wheels, these clusters of hurled lightning bolts, this grinding underfoot, this rearing and collapsing, this endless straining to twist upward out of grainy boulders. And how gracefully curly the hair, how elaborately gathered and girded the lightweight mantle, how delicate the ornamentation on the straps of the shield, on the bulge of the helmet, how gentle the shimmer of the skin, ready for caresses yet exposed to the relentless rivalry, to slaughter and annihilation. With mask-like countenances, clutching one another and shoving one another away, strangling one another, clambering over one another, sliding from horses, entangled in the reins, utterly vulnerable in nakedness, and yet enrapt in Olympic aloofness, appearing indomitable as an ocean monster, a griffin, a centaur, yet grimacing in pain 4 and despair, thus they clashed with one another, acting at higher behest, dreaming, motionless in insane vehemence, mute in inaudible roaring, all of them woven into a metamorphosis of torture, shuddering, persisting, waiting for an awakening, in perpetual endurance and perpetual rebellion, in outrageous impact, and in an extreme exertion to subdue the threat, to provoke the decision. A soft ringing and murmuring resounded now and again, the echoes of footfalls and voices surrounded us for moments at a time; and then once more, only this battle was near, our gazes glided over the toes in the sandals, bouncing off the skull of a fallen man, over the dying man whose stiffening hand lay tenderly on the arm of the goddess who held him by the hair. The cornice was the ground for the warriors: from its narrow, even strip they threw themselves up into the turmoil, the hooves of the horses banged upon the cornice, the hems of the garments grazed it, and the serpentine legs twisted across it; the ground was perforated at only one place: here, the demoness of the earth rose up, her face hacked away under her eye sockets, her breasts massive in a thin covering, the torn-off clump of one hand lifted in a search, the other hand, asking for a standstill, loomed from the stone edge, and knotty, long-jointed fingers stretched up to the profiled corbel as if they were still underground and were trying to reach the wrist of the open thumbless female hand, they moved along under the cornice, seeking the blurred traces of incised script, and Coppi's face, his myopic eyes behind glasses with a thin steel frame, approached the letters, which Heilmann deciphered with the help of a book he had brought along. Coppi turned toward him, attentive, with a broad, sharply drawn mouth, a large, protruding nose, and we gave the opponents in this melee their names and, in the torrent of noises, discussed the causes of the fight. Heilmann, the fifteen-year-old, who rejected any uncertainty, who tolerated no undocumented interpretation, but occasionally also adhered to the poetic demand for a conscious deregulation of the senses, who wanted to be a scientist and a seer, he, whom we nicknamed our Rimbaud, explained to us, who were already about twenty years old and who had been out of school for four years by now and were familiar with the world of labor and also with unemployment, while Coppi had spent a year in prison for circulating subversive literature—Heilmann explained to us the meaning of this dance round, in which the entire host of deities, led by Zeus, were striding toward victory over a race of giants and fabulous creatures. The Titans, the sons of the lamenting Gaea, in front of whose torso we were now standing, had blasphemously mutinied against the gods; but other struggles that had passed across the kingdom of Pergamum were concealed under this depiction. The regents in the dynasty of the Attalids had ordered their master sculptors to translate the swift transience, paid for with thousands of lives, to a level of timeless permanence, thereby putting up a monument to their own grandeur and immortality. The subjugation of the Gallic tribes invading from the north had turned into a triumph of aristocratic purity over wild and base forces, and the chisels and mallets of the stone carvers and their assistants had displayed a picture of incontestable order to make the subjects bow in awe. Historic events appeared in mythical disguise, enormously palpable, arousing terror, admiration, yet not understandable as man-made, but endurable only as a more-than-personal power that wanted enthralled, enslaved people galore, though few at the top, who dictated destinies with a mere stirring of the finger. The populace, when trudging by on solemn days, scarcely dared to glance up at the effigy of its own history, while—along with the priests—the philosophers and poets, the artists from elsewhere, all full of factual knowledge, had long since walked around the temple; and that which, for the ignorant, lay in magical darkness was, for the informed, a handicraft to be soberly assessed. The initiates, the specialists talked about art, praising the harmony of movement, the coordination of gestures; the others, however, who were not even familiar with the concept of "cultured," stared furtively into the gaping maws, felt the swoop of the paw in their own flesh. The work gave pleasure to the privileged; the others sensed a segregation under a draconian law of hierarchy. However, a few sculptures, said Heilmann, did not have to be extracted from their symbolism; the falling man, the man of Gaul taking his own life, showed the immediate tragedy of a concrete situation; but these sculptures, replied Coppi, had not been outside, they had remained among the trophies in the throne rooms, purely

in order to indicate from whom the shields and helmets, the bundles of swords and spears had been taken. The sole aim of the wars was to safeguard the territories of the kings. The gods, confronted with the spirits of the earth, kept the notion of certain power relationships alive. A frieze filled with anonymous soldiers, who, as tools of the higher-ups, fought for years, attacking other anonymous soldiers, would have altered the attitude toward those who served, boosting their position; the kings, not the warriors, won the victories, and the victors could be like the gods, while the losers were despised by the gods. The privileged knew that the gods did not exist, for they, the privileged, who donned the masks of the gods, knew themselves. So they were even more insistent on being surrounded with splendor and dignity. Art served to give their rank, their authority the appearance of the supernatural. They could permit no skep-
6
ticism about their perfection. Heilmann's bright face, with its regular features, bushy eyebrows, and high forehead, had turned to the demoness of the earth. She had brought forth Uranus, the sky, Pontus, the sea, and all mountains. She had given birth to the giants, the Titans, the Cyclopes, and the Furies. This was our race. We evaluated the history of the earthly beings. We looked up at her again, the demoness stretching out of the ground. The waves of loosened hair flowed about her. On her shoulder, she carried a bowl of pomegranates. Foliage and grape vines twirled at the back of her neck. The start of the lips, begging for mercy, was discernible in the raw facial plane, which veered sideways and upward. A gash gaped from her chin to her larynx. Alcyoneus, her favorite son, slanted away from her while dropping to his knees. The stump of his left hand groped toward her. She was still touching his left foot, which dangled from his stretched and shattered leg. His thighs, abdomen, belly, and chest were all tensing in convulsions. The pain of death radiated from the small wound inflicted between his ribs by the venomous reptile. The wide, unfurled wings of the kingfisher, growing from his shoulder, slowed down his plunge. The silhouette of the burst-off face above him, with the hard line of the neck, of the hair, which was tied up and tucked under the helmet, spoke of the pitilessness of Athena. As she swung forward, her wide, belted cloak flew back. The downward glide of the garment revealed, on her left breast, the scale armor with the small, bloated face of Medusa. The weight of the round shield, her arm thrust into its thong, pulled her along to new deeds. Nike, leaping up, with mighty wings, in loose, airy tunics, held the wreath, invisible but implied by the gesture, over her head. Heilmann pointed: at the dissolving goddess of the night, Nyx, who, with a loving smile, was hurling her vessel full of serpents toward a downcast

creature; at Zeus, who, in his open, billowing cloak, was using his woolen aegis, the goatskin of doom, to whip down three adversaries; and at Eos, the goddess of dawn, who was riding like a cloud in front of the rising team of the naked sun god, Helios. Thus, he said gently, a new day dawns after the dreadful butchery, and now the glass-covered room became noisy with the scraping of feet on the smooth floor, with the ticking echoes of shoe soles on the steep steps leading up the reconstructed western façade of the temple to the colonnades of the interior court. We turned back toward the relief, which throughout its bands demonstrated the instant when the tremendous change was about to take place, the moment when the concentrated strength portends the ineluctable consequence. By seeing the lance immediately before its throw, the club before its whizzing plunge, the run before the jump, the hauling-back before the clash, our eyes were driven from figure to figure, from one situation to the next, and the stone began to quiver all around us. However, we missed Heracles, who, according to the myth, was the only mortal to ally himself with the gods in the battle against the giants; and, combing the immured bodies, the remnants of limbs, we looked for the son of Zeus and Alcmene, the earthly helper whose courage and unremitting labor would bring an end to the period of menace. All we could discern was a sign bearing his name, and the paw of a lion's skin that had cloaked him; nothing else testified to his station between Hera's four-horse team and Zeus's athletic body; and Coppi called it an omen that Heracles, who was our equal, was missing, and that we now had to create our own image of this advocate of action. As we headed toward the low, narrow exit on the side of the room, the red armbands of the men in black and brown uniforms shone toward us from the whirling shifts in the throng of visitors; and whenever I spotted the emblem, rotating and chopping in the white, round field, it became a venomous spider, ruggedly hairy, hatched in with pencil, ink, or India ink, under Coppi's hand, as I knew it from the class at the Scharfenberg Institute, where Coppi had sat at the next desk, doodling on small pictures, cards from cigarette packs, on illustrations clipped from newspapers, disfiguring the symbol of the new rulers, adding warts, tusks, nasty creases, and rivulets of blood to the plump faces looming from the uniform collars. Heilmann, our friend, also wore the brown shirt, with rolled-up sleeves, the shoulder straps, the string for the whistle, the dagger on the short pants; but he wore this garb as a disguise, camouflaging his own knowledge and camouflaging Coppi, who was coming from illegal work, and camouflaging me, who was about to leave for Spain. And thus, on the twenty-second of September, nineteen thirty-seven, a few days before my departure, we stood in front of the altar frieze, which had been brought here from the castle mountain of Pergamum to be reconstructed, and which, painted colorfully and lined with forged metals, had once reflected the light of the Aegean sky. Heilmann indicated the dimensions and location of the temple, as the temple, still undamaged by sandstorms or earthquakes, pillage or plunder, had shown itself on a protruding platform, on the terraced hill of the residence, above the city known today as Bergama, sixty-five miles north of Smyrna, between the narrow, usually dried-out rivers Keteios and Selinos, gazing westward, across the plain of Caicus, toward the ocean and the isle of Lesbos, a structure with an almost square ground plan, one hundred twenty by one hundred thirteen feet, and with a perron sixty-five feet wide, the whole thing dedicated by Eumenes II, to thank the gods for helping him in his war—the construction having begun one hundred eighty years before our era and lasting for twenty years, the buildings visible from far away, included among the wonders of the world by Lucius Ampelius in his *Book of Memorabilia*, second century A.D., before the temple sank into the rubble of a millennium. And has this mass of stone, Coppi asked, which served the cult of princely and religious masters of ceremony, who glorified the victory of the aristocrats over an earthbound mix of nations—has this mass of stone now become a value in its own right, belonging to anyone who steps in front of it. It was no doubt highbred figures who trod barbaric mongrels underfoot here, and the sculptors did not immortalize the people who were down in the streets, running the mills, smithies, and manufactories, or who were employed in the markets, the workshops, the harbor shipyards; besides, the sanctuary on the thousand-foot-high mountain, in the walled district of the storehouses, barracks, baths, theaters, administration buildings, and palaces of the ruling clan, was accessible to the populace only on holidays; no doubt, only the names of some of the master artists were handed down, Menecrates, Dionysades, Orestes, and not the names of those who had transferred the drawings to the ashlars, had defined the intersections with compasses and drills, and had practiced expertly on some veins and shocks of hair, and nothing recalled the peons who fetched the marble and dragged the huge blocks to the oxcarts, and yet, said Heilmann, the frieze brought fame not only for those who were close to the gods but also for those whose strength was still concealed, for they too were not ignorant, they did not want to be enslaved forever, led by Aristonicus they rebelled at the end of the construction, rising up against the lords of the city. Nevertheless the work still incorporated the same dichotomy as at the time of its creation. Destined to emanate royal power, it could simultaneously be questioned about its peculiarities of style, its sculptural persuasiveness. In its heyday, before falling to the Byzantine Empire, Pergamum was renowned for its scholars, its schools and libraries, and the special writing pages of cured, fleshed, and buffed calfskin made the fruits of poetic invention, of scholarly and scientific investigation permanent. The silence, the paralysis of those fated to be trampled into the ground continued to be palpable. They, the real bearers of the Ionian state, unable to read or write, excluded from artistic activity, were only good enough to create the wealth for a small privileged stratum and the necessary leisure for the elite of the mind. The existence of the celestials was unattainable for them, but they could recognize themselves in the kneeling imbruted creatures. The latter, in crudeness, degradation, and maltreatment, bore their features. The portrayal of the gods in flight and of the annihilation of urgent danger expressed not the struggle of good against evil, but the struggle between the classes, and this was recognized not only in our present-day viewing but perhaps also back then in secret glimpses by serfs. However, the afterdays of the altar were likewise determined by the enterprising spirit of the well-to-do. When the sculptural fragments that had lain buried under the deposits of Near Eastern power changes came to light, it was once again the superior, the enlightened who knew how to use the valuable items, while the herdsmen and nomads, the descendants of the builders of the temple, possessed no more of Pergamum's grandeur than dust. But it was a waste of breath complaining, said Heilmann, for the preservation of the showpiece of Hellenic civilization in a mausoleum of the modern world was preferable to its traceless entombment in Mysian detritus. Since our goal was to eliminate injustice, to wipe out poverty, he said, and since this country too was only going through a transition, we could imagine that this site would some day demonstrate the expanded and mutual ownership intrinsic in the monumentality of the formed work. And so, in the dim light, we gazed at the beaten and dying. The mouth of one of the vanquished, with the rapacious hound hanging over his shoulder, was half open, breathing its last. His left hand lay feeble on the forward-charging leather-shod foot of Artemis, his right arm was still raised in self-defense, but his hips were already growing cold, and his legs had turned into a spongy mass. We heard the thuds of the clubs, the shrilling whistles, the moans, the splashing of blood. We looked back at a prehistoric past, and for an instant the prospect of the future likewise filled up with a massacre impenetrable to the thought of liberation. Heracles would have to help them, the subjugated, and not those who had enough armor and weapons. Prior to the genesis of the figurations, there had been the bondage, the enclosure in stone. In the marble quarries on the mountain slopes north of the castle, the master sculptors had pointed their long sticks at the best blocks while eying the Gallic captives toiling in the sultry heat. Shielded and fanned by palm branches, squinting in the blinding sun, the sculptors took in the rippling of the muscles, the bending and stretching of the sweating bodies. The defeated warriors, driven here in chains, hanging from ropes on the rock faces, smashing crowbars and wedges into the strata of glittering, bluish white, crystalline-like limestone, and transporting the gigantic ashlars on long wooden sleds down the twisting paths, were notorious for their savagery, their brutal customs, and in the evenings the lords with their retinues passed them timidly when the stinking prisoners, drunk on cheap rotgut, were camping in a pit. Up in the gardens of the castle, however, in the gentle breeze wafting up from the sea, the huge bearded faces became the stuff of the sculptors' dreams, and they remembered ordering one man or another to stand still, opening his eye wide, pulling his lips apart to view his teeth, they recalled the arteries swelling on his temples, the glistening nose, zygomas, and forehead emerging from the cast shadows. They could still hear the lugging and shoving, the stemming of shoulders and backs against the weight of the stone, the rhythmic shouts, the curses, the whip cracks, the grinding of sled runners in the sand, and they could see the figures of the frieze slumbering in the marble coffins. Slowly they scraped forth the limbs, felt them, saw forms emerge whose essence was perfection. With the plundered people transferring their energies into relaxed and receptive thoughts, degradation and lust for power produced art. Through the noisy maelstrom of a school class we pushed our way into the next room, where the market gates of Miletus loomed in the penumbra. At the columns flanking the gates, which had led from the town hall of the port to the open emporium, Heilmann asked whether we had noticed that inside, in the altar room, a spatial function had been inverted, so that exterior surfaces had become interior walls. In facing the western perron, he said, we had our backs to the eastern side, the rear of the temple, that is, in its merely rudimentary reconstruction, and the unfolded southern frieze stretched out to the right while the relief on the northern cornice ran to the left. Something the viewer was to grasp by slowly circling it was now surrounding him instead. This dizzying procedure would ultimately make us understand the Theory of Relativity, he added when, moving a few centuries deeper, we walked along the claybrick walls that had once stood in the cluster of Nebuchadnezzar's Babylonian towers, and we then suddenly stepped into an area where yellowing leaves, whirring sunspots, pale-yellow double-decker buses, cars with flashing reflections, streams of pedestrians, and the rhythmic smashing of hobnailed boots demanded a readjustment in our bearings, a new indication of our whereabouts.

We are now, said Coppi, after we crossed the square between the museum, the cathedral, and the Armory Canal, in front of the motionless field-gray steel-helmeted sentries at the monument, whose dungeon still has room enough for the mangled marchers who, having bled to death, are en route here, willing or not, in order to lie down under the wreaths with silk ribbons. Heilmann, beneath the foliage of the Lindens, pointed between the Brothers Humboldt, who, enthroned loftily in armchairs with griffin feet, were brooding over open books, and he motioned across the wide forecourt, toward the university, where, reckoning with an accelerated high school diploma, he intended to study foreign affairs. He already knew English and French, and at the night school where we had met him, he had been seeking contacts for teaching him the taboo Russian language. The municipal night school, a gathering place for proletarians and renegade burghers, had been our chief educational institution after Coppi had left the Scharfenberg School Island at sixteen, and I, one year later, had likewise taken my last ferry to the mainland near Tegel Forest. Here, basic courses on Dostoyevsky's and Turgenev's novels served for debates on the prerevolutionary situation in Russia, just as lectures on economics guided us in our perusal of Soviet economic planning. The Association of Socialist Physicians plus scholarships from the Communist Party, where Coppi belonged to the Youth Organization, had enabled us to attend the Scharfenberg School, a progressive institution at that time. Our chief advocate had been Hodann, a municipal physician, head of the Health Office of the Reinickendorf district and director of the Institute of Sexology. We had met him at the question-and-answer evenings in the Ernst Haeckel Auditorium, and until his imprisonment and escape in nineteen thirty-three we often participated in the regular discussions on psychology, literature, and politics taking place every second week at his home in a settlement on Wiesener Strasse, Tempelhof. After the summoning of the National Socialist government, known as the *Machtübernahme*, the takeover of power, when it was no longer possible for us to go to school, Coppi had begun training at Siemens, and I had gotten a job as a shipping clerk at Alfa Laval, where my father had been foreman in the separator assembly department. Here, in one of the low elongated brick buildings on Heidestrasse, between the Lehrter freight station, with its workshops, warehouses, roundhouses, and shunting trains on the one side and on the other the thronging barges on the canal, which linked Humboldt Harbor to North Harbor, I was busy receiving equipment parts from Hamburg, from the Bergedorf Ironworks, and from company headquarters in Stockholm, as well as packing the finished separators for dairies. In late nineteen thirty-four, my parents had decided to return to Czechoslovakia, the country to which our passports assigned us after the conclusion of the peace treaty of Versailles and Trianon; I myself had kept my job in order to continue the evening classes for my high school diploma. When my parents left, I rented out the room in our apartment on Pflugstrasse, near Wedding, to a family, while I, as I had done earlier, slept in the kitchen, where the incessant nightly rattling, clattering, and hissing from Stettin Station alternated with the roaring at my job in Moabit. In the spring of thirty-seven, after becoming an assistant fitter, I had been laid off because of staff reductions, and I had been looking for odd jobs ever since, constantly at risk of being deported or, given the demand that I apply for German citizenship, in danger of having to report to the army, an obligation that, following a draft notice from the Czechoslovakian embassy, was hanging over me this fall, in my unfamiliar homeland. However, my high school equivalency classes and my studies of medicine and economics, which I had pursued on the side, were done with anyway for the moment, while my military duty had to be delayed since I was looking ahead to activity in Spain. For me, as was true for Coppi and so many others, the lack of solid career plans was part of a natural development, we saw political action as our chief task, and my road led out of the country in which I had grown up. Coppi had to get his bearings here; after his prison term he, a trained latheman, had been forced to go on unemployment, he had sold shoelaces and also newspapers and ice cream at a stand by the Red Mill Movie Theater at Halensee Station, and now, still a member of the illegal Communist Party, he was being conscripted for labor service to build an expressway outside Spandau. For Heilmann the schooling was still regulated. Once his father, after teaching at Dresden's Technical Institute, had taken over a leading position at Berlin's Municipal Construction Agency, Heilmann had started at the Herder School and was living with his parents on Hölderlinstrasse, right off the square that we called Reich Chancellor Square, where we spit whenever we passed any of its present street signs. The gray men planted there, with straightened hams, each rifle placed on a flat hand on the shoulder, should, said Heilmann, stand in front of the temple not to commemorate the conquests but to make sure no further marching orders were given, and the only people honored in the tomb should be those who resisted the tyrant. Taking detours, roundabouts, from the turmoil of Friedrichstrasse into the vaults and embranchments of the passageway, past the waxworks and the shop windows of the court painter, who, in accordance with the Chancellor's taste, daubed the oppressive mendacity of the Greater German intoxication into the nakedness of ecstatic maidens and youths, then into Georgenstrasse, past the elevated lines, amid the thunder of the municipal trains, back to the Copper Ditch, on the bridge to Monbijou Castle, in the riverbanks areas, past Chamisso with shoulder-length hair on the red marble pedestal, leaving the stock exchange behind us, turning into Hackescher Markt, all the way to Rosenthaler Strasse, corner of Linienstrasse, where the Coppi Family lived three flights up in the second back court, Heilmann, occasionally referring to Heracles' project, elucidated something he had been recording in notebooks for years now, his concept of a future society that, after the experiences of coercion, deception, degradation, and all manner of torture, would eliminate the familiar systems, laws, and taboos. Any fear of authority, any submissiveness, any blind performance of work would, he said, give way to a sigh of relief, confusion was over, the collective best was identical with one's own best, everything would be voluntary and completely balanced, there would be no more ranks, no secret decisions made behind closed doors, everything would take place in public, allowing access and monitoring at any point. This society, where every measure, every assignment would be determined by the participants themselves and where the products would belong to them, where everyone could continue his education according to his own needs, was certain to be characterized by self-confidence, by pride and pleasure. Such a structure, borrowing, said Coppi, from the ideas of Saint-Just, Babeuf, Proudhon, can only lead to anarchism, to chaos. Your state, which makes itself superfluous by having no ruling class to support and no one left to keep down, recalls the generation that Lenin said was capable of discarding all the old garbage, ask about that preparatory phase, which you leave in mythical murkiness, and in which the most authoritarian thing that exists, the revolution, is reality. The victors would have to use weapons to force their will upon the vanquished and weapons that inspire terror to assert their power, and before talking about the demise of the state, they would have to set up a new state, with the rules of a new life together, and this would launch the everyday efforts, in which any theory has to demonstrate its usefulness. Perhaps it was the hustle and bustle of the surrounding traffic that made Heilmann's words unclear, but he insisted that the very thing that Coppi labeled an illusion, the figment of an imagination run riot, was, to Heilmann's mind, built on solid ground, for we were, after all, sufficiently familiar with programs, with the strictures of rules and regulations, we knew that obedience, trust in superior leadership were meant to weaken our own faculty of judgment, invalidate our discernment, and promote inferiority and powerlessness. What we must do, he said, is overcome the patterns that have been taken over since time immemorial. His statements, however, which got lost in the din, bouncing against unknown faces, had long since been refocusing on the step that Heracles had taken, away from the privilege of an alliance with Mount Olympus and toward the earthly, and it was only gradually that we could follow the thoughts about what sort of changes Heracles had thereby wrought, what mistakes he had made, and, perhaps, what knowledge he had gained on his travels. The direction he thereby took was traced out from the very start, for as a baby he had already rebelled against the intrigues of the powerful. In her jealousy, Hera, sister and wife of Zeus, had acted to delay the birth of Heracles by clamping up the womb of Alcmene, who, impregnated by the father of the gods, was now in labor. This, said Heilmann, showed the breach leading to irreconcilable conflict, for the revolt against the status quo had been prefigured in the embryo, and intrigue and cunning had been used in the attempt to preserve tradition. On that day, as Zeus solemnly announced to the gathering of the great, a new ruler was to come into the world, a highly promising man. Zeus's drift was, as usual, unfathomable to mortals, but the queen of heaven smelled disaster, for she was sufficiently acquainted with her spouse's machinations, and something inspired by a sudden whim, by a divine pleasure, seemed to be in the making, something that could shake the entire venerable structure. The events had shifted from the upper sphere to the earthly level. The man of promise was to be born to Amphitryon, a nobleman in Thebes, a descendant of Perseus. Hera, striding through the air, hurried into the chambers of another lofty personage, likewise a kinsman of Perseus, Sthenelus, whose wife was pregnant, in her seventh month, and the goddess, using acrid potions, made her give birth prematurely, so that, instead of Heracles, Eurystheus was pushed into life at the designated hour. Outfoxed and belated, the person whom Zeus had chosen for grand deeds appeared next to the one preferred by Hera, and Heracles was well formed, he promptly opened his eyes and reached about while the other lay motionless, grimacing, with a bluish cast. We will see, said Heilmann, the fruits of this rivalry, in the course of which the misshapen boy came to power and the strong and well-proportioned boy had to endure all burdens and afflictions. Enviously Hera followed the growth of the healthy baby, for whom the normal basket was soon inadequate, and in golden sandals that did not graze the ground she stole over to him, bathed in ambrosia, heavy pendants on her ears, and, in her voluptuous arms, two serpents to snuff the rival's life. She bent deep between the mosquito veils, which were pushed aside, and the child reached out his hands as if to stroke her tenderly, but then spit in her face and strangled the adders. While Eurystheus was still woefully bawling in his pillows and being coddled to health by the nurses, Heracles was already tending the flocks of sheep on his parents' large estate and gaining his first renown in the rustic population since he tore the throats not only of the attacking wolves but also of the supposedly invincible lion that had been devouring the livestock in the environs for years. Eurystheus, his cousin, tearfully recited poems, accompanying them, off-key, on the lyre, but when Linus, the tutor, tried to inveigle Heracles into believing that the only existing freedom was the freedom of art, his pupil yanked the man's hat down so hard over his eyes that he broke his nose, and when the schoolmaster then claimed that art was at all times to be enjoyed independently of the contemporary chaos, Heracles thrust him headfirst into the cesspool, drowning him to prove that unarmed aestheticism cannot withstand the simplest violence. He had already once beaten the daughter of Mnemosyne, she too a relative, for daring to presume that she alone could settle all issues of dance, music, song, and poetry, Heracles preferred the ditties sung in the streets and the shrill reed flutes, the caterwauling bagpipes, the whacking of drums in the taverns. Wandering around the urban outskirts despised by the muses, he got to know the poverty that was at home in shacks and basements, and it was always the maids and farmhands, the cringing domestics, the day laborers, the small shopkeepers, who starved and were sucked dry by the inflicted tributes, while the castles had overabundant meat, fruit, and vegetables, just as the wine vats there, and the treasure chests, were always filled. Heracles could not believe that the terror gripping his native city Thebes could be blamed on Erginus, the mystical prince, whom no one had ever seen, for why did Creon, the king, and the entire royal household belch and puke in surfeit, why did the aristocratic ladies don new frocks every day, if they were ruled by a despot who levied incessant taxes. To show that it was solely the blue bloods who held the ignorant mass of workers down by deluding them and forced them into drudgery by bribing and buying their leaders and masters and threatening the workers with unheard-of punishments, Heracles sailed to the island of marble quarries and came back with a retinue that commanded respect. He did not need to explain very much to the slaves who sat coughing in the basin, their lungs full of stone dust. With marble chips in their beards, with pebbles between their toes, armed with their big saws and crowbars, they accompanied him, and they made short shrift of any sentries, the only surprise was when people asked why this had not happened earlier. Heracles arrived in Thebes with the freed slaves and spread the news that he had drawn and quartered Erginus and tossed him to the ravens. Before he even entered the royal castle, songs were being sung in the city, hastily composed for everyday use, with striking rhymes and catchy tunes, describing how the mortal enemy had been dismembered, his limbs scattered in all directions, and how Thebes had finally been delivered. Since neither Creon nor his cagiest priests and philosophers could produce the monster that had ruled over them for so long, Heracles had to be celebrated in the highest echelons, and Creon gave him his daughter Megara as his bride, distributed food and drink to the populace, ordered three days of feasting, and opened the gates of a few labor camps. The king and all the dignitaries now informed Heracles that he was the best, the strongest, that he deserved the rank stolen from him by the weakly inferior Eurystheus, but they simultaneously maneuvered the earlier born upon the throne of Mycenae, from where he ordered the capture of the runaway slaves and sent heavily armed troops across the land to massacre the rebellious peasants. That was the time of Heracles' derangement, said Heilmann, while, from the central market hall, trucks piled high with empty crates and cartons drove toward us. Heracles, beguiled by Megara's charms, did not even notice that his bodyguards had been murdered and buried, no warning cry came up to him over the castle walls, and when, in a silk garment, he first went out again through the gates, into the city, where he thought the epoch of prosperity had begun, he found only beggars and children running wild and throwing rocks at him, and a few passing craftsmen turned away when he called to them. A single moment of inattention had managed to destroy all his achievements, and now months had passed, perhaps years, ones that he had spent idly and that the enemy had used. The state was armed better than ever to forestall any recurrence of surprise attacks. The court authors had likewise learned a bit more and, in the patois of the streets, composed satirical poems about Heracles' swindling of the poor, his braggadocio, his bumptiousness, while Eurystheus, the sage, installed by the grace of the supreme god, was praised in many verses for his fatherly love of the populace. The populace, who it was said, always needed something it could believe in, could venerate, was offered parades on the public squares, with a visual delight of chariots, plumed helmets, standards, while exalted speeches voiced the hope that the final conspirators, who stood in the way of renewal, would soon be eliminated, and the regent told the weary and famished that he was worried about them and shared their suffering, and the listeners learned in hushed amazement that what had been imposed on them was a state of emergency. How, we wondered, on the canal, leaning against the sooty iron railing, its knobs splotched white by bird droppings, how could Heracles have assumed that others had already been there to continue what he had begun, how could he have believed that an isolated deed sufficed as an example of how to achieve the upheaval. He howled with anger, said Heilmann, he raged in his bedroom, less because this had happened to him, a man who did, after all, know how to defend himself, than because he had run out on the countless others who were weaker and without influence. Before fighting his way out of the spears encircling him, he killed his wife and also the children she had born him, everything that bound him to the higher ranks, any kinship had to be snuffed out, no reconciliation was possible here, and we were endorsing his frenzy when a squad of black gravediggers, with skulls on their caps, moved past us, bawling. But we did not understand why, wrapped in a sack and strewn with ashes, he then went to Mycenae to submit to Eurystheus. He humbled himself, begged forgiveness, said Heilmann, he took every degradation upon himself because it was necessary for him to survive. Instead of winding up in the torture chambers that were prepared for him, he offered to serve the monarch and carried out a series of dangerous missions for the ruler, who could pique himself on his ally. Understanding the negligence and the changed situation in the land, Heracles now had to focus on a lengthy plan, with which he hoped to overcome the system of malevolence, assassination, and lust for power maintained by Eurystheus with Hera's help. Initially, the purpose of Heracles' actions was not obvious, and this uncertainty has been preserved up to the present day in the legends that were spread about him. The scholars tersely announced that Heracles was risking his life for the beloved Eurystheus in order to wipe out the hotbeds of rebellion and hostility throughout the country and later in distant areas as well. The storytellers in the markets embellished the envoy's deeds with details. Way up in the northeast, close to Nemea, he had slain yet another lion by getting him into a headlock with his left arm, boring his thumb and forefinger into the brute's nostrils, and plunging his right fist through the gaping jaws, deep into the gullet. Cloaked in the beast's skin with the paws joined on his chest, the open maw thrust over his head, Heracles had moved on, this time southward, to the marshes of Lerna, where the nine-headed Hydra dwelled. Since it was known that whenever one of the reptile's heads was chopped off two grew in its place, people in the bazaars were already saying derogatory things about Heracles, what good is his big black sickle, they said, if all he does is leave a bigger tangle of serpents than before. He would not be Heracles, came the retort, if he ended an adventure without victory. What happened was that he took a glowing tree trunk and burned out the neck stump of every decapitated head, thereby preventing any new growth. The listeners shook their heads, clicking their tongues in disbelief. But then when Heracles came from the mountains of Erymanthus with a captured boar, holding the tremendous drooling beast by its rear legs as he paraded it into the palace and into the throne room, where the God-sent king, quaking with fear, crept into a clay jug, there was loud mirth despite all the misery, and some people got an inkling of what Heracles was planning. Ever since, his fame resurged among those who had already given him up for lost, and when they heard that he was at the lake of Stymphalus, about to eliminate the giant birds that plagued the countryside, nesting on the farmland, the children acted out these stories, shooting their arrows aloft with lightning motions and, surrounded by feathers, pointing triumphantly at the heaps of prey. Granted, many people still felt that all the game he had hunted, all the herds of cattle he had brought in benefited not them, but only the gentlemen of the court; but others set out to emulate Heracles and explore the regions beyond the Archipelago. A time of ocean voyages, of epoch-making discoveries commenced. While the aristocrats drove their thinkers to ever-greater exertions in depicting the distant feats of Heracles to their advantage, the have-nots talked about him as one of their own. What's the news about Heracles, was constantly asked, and just as they were proud of him for wresting the fire-breathing bull to its knees, taming the man-eating horses, felling the three-headed giant, and winning the friendship of Atlas, so too their anger mounted against Eurystheus, who, with Hera's whispered promptings in his ears, attempted once more to pursue the hero with disaster and bring him down. It was time, said the workers gathering secretly at night, for him to return, since no one now had any doubts that he was superior to Eurystheus with all his landowners and generals, and the workers wondered what he had done among the Amazons, what the pillars meant that he had erected on the shores of Okeanos, and why he was staying on so long in the gardens of the Hesperides. He had, came the answer, to measure the entire world with his steps in order to determine where a superior enemy force or a potential for free development could be found. Meanwhile the workers geared up for the day when he would rejoin them. During the inroads of the mercenaries, the workers remained calm and collected. They gathered pitch in secret cellars in order to set the arsenals ablaze at the appropriate moment. When they had to erect new walls around the royal castle, they made sure these ramparts contained passageways to be opened quickly. They knew that Eurystheus wandered sleeplessly through his sumptuous halls, hearing all the walls whispering that Heracles would soon be returning. By now it was too late for the rulers to bewail Heracles' release, for the whippers to order the soldiers to remain extremely watchful, for the governors to distribute alms in the cities. The disquiet that had been spreading could no longer be denied, the security of the nobles was undermined, no prayers or parades could wring devotion from the populace. The torturers were still raging, and the dungeons still filling up with any people arbitrarily suspected of dissatisfaction. But the whereabouts of the real prisoners were shown one morning, before sunrise, when Heracles arrived in Thebes, accompanied by a gigantic hound, at whose howling all those who had a solid house crept under their beds, while those in shacks and those who slept outdoors pricked up their ears and dashed toward Heracles as if called by a cheery trumpet. The guardian of infernal order, who had been depicted as unassailable since time immemorial, had been pulled out of the earthly depths by Heracles, easily, with a song, it was said, during his last raid into the interior of the world structure, and in the marketplace, which had been abandoned by the warriors of the upper ranks, he showed the maids and farmhands, the craftsmen and the day laborers, and the loitering rank and file: Cerberus, the shabby cur, who, upon viewing the vast assembly pulled in his tail and started whimpering. Heracles had also brought a caged eagle, a further celebrity in the system of coercion and menace; the eagle had served to torment the defiant, the valiant, the self-confident, to devour the livers of the rebellious, over and over, and now all this, as the inhabitants of Thebes could see, was about to end. They saw what scabby scraggy legs had propped up the reign of fraud and lies and how wretchedly the feathers dangled on the bird that had only just been throning proudly over Prometheus, how dull the membranes were that had drawn over the bird's eyes, which had otherwise glittered so dangerously. An end thus to fettering anyone to anguish for thinking new thoughts, everything was open in Thebes, in Mycenae, for the age of justice. But, we wanted to know, did the inhabitants manage to spread so much conviction that the aristocrats in the palaces, in the patrician buildings, came crawling on their knees, begging for mercy, were they not, after a little doubting and waffling and not even necessarily a betrayal, but rather that routine tolerance, given a chance to defend themselves, to strike back. For it was not peace that now followed, we would, after all, have heard about it; instead new campaigns were launched, wars, vaster than ever. From now on, however, Heracles could not be imagined anywhere but on the side of the enslaved, said Heilmann amid the screeching of the wheels of a packed trolley, which, coming from Alexanderplatz, turned into Rosenthaler Strasse; Heracles, Heilmann went on, had made it clear that all magic spells had been broken, all legendary creatures subdued, and it was a mortal who could perform such feats. His apprenticeship was over, everything he now did would be marked by tremendous changes, he already had powerful allies, including the carrier of the firmament. And yet, said Heilmann after a while, as we entered the worn building entrance, which was shored up by buckling titans, and yet Heracles perished in dreadful agony, no one managed to grab the shirt soaked in Nessus's poisoned blood, tear it from his skin, stop his pain-induced madness, and prevent him from throwing himself into the ever-burning pyre on Mount Oite.

Leaving behind the rows of telescoped carts in the courtyard, the creaking boards of the stairs, we opened the door with the ribbed glass pane, with scratches and peelings in the greasy, blackish brown paint, with the letter box of bossed black metal, with the cracked white enamel of the oval nameplate, with the nailed spotted cardboard bearing the ornately printed text, Reader of Der Völkische Beobachter, and we entered the kitchen. In the smoky light falling through the window, we could recognize stove and sink, and, at the table, under the green porcelain shade of the ceiling lamp, Coppi's mother, upright on the chair with the slanting arm. After returning from her half-day shift at the Telefunken Works on Hallesches Ufer, she had taken off her shoes and stockings and sunk her feet into a bowl of steaming water. At first only dimly perceptible, their contours dissolving in front of the six rectangles of the window, the details of her shape emerged as we joined her at the spic-and-span table. From the edge of her gray hair, which was tied back in a knot, thin creases fanned down her forehead to the root of the nose, between thick eyebrows. Her nose arched out, deep notches ran from its wings, past the corners of the mouth, to the chin, her lips were narrow, moistened by the tip of her tongue, she wiped the back of her hand across her closed, yellowishly discolored eyelids. Her thin neck rose rigidly between the stooped shoulders, she wore a light blue dress, with dark blue vertical stripes and a white collar with a brooch, its white bead reflecting the window intercepted in the mirror on the opposite wall. The effigy of the window likewise shone in the pupils of her eyes, which now opened. The window halves were hooked fast, the front door was locked from the inside with the key, the blanket pulled across on its brass rings. From the walls a dull green poured into the room, except for the mirror nothing hung on the walls but a calendar and a clock in a round white case. A door led to the room containing the bed of Coppi's parents. Coppi himself slept on the sofa in the kitchen, between a chest and a low bookcase, everything resembled the furnishings in our apartment on Pflugstrasse when I had lived there with my parents. The kitchen space, gradually filling with shadow while the filaments of the lamp grew sharper, formed a seclusion that attempted to impose a sense of overwhelming defeat on us as we sat at the table. Outside this cell, beyond the crumbling walls, the framework of the stairs, the courtyard shaft, there was only hostility, occasionally interspersed with similar small locked rooms, which became scarcer and scarcer, more and more difficult to detect, or were no longer to be found at all. Every word had to be picked out of the powerlessness in order to strike the tone we had been using for over four years to inspire one another with confidence, perseverance, and vitality. Overcoming the catastrophe we had suffered was always a premise for everything we undertook, whether alone or with like-minded people. Usually this fortifying ensued imperceptibly, out of habit, it required only a few moments of silence. Even when our conversations then seemed commonplace or began to focus, they were always haunted by the closeness of a mortal danger. Any knowledge we had gained during the past few years was related to this interplay between necessary isolation and extremely alert reconnoitering in an enemy realm that kept widening its borders. We refused to acknowledge that fatigue and overexertion could sometimes take the upper hand, we declared such manifestations of physical and mental weakness to be components of our function. Whenever they set in, we ignored them, waiting for them to pass, and we remembered the prisons, the peat bogs, the torture fields fenced in with barbed wire, and after a while we found ourselves back in a structure containing certain guidelines and reference points despite the seeming hopelessness. After the failure to make common cause, after the shattering of our organizations, we, in the greenish darkness of the room, shared a number of unshakable ideas for which news and instructions were transmitted to us from the outside. While the inside of the kitchen, where Coppi now covered the windows with blackout paper, was sealed almost hermetically, we nevertheless already had viewpoints that tied us to actions leading to violent conflicts and clashes in places that could be geographically pinpointed. Once we had eluded the surveillance that dogged our every step, we could discuss the directives that gave us stability and enabled us to keep working. Leading functionaries of the outlawed parties, having managed to evade prison and murder, had set up their bases outside the borders, sometimes they came back, and in the small conspiratorial groups at the factories, in the bogus clubs of bowlers, singers, athletes, Sunday gardeners, we learned, mostly just in twos, in threes, in fours, about any resistance measures created within the larger circumference. Often the names of places where meetings had been held were changed. Thus the discussions in Moscow, during the autumn of nineteen thirty-five, on the buildup of illegal activities and on the necessity of unifying the workers' parties, were attributed to Brussels, where, at the start of the century, the Russian Social Democrats had held their congress, originally called the Party Day of Unity, but then leading to the division into Bolsheviki and Mensheviki. The reference to this historical point of departure contained dialectical irony, for as of July nineteen hundred three, one could follow not only the breach within the Russian party but also the antagonistic opinions of German and Russian Social Democrats, which ultimately resulted in a split into the Second and Third International. The name of Brussels reminded us of the grain elevator where, suffocating in the heat, plagued by fleas and rats, huddling on boards, haunted by prowling informers, the émigré Russian revolutionaries, under Lenin's leadership, established their strategies. Brussels evoked the stubborn and resolute and also uncompromising presentations of viewpoints, yet the choice of name simultaneously indicated the effort to regain something of a fundamental togetherness that had been lost. The three decades that had worn by constituted a very brief period, but the severing of the proletariat into the two major parties and then the further splinterings forced by the discord had nurtured an ill that lurked constantly, knowing how to catch any sign of weakness and exploit it for its assaults, and now, in its vast proportions, planning to quash any attempts at renewal. The struggle, verging on mortal enmity, between the labor parties, the destruction of solidarity, the impact of factionalism, all these things were stirred by the memory of Brussels, and it struck us as all the more courageous to begin precisely with the current irreconcilability of the political lines, the source of controversy, thereby pointing out how difficult the enterprise was. The discussions on united action between Communists and Social Democrats were based on the resolutions, passed several weeks earlier at the Seventh World Congress of the Comintern, to orient policies toward forming popular fronts. In the dark about the details of the debates, we had viewed pictures of the edifice of the Communist International to at least behold the headquarters of the men whose deliberations shaped our destinies. The symmetrical multi-windowed building, right next to the Troika Gate of the Kremlin, was given a pink glow under the small frittered clouds of the evening sky, and we also pictured the golden cupolas rising from the red brickwork, with the lily-shaped loopholes, and above, in front of the gigantic open square, the compact cube, the black Kaaba, containing the glassy man, the vanished man. We tried to fit our tiny hidden precinct into the grand pattern and to accord our isolated experiences with guidelines, with slogans, whose diverse issues had been compiled, compared, assessed, revised, and hardened by the delegates and purified in disputes. During our childhood, incessant efforts had been made to establish the United Front; then, for half a decade, all the way into the open power of fascism, those endeavors had bogged down, been blocked, but were now once again pressing for a solution, for a way of overcoming earlier mistakes. The sparse news reaching us eighteen-year-olds, information that could be articulated in the underground, was repeatedly readdressed, reexamined, and also re-scrutinized in terms of its consequences. For us, a basic proviso was that large-scale events must never become something incomprehensible, enigmatic, that we must never view our isolation as a liability. We clung to the belief that something existed abroad, gaining strength and preparing to strike back, and the harder it was to take up contact among the leftovers of illegal groups, to provide mutual help and inform one another about plans, the more meaningful even the slightest detail became for drawing inferences about the status, the courses of action outside our borders. Yet for a year now, aside from the total control, which barely permitted movements in a wider perimeter, the Soviet Party had been experiencing changes that imposed additional caution and anxiety on us and that, concealing their underlying causes, demanded that we focus harder on everyone we had previously trusted. Since I myself had begun working only after the start of the fascist regime, the premises for the political activities of our parents had become defunct for me. At their jobs, our parents had had mutual everyday interests overriding the diversity of party memberships and ideological conflicts. The bias of generational antagonism was all that was nullified; but stronger than ever was the sole existing demarcation, drawn by the class struggle, and this line ran straight across all age groups. The only question asked was on which side of the front one stood, though eventually this was shown in nothing but tacit concurrence with joint actions. Our personal development took place in drastic confinement, freedom of cultural movement was unthinkable, anything we learned could only be picked up on the sly. In nineteen thirty-seven, amid paradoxical signs of the striving for a broad unified front, of the interior distrust, of the disintegration in our own ranks, we were forced, with every impetus we received, to interpret it by our own lights, often in a visionary way, thereby giving it Idealistic Form. The things we heard about Spain, about the revolutionary movement in China, about the riots and rebellions in southeast Asia, in Africa, in Latin America, or about the mass strikes, the coalition of unions and labor parties in France, led us to assume that the thought of victory over the reactionary forces in the world was not so far-fetched as the shrieking claptrap of *Gleichschaltung*, forced conformity, in our country would have it. Yet whenever we tried to detect clues of changes in the factories and organizations, hints of recalcitrance, of sabotage, practically all we found was resigned accommodation, wordless witnessing, and our utopias could not blind us to the fact that many of those whom we had seen, in January of thirty-three, freezing, ill clad, going to the Liebknecht House, were now marching under the flags in whose red the crossed tools of work had been replaced by the glaring angular symbol of devastation. While it was imperative that Heilmann's parents learn nothing about their son's plans, and we visited him simply as buddies from the Eichkamp Sports Club, with the soccer ball in the net bag, Coppi's family, like mine earlier, participated in all discussions on the dubious aspects of political life. This possibility of also thrashing out even our own perplexities and fallacies was crucial to our progress, and Heilmann belonged here in Coppi's kitchen more than at his parents' home in Berlin's West End. Just as for us a generation gap was a feature of economic dependency in a society we were striving to abolish, so too we had violently ended the division of education according to class privileges. Lack of interest in social, political, scientific, scholarly, and esthetic issues of the day, dull inactivity, intellectual and spiritual impoverishment, noncommittal opinions were more frequent among philistines and also members of the bourgeoisie than in the masses of those who were cut off from the cultural institutions and ground down by hard, monotonous labor. Since my early youth, I had been accustomed to hearing clear and cogent statements about property conditions and the workings of the economy, about the state of research, about artistic production, about the situation in our country and in other countries and continents from people who had gained their experience in places of confrontations between antithetical forces, who were drawn directly into the storm centers of the social process, and who not only knew which inventions and discoveries served the powers that be and which were of popular benefit, but who could also provide information on where to find the beneficiaries, what their faces and names were, and what profits they had scraped off the backs of the workers. At issue were elementary things, the investigation of crimes and racketeering in companies and in the housing market, in the municipal and central governments, in international diplomacy and in the strongholds of trusts and monopolies, at issue were press debates, art exhibits, and newly published books, the assessments of party politics and worldwide power constellations, and before the reign of madness we had participated in the critique of the delegates in businesses and unions, in the discussions on wage demands, industrial safety, or strikes, and all of us knew about the conditions in the laggard southern European countries, in the ghettos of the United States, and in the colonies, where nations were launching their struggle for freedom. Many people certainly refrained from speaking out, degraded as they were by upbringing, numbed by defeats, but once they began talking they showed how familiar they were with the processes they were embroiled in, and wherever I went I always heard an apt judgment, a new indication toward understanding a current issue. On Saturday evenings and on Sundays, fellow workers of parents, neighbors, at times also foreign guests, metal workers from Bohemia, Italian and Spanish comrades, with whom my mother, a native of Strasbourg, used scraps of French to help them communicate, we would often sit in the kitchen, which was our parlor. My father, a Social Democrat since adolescence and certainly the only political prisoner ever detained by the police in his native Hungarian village of Nagy Emöke, for agitation against the war-mongering of imperial royal Austria, had been forced into military service, had been critically wounded on the Galician front and shipped to Germany in the spring of nineteen sixteen, and then, after his release from the army hospital, had settled in Bremen. That was where I was born on November eighth, nineteen seventeen. My father had found a job at the Weser Shipyard and, through his activities at the Workmen's Educational Alliance, come into contact with *Arbeiterpolitik* [Workers' Politics], a newspaper closely linked to the Spartacus League. In November of nineteen eighteen, after Liebknecht's proclamation of the Socialist Republic, my father was in Berlin and then with the revolutionary insurrection in Bremen, during the Twenties he studied on his own and eventually took the state engineering examination, but, having no possibility of professional advancement, continued working in dockyards, in fine-mechanical workshops, until we moved to Berlin, where, thanks to technical improvements that he had introduced at his workplace, he was promoted to foreman. After belonging to the Independent Social Democrats during the time of political radicalization, he had rejoined the Majority Party in March of nineteen twenty-one because he felt it offered him greater opportunity for operating inside the union organizations. Although the party leaders sided with the adversary during the fighting in Berlin and Bremen and he subsequently kept clashing with their policies, he nevertheless clung to his belief that the masses of workers could push the party toward a United Socialist Front. Despite his striving for united action, he had an anarchist, a syndicalist streak, and just as he always distrusted officials, officers, bureaucrats, and managers, so too he was repelled by the functionaries and high muckety-mucks in

his party. The party, for him that was his fellow workers, and he never abandoned his expectation that they would give the party its physiognomy. He did not join the Communist Party because he was unable to sympathize with its centralism. He viewed the command power of the top brass and the obedience of the subdivisions as a principle that was inconsistent with his concept of democracy. He also rejected the mandate of absolute faith in decisions because he said it had a religious character and reminded him of kowtowing to authority. By sticking up only for workers, whether Social Democrats or Communists, and opposing the burgeoning anti-Communist tendencies in the union, he voted for the Social Democratic Party, though always vehemently attacking its latest maneuvers of retreat and compromise, yet trusting that through this party the workers, without smashing the state, indeed using it, would eventually supervise and gradually take over production. The dichotomy between reform and revolution was our constant theme, and it may have been my father's experiences during the postwar uprisings that convinced him that social change could be achieved not by violent actions but purely by gradually strengthening and expanding the labor movement, not by armed struggle but along a parliamentary route. When asked whether the fighting spirit had not been broken long ago by opportunism, the toleration of bourgeois power positions, and the postponement of intrinsic demands, he merely replied that the forces carrying the two major parties had always been willing to join together and that only the leaders had not yet found the way, and even in the early Thirties, when the rapid growth of the fascist menace could not induce his executive board to come to terms with the Communist Party leaders, he still considered the emergence of proletarian common sense possible and, shortly before January of thirty-three, he actually reckoned with powerful counter-demonstrations that would, in the last minute, avert the ruin of the working class. During such reflections, he would pull up his left shoulder, which had been stiff since being struck by a bullet during the skirmish on Bremen's Kaiser Bridge, and this half-shrug made him look like an eternal skeptic. He was friends with Merker, who was on the Central Committee of the Communist Party and who, at union meetings, advocated cooperation at a time when the Social Democrats were being labeled Social Fascists by the Communist slogans, and who offered his support when Social Democratic groups were being formed for illegal work inside the borders. Merker, Dittbender, Münzenberg, Ackermann, and Wehner were only a few of the numerous Communists whom he got to know at work and through the Berlin Red Aid (which looked after comrades from abroad), and who encouraged him in his efforts toward overcoming the partisan conflicts. After the collapse of the labor parties, after the terrifying acquiescence of the greater majority, scattered names survived with which we, in our isolation, long associated a tradition, that, having now grown shaky, could not be personified with any certainty. Earlier, people like my parents, like Coppi's, used to be found throughout the working population, they were internationalists in their attitude, whether Social Democrats or Communists they kept aloof from party feuds, and while the decisive politics were being conducted over their heads, these people, never much talked about and ideologically seeking cooperation instead of separation, always had the courage of their convictions. Hoping, like many others, for the counterforce, then, after a year, confronted with the humiliating realization that the time of waiting, of hibernating would drag on for years, for decades, my father had moved to Czechoslovakia to look for work once again. The readjustment was tough on him and my mother, and although, with the help of the party and the union, he was soon hired by a textile plant in the north Bohemian town of Warnsdorf, the letters I received from my parents talked about the difficulties of adapting and covertly hinted at an instability that kept gaining ground there too. At a time when Czechoslovakian citizenship still provided a certain protection, my parents had succeeded in escaping political persecution, and with my Czech passport I could continue my education so long as I could show I had a job and a permanent residence. It was harder for the Coppi family to endure the pressure, the father, a body painter at the defense plant of the Mechanical Workshops, Berlin, was instantly dismissed for refusing to join the National Socialist organizations, and then, having to buckle after all, he was given a subordinate job with a salary that, together with the low pay from the mother's part-time work, was barely enough to survive on. Only the beans, turnips, and potatoes grown on the parcel the Coppis owned in Forest's Edge, the allotment association in Tegel, could tide them over in emergencies. Nevertheless, the burden of uncertainty did not prevent us anymore than earlier from seeking cultural stimuli. Granted, we had no wealth of literature on our shelves, we borrowed books every week from the public library, during Hodann's absence I had lugged piles of them from his apartment to ours for he was glad to lend them, but the volumes that belonged to us were carefully picked, they had become part of our life, acquired by Father, by Mother. Freighted through countless moves, some books having been obtained way back in Bremen, they were our sole permanent property along with some dishes and bedding and the packed-up clothing, for we regarded the furniture as simply random goods, purchased cheap and used, handcarted to a new apartment, hurriedly sold before our relocation to a different city. We owned a selection of Mayakovsky's poems, some writings by Mehring, Kautsky, Luxemburg, Zetkin, Lafargue, a few novels by Gorky, Arnold Zweig, and Heinrich Mann, by Rolland, Barbusse, Bredel, and Döblin. Instead of a lace tablecloth, a porcelain vase, my parents had always bought these small blocks of densely piled paper covered with knowledge, suggestions, and instructions, and even when money was scarce my father or my mother might come home with a new book by Toller or Tucholsky, by Kisch, Ehrenburg, or Nexö, and we would spend evenings under the kitchen lamp, taking turns reading aloud with all of us discussing the contents. How meaningful these books were and how powerfully they held us together was shown during the period when the police kept breaking into one or another of our homes and using the authors' names as incriminating evidence, so that owning a volume of Lenin was tantamount to high treason. That was why the number of books we stored in our apartments kept shrinking, under the kindling wood next to Coppi's kitchen stove there was room for nothing but a paperback introduction to *Das Kapital*, a few news clippings of speeches by Dimitrov and Stalin, the latest issues of *Die Rote Fahne* [The Red Flag] thrust into *Der Völkische Beobachter* [The People's Observer], and the tattered pamphlet that, disguised as a paperback edition of *Wallenstein's Camp*, had gone from hand to hand, the *Brown Book of the Reichstag Fire Trial*. During these years the bleakness and squalor in the workers' flats spoke less than ever of a cerebral vacuum, the political activists were all well known, in the past no one had ever made a secret of his party allegiance, the membership lists were in the hands of the State Police, we lived from moment to moment, watched by janitors, shop stewards, block wardens, district heads, Storm Troopers and SA men; relatives, close friends were in prison, in detention camps, or in exile, and those remaining made do with the barest necessities. The latter were as usual clean and tidy, the rooms where many people lived crowded together were never dilapidated, the meagerness expressed a tacit and tenacious revolt against the storm of demoralization and stultification.

The wet footprints on the dark green linoleum marked the path that Coppi's mother had taken to empty the bowl into the sink and refill it with hot water from the kettle on the stove. The altar that is now in our museum, she said, carrying back the bowl, was the property of kings, we can, if we have time, stand in front of those things, but if we want to understand what they mean, and above all if we want to claim them for ourselves, we have to make up for everything we were not taught at school. After all, we barely learned, she said, sitting down and putting her feet back in the bowl, how to read and write, and looking at pictures never entered anyone's mind. For most of us, these marble figures have no more value than the giants down at the entrance, and if they are torn down, it bothers us as little as the ancient builders who had to erect new walls from the blocks. When they broke the stones out of the walls, they did what was practical, they did not have to drag them up from the valley, they could get them from close by, and besides they had to act fast, the enemy was on the march, the stronghold was threatened. Whenever I pass between the Atlases, I feel sorry for them, I wish they could finally be rid of their burdens, no one ought to be bending by doors like that, reminding us of our own hardships. If we toppled them across the roadway, as a barricade, they would have some purpose. For the laborers on the acropolis, the ashlars were nothing but building material, they walled them up with the smooth backs on the outside after lopping off the heads and limbs because anything that jutted out interfered with the fitting. How can we, she asked, ever get away from the fact that for our kind all that construction involved nothing but drudgery and deprivation, plus a pent-up rage toward the people who took the credit. And how can we then say that the salvaged ruins represent something that enriches our senses. To the Mohammedans, said Heilmann, who invaded Pergamum earlier the Hellenist artwork looked as barbaric as to the Byzantines, who were defending their possessions. After all, the Arabs did have grounds for smashing the buildings, since they came as conquerors, and destruction was a law of war, while the Byzantine lords of the castle used their self-defense to make a clean sweep of the pagan remnants. The faces of the gods were hewn off, the sons of the earth were spared. Both Islamites and Christians annihilated anything that flouted their religions, anything they found exotic, a feel for bygone cultures had existed only in the highly developed Pergamum. When we look at the athletes in loincloths beneath, we can guess the period when they were produced and read the mendacity of industrialism, which needed new slaves, and by the same token the frieze sculptures take us to an epoch that teaches us something about the origins of the society whose final abuses we are now experiencing. We debated what Pergamum had represented, how it had emerged, the way it crumbled and passed to new phases, and every sentence involved learning how to think, learning how to speak, the gulf between knowledge and speechlessness, which had to be bridged. With its position of power, in which it wanted to become a second Athens, Pergamum also took over the gods of the motherland. The giant figure of Athena, copied from Phidias's statue with its gold and ivory trimming, rose in the inner courtyard of the library, whose archways housed two hundred thousand scrolls on wooden shelves, between stone ledges. Realizing the significance of traditions, Pergamum had set up art collections with copies of classical works and with originals bargained for or else looted by military expeditions. This wealth permitted a look back at the achievements of other centuries, giving the elite of Pergamum the awareness of belonging to a modern era. The teachings of Anaximander and Thales of Miletus were a cultural fundament for a materialistic view of life. These two great forerunners of Pergamene thinkers were less philosophers than construction supervisors, scientists, mathematicians, astronomers, and politicians. They belonged to the class of merchants and seafarers, and their investigations were always sparked by concrete tasks. Bridges, harbors, and strongholds had to be put up. Competitors had to be eliminated, enemy expansions checked. Transportation routes over land and sea had to be extended, raw materials tapped, colonies won, and toward these ends they had to learn the characteristics of the elements and explain the world in terms that renounced any divagations into mystical regions. Coppi pointed out that as a result the entire system of gods had long since become merely part of the superstructure, used for intimidation by the regents, like today's religion, with which the enlightened lulled the ignorant to sleep. The populace was entitled to the plain, the simple, the uncomplicated, the hope for an afterlife that would reward them for all miseries, the faith in the goodness and assistance of the invisible and the fear of the wrathful and punishing deities who scrutinized their every rebellious thought. The upper crust had shrugged off such superstition, they smiled at the childishness of the lower classes and, with fashionable excursions to view shepherds, grape pickers, they could admit that an occasional poetic utterance might come from these illiterates too. For the schooled, there was no existence after death, they had to gain everything here, while alive. The gap between the classes was a gap between diverse realms of understanding. The world was the same for both, the same blue sky, the same green of the trees, the same waters, the same stars could be seen, yet separated from the servants, the untutored, there was knowledge that did not alter things themselves but gave them additional values and functions to be used by the insiders. The man who believed that the earth was a disk surrounded by the torrent of Okeanos, from which the lamps of the gods were withdrawn at night, the man who believed that Selene with her brightening and darkening moon-mirror dictated the lightness and gravity of coming events and that Poseidon blew the waves to the shores and hurled lightning from the clouds at seafarers, that man would not venture abroad on his own, he had to entrust himself to protection by the leaders and the armed men. Wood, fire, wheat, minerals, and metals looked the same in the eyes of those who worked things with tools and those who received the products and harvests, but the advantage enjoyed by these recipients was that they could already calculate the net profit, for they owned the ground that yielded the desired things and owned the market for selling them. The slave held the heavy chunk of ore in one hand and the light leaf in the other, he saw the veins and the glitter of grains and stripes, the thin tissue had been broken from the branch, the fragment had been removed from the split rock, the light, which the lord of the land also saw, played upon the ore, but he knew that matter was composed of infinitesimal particles, the atoms, which, in a wide variety of characteristics and attributes, gave every phenomenon its shape. Whenever he walked across the same soil as his underling, peering across the vast rondure, with its hills, its flocks of cranes, and the hazy mountain crests, he, the lord, was aware of utterly different proportions than the cottager. Driven by the urge to understand what he needed, he had stepped into the four-dimensional conception of space: after curving the plane of the earth, finding its roundness, gaining the possibility of returning to the starting point by following a straight line, and thereby discovering that he was located in infinity, on a rotating sphere, which, together with other spheres, revolved around the sun, the lord had added the relationship with time to his thinking. Lying stretched out, in the clear nights, on the Aegean Sea, and in Egypt, mapping the positions of the stars on the celestial chart, learning the rules by which the moonlight waned and waxed, he established his calendar, precisely reckoning the length of the earth's rotation, the time it took the moon to circle the earth, the earth to orbit around the sun, and the participation of the sun, with its planets, in the system of the millions of stars, which altogether, an utterly remote and milky concentration, formed a gigantic ring with which the infinite closed itself up. Just as he understood what he needed, so too the simplest explanation was the true one. Earlier it had been simple and true that the gods had created the world with all its life, but after forging across the mountains and oceans and extending his view aloft, he was no longer dizzied by the thought that the earth, left alone by the gods, was flying with him through the universe. From a well in Egypt's Syene he took bearings of the sun at its zenith. The string of the plumb bob transmitted the line that could be drawn from the fiery star to the center of the earth. Since by measuring he knew that the rays of the sun were parallel when hitting the earth, an angle had to emerge between the ray falling at the same time in Alexandria to the north and the vertical line he had set. With the aid of this angle and the distance between the two places, he could find the degree of the curvature of the earth and then its circumference, almost down to the exact kilometer. However, just as here, in the valley basin, in the olive plantation, he kept the reasons for the lunar darkening, the solar eclipse, ebb and flow, thunderstorms and rainfall to himself, so too he never let on that masses of primal matter had once torn loose from the universe and linked up in the void, that worlds had been created and destroyed by collisions before the fiery lump of the earth crusted over, the flaming storms were snuffed, the continents ascended from the boiling water, and the first fishlike creatures developed in the slime, ultimately producing human beings. The dynamics of the whole thing, it was said when people asked about the purpose of existence, was the law of necessity, and anyone who recognized this law also mastered it with his free will. The action of this freeness was solely an abiding by necessity. Driven to increase his possessions, he explored the earth all the way to the icy isle of Thule in the north and southward all the way to the African cape, westward beyond the Pillars of Heracles and eastward to the widely branching flow of the Ganges, while the peasant, measuring clumsily, paced off his scrap of farmland. The bound man sat on the thwart down in the galley, all he had was the unvarying forward bend and the brief hard backward bounce to the slave driver's drumbeat, the navigator on deck possessed the vast reaches of the sea with its currents, monsoons, and trade winds, which he harnessed on his cyclical voyages, locating his whereabouts by the constellations. For the unfree man there was never anything but what was immediately before him, and all his efforts had to be used up to cope with it. For the free man there was always the suspense of the new, he mapped coastlines and geographic formations, located seaways, strikes of raw materials, opportunities for trading. The people condemned to servitude rapidly withered in the monotony, but he, who had initiative and variety, grew younger. He did not, amid the masses conducted by the priests, need to pray for being saved from illness, for healing, the physicians had spelled out the workings of the organs, the pulse, the nerves, the circulation of blood and prepared all sorts of medicaments for him. The have-nots made sacrifices on their altars to the gods of fertility and weather, of the lower and upper regions of the world, deities whom their ruler barely knew by name, and the purpose of the offerings was to move the deities to let them have a sliver of the abundance. The well-to-do could attain anything they desired, with minted money, with banks, with expeditionary troops. Their philosophers found that the giving and taking, the continual counteracting and interacting was consistent with the essence of all living things, every object was formed by compounding and separating, by thinning and thickening, by attracting and repulsing, there was no matter that did not consist of pairs of opposites. Just as knowing the world meant controlling it, so too control was bound up with the right to power and violence. With their filled silos, their laden freighters, their country villas, palaces, and art treasures, the entrepreneurs demonstrated the correctness of their actions. They stood on the side of progress, they doled out the work, they called for whomever they needed, they dismissed whoever no longer suited them, they started workshops and manufactories, they sped up the production of skins for writing after the competing Egyptian authorities outlawed the export of papyrus, they developed the technique of dyeing sheep's wool. Weavers, tailors, sandal makers, and blacksmiths worked for them, their caravans brought back ivory, jade, silk, and porcelain from China, spices, perfumes, salves, and pearls from India. For their shipyards they had the workers haul timber from the high forests, they had them extract copper and iron ore, gold and silver from the mines, tend the herds of cattle, raise horses, and bring in the grain and wheat, so that this agricultural profusion earned their country the rank of the granary of Asia Minor. That, said Coppi, was when they gained their advantage over us, which keeps confronting us with the fact that everything we produce is utilized way over our heads and that it trickles down to us, if at all attainable, from up there, just as work is said to be given to us. If we want to take on art, literature, we have to treat them against the grain, that is, we have to eliminate all the concomitant privileges and project our own demands into them. In order to come to ourselves, said Heilmann, we have to re-create not only culture but also all science and scholarship by relating them to our concerns. We have stated common knowledge about the shape of our planet and its position in the universe, but for us there is something odd about this simple lore. When we say the world is round and turns on its own axis, we are confirming that there are haves and have-nots. If we state principles of physical orders, they involve the division of labor into doers and drivers, a split as old as science. Whenever the image of the world as established by ancient scientists is taken over in its full scope, it always expresses the tie to the existing rules of social conditions. Only by realizing that we are on a rotating sphere and by forgetting all the connected things that are taken for granted can we grasp the horrors that mold our thinking. Two thousand years had elapsed since the highest stage of the Pergamene Imperium, yet nearly one century after the *Manifesto* the rulers, whom we had always helped to bring to power, still claimed all discoveries for themselves. Decay was already seeping in, but so huge still were the superior strength of the idea of being chosen and the commandment of subordination that nothing could as yet make the workers understand that it was they who carried every advance to the next phase of society. On the mountain over the fruitful fields of Mysia, over the hustle and bustle of the port of Elea, the nobles in the castle devoted themselves to their skills, the fundamental questions about the mechanics of the world were clarified, the government watched over the interplay of exploitation and profit, the business was conducted by specialists, the governors had subaltern bureaucrats and functionaries, who made sure the production quotas were met, the rents collected from the small landowners, the taxes levied in the villages, often under the pressure of troops from the garrisons, the town councils ensured the order in the towns, foreign politics was conducted by the Supreme Council, and in the courts, halls, and covered walks of the gymnasium, originally built to train the youths for military service, teachers and pupils could focus undisturbed on the disciplines that next to solidity and rigorous organization were inexhaustible, epics, elegiac and lyrical poetry, painting and sculpture, music, dance, and drama, singing and calligraphy. To haul art down to us, we had to head for the peak encircled by dazzling white walls and lined with cypresses and flower beds, the mountain top where art led a life of its own. The directors of the academies dubbed themselves skeptics, for their task was to examine, to mull and doubt, and they bore the honorary title of critic because they took on nothing without analyzing it and subjecting it to change. On the basis of their authority in the ruling world they could question everything they dealt with, they could forge ahead into previously unknown intellectual regions because the ground they were on was stabilized and systematized. And when we stand next to a self-perfected man like Crates, said Heilmann, in his customized park and listen to him defining the features of language, we can jot down his every last word, and he opened his notebook under the kitchen lamp. Literary criticism, according to Crates, had three tasks, first of all, to test diction, syntax, and sentence articulation, secondly, to evaluate phonetics, idioms, style, and figures, and thirdly, to make a historical assessment of the ideas and images used. For him and his school, linguistic qualities could be ascertained only if all obscurities found their rational explanations, so that every statement was compared with empirical observation and practical experience. The boundaries of conception were widened on the basis of logic, and beauty was attributed to anything that had found name and form out of the unknown. Hence understanding was always given priority over the sensation of the marvelous, art was a science like geometry and statics. Thus the sages at the court of Pergamum acted on the same perspectives established by the early naturalists, everything they found was weighed in terms of its usability, they set rules that still held sway two thousand years later, they served the further evolution of the intellect, thereby also serving those who permitted its development. This kingdom of the mind had sprung up by means of violence, every utterance of art, of philosophy was grounded in violence. And the grander and more sublime the creation, the more furious the reign of brutality had been. The heyday of the Pergamene Kingdom lasted for only a few short decades, and it had been preceded by over a century of unabated warfare. This was the pattern still inherent in most polities today. The laws of the ancient slaveholding society were still in effect. All revolts notwithstanding, the majority of the populace still had to take the field for the elite. More than two thousand years had passed since the conscripted farm boys, the prisoners captured during the military operations had been driven the length and breadth of Asia Minor by their respective commanders, bleeding to death in battles that led to the ruin of one usurper, the rise of the other. Only twenty years ago, our fathers had returned from their massacres, and minuscule was the period since the October when the signal had been given for a fresh start after the long history of murder. The superiors had always asserted their rights, and they had always insisted on their hegemony until they were replaced by other powerful men, and we had never managed to get beyond buckling and submitting, and once again we faced a burgeoning tyranny that we had not seen coming. In our sealed-off kitchen, we pictured the continent as Alexander had left it, with its Greek settlements, its mix of nations, its fortresses, where the generals who had conquered the empire for their ruler now administered their own kingdoms, having switched from partners to adversaries, jealously pressing to expand territories, siccing their troops on one another, from Macedonia, from Thrace, Bithynia, and Pontus, from Cappadocia, Babylonia, Syria, and Egypt. The lands of the Diadochi lay on the bare surface of the table, Coppi sat leaning back in front of the Hellespont, from where Lysimachus, former bodyguard to the army commander, had thrust southward, along the Aegean coast, and installed Philetaerus, a young captain from Tius on the Black Sea, as governor in Pergamum. Coppi's mother bent over the Taurus Mountains, which formed the northern border of the realm of Seleucus, king of Babylon, Heilmann's hand slid up from Alexandria, the seat of Ptolemy, across the sea, toward the center that was to become the residence of the Attalids. Assigned to build up the garrison and protect the work of the governors, Philetaerus promptly realized the possibilities afforded him by his authority, instead of serving Lysimachus he now wished to challenge his monopoly. He took the money box stored in the mountain tower, its nine thousand talents equal to thirty-two million gold marks, and he instantly invested funds to concentrate forces from all regions for shielding his venture. Who cares about demands, he could ask when his ruined boss reminded him of the obligations he had agreed to. No dangers threatened Philetaerus from that source, and with Seleucus, his southern competitor, he entered into an alliance based on mutual respect so long as the balance of the military potential could be maintained. This was styled a friendship treaty, and according to the terminology of the market administration he established a protectorship over the coastal cities, which had regained some of their earlier freedoms after Alexander's routing of the Persians. The catchwords verbalized by the great conqueror, who claimed that he meant to restore democracy and that the Greeks had precedence over all other races, suited the polis just fine. During his ten-year march across the Asian interior, where he established military bases all the way to the Indus, naming them after himself, and did likewise with fortified colonization sites for specially tax-privileged merchants, the Alexandrian slogans changed. In order to unify the empire he had grabbed in his boundlessness and his passion for fame, he had to forswear racial discrimination. Now, reconciliation was the watchword, a melding of West and East, community and unity, and yet this spelled nothing but an insatiable need for victorious battles, for enemy potentates slain or tortured to death, for captives to be used as slaves, as army reinforcements, for women given to officers and meritorious soldiers. Supposedly Alexander saw the light before his untimely death and was well-nigh stricken with humility, but what really struck him was intense hysteria, which erupted regularly with mutinies of impatient troops. In a cadence not attained by even the corporal who was now trying to climb to the rank of world ruler, Alexander drew the doubters, the exhausted back to his side by promising them anything. Had the fever not snatched him away at thirty, he would, after a time of raging, have perished in his gigantic, untenable, ubiquitously crumbling structure. He left behind chaos, ruins, and hostility. Reared in the spirit of graft, Philetaerus granted privileges to the landowners and merchants, whose support he initially required, the latifundia could be expanded, the warehouses had free access to the colonial goods, for a while the citizens could gorge themselves, the tributes and rentals were collected from tenant farmers, craftsmen, and workers. For the inhabitants of coastal cities, which had previously been sucked dry by a Spartan or Athenian military junta, a Lydian king, a Macedonian, Thracian, or Rhodian admiral, a period of economic prosperity seemed to be heralded by the founding of the Pergamene Kingdom, and it was in the interest of those coastal dwellers for the regent in the acropolis to surround himself with glamour and prestige, for the more portentous he made himself the more he was respected by the neighboring empires. It dawned on nobody as yet that he was depriving the polis of more and more clout. The walled cities still had the class division between citizens, foreigners, soldiers, freemen, and private, public, and imperial slaves; the citizens had a say in the seemingly democratic government, practiced by the legislative assemblies of the House of Representatives and the Council, the members of the Municipal Council could be elected by the people. Alien mercenaries who had proven their loyalty to the army obtained citizenship, lands were distributed to officers, arable patches to soldiers who had distinguished themselves in combat, the transition from the society of Greek city states to the absolute Hellenistic monarchy occurred in the education of a broader propertied stratum that had an interest in maintaining its cultivated grain, its cattle and orchards. A national feeling was thus developed by a prudent Philetaerus, who had aroused the willingness to undertake an armed defense of the state. Not only was he exposed to the greed of the kings in the south and the east, but now he also needed the allegiance of the cities and the countrysides, chiefly to ward off the Celtic tribes, which, driven from their Gallic homes by dry spells and by the Germanic invasions, had followed the Danube, migrating through

Thrace and ferrying across the strait to the Ionian coastal areas. Founding the dynasty of the Attalids, named for Attalus, his father, who had served as a general under Alexander, Philetaerus craved an intercession by the gods and a connection with mythology in order to show off more effectively to the soldiers, whom he conscripted in great numbers. Just as Alexander had claimed Heracles as his ancestor, so too Philetaerus asserted that he was a direct descendant of Telephus, Heracles' son, who, after the death of his mother, Auge, in a shipwreck, had found a home on the mountain of Pergamum. Presenting the history of those fifty years, during which Philetaerus and his brother Eumenes defended themselves against the Gauls until their successor delivered the land from the enemies and declared himself king as Attalus the First, was, said Heilmann, like trying to unpuzzle the muddle of a nightmare. Eventually, Heilmann went on, he wanted to consult the sources in order to investigate the motives of that phantasmagoria, which, of course, involved the same dynamics as the events that had occurred here during the past fifty years and that two thousand years from now would again leave our heirs bewildered. The Gauls were beer drinkers, the Hellenes were partial to wine, he said, at first that was the only distinction by which the local populace recognized the new invaders, the customs of the warriors, who came with their horn blowers, their families in columns of carts, were scarcely cruder than the earlier mercenaries, who had looted and plundered their way through the region. The Gauls were seeking landscapes where they could settle and raise their hops, and just as their homes had been taken from them, so too they drove others from their households. They did not sidle up to the fortified towns, they were content with cutting off the approach roads and demanding tolls from the inhabitants, which was legitimate for them in their plight and also, in that despotic era, consistent with odious measures. Beleaguering the wealthy commercial centers, offering their protection, taking recompense in wares, occasionally also storming granaries, occupying harbors, several of their tribes spread through northwestern Asia Minor while others struck off into the central highlands, obtaining a sanctuary between Phrygia and Cappadocia since the men were willing to hire themselves out for the armies of the kings of Bithynia and Pontus. They could sell their manpower best as troopers or foot soldiers, and while marching back from the northeast, in the regiments of Nicomedes and Mithridates, to the Pergamene realm, some fellow tribesmen had entered the armies of the Attalids, which were advancing against the Gallic clans in the north of the country. Just as Gauls fought against Gauls, so too Macedonians and Thracians, Persians and Syrians charged against one another, and all the units included lansquenets from Crete, Rhodes, and Cyprus, and straggling groups of Mysian nomads with their chieftains, their own gods and cults, and Cyrtians from the remote Euphrates, leftovers from Alexander's wars. In this commotion, the country boys were recruited, for a drachma a day, for food and drink, for tax exemption and the assurance that they could keep their booty and that in case of their demise their pay would be handed over to their families. For the soldiers there was no fatherland. The recruiters, the officers could talk a blue streak about sacred missions and duties, but the troops barely knew the names of the rulers under whose standards they rallied. As day laborers they trudged ahead to get land, mineral resources, and raw goods for the king, and the most important means of production, the slaves. They, the workers, locked horns, plunging one another even deeper into serfdom, and so, in the embittered mercantile ventures, which, from the south, the Seleucids and the Ptolemaeans joined, taking advantage of the situation, the soldiers often wound up in the enemy camp. To divert them from the real goals of the actions, Pergamum's propagandists hollered once again about savage inferior races, about barbarians who had to be eliminated, and the last vestiges of the illusion, spread by Alexander, of a peaceful coexistence of nations went under in the marketplaces, in the speeches about the robbing, looting, raping, and burning perpetrated by the foreigners. Dazed by the image of the occupiers' reign of terror, alarmed by the threat of wholesale enslavement if they did not sacrifice everything for Pergamum's victory, the urbanites handed over their final cash reserves, the landowners their crops and cattle. For a long time now, all decisions had been made exclusively by the court officials in the administration, the deputies were no longer freely elected, they were installed at the ruler's recommendation, the sokemen could no longer make up the losses their masters suffered because of the increased tributes, and by the start of the brief phase of flowering civilization, which culminated in artistic riches, the old class hierarchy had yielded to a flagrant division between a small privileged caste and an amorphous mass in which disempowered burghers, indigent tradesmen and artisans, and slaves of all backgrounds resembled one another more and more in an all-encompassing impoverishment. In regard to the implementation of Pergamene absolutism, he could not, said Heilmann, pacing up and down in front of the blanketed door, picture anything other than a clashing of spearheads of continually incited brutality. The historians did not report how many hundreds of thousands of inhabitants had lost their lives, but after the victory at the sources of the Caicus, the chroniclers did cite the figure of forty thousand captured Gauls, which implied many times that number of exterminated victims and refugees fleeing to the eastern mountains. In the stillness, which hung thick on the walls, we listened for several moments, since the rattling of arms and armor was sure to be heard soon, the numbing efforts at advancing, the slamming of the iron penetrating flesh, and then, for the length of a second, the close combat raged in the kitchen, the swords and helmets flashed under the lamp, the wives and children of the Gallic warriors lay slaughtered. However, said Heilmann, the pacification of the kingdom was, as expected, a mere shadow, since the accumulation of foreign slaves, the progressive exploitation of the populace were bound to feed disquiet. Supported by an officers' caste, by a corrupt administration, and by the feudal families, who now controlled the lands and emporiums, Attalus, the rescuer, solidified his military regime and prepared the Realpolitik that enabled his son, Eumenes the Second, to make Pergamum world famous. He formed alliances to ward off the southern rivals, who, however, did wipe out his dynasty within two generations. Instead of battling the Romans, who, now pressing toward dominating the Mediterranean, would have defeated him, he offered them commercial ties, allowed them to establish trading posts, initiated a cultural exchange, and assisted them with their wars of conquest in Macedonia, while the Romans helped Pergamum to beat Antiochus of Syria and Pharnaces of Pontus. Had it not been for the pact with Rome, there would have been no Temple of Zeus with its frieze, which formed an uninterrupted band running in an astounding and novel fashion around the outer walls. Of the forty years of a peace secured by conferences, by nimble diplomatic games the last two decades were devoted to the total isolation of the spirit, which, straining to the utmost, was meant to draw a synthesis from centuries of art appreciation. Creating pieces that transcended all contemporary events with special features, the sculptors were dependent on Eumenes, who called himself the Benefactor, and who for his part needed the favor of Rome to frighten off potential attackers, while his kingdom, stretching from the Hellespont to the Taurus, offered the Romans a shield against the aggressive Asian regents. The sculptors, working for the ruler, who wanted to adorn his exertion of power with the aura of artworks, were enclosed in a small circle amid abundance and widely surrounded by servility, confusion, and effeteness. Not that their oeuvre repudiated the authorities, after all it indicated clearly enough whom to glorify and whom to humble, but if we now recalled the worked stone, the facial features of the gods were cold and rigid, their appearance was unreal in its standoffish grandeur, while the defeated, albeit disfigured, remained human, marked by fear and suffering. Yet did that mean the master sculptors sided with the victims, asked Coppi, were they open to the turmoil fermenting down in the cities, or did they take the surrounding conflict, fragmentation, protest merely as inspirations for sculpted forms, motions, contrasts. They must have known about Aristonicus, the son of Eumenes and a concubine from Ephesus, a harpist's daughter; Aristonicus, excluded by Eumenes from his successorship, had soon gotten close to the populace, learning about its plight, said Heilmann. The sculptors must have known about Aristonicus's preparations to join with the landless peasants, dissatisfied soldiers, and slaves in defying the reign of swindlers and pillagers and founding a more just state. Nor was such a revolt new to the artists, the slaves rebelled in the Hellenistic colonies, the poor had once risen up in Cassandra, and in Sparta the Macedonian patriarchs had to yield to the rebellion of Agis and Cleomenes. Now, however, inherent from the very outset in Pergamum's hierarchical structure, its downfall began as the power was shattered by its ultimate intensification. In the social polarizing, it was not the forces aiming at social progress that carried the day but the eventually self-destructive conservatism. The Roman cohorts had long been ready, waiting for marching orders from their envoys, yet before a favorable moment came for the invasion, Attalus the Third, son of Eumenes and heir apparent to the throne, the last of the Attalid dynasty, asked the Romans to come and help him fight his half brother, for the ruler preferred handing them the kingdom to letting it be ruled by the people. The Roman commanders had already demonstrated in Corinth and Carthage what they meant by building an imperium, and with a view to their further plans they promptly named the Hellenistic acquisition "Asia." After the transfer of battalions, the installation of prefects and tribute collectors, after the crushing of armies invading from east and south, and Sulla's establishment of a network of fortifications, Anthony came and got hold of the knowledge rolled up in parchment at the library and shipped it to Alexandria as a wedding gift for Cleopatra, his Isis, his queen of kings, and soon his statue, as god and benefactor, along with the monuments and columns of Trajan and Hadrian, loomed over the relics of forgotten majesties and idols. New temples, for the cult of Roma and her caesars, arose from the foundation walls of the Attalid palaces, colossal buildings, arenas, therapeutic hot springs surrounded the mountain, and once again notables and celebrities were present at the clay baths of Caracalla, the theatrical performances, the music and dance recitals, the artistic contests and the learned conversations, and down in the sewer gutters, in the dockyards, smithies, and manufactories, all working at high pressure, the plebeians collapsed under the whip and consumption. And yet the Roman might, with its whirring blows, its furious kicks, its profiteers, its intricately organized militarism, could not hold a candle to the system that Byzantinism had in readiness. Under the Romans there had been at least some reform efforts, there had been an interest in education, teachers, doctors, scholars, scientists were encouraged, but in the Byzantine Empire the sucking of the final strength of the land was celebrated with tremendous hollow pomp, and over the oppressed loomed the hierarchies of the religious and secular aristocracies, which, surrounded by toadies and sycophants, were neither assailable in their stolen dignity nor liable for their crimes. Her broad bony hands lying in her lap, her legs, with swollen blue arteries, standing straight and parallel in the bowl, Coppi's mother said she could not help wondering whether the burden of torments that paid for the creation of the artworks might not give them a repulsive touch for all time. She could, she added, understand the lime burners who had set up their ovens next to the deposits of the ancient shrines. The rubble of capitals, cornices, and statues was merely a marble quarry for them, and when they occasionally saw a face, a body, an animal hewn into the blocks, it could not prevent them from concentrating on the lime that lay bound here. Just as the ashlars were building stones for the masons, so too they were raw material from which the lime burners could extract marketable mortar. For centuries, lime had been produced from the wealth of marble ruins, and this manual labor, like hauling stones in shabby carts to the surrounding villages, was terminated by the arrival of an engineer with an archeological background. Coppi's mother wanted to know whether the lime burners had been recompensed after Humann, while building a highway through western Asia Minor for the Turkish government, had discovered the ancient fragments during an outing to the mountain peak and then expelled the workers from the discovery site. At the orders of Grand Vizier Fuad Pasha, said Heilmann, they had to leave with their tools and migrate eastward, into the mountains, from which, it was said, they had originally issued and which had once belonged to Galatia, a land settled by Celtic refugees. Once again, these bearded primordial figures, who had lent their appearance to the giants, were driven away. They, the living, perished in steppe, desert, and gravel so that the stone could awaken. On a clear morning in September eighteen seventy-one, after a hazy night amid cypresses and mulberry trees, Humann wiped the sand out of the frizzy hair, the eye sockets, the torturously opened mouth of Gaea's son, who lay embedded in the parched earth. Humann went through years of preparations and small excavations before he could start the real work in June eighteen seventy-eight. Who paid for the project, asked Coppi's mother, and what did it cost. For the first period, slated to last twenty-five days, Humann had twenty men, mostly Bulgarians, at his disposal. Their combined wages for this time frame totaled eight hundred marks. The overseer received one hundred marks. Five hundred marks were estimated for tools and technical equipment. Humann's honorarium was one thousand marks. Counting travel and other overhead, the complete outlay was three thousand marks. The money came from the royal reserve fund once His Imperial and Royal Highness, Crown Prince Friedrich Wilhelm, grew interested in the enterprise. The victory over France, the crowning of the Prussian king as emperor, and the founding of the German Empire, and then the smashing of the peril to the French capital, the Commune, were followed by a period of industrial expansion, of control over continents, and the German capital, the seat of the court, demanded treasures for emphasizing the artistic sensibilities of the monarch and colonial lord. That was why the digging on Pergamum's mountain went on, undisturbed by the war that had broken out between Turkey and Russia. Initially one-third of the artworks was to belong to the finder and two-thirds to the Turkish state, but in its dependent relationship the Turkish Grand Vizierate in Constantinople promised the German government two-thirds and then also waived the last third for a fee of twenty thousand marks and a donation in the same amount for the indigent population of the country. By eighteen eighty-six, after the completed excavation of the acropolis and the shipping of over a thousand crates of columns, sculptures, and frieze panels to the museum designed by Schinkel, three hundred thousand marks from the reserve fund and the government cultural budget had been spent on Pergamum's marbles, a negligible sum compared with other art purchases and with the overall value of the find. And yet something that is cruel can never contain beauty, said Coppi's mother, and shouts came up the courtyard shaft, windows were slammed, doors banged; despite the blackout ordered for the air-raid drill the janitor had discovered a gleam of light, there was a trampling in the staircase, we sat still, listening as stifled fear and fury, bottled-up disgust, repressed frenzy were suddenly vented, to erupt in scolding and raging and then just as quickly peter out. Somebody sneaked down the stairs, Phoibe, the glorious, radiant one, aimed her burning torch at the face of the flinching winged giant, and Asteria, her daughter, the bright goddess of the stars, grabbed the hair of the serpent-legged opponent, who had been yanked down by the hound, and, unhindered by the fallen man's hand on her arm, she plunged the sword through his clavicle, piercing deep into his chest. Thus they all arose, the deities, in their gestures of superiority, Leto rammed her flame-thrower into the screaming mouth of the sunken Tityus, whose foot was digging into her loin, and she carried on her fame as mother of Artemis and Apollo, while the savage had to atone forever in the underworld, devoured by vultures. Aphrodite, goddess of love and beauty, pressing her richly adorned sandal into the forehead of Chtonius, supine on a heap of cadavers, fixed her full strength on pulling the lance out of his body, the felled demon would molder, becoming food for the forest vegetation, but the foam-born goddess was destined to win countless more victories and enjoy inexhaustible worship, the Moirai, chosen to spin the threads of life, distribute the lot of life, and also to halt the course of life, were raging over their victims, the smoothness of their faces hovered unruffled above the storm of war, misery, and terror that the huntresses brought along, leaving corpses behind they hurried on, and Hecate, the Helpful, equipped with three pairs of arms and three heads and shielded by the great buckler, aimed the fiery staff, the spear, and the sword at the boorish giant, whose hand was clutching a piece of stone as a projectile and whose features bespoke the ineluctability of his doom. All they have is stones, said Coppi's mother, to defend themselves against armored and heavily armed opponents, they kneel, crawl, shatter, and fall into torn-up asphalt, the targets of water cannon, gas grenades, and machine guns. She saw the fighting in our occupied city, our occupied country, and it did not help Gaea to plead for mercy for her son Alcyoneus, he was in Athena's power, the murderous bite of the serpent in his breast was not enough for her, she wanted him torn to shreds. The unarmed, ganging up behind barricades, were condemned to annihilation by the chosen, who had given themselves imposing names and had spread the news that they were invincible, that their goal was a sublime order of the world. After emptying the bowl, Coppi's mother, hunching over in her chair, the towel on her legs, stared at the ghostly screen, and throughout our descriptions she detected only the triumphs of the tormentors over the milling throng of the disempowered. And after a lengthy silence, Heilmann said that works like those stemming from Pergamum had to be constantly reinterpreted until a reversal was gained and the earth-born awoke from darkness and slavery to show themselves in their true appearance.

Inseparable from economic advantage was the superiority of knowledge. Ownership involved greed, and the advantaged tried as long as possible to block the road to education for the have-nots. The privileges of the ruling class could not be eliminated until we gained insight into the conditions and acquired fundamental knowledge. We kept getting repulsed over and over because our ability to think, deduce, and conclude was insufficiently developed. This state of affairs began changing with the realization that the upper classes essentially opposed our thirst for knowledge. Ever since, our most important goal was to conquer an education, a skill in every field of research, by using any means, cunning and strength of mind. From the very outset, our studying was rebellion. We gathered material to defend ourselves and prepare a conquest. Seldom haphazardly, mostly because we continued with the things we understood, we moved from one object to the next, fending off weariness and familiar perspectives as well as the constant argument that we could not be up to the strain of self-education at the end of a workday. While our numb minds often had to squeeze out of a void and relearn nimbleness after monotony, we did not want paid labor to be either derogated or despised. In rejecting the opinion that it was a special achievement for people like us to deal with artistic, scientific, and scholarly problems, we wished to maintain ourselves in work that did not belong to us. When Coppi's father, in a dark suit shiny from many brushings, a collarless shirt, a beret pulled way back from the forehead, with a battered briefcase under his arm, entered the kitchen and stood by the table, we all felt the day hanging down on us and the huge gap we had to overcome before laying claim to imagination, excessive mental pressure, or meditative leisure. Once, we had furiously refused to admit that reading a book, going to an art gallery, a concert hall, a theater would require extra sweat and racking of the mind. Meanwhile our attempts to escape speechlessness were among the functions of our lives, the things we thereby found were first articulations, they were basic patterns for overcoming muteness and measuring the steps into a cultural realm. Our idea of a culture rarely coincided with what constituted a gigantic reservoir of goods, of pent-up inventions and illuminations. As have-nots we initially approached the accumulations with anxiety, with awe, until it dawned on us that we had to fill all these things with our own evaluations, that the overall concept might be useful only when expressing something about the conditions of our lives as well as about the difficulties and peculiarities of our thought processes. The topic had been taken up by Lunacharsky, Tretyakov, Trotsky, whose books we were familiar with; we also knew about the initiative that had emerged during the twenties for educating worker-writers, and in study groups we had discussed the statements that Marx, Engels, and Lenin made about cultural issues. All these things may have been informative, stimulating, and perhaps also indicative of the future, but they did not chime with the totality we were striving for, instead they expressed traditional notions, conventions that ultimately did not renounce the standards of the dominant class. We too, as we were told by progressives, should benefit from what was known as culture, we recognized the greatness and power of many works, we began understanding how the social stratifications, contradictions, and conflicts were mirrored in the artistic products of eras, but we did not yet achieve an image that included us ourselves, everything that was supposed to jibe with us was a conglomerate of forms and styles borrowed from various sources. Whatever we read into completed things could only confront us with our own exclusion, and when we were in the midst of discovering timeless and powerful things, we ran the risk of estrangement from our own class. Our using new names, new associations aroused the distrust of those who had been so violently raped by the predominance of bourgeois ideology that they did not even contemplate gaining any access to intellectual levels. Yet we only had to glance at their faces to recall the expressive power concealed in them. Before nineteen thirty-three, when I sometimes visited my father during lunch breaks at work, a representative of an educational alliance might be lecturing or reading poetry in the canteen, and I realized how impossible it was to establish a link to intellectual regions in this way. There the workers sat over their metal boxes, their thermos bottles, their sandwiches unwrapped from greasy paper, their ears half deaf from the smashing of metal and the riveting hammers, with only twenty minutes allotted them for eating, and the reason they kept averting their faces from the speaker and crouching deep over the table was not that they had to wolf down their food, but that they were embarrassed at failing to make head or tail of the well-meaning presentation they were offered. When they subsequently applauded, about to dash back to the factory halls, they clapped out of politeness, he, the artist, got something from them, but they left empty-handed. This was so, as I already understood, because nothing could impress us from outside, from above so long as we were prisoners, any attempt to grant us a vista could only be awkward, we wanted no rations, no doled-out patchwork, we wanted the totality, and this totality was not to be a traditional thing, it had be to newly created. Our primary needs were situation reports, elucidations of political measures, organizational plans, and these things could come only from our own ranks. When we were among ourselves, practical considerations also led us to this entity known as culture, to which the qualities of questing voices adhered, with the gestures of generations of experience, the beginnings of pride and dignity. Our road out of intellectual suppression was a political one. Anything referring to poems, novels, paintings, sculptures, musical pieces, films, or plays had to be thought out politically. This was a groping, we did not yet know what use our discoveries would be, all we understood was that in order to make sense it had to come out of us. Coppi's father, having deposited his briefcase on the table, took out folded wrinkled paper, a bottle, a two-part sandwich holder, he washed up at the sink, coffee was put on, Coppi's father, bare-chested, scrubbed his throat and face, then put on a woolen jacket with a row of embroidered stag heads in front, and once again we talked about things we would someday acquire, about achievements we were striving to understand. In the evening, my arms are seven feet long, said Coppi's father, when I walk, my hands drag along the ground. This image captured all the art and literature that had come close to us during years of our growing-up. At the factory loading ramp, Coppi's father had shoved, pulled, and lugged crates for eight hours, ordnance parts were packed in them, and Coppi's mother, at the Telefunken Works, had built maneuvering devices for war planes. Every delivered item, every package was accompanied by a checklist naming all the people involved in the procedure, which could make each one personally liable. A loosened screw, a few grains of sand in the gears, a missing or misplaced wire, those were concrete things by which to measure the results of reading, of looking at a picture. We wondered if the themes of the books we read were germane to our experiences, if they depicted people who were close to us, if they took a stand and offered attempts at solutions. There were works that, though not directly related to our norms, sparked our interest precisely because of their unfamiliar contents. When stumbling upon a text or a painting in a magazine, a museum, we would usually test it to see if could be used in the political struggle, and we accepted it if it was openly partisan. But then again we also stumbled on things that did not reveal an immediate political impact and yet had disturbing and, we felt, important qualities. If books or paintings of this sort, especially when decried as degenerate by the new rulers, were removed from the public collections, then we felt all the more strongly about including them in the registers of sabotage acts and revolutionary manifestations. We had already been impressed by Surrealism when Hodann, in Haeckel Hall, proceeding from numerous questions about the origins of neuroses, depressions, and obsessions, pointed out the links between social conditions and illness motives, the dream impulses, and explained their repercussions in an art that followed the unhampered torrent of inspirations. This kind of expression, transcending logic, acknowledging all exotic, terrifying things in order to thrust forward to the causes of personal behavior, was right up our alley in our search to find ourselves. After all, we too distrusted anything that was definite and solid, and beneath the envelope of legitimacies we saw the manipulations that were destroying many of us. Dadaism likewise evinced some of our tendencies, it had spit into the elegant parlors, it had toppled the plaster busts from their pedestals and shredded the garlands of petty bourgeois self-aggrandizement, that was fine with us, we endorsed the ridiculing of dignity, the deriding of holiness, but we had no time for the call for a total annihilation of art, people who were sated with culture could afford such slogans, but we wanted to take over the cultural institutions left unscathed and see which of their contents could be made serviceable for our craving to learn. In the paintings of Max Ernst, Paul Klee, Kandinsky, Schwitters, Dali, Magritte, we saw dissolutions of visual biases, lightning flashes exposing rot and ferment, panic and upheaval, we drew the line between attacks against worn-out, perishing things and mere thumb-nosing that ultimately left the market in peace. We thrashed out the conflict between those who preferred to depict the present in its intricacy, fragmentation, and chaos, making it blaze and burn, like Nolde, Kokoschka, or Beckmann, and those who preferred to render the disintegration objectively and accurately, like Dix and Grosz, who painstakingly dissected and measured the existing reality, like Feininger. Spurred on by the fiats, by the edicts mandating what art now meant, by the censoring measures that disclosed the undermining abilities that the rulers ascribed to painting and literature, we constantly sought out books and magazines containing testimonies by the pioneers, who were now working surreptitiously or had gone abroad. As we wondered if secret poetic languages, image codes, and magic symbols were appropriate for depicting obscure, seemingly irrational processes or if, confronted with the unintelligible, an unambiguous rendering was necessary, Heilmann joined us after reading us his translation of Rimbaud's *Une saison en enfer* at Gleisdreieck Station on the way back from night school. Both sides are correct, said Heilmann, the lunge that yanks the ground out from under our feet as well as the effort to establish a solid basis for investigating simple facts. Most people are all too remote from such inquiries, said Coppi's father, to see any necessity in them, your words fly past them. There was a humming in the ears, it would not be penetrated by words coming from a stage, from the notes emitted by the strings and woodwinds on the platform, and besides, sitting with a painful back on the folding chair was impossible. The to-and-fro of the arms in the blackness of the tuxedo and the stuff hammered into the keys and gushing out of the yawning piano up front would be torture for a head in an iron ring. Before starting with their painted lips, their ambivalent gestures, spotlighted in their rich colorfulness, surrounded by artificial spaces, they had to comply with their need to sleep. They hung fast, to the limits of endurability, between the straps of the workbenches, and the cold hardness of the concrete floor banged incessantly against their feet. These people had been up since three or four A.M., and if they tried for a while, said Coppi's mother, to escape the place where they were beaten to a pulp, they would not sink into the cushions of a seat between Rembrandt and Rubens, they would feverishly pull the blankets over their faces. There could be no question of getting to understand the things written in thick tomes, going to windows, filling out forms, specifying wishes, which meant admitting to total ignorance. From the metal factory, from the railroad roundhouses, from the terminals of buses, beaten paths were all that led in directions that could be taken with half-shut eyes, mechanically dragging feet. The problem was not how one style developed from another, but what would happen if one day of sickness were followed by a second day of feebleness, for given the paltry government support the third day would bring naked need. It was more likely for illness to assault the toiler than for knowledge to come to him, his eyes stumbled over the lines along which his fingers moved, his lips murmured something that his brain promptly forgot. Catastrophe invaded the room where the rent could no longer be paid and where the landlord now barged in without knocking. Things leading to catharsis in the lofty admired dramas were now mercilessly transplanted into daily practice amid utter secrecy and discretion. Working, said Coppi's mother, becomes even harder after an interruption. Nevertheless, replied Coppi, we have to keep asking ourselves what our mission is, no one else can explain to us the structure we are caught in. And that was exactly what allowed us to talk about things that could not really be accessible to us. To interpret theories that might say something about the ways and means of our liberation, we first had to understand the system we were moving in. The fact that we had not yet achieved anything was shown now that the loss of self was greater than ever. Cultural work was Coppi's term for the transition from the enclosure in the factory to the openness of the night school class, for getting there was the achievement, it had to succeed, it had to overcome the exhaustion that tried to hold us back. More than half the participants dropped out after the first few sessions. The foreheads striking the desks, beaten down by twelve hours, were made of lead by seven P.M. The school system took these casualties into account, the survivors held their eyes open with their fingers, gaped at the blurring blackboards, pinched themselves in the arm, scribbled up their notebooks, and during the final phase more participants dropped out, they only had to lose a week because of apartment hunting, job hunting, because of an accident or simply because of discouragement, and they were yanked out of the class. It would have been presumptuous to try and talk about art without hearing the shuffling as we shoved one foot in front of the other. Every meter toward the painting, the book, was a battle, we crawled, pushed ourselves forward, our eyelids blinked, sometimes this squinting made us burst out laughing, which helped us forget where we were going. And the thing then shown to us when we viewed a painting was a web of threads, shiny threads, clotting into lumps, flowing apart, shaping into fields of brightnesses, darknesses, and the switchgears of our optic nerves marshaled the oncoming storm of tiny luminous dots into messages that could be deciphered. We could recall all the circumstances along the road to knowledge because we remained in a constant stage of preparation, because we sometimes never got beyond the start, because nothing was handed to us on a silver platter, because the encounter with a literary, an artistic subject could never be taken for granted. It was only with the works of Socialist Realism that we held back our questions about style and form, acknowledging only the content, which differed fundamentally from that of all other art movements. We were acquainted with the stages that led to these painting trends, which demanded acceptance purely on the basis of their novel expressiveness. They bore in on us from the nineteenth century, from a strenuous darkness, evincing the forerunners of those who were now powerfully rising up, freed and proud. The tremendous feat was even plainer in that behind it the slaves, the parched, the impoverished became visible, generations of them thronging against the superior strength, which seemed invincible. Nothing but humiliation, suppression, and imprisonment existed in the paintings of the Russian Realists, yet in their rapport with the people that they portrayed, in their depiction of the injustice that afflicted them, they were already siding with the planners of a renewal. There were Repin's boat haulers hanging in the straps, Savitsky's forced laborers toting soil for building the railroad embankment, Perov's children dragging water barrels through the blizzard, there were Yarosyenko's haggard stokers, singed by red heat, locked in the low-ceilinged furnace room, clutching the pokers in their swollen thickly veined hands. The faces of the ragged bearded serfs, barefoot or in tattered sandals and straw boots, trudging through the sand of the shore, were snuffed out, drained of all hope. The children pulling the sleds were emaciated, their features waxen, dull with exhaustion. It was the year eighteen seventy-four, when the road workers, guarded by soldiers, braced themselves over the fully loaded cars by the dusty embankment. In the wasteland, in the devaluation of their lives, they had never heard of the revolutions in France, the Commune, for them the Middle Ages were still present. Nor were Courbet's stone breakers granted any relief, yet their drudgery in the detritus was no longer marked by hopelessness. Their clothing was shabby, seedy, but their motions imparted something of the strength of the rebellions in February and June eighteen forty-eight, and though the revolts were quelled, the jolt with which the young worker heaved up the basket of stones, and the older man's hard grip on the hammer shaft resembled the gestures at the building of barricades, at the furious clashes. Both men had their backs to the viewer, the reproduction showed them against a swarthy background, there was a dented pot of food for the road, a couple of pickaxes lay ready like weapons, if the men turned their movements would be forceful. We had found a great deal from our own lives in such paintings, as imperfect and allusive as we had seen them in books and magazines were our own concepts and schooling. Anything we expressed about them could only be a sketch, a draft. Decades would be needed for our approximate insights to mellow into knowledge. By way of experimenting, usually very remote from encounters with the originals, we investigated what appeared as the shadow of an artistic reality, thus sharpening our eyes for the typical, the gesture, the relationship between the figures, for everything that could be gleaned even from a smudged gray. The workers in Doré's suite about the London waterfront were in the same abysmal murk that dominated his illustrations for Dante's *Inferno*, however these laborers were not deserted by the world, they slogged on in a living circle, whose hallmark was the steam and the smoke, the fiery glow, the seething water. For Millet, whose colors we did not yet know, daily work was an incessant, necessary torment, his country folk existed in a haze that blended the sweating of bodies with the smoldering sunlight, they were grafted on their tools, they were entangled in the strawstacks, they wrestled with the harvest, stood like clods of earth in the sultriness. Yet they too did not own the soil they tilled, and while the day likewise gave them nothing but sweat, physical emaciation, and the few coins necessary for food to ride out the coming day, they were nevertheless fully engrossed in what they were doing, the work was not alien, not forced on them, they participated in every push and pull, when knuckling down they felt their stamina, there was never anything sullen or broken about their bodies. They were represented as natural beings, creature-like they bent way over to pluck out the haulms, a row of three women, in a continuous motion, the first hand about to grip, the second hand clutching the spikes, the third gathering the sheaf, all figures equally heavy, equally important, their slow, bent striding unstoppable, yet still vegetative, not seen as a component of a specific production process. The uprisings of the year eighteen forty-eight were communicated in the gestures of the workers but did not yet challenge their social existence even though, monumental, they occupied the entire pictorial space, leaning on a hoe, jabbing a spade into the ground, swinging their arms way out when sowing, it was as if they were nonetheless bowing to their fate. Millet himself had grown up among them, not as a cottager but as the son of well-to-do farmers, he had sucked in the smell of grain, had, like Heracles, tended the sheep, peered up at the cloud formations, stared at the high rocks, imagining Prometheus fettered to them, and this mythological vastness was still present in his paintings. The revolutions had, at first glance, accomplished little, and any gains had instantly been shattered by the power of the bourgeoisie, but the exertion of force, the stretching, the leap were an achievement that could not be denied, and Millet knew how to capture and render this proletarian energy. He was no politician like Courbet, he did not follow up on the consequences of social turmoil, he merely rendered what he encountered, as a realist he portrayed the new resoluteness in human behavior, he could not see the workers possessing a power that was still utopian, but he showed them with the dignity they had fought to attain. His pictures revealed an interlude, the physical expressions of the figures had to be ascribed to the revolutionary experiences, but the step toward their self-awareness had only just been initiated, the violence they were capable of appeared only in a rudimentary form, and yet by lifting such life into the salons of society, by removing the sweaty figures with their earthy features, their loamy weight from where they had endured anonymously and placing them in between the well-groomed portraits, the nymphs and shepherdesses, he did something on a par with the revolutionary aim. However, the mere appearance of such figures in the very midst of the bourgeois precincts was a slap in the face for the connoisseurs, since those people ought to remain outside, in their filth, where they belonged. But now they were no longer to be rebuffed, intimidating as they were, even when standing during the Angelus, in this devotion, this mystical absorption, which could settle on Millet's fields, the farm laborer then blatantly ominous, in the klutzy sabots, breathing heavily over the hoe, and the sower, black, inky, somber, plodding through the soil, barely a trace of sky, he had started trudging before dawn, he would not stop before onset of darkness. These impressive gestures belonged to the revolution, all at once the maids and farmhands had broken into the venerable precincts of academicism, into middle-class security. The harvesters in Lhermitte's canvas were getting their day's pay from the estate manager, standing upright, without humility, one of them stretched out his receiving hand, another meticulously counted the coins, a third sat proud, massive, with the sharp gigantic scythe in front of him. The wage issue was again broached here, as was the cheating of manpower. They were worth no more than what they received this evening, the wealth of grain lying before them belonged to other people, yet there were five of them and only one leaseholder, and their superiority was shown not only in this ratio but also in the effect of their physicality. Meunier's miners, dockers loomed motionless, deeply earnest, imbued with strength, yet they did not raise a hand. Very seldom in this century, when the worker became a foreground figure in art, were they shown with a gesture of resistance, attack. Still, their emergence as a new class, their lifelike appearance in front of the flabbergasted spectator, those were artistic feats enough. Behind them lay a string of revolts and revolutions, and although driven back each time, they had gained experience each time, and perhaps they would be better equipped for the next charge. By approaching them, by seeking motifs from the workaday world, the painters showed that art too was freeing itself from old obligations, that energy coming from the populace was forcing itself on art, energy that had to be articulated, at first by those capable of speech, of expression that mediated. The painters understood this exhortation, they were as yet unable to apply it to the overall system they lived in, but they accused, they emphasized the plight, they saw the workers as their patrons, they protested on their behalf, they occasionally identified with them, but then they also let themselves be inveigled anew by the lures of conventions. As usual the contradiction was that things emanating from the populace found shape only on a higher level, and there they were no longer reliable as authentic utterances, they did not need to be idealized or dramatized, but in a world of forms and colors they easily took on a life of their own. The realistic works of the past century could help the workers only indirectly. Long after their effigies began spreading through the sphere of art, they, the inspirers, were still excluded from it, they barely caught a glimpse of what the masters had captured of their life, but the privileged learned to focus on them, to deal with their problems. For the time being, that was the only possible course of development. Just as the basic actions of the revolutions had always been taken over and utilized from above, so too the thoughts and hopes of people who wanted to move up were precipitated in the basin of culture to be sublimated there. The society, often full of compassion, gave the masses something that belonged to them anyway. Breaking through this cycle, which was a steady insult, a rebuke, this had to be our goal. This was why Coppi and I unreservedly confronted the pictures showing the first major breakthrough of the laborers, their victory, the establishment of their rule. In our eyes, the works were exactly as they had to be, unambiguous, true to nature, consistent with the events, they came not from above, where artistic activity usually had its seat, but directly from the ranks of those who had waged the struggle and wanted to recognize themselves here. Those people followed a familiar manner of painting, they did not demand a turnabout of visual habits, there were more important, more fundamental things in education than dealing with new style trends in order to understand the depictions of the revolutionary events. A tremendous leap had been taken, from the time when the workers had received their pay, mute, withdrawn, hired out, to the day when they lifted their own tools, switched on their own machines. The image of reality was continued intact, but the despotism hanging over the old Russian portrayals of the life of the people was swept away, the figures no longer stood waiting as condemned men, they now had a pride, a laughter such as no one had ever seen them having before. Still, the fact of this revolutionary process, said Heilmann, does not exempt us from asking how this process is captured in the painting. When acting, people likewise, he said, carefully considered what was right and what was wrong, what could imperil the subsequent movements and what could safeguard them and move them further ahead. Reflection, he went on, had been the hallmark of violent action. That was why we had to examine how human energy, enthusiasm had been transformed into the value obtaining for the artistic handicraft. So long as such a quality could not be ascertained, he said, the object remained a mere byproduct of the realm of external action. This kind of art, Coppi retorted, has broken with all earlier criteria. It issues straight out of reality. Perhaps the rags and chains were painted better in the old political system, perhaps the compositions, the color contrasts, the effects of light and shadow attained perfection in the portrayals of the dungeons, perhaps new art movements could be inferred from the renderings of poverty and misery, but these paintings here express something that never succeeded before, the event in which labor takes possession of itself. The realism in this altered situation, said Heilmann, had yielded to an idealizing and heroizing, a stance reemerged after being overcome by the realists at the turn of the century, that was why, he said, the true events lost their authenticity in the paintings. The painters of battles and allegories, he added, are still at work here, though with different contents. Our normal critical approach, said Coppi, will not get at the heart of these pictures. The triumph in them is their truth. To the person for whom the construction of Socialism is meaningless, such art may seem like sheer decoration, and the rapture like empty glorification. But in a place where the step to freedom has been taken, which we do not dare to do as yet, excessiveness corresponds to reality. In judging such art, said Heilmann, we let ourselves be guided by our respect, our admiration for the workers' state. But when dealing with artistic issues we cannot make emotional and ideological allowances. Anything that is to be part of our cultural foundation must stand the test. These paintings encourage us, said Coppi's mother, we need such help now that so many of us are throwing in the towel. But Heilmann stuck to his guns. These paintings do show achievements, accomplishments, he said, but they cover up the contradictory processes in which new things emerge. Their contents cannot be evaluated as something self-contained. Just as the thought of revolution was not yet the revolution but only demanded its deeds, so too the pictorial idea called for its implementation in form. Content and form do not coincide here. A worn-out style mixes into the effigies of revolutionary events. The painters who want to champion the future are resorting to the methods of a romantic naturalism, which looks back, toward the bourgeois era. Their naturalism, said Coppi, shatters everything that was a visual delight for the philistine, it is precisely by evoking the old and the familiar that their naturalism shows how it transcends the earlier idylls of profit and exploitation. Moreover, he went on, in this urgent situation, art could not aim at setting up ultimate things, essentially it had to point out the strength and desire to defend the gains. We had to approach these paintings morally, he said, and also accept defects until an art was found that fully corresponded to the greatness of the achievement. We declare all our studies null and void, said Heilmann, if we knowingly acquiesce to an artificiality, a pose, if we halt at a point where advances have long since been traced out. A cultural counterrevolution, he said, is sneaking into our image of society. Philistinism is forcing itself on us, undermining our conceptions, and we fail to notice it. He believed, he said, that it was because in the formation of their taste numerous political activists had bogged down between plagiaries and surrogates. This was understandable, he said, since compared with a total absence of artistic objects the mixture of fustian, pinchbeck, and sentimentality in the philistine home could certainly represent something loftier, and many who started by looking for a road to education stumbled upon these rudimentary things and mistook the disguised misery for tokens of culture. The struggle for our art, he said, must simultaneously be a struggle to overcome petty bourgeois leanings. We need only reach for a sketch dashed off by van Gogh, and the clumsy strokes will reveal the beauty to which the colossal gold-framed paintings aspire in vain. I would also, he continued, put up with the one-dimensional optimism if it did not claim absolute validity, a hegemony that shoves any other statement aside. He recalled the other things that had come about, especially in the area of the film, where in the year before the Collapse we had received impressions that were crucial in molding our political conviction. In Gorky, Ostrovsky, Gladkov, Babel the characters were never stereotypes, and during the years around October, painting and architecture had drafted constructive possibilities that tallied with the essence of the Revolution. Why, asked Heilmann, were they receding way behind the previous gains, why was a revolutionary art being denied and outlawed, why were the works that gave voice to the experiments of their time, that were subversive because the life surrounding them was changing through and through, why were these bold stirring metaphors of awakening replaced by ready-made things, why was a narrow limitation of receptivity introduced if a Mayakovsky, Blok, Bedny, Yesenin, and Bely, a Malevich, Lissitzky, Tatlin, Vachtangov, Tairov, Eisenstein, or Vertov had found a language identical with a new universal consciousness. The things the Cubists and Expressionists churned up in the decade before October, said Coppi, occurred in a world of forms with which only specially trained people were familiar. It was a revolt by art, a rebellion against the norms. Granted, the turmoil in society, the latent violence, the yearning for a radical upheaval found expression, but the workers and soldiers in November of nineteen seventeen had never seen or heard of these artistic metaphors. The Dadaists and Futurists in Moscow continued the transformations on a level with which the fighters were not intimate. Henceforth, art was to belong to them. But what came upon them now originated in the western European countries, where the representatives of the intelligentsia had received their impressions, this was not their own property, once again something was being served to them, the goods of émigrés, of literates were grafting things. It was fruitless for them to be told that the revolution of forms was now to be united with the revolutionary transformation of the whole of life, what the vanguard in literature and painting designed was bound to be unintelligible to the Russian workers. No paintings hung in their basement hovels, at most they had a color picture from a magazine as we do. For the time being, Modernism, Abstraction had to remain the privilege of people who dealt with artistic problems, no proletarian art could arise from there even if the artists believed they were speaking the true language of a revolutionary nation. During this state of transition, people asked which was better, things that nourished the highly developed intellect or things that helped the beginner along. These ponderings included the opposition between the national and the international guidelines. Had the Revolution spread, then art would likewise have maintained a revolutionary versatility. The temporary isolation of the Revolution, the necessity of continuing a lone struggle, of preserving and defending oneself, of entrenching oneself against the enemy pressing in from abroad, forced art too into this position, where every work had to be utilized as a social weapon, every statement had to be precisely examined for its immediate usefulness in resistance and production. As a result, everything showing signs of complications, conflicts was rejected, it would have served neither the Soviet state nor us on the outside. The paintings there could not be shattered, dissolved, fermenting, laboring with new elements again and again, like our art, there was no room for subjective contemplation, they demanded concrete things that could be tested, criticized, like an engine, a building construction. The workers in the iron plants, the machine factories, the shipyards, the kolkhozi saw themselves confirmed in these paintings. Their milieu, the processes of their labor, the handling of the tools had to be rendered correctly. That was the goal. What was portrayed functioned, it was a component in a social, a technological plan. This art, said Coppi, takes its place next to the dams and collective combines, next to the electrification, the agrarian reform, and the workers' universities. This art is utilitarian, just like schools, political organizations. Practical demands are made on it, it has to respond not to the cogitations of an individual but to the expectations of the majority. And yet, Heilmann retorted, this art cannot suffice for the worker. No matter how squarely it places him in the middle of the events, it nevertheless underestimates him by granting him only one aspect of reality. He must feel that tailored themes prevent him from making up his own mind. With the significance allotted to Socialist culture, the worker who has begun studying, reading, who wants to express something himself in painting, in writing, realizes that important, indeed crucial things are being kept from him. He sees situations rendered with photographic accuracy, yet instead of nearness they produce detachment, alienation, because the material is not worked on, because it contains nothing but externals. No matter how precisely the detail is captured, it remains an imitation, a deception. For centuries now, art has been striving to overcome such knock-offs. Why, he asked, did the Impressionists, the Cubists, and the Futurists disintegrate that which presented itself to the eyes, certainly not to get away from the tangible, but to lend new solidity to the impalpable. Now that photography makes the realm of authenticity and documentation visible for our image of history, now that the light issuing from objects can be directly captured and preserved, painting is less capable than ever of feigning reality by diligently transferring a specific cut-out of space to a flat surface. Art has always convinced us only by filling the painted plane or the written pages with a life of its own. Whenever precautions are taken to steer art, they merely confirm that it has a mind of its own. The more tightly art is bound, the more people fear the danger of its explosive energy. From this insight it is not far to the suspicion that not everything that claims to be exemplary conforms to the facts. Is he the lord over everything he has conquered, the thinking man will ask when he recognizes the skimpy freedom of movement allocated to artistic activity. He is then bound to be distrustful, said Heilmann, toward the icon that, in its edition of ten thousand copies, places itself above all artistic work, constantly referring to a supreme being, an omniscient mustachioed father who guards the totality. On Sundays, when scores of Russian workers, said Coppi's mother, visit the museums, the painting exhibits that are now their property, they focus hard on their history and also on the clashes during the years of struggle, of enemy invasions. The most important thing for them is that they stood their ground. She could never, she said, forget a film she had once seen at the Liebknecht House, about Kirghiz and Turkmene collective farmers visiting the Tretiakov Gallery, the way the openness and brightness in the faces, the joy and wonder reflected the depictions. It is only in the variety, said Heilmann, with which art depicts human experience that we can recognize the liveliness of its native land, and the degree of its restrictions also shows the repressions that operate in the land. Mayakovsky's suicide, he went on, had anticipated the disaster that was now swooping down on the Soviet state. We had heard about the rumors and testimonies concerning acts of sabotage and attempts at division, subversive plans and conspiracies to assassinate the Party leader. Vermin, leeches, parasites, subhumans, that was what they called the men who two decades ago had carried out the Revolution and founded the Soviet state. They, Lenin's comrades, wanted to annihilate Socialism, smash industrial life, sell large portions of the country to the fascists, and reintroduce capitalism. But indirectly, said Heilmann, this is a terrible indictment of Lenin, for he, whose acumen, whose understanding of the future always inspires us, had sought colleagues and confidants who now had all been exposed as criminals, mangy dogs, enemies of the people, and yet from the very start they would somehow or other have revealed their plans to destroy all achievements. Why had Lenin not seen through the riffraff, asked Heilmann, which had become known to us as the Bolshevik Guard, why did only one man survive who was supposedly worthy of succeeding him. The situation during the final year of Lenin's life was different from the situation after his death, said Coppi. The cohesive energy issuing from his personality enabled his closest comrades-in-arms to develop their most valuable qualities. He also saw their weaknesses, he kept warning them about the power struggles, the schisms that were bound to be lurking where such a collection of obstinate men was trying to build up something completely new. The internationalists, who had spent years in exile with Lenin, who had oriented themselves by the outside world, clashed with the people who had stayed at home, who were rooted in the people. In the decisive situation, when the revolutions failed to materialize in the West, when all energy had to focus on preserving the isolated Socialist state, the secretary-general, whom Lenin managed to criticize for his crudeness, his intolerance, had become the figure who connected and concentrated everything, he had kept aloof from the rancor, rivalry, and factionalism that emerged as Lenin lay dying, it was the secretary-general who represented calm and control, who arbitrated, who offered his verdict when the struggle for succession erupted. History, said Coppi, would show whether he was self-seeking when he held back or acting in the best interests of the people, but the authority had been delegated to him by the Party congress because no one seemed more capable of assuring the unity of the Party in the period of mortal danger. Amid the rage and cunning of fascism, which was setting out to mobilize every available force against the workers' state, it was possible for the fascists to win over even individual people and groups in the land of Socialism by exploiting the infighting and to turn them against the leadership, so that it became justified and necessary to eliminate all those working against adherence to the official policies. Yet, retorted Heilmann, not only were spies, assassins, and traitors dragged out of the government administration, the economic sector, and the military, but many artists who had familiarized us with revolutionary experiences were suddenly labeled scum, decadent, contaminated with bourgeois ideas, books were pulped, movies destroyed, theaters shut down, some artists, like Babel, Mandelstam, Meyerhold were arrested and may have already been shot, liquidated. These words, said Heilmann, the words of defamation, to which we close our ears here, in the precincts of murder and robbery, should we accept those words when they come from people on our side, and what about artistic investigation, should we surround it with taboos, with atavistic and irrational omens, and let ourselves be persuaded that all this is justified, meaningful only because we feel close to the country in which such orders are given, because nothing must imperil this country, because it must be kept alive, defended, not only by our acting, but also by our incessant thinking. How could it happen, he asked, that such distortion, such scorn could seep into what we considered clarity, and how should we muster the strength to keep championing something that has been tainted. In the cramped kitchen, where Coppi's father was pacing to and fro, letting his shadow shrink in front of him, grow in back of him, on the door wall, on the window wall, all we could think was that they had proved every detail of the misdeeds of the defendants, who had been on trial for a year now, after all, authors like Feuchtwanger, Heinrich Mann, Lukács, Rolland, and Barbusse, Aragon, Brecht, and Shaw believed the revelations and had bowed to the evidence. No doubt must arise about the legitimacy of the proceedings now that the Anti-Comintern Pact had been signed between Germany and Japan, now that the Chinese armies were retreating from Shanghai, Nanking was being bombed, and Peking threatened, now that Italy was about to join the Pact after conquering Ethiopia, now that the Germans and the Italians, supported by the nonintervention policies of France and England, were stepping up their aid to Franco, and now that voices were talking louder and louder about the Greater German Empire, the right to colonies, the drive to the East. The thing is, said Heilmann, we are confronted with events that we have to put up with silently, that we are not allowed to touch on, suddenly our thirst for knowledge, which is part and parcel of dialectics, is supposed to be all we need to damn us. It is precisely because we have to hold up this country as exemplary to the world, said Heilmann, that I have to ask myself what is going on there, and if I had previously avoided trying to understand the historical connections, I would have remained on the other side. It is up to the Soviet people, said Coppi's mother, to take a position on the events and eventually explain them to us. Do we expect that such a gigantic country, such a continent, with its two hundred million people, its fifteen republics could be turned inside out within twenty years, and that everything should promptly be top-notch after so much deprivation. After all, what did we do, here, we left them on their own, back then when they were starting out, we exercised patience instead of doing what they called on us to do. Let us trust them, for they are ahead of us. But at that moment Coppi's father found the cramped kitchen unbearable, he had to have a breath of air, he switched off the light, we heard him trudging through the darkness, he would have shattered the panes if the window had been bolted, he would have dulled his fingernails on the wall if there had been no window, the blackout paper fell off noisily, he swung the window open, coolness came in and the smell of moist dust, and our field of vision expanded to include a few dark gray façades with black squares, and mirrored clouds drifting across them.

It was not until two thousand years after Aristonicus that the revolution succeeded. The leader of the Pergamum rebellion wanted to name the citizens of his new state Heliopolites after the sun, the symbol of justice. But what they got instead were mass graves or slave chains. Aristonicus was thrown into the bilge of a trireme and brought to Rome. His dream of an independence movement ended in the Forum, where, harnessed to the stocks, he was gawked at and spit at. As he lay dying, he saw the shining temples of his subjugators rising about him. Two millennia of the slaveholding society had passed, in its ancient, its feudal, and its bourgeois stages, history, climbing, as it was put, from level to level, had made progress because of the constant pressure of the masses, every improvement was based on an eruption of despair, but the system of domination had remained the same, every push by serfs, thralls, wage slaves had always been countered with new weapons, and the greater the thrust of self-defense, the more comprehensive the annihilatory blows. For two thousand years people had talked about the men who ascended to power, shoving aside their predecessors, settling in the higher ranks, until the next ones came, impatient, reckless, and in the descriptions of this steady motion all that was said about those remaining in the depths was that the time was not yet ripe for them. The conflict in society, it was said, was not yet sharp enough for them, the revolt was inadequately organized, the populace too unenlightened, the people in the underclasses were too deeply marked by misery to grasp the idea of a fresh start, to succeed in overthrowing the government. History had been handed down from above, it was convincingly pointed out that every uprising could be crushed, and the profiteers likewise changed as a matter of course. Everything took place according to unalterable principles, for the people who bequeathed the image of the world always sided with those who laid down the rules of the world. Adversaries existed from the very outset, for them history was one long sequence of horror and rebellion, but they never got a word in under all the oligarchies, and from the papyrus scrolls to the yelling radios the truth was throttled by demagogy. Had the scribes, the savants been linked to the class of the laborers, the visions of a life in equality would not have had to wait until our century to come true, but intellect, said Coppi, was simply inseparable from finance, and even today very few individuals tear loose from the intelligentsia to join us. The sculptors in the acropolis, he said, approved of eliminating the turmoil down in the streets, for had they not been agreeable, they would have been incapable of making the frieze so sublime and definitive. The harmonious picture of the gods, radiating calm and restraint, was part of their ideal. Had the portrayal of sin and impurity revealed their social conflict, they would have been unable to get on with their undertaking. Any humane stirrings in their oeuvre entered unintentionally, thanks to their

craftsmanship, which involved observing, rendering concrete experience. Only the awareness of the actual power conditions would enable someone to stand up against the patrons' wishes. But they put off such a course of action by seeking refuge in a self-containment and isolation of their art. They remained devoted to the princes and prelates, to the speculating Maecenases, and they paid off their debts with carefully and lovingly drawn minutiae that they allowed their senses to filter in from the outside. The underpinning provided by the stockpiled money was a guarantee that lofty things could be accomplished in the first place; where frugality existed there could be no fostering of art, the more unbridled the violence, the deeper the contemplation became, the vaster the booty, the more significant the artistic embellishment became. In their position between those living below and the rulers, whose power they accepted, the artists gave themselves over to the game of materialization. Only the notion that their accomplishments had an intrinsic value could explain their tireless efforts, their devotion to their work while the terror spread all around, while the spontaneous disorderly military campaigns turned into carefully planned and smoothly functioning war machineries, while the executioners' henchmen perfected their tortures, the incarcerations proceeded like a conveyor belt, and the slave markets were transformed into immeasurable detention camps that abolished every last right and any prospect of freedom. With the French revolutions, the structure they had erected began to wobble, a few artists discovered that they belonged to the proletarian element, and once again this realization had been forced by the fighting in the street. Yet goodness knows what it requires, said Coppi's mother, to translate knowledge into action. It took us two thousand years to find a scientific explanation for why we have always served as nothing but a footboard for others in all uprisings and rebellions, why we have never succeeded in establishing our own power. Any glimpse of our own history could sometimes make it appear that we had always been the underdogs, that nothing had changed in the might we have faced, but then October proved that all those onsets had stored up an energy more powerful than all our previous fetters. In the spiraling tableau of the development, we occasionally saw ourselves right next to the defeated of earlier centuries, we conjured up their raging and lethargy, but then, instead of hopelessness, a new effort began, and no matter how close we were to the slaves and serfs, we were now in an era when our goals were starting to be attained. We were rising up not in groups but as a class, the added knowledge we had gained about the past had not only burdened us with the plights of bygone generations but also made us aware of the continuous suppression in the underdeveloped countries, the colonies. The yoke had been equally heavy everywhere, what we had in common was not a country but a responsibility that we all bore, and thus the consciousness of solidarity, of internationalism had emerged. Perhaps it sounded paradoxical to mention such things in our situation, what with the millions of workers in our country who were letting themselves be drawn away from the duties of their class. In these beginnings, socialism too had disunity and rivalry, intolerance and arrogance, the people who wanted to build the new were themselves still stuck in the old, everyone dragged the legacy around, the future had to be incomplete as yet, decipherable only from hints, suggestions. Political training courses had become impossible, we had to form a judgment about the situation by reading a secretly circulated copy of an illegal publication, we had to go by our own lights when championing what was right for us. And just as our political decisions were based on fragments, dissonances, hypotheses, resolutions, and slogans, all borne by a conviction deriving from our own life experiences, so too we could not conceptualize art without including its ruptures, fluctuations, and oppositions. And if it were deprived of its contradictions, then only a lifeless stump would remain. From its very inception, the expressiveness of art had its ascents and declines, they were part of every era, showing up in the dynamic and static phases, in expansive originality and regression, in authenticity and imitation, the quality of one style could scarcely be set off against another, features called primitive in Paleolithic stone sculptures and body forms carved into rock, in the monuments on Easter Island and the African and Indian masks, were so true to the mark that they became models for today's art, though retaining a more powerful symbolism, the cave paintings in Altamira and

Lascaux possessed a magic that was supplanted by decorativeness in Expressionist works, the Cretan frescoes, with their loose airy tonalities, their blurred contours, were similar to the Impressionists' conception of nature, the floral patterns of Knossos already contained Art Nouveau, the shifts of aspect in Egyptian reliefs paved the way for Cubism, Surrealism actualized the Babylonian and Aztec figures, the sculptures of the Hindus and the Khmer or the Sumerian and Coptic forms broke into the plastic art of modernity. Antiquity, Middle Ages were labels for the categorical pigeonholes of the theoreticians, obfuscating the fact that everything in art was new and current. Realism and abstraction, ritual and the fantastic had always existed, at one time clarity was achieved with flatness, at another with a volumetric effect, central perspective was to be regarded not as an improvement but as a different way of transmitting illusion. Art was always goal-oriented and self-willed, rigorously constrained and leaping to surprises. The history of art likewise resembled a spiral in which we were always near the past and all components perpetually looked modulated and varied anew, and if any alteration was important for us it was because we had rediscovered the initial value of art, for as long as thinking had existed art had been everyone's property, interlaced with our impulses and reflexes. We refused to accept the notion of an exclusive art created for specifically educated people, nor, likewise, could we be satisfied that there had to be an artistic parlance customized for the working class, a language that had to be very intelligible, solid, and vigorous. For us, art could not be versatile and inventive enough. We agreed with many studying comrades that the paintings that were supposed to mislead us about antithesis had little in common with our goal, no matter how well defended they were. We wanted to find out for ourselves what spoke to us and what was worn out, what was in the service of the demagogues and what might help us in our efforts to track these things down. Painters, poets, philosophers reported on the crises and confrontations, the concretions and awakenings of their time. In the passages from one style to another, in a sudden liberation of movement, gesture, color, one might read social upheavals, yet in the multiplicity of mirrorings, of visual concentrations, one could always find a unity, everything nourished, questioned, answered everything else, and nothing was so remote as to be unfathomable. At one point we wondered if despite the necessity of obeying the wishes of their patrons, the artists' dependence on clergy and royalty had not made their work more secure and stable than in later periods, when they were on their own and responsible only for themselves. The slow calm execution of a work within a sequence solidified by tradition was replaced by a demand for originality, newness was attributed not to mature craftsmanship but to genius, and this pressure to be singular, to dedicate oneself to individuality led to isolation, to brooding, to the dominance of personal suffering, to surfeit, so that eventually art per se was called into question. Dürer's woodcut of the Prodigal Son and his *Melancholia* clearly pointed out the gap between hierarchical art and art left completely to its own devices and forced to make its choice all by itself. We debated whether one therefore had the right after all to claim exclusivity in order to impose a guideline on art, and whether stipulating a specific function in that way might elicit a conviction, a consequence. Yet a style could not be inflicted on anyone, it had to grow organically. It was intrinsic to the period we lived in that the entire past, which we were the first to get to know in its full scope, was plunging into a melting pot, the style of our era had to be a continuous seeking and rejecting. And how, asked Coppi's mother, was it possible for earlier artists to produce things of lasting value while working under tyrants. They could do so because they did not see the extent of suppression, did not challenge the power structure, replied Coppi, they stated what they considered to be true. The enlightened artist today who makes himself available to the dictatorship can only toady and fool himself. The monuments of fascism, based on Greek, on Roman models, communicate nothing but plaster emptiness. That is why, said Heilmann, the advocates of truth live in exile or captivity, or if they dare to express their opinions to the rulers, they have to pay for their openness with their lives. Prison and torture, a ban on one's working, escape, banishment, and autos-da-fé, he said, became part of the artist's lot ever since he started repudiating the powers that be. All art, he went on, all literature are present inside ourselves, under the aegis of the only deity we can believe in, Mnemosyne. She, the mother of the arts, is named Memory. She protects what our own knowledge contains in all achievements. She whispers to us, telling us what we yearn for. Any man who presumes to cultivate, to castigate these stored assets is attacking us ourselves and condemning our powers of discernment. Sometimes I am repelled by art historians who while raising an index finger forget all about the multivalence of every single work, but those who apply restraints based on political considerations know nothing about the essence of art. By smashing images, burning books, fighting against disagreeable views, they present themselves as members of the Inquisition. Ideology bluntly barges into a field with which it could be linked, but which must turn a deaf ear when ideology demands subordination. Marx and Engels knew that, nor would Lenin have ever exploited his position to force his artistic views on others. In their notions of beauty they were traditionalists. Their appreciation of art derived from the bourgeois schools. Yet from the works they gleaned the values that were connected to social progress and that cleared the ground for the universal ownership of art. Once the mechanisms of suppression were shattered by the revolution, then not only would art remain intact, it would finally show off its harmony and grandeur. They cared little for upheavals à la Blanqui, Proudhon, or Bakunin, and just as they opposed extreme radicalism, avant-garde rhetoric, so too they preferred the intrinsically solid classics to restless minds like Hölderlin, Novalis, Kleist, or Büchner, they favored the French novelists over Rimbaud, Lautréamont, Verlaine, Baudelaire, they sided with the melodious symphonists, while atonality must have been agony for them. Lenin regarded the contemporary artworks as an insult to nature, he was angry that his ideals had not passed unscathed through the chaos of revolution, but for the art blossoming in the workers' state he likewise desired symmetry and harmony instead of the anatomical dissolution, the bedlam of shrieks, factory sirens, and turbines, so his claim to partisanship would have to have a face devised anew by every artist. What he, as an authority, considered partisanship was ethical in nature, he ascribed an inherent vitality to art, but among his successors his generosity became flat and petty, prototype won out over spontaneity, method and correctness over free growth. Now when the schoolmasters, we asked in discussions, recommended that we study the art and literature of the nineteenth century, when they praised Balzac, Stendhal, and Goethe, Rembrandt, Bach, and Shakespeare for their maturity and knowledge of human beings, their circumspection, their sophistication and universality, when they saw timeless conflicts humanistically exemplified in patricians and lieges, in aristocrats, ladies-in-waiting, and kings, then why should the works of late-bourgeois brooders and experimenters not be likewise informative and arouse our interest. Hadn't Marx, Engels, Luxemburg, and Lenin sparked the idea that cultural utterances are not always made as a result of the material conditions of their era, but rather in contrast with them, that artists applied cunning, defiance, and irony to smash through the barriers and factors of the relations of production, the new knowledge helping to alter consciousness. Thus, next to its specific class character, art had a feature that made it superior to the social, economic, and political processes determining our lives, art often found itself on the brink of the changes of social being, and it was precisely this characteristic that perplexed the ideologues. They were unable to go through with the idea of letting art function as a constant ubiquitous force for renewal, instead they demanded the same disciplining for the artistic media that was necessary for them, the politicians. Whenever they interfered, patronizing, reprimanding, they were difficult to criticize since their intentions were always the best. Socialist art was to be kept pure from the brutalization in capitalism's culture business, and any measure eliminating the glorification of war, of racism, of sadistic violence, had to be approved, but it was hard to pinpoint the line between freedom of opinion and the fight against reactionism. We did not agree that pulp was the price to be paid for freedom of choice, we condemned the sleaze that the cesspools of the mass media poured daily over the populace, but true literature and fine art must not be customized. Thus our education not only ran contrary to the obstacles of the class society, it also flouted the principle of a socialist view of culture that had sanctioned the masters of the past but excommunicated the pioneers of the twentieth century. We insisted that Joyce and Kafka, Schönberg and Stravinsky, Klee and Picasso were of the same rank as Dante, whose *Inferno* we had been studying for some time now.

The *Divina Commedia* was as unsettling, as rebellious, and in form and theme apparently as remote from anything familiar as was *Ulysses*, which we had only just gotten to know fragmentarily, as a kind of rebus. What was happening here, we had been wondering since the summer of this year after starting our trip into the strange upside-down dome sunken into the earth, with its circles coiling deeper and deeper, trying to take an entire lifetime, whereas after the complete passage they promised ascent, likewise in rings, to heights beyond imagining. We had come no further than Francesca da Rimini and Paolo Malatesta, spending a lot of time reinterpreting Gmelin's translation in a Reclam paperback and Borchardt's in the Cotta pocket edition, comparing the German tercets with the Italian terza rima, which Heilmann read aloud to us on the basis of his knowledge of Latin and French. Forging ahead from the linguistic imprecisions, the smoothened metaphors, the lost rhythms and melodies of the outer layer and plunging into the internal dynamics of an everlasting fire, we felt things awakening within us, experiences we had never known about, laid out inside us and now made operative only by the poetry. When reading, we wanted nothing mystical, irrational to emerge and we tried to break every association down thoroughly into its components, but the conversations about the forest that we entered with the wanderer lasted for weeks, and later we often harked back to them, aware of having grasped only a few motifs of that canto. The depiction of the overall enterprise ran simultaneously with the motion of groping one's way toward a specific place that could not be found in the world of perceptions and whose entrance and forecourt were described as concretely as the dark woods with their animals, their topographic features, and their light slowly oozing forth. The opening lines already made it sound as if anything portrayed here could not really be expressed in words and images, and as the impossible then moved from verse to verse, section to section, in a consistent articulation steadily accompanied by marginal numbers, knitting together into a stable, harmonious unity that could not be pictured in any other way, it clarified the triumph of the imagination over chaos, misguidance, and absolute uncertainty. It revealed not only the path into the spiritual structure of the inferno, where the raw material of an epoch concentrated into a subjective vision, but also the step into the mechanism of artistic labor. The approach to art was linked to the thought of death. The writer of the poem found himself at the midpoint of his life, yet in his work he not only put himself in the hands of a dead man, he encountered only the dead. Upon setting out he had placed himself in this vicinity of death, he was still breathing, but filled with demise, he contained the mirroring of those who now possessed nothing, and thus, in pondering what they had given him, what survived in him alone, when he penetrated the regions in which, as was natural, at most only his skeleton could be found, he felt as if he too were perishing. We could compare the start of his journey with somnolence, we were familiar with the abrupt sagging of something within reach, the start of a dream, the moments when the grab-hook dangling from the crane might hit your skull, the drive belt of the machine might rip off your arm, or at night, at dawn, when you could not tell whether the room you were in was part of a dream or whether the dream pounced on your room, and in this intermediate stage, cloaked by heavy fatigue yet able to see and hear something, searching for thoughts to transform surfacing palpable things into objects, he put letters on paper. We could not yet visualize the making of a book, a painting, so far we had encountered art only receptively and, aside from a few poems by Heilmann, at most occasionally written notes, chiefly about experiences in the realm of work, which always indicated the infinite difficulty of focusing the mind, gaining a wider overview. And when speaking about the complex offered us by the Dante book, we felt remorse. Though insisting on our right to books, we never read without timidity. Not even Coppi's parents were involved here, this showed how utterly impossible our leap was from the given to our own, we saw all too sharply our separation from those who, like us, could read but had not learned in time how to take hold of a book and open it. Though we talked with so much conviction about our cultural self-awareness and though we knew how it had already solidified in a few groups, and how many were pushing up, we could not help thinking of the terrible paralysis of most of the others, whom brutal autocracy deprived of initiative, leisure, stimulus and education for reading. It was not enough to point out that the libraries were open, first you had to overcome the generations-old compulsive idea that the book did not exist for you. On Sundays we sat in the Humboldt Grove or in St. Hedwig's Cemetery, near Pflugstrasse, trying to find out what the *Divina Commedia* had to do with our lives. At first we assumed that disembodiment was a prerequisite for making art, that the producer gave himself up in order to gain something outside himself. Yet this sounded irrational, for after all, we were convinced that art depicted utmost reality, which could be achieved only by straining all vital energy. It then turned out in the measured, consciously implemented course of composition that touching on the thought of death, that life with death and with the dead in it, could trigger the drive to make art, but that the finished product was meant for the living, so that it had to be executed according to all the rules of living reception and reflection. Dante showed this method of doubleness, in which the fear of perishing overcame itself by leaving behind signs that outlasted one's own life, and though it initially seemed as if this transformation were hidden under symbols and allegories intelligible only to people grounded in Scholasticism, the filigree of metaphors and similes could be probed more and more for details speaking from a reality observed up close. Regarding what was said, it was not necessary for us to understand it as it may have been meant six centuries ago, it simply had to be transferred to our time, take on life here, in this park, next to the playground, here, amid these freshly filled graves below St. Sebastian's Church, for this was what made the statements permanent, the way they aroused our own deliberations, the way they asked for our answers. Although we were surrounded by perdition, it had never dawned on us that our lives, only just begun, could be cut off prematurely, but now our own deaths, emerging momentarily from blurriness, came into focus and receded again, yet only, we now knew, to resurface later on, more clearly each time. Dante had perished, but circled by embodiments, furry, haggard, snarling, ranging about, as a lynx, a wolf, eventually roaring with a lion's voice, pushing it back, making it sink away, and what else was the rescuer, the guide, but memory, which produced endurance where instability had just been. The man from Mantua, the Lombard, reminded him of the continuity beyond life and death, and in this way, at the limit point, where dissolution waits, the easy-to-lose world could once again grow mightily, violently, tumultuously, pitting against him everything that had driven him to poetic, political activity, that had shattered his hopes, chased him out of Florence, inflicted exile and poverty on him, and that had also kept him alive after renunciation and loss of love. Upon entering the realm of the lost, before Charon's boat might even cast off to cross the Acheron, it had become obvious that this was not an afterlife corkscrewing into the earth, it was really the inhabited world, which Dante had upended at the cusp between the thirteenth and the fourteenth century, with all that there was of hubbub and wickedness, jealousy, anger, and blindness. Amid the crush of figures, each trapped in his own obsessions, he kept highlighting certain ones after first leaving them to Virgil's cool pointing, and, not just stripped to the skin, with their scars, deformations, characterized in their madness, they also appeared as representatives of specific class interests. At times emotionally overpowered by the sight of people he had confronted in schemes and struggles, he nevertheless managed to trace out a social pattern that must have been unheard of for his time. Here all the grandees of the era, even the popes and emperors, were portrayed, by name, by individual traits, and their passions had grown into a fire, an eruption, a glaciation that devoured them for all eternity. No sooner had we leafed through the pages recording the disasters they had perpetrated than we managed to see how the tremendous profusion was systematized. The hallucination in which the murdering and torturing fell back upon the culprits, in which every perversity made itself unredeemed, was simultaneously an almost pedantic catalogue of all the attributes involved in rising to power. And yet, Coppi had said, this moralist, who delivers every one of his enemies and antagonists to damnation remains unsullied himself, he may weep, may faint because of all these pains endured by the people who inflicted them, or even because of his own suffering, but it never strikes him that he too, through a hesitation, an omission, a silence, a denial, may be guilty in someone else's eyes, he passes through the evil, knowing that so long as he clutches the hand of the tutelary genius, of the artistic consciousness, no harm can come to him. Is not this too, Coppi had asked, an arrogance that we should guard against in art, and Heilmann had responded that this insensitivity might be the same that we know in dreams and that enabled us to get through what we see. If the beasts actually injured Dante, if the furious dead all around him struck the blows they threatened, he would have nothing more to report. The agony of dreams and literature, Heilmann had said, was to be at the mercy of an inescapable situation, everything happened to us there as if it were true, except that in a dream the no-longer-endurable led to awakening, just as in literature it is freed by the translation into words. Anesthesia, he went on, was likewise part of extremely participatory art that took a stance, for without the help of an anesthetic we would be overwhelmed either by feeling compassion with other people's torments or by suffering our own misfortune, so that we would be incapable of transforming our falling-into-silence, our paralyzing terror into the aggressiveness necessary for eliminating the causes of the nightmare. The same thing applied to the transparent fluoroscope of the decisive battle between death and survival in certain paintings. When I was still working in the assembly hall at the separator plant, there was a period when we lived with the dreams of Piero della Francesca. This was not a book that, tied to no locale, could be taken up at will to show itself in its freestanding special features, it was a series of pictorial excerpts only hinting at the totality they belonged to and filled with so much tension that every glimpse aroused the desire to encounter the real dimensions of the frescoes in Arezzo. Shadowless, in a space without depth, the figures, with their weapons, banners, and war horses, were telescoped into one another, the farthest the same size as the nearest, and every detail, whether a catapult chain, a buckle, a hinge, a panache, a soldier's or a horse's eye, was of equal value, subject to no other laws than those promulgated by the composition surface. The harmonizing of the gray-white, gray-black, and umbra of the steeds, the reddish violet, gray, green, and blue shades of the garments, the red of the bloodstains, the shining of the swords and armors, the copper fittings on the dull leather, the glimpse of a bend in a glossy river with swans, the white sand of the banks with grass and bushes as transparent dabs in the lime plaster, the geometrically unfolded walls of a city, the green-blue of sky taken up by the oddly smooth unscathed ground, all this had been transferred by an utterly unemotional view to the monumental efficacy of carefully harmonized forms. Coppi found this gaze cold, restrained, the definitiveness of the depiction struck him as fatalistic. The noblemen stood on their own, circled by armed men, by standards, shielded by a starry firmament, while off by themselves, forever wedged into the gestures of mutual annihilation, were the warriors. Neither the galloping legs of the horse, nor the swung ax, nor the spear clutched for hurling contained the possibility of further movement, of a change of situation. No sinking forward or plunging back was conceivable in the balanced postures, no twisting or turning. Nothing existed but the uniqueness of this second observed in deep concentration and sacrificing any feeling to a guilloche of visual relationships made up of the lines of swords and lances, bridles and banner poles, the curves of shields, helmets, and horse shanks, the columns and pillars of legs, the echelons of arms, hands, and faces, the vision lines of eyes under dark brows. The strange, the estranging character of the painting came from its refusal, despite its figurative content, to imitate nature in any way. It possessed its own light, and the event within it was an accord of colors. Such a statement was speculative, said Coppi, and did not advance our cause. The issues being fought out over there had nothing to do with our struggle. However, the objections we raised often served merely to sharpen our judgment. Why, we asked, were we interested in this painting, in which the choice of groupings is based on class division. Because we have to know such works, which are unerring in their way, we said. We needed these exclusive, demanding achievements of art, of literature to complement what we were familiar with on the other side, which has no monuments, the side of poverty and deprivation. The reaction could be hostile. But in regard to things that were unfriendly, indifferent toward us, we felt a greater urge to treat them as if they existed solely to provide us with study materials. Just as shadows, which give bodies air and animation in a varying interplay, were banned from the painting, so too no imprints of feet or hooves were present in the ground plane despite the thronging of legs. From the teeming mass, the bodies towered statuesque, laden with shields, brassards, and coats of mail, and yet no man had a weight of his own. The faces of the warriors, under gigantic helmets, gaped motionless and unaffected from the crisscross of weapons. Sometimes my memory projected a detail of the painting into the boilers, cylinders, and pistons of the cream separators I was occupied with. Mostly I projected the faces, unfeeling yet strongly expressive, earnest, silent, in the throes of the conflict that I saw before me, three of them, primed in Verona green and in white highlights, were squeezed together between armor ornaments, swords, and pikes, one face at a frontal angle, framed by a salt-and-pepper beard, the second face in profile with an arching beaklike nose, a jutting lower lip, the third face behind that one, the teeth glittering in the open mouth, the cheek split by a stroke, bloody, and yet in leaning upon one another each face remained by itself, with the same thoughtful gaze. Wedged between a closed sharply protruding visor, a trumpet, a club, a horse's head, another figure very attentively ogled the viewer, and this soldier was so absorbed in his scrutiny that he failed to notice what was happening to him, for behind him a fist was clenching on the pommel of a dagger whose blade was boring into his throat. The drama of the dagger, a component in this section of the *History of the True Cross*, took place at the exact same height in a second spot, though not hemmed in, not hidden, but presented wide open, for instruction, as it were. On the straight blue outstretched arm, the hand was lightly and loosely clutching the artfully chiseled shaft and plunging the long thin edge into the adversary's steeply bent-back throat. The adversary was turning his profile with his chin up, his skull lying in the basin of the helmet with its painted floral pattern, and the dissector's face high above him expressed the same careful matter-of-fact deliberation that must have guided the artist in making his painting. And now we also saw that the works dedicated to the chosen and privileged brought out the faces of the soldiers and squires, accentuating them as more convincing, more powerful, more experienced than the faces of their masters. In Mantegna and Masaccio, Grien, Grünewald, and Dürer, in Bosch, Brueghel, and Goya, the workers stepped into the foreground. In paintings by Poussin, the shepherds and fishers, who had once put up with their decorative functions, suddenly lost their simplicity and gentleness, bearing passions such as had been described in classical tragedies. A blacksmith or a carpenter in La Tour was so towering with his labor that he occupied the pictorial space all by himself, without a patron or purchaser. Vermeer, Chardin did not reserve beauty and maturity for the nobles, they assigned them to the seamstress, the laundress, the maid. Once the historically determined hierarchies, the proportions of a specific era were exposed, we were confronted with a permanent image of reality, and we could discern to what extent the artist had prepared the future development and what stance he had taken on the suppression carried from century to century. In many works, no matter whether princes, prelates, or speculating patrons had laid claim to ownership, the artist, following his own sense of truth, overcoming biases and boundaries, had always included the element of classlessness. Social renewal, the removal of discoveries and conquests from the hands of the rulers, the creation of our own power, the establishment of our own scientific thinking, those were subjects we could imagine in art, in literature. But given the countless possibilities of expression that we had gotten to know, and weighing the various receptivities, reactions, and lines of sight within ourselves, we became convinced that a new art would develop among people who thought in socialistic terms, and that the path taken by like-minded people had a more certain direction than all programmatic directives. Aberrations and abortive efforts were also good enough so long as they were on the side of the revolution, and everyone ought to look at the available possibilities and pick out any old or new things consistent with his personal trains of thought. We, who of our own free will kept abreast of current events, who drew our own conclusions from them and had chosen our political affiliation, demanded that the party we belonged to or were close to should appreciate our selection in the cultural realm. The very fact that we young workers, like our fathers and mothers, who had grown up during the years of war and want, were even dealing with art and literature, the very fact that we could contest the oppressive living conditions precisely with our own discoveries indicated that our future culture would come out of ourselves and that toward this end we would need to rely chiefly on our own abilities. All that was a sketching. Now, on this last day in Coppi's kitchen, I saw the full extent of what we had begun, what we had gathered, and that was why the brief hour before the start of the air-raid drill was crowded with books and streets, pictures and workplaces, museums, ideas, and political realities. The years I had spent in this country

had become densely tangible, I found myself at a turning point, in a transition to a new period of my life. But was this really the correct term, we asked when discussing my imminent departure, was the change of place still meaningful, since the tasks facing us were the same everywhere and bound us with one another. After the victory in Arezzo, said Coppi, repeating the salute from our Francesca period, and he handed me one of the pictures from the outset of our artistic agitating. The picture was part of the series of world-war military commanders and Fascist Party bigwigs, whom Coppi had lampooned in his caricatures. They were provided with balloons in which they bawdily confessed to being what they were, document forgers, thieves of the people's property, racism mongers, mass murderers, and, further clarifying their goals, they brandished a knife, an ax, a pistol. These cartoons, which he attached to bus schedules and subway bulletin boards or pasted on kiosks and on posters for mass rallies, eventually led to his home-mimeoed leaflets and his arrest while distributing them outside a factory entrance. But Heilmann took the picture away from me. You people still, he said, underestimate the enemy's machinery of violence. Heilmann offered to take Coppi's drawings, along with the writings hidden by the stove, and safeguard them in the basement of his parents' building, where they would elude detection, and for safety's sake he advised hanging, aside from the nameplate on the door, a portrait of the Führer inside the apartment, so that all who entered would be impressed in various ways.

As I hurried from the subway station at Schwartzkopfstrasse, across Chausseestrasse, to Pflugstrasse, amid the howling of the air-raid sirens, yelled at by block wardens trying to drive me into the nearest air-raid shelter, pursued by the screeching of their whistles, I was haunted by a question, and as cars and buses stopped, people hastily vanished in the holes indicated by white arrows, and I merely took the next corner all the more swiftly in order to get home, the question demanded an answer as to whether all our perusing of books and paintings had not been an escape from the practical, overwhelming problems, the same breathless panicky escape as this dash across rain-glistening asphalt, through the double door with the carved posts, along the corridor, across the courtyard, up the stairs, into the cold cleared-out apartment. And I only had to see the linoleum mat with the abraded lines and cracks at the protruding edges of the floorboards, with the trodden paths running to the range, the sink, the door to the next room, and then glance into the bedroom, where the bed legs had left four cavities in the floor covering, and I could once again sense the pattern of poverty and admit that the things we had striven for so wearily and dizzily did not really exist for us after all. But then, standing at the open window, high above the tangle of tracks, the thicket of transmission poles in the approaches to Stettin Station, the resistance that belonged to doubt commenced, and I told myself, now under the roar of the maneuver formation, that absurd as our exploration of intellectual riches might seem in our poverty, we were doing our bit in the struggle for survival, and that with their stylized spareness Giotto's rectangles at Assisi and Padua fit into our empty grayish green rooms. Why, I wondered, must we always let ourselves be driven to deny ourselves even something that costs us nothing but our mulling, merely to confirm that we have been dispossessed once and for all. And almost feverishly I had my father, in his green loden coat, with his left shoulder pulled up, step from the geometry that outlined the life of St. Joachim at the Arena Chapel, and on the floor, in front of the wooden frame that was my bed, my mother, in her long brown slip, was kneeling like St. Anne, to whom something was announced through the wall. My parents had been driven from this dwelling, I was moving out too, and several days ago the proletarians with their two children had left the room next to the kitchen and, with their belongings on a cart, were looking for a different refuge to lodge in. Nothing was left in the kitchen but the shabby valise containing my clothing and a couple of books and notebooks, and, on the wall, a discolored poster with torn edges, depicting a worker against a gray background, bursting his chains with a mighty gesture. He was to keep hanging here, as a final appeal, before being swept away, it was necessary that something remain of our earlier life, for the walls were already gnawed at by the dribbling and crumbling, and there was no more thinking about the smooth table with the two small loaves and the round wooden slab with the fish, above it St. Francis severely raising the knife, compared with these frescoes everything here was a procession through dust and rubble. Spotlights broke through the smoke with circular movements and got caught in the low-drifting clouds. The squadrons had flown off, the clearer zooming of reconnaissance planes could be heard, and loudspeakers in neighboring apartments or in the station emitted the voice of an announcer, now and then with a few recognizable verbal shreds, indicating the successfully completed drill after the drawn-out all-clear signal. At one swoop, the lamps in the station concourse went on, casting long ribbons of light and shadow across the tracks, the switch pistons, the trains rolling in and lumbering out, with the names Stralsund, Rostock, Stettin visible on their signs. Freight cars were shunted on the sidings, accompanied by whistles, by blue lanterns being swung back and forth. Behind the moistly blinking wires and rods of the railroad area, above the housing blocks along Ackerstrasse, the advertising sign at the meter factory of the General Electric Company flamed up, and between the dusky masses of the park around Lazarus Hospital and the graveyards along Liesenstrasse stood the blue-gray spire of St. Sebastian's Church, cloaked in locomotive steam. Buses and elevated trains began moving, the side streets were again filled with shouts and footsteps, the lightbulb dangling naked from the kitchen ceiling could be switched on, I sat down on the floor, leaning against the wall below the window, I would lie here tonight, stretched out, covered with newspapers, and tomorrow too, for though everything was packed, the furniture sold, the rent paid, the departure would not take place for another few days, and I had to ponder the reason for the delay. At that moment, I did not know what else had to be done, the change-of-address forms would have to be filled out at the police station, another visit would have to be paid to the Czechoslovakian consulate, but nothing else came to mind, I already had the train ticket, only an empty waiting lay ahead in an empty room. Perhaps I had miscalculated something in my plans or, I wondered, had I felt that before leaving I needed to muse for a long time in order to review the years I had spent in this country. But now it was again clear that no deep incision was occurring, that the date of the trip could not be separated from the subsequent dates, that time was a single indivisible continuity, always to be thought about and observed only as a totality, and the further away a period was from the center of vision, the more uniformly it dovetailed with its before and after. Thus this hour also contained all coming ones, and I wondered how the twenty-second of September nineteen hundred thirty-seven, a Wednesday could be characterized several days later in Warnsdorf, a few weeks later in Spain, three or four decades later in an unknown place, how could it be identified except as the cube in which I sat in the angle between two planes, ferreting out the holes left by nails, the imprints of furnishings. It was also part of the escape that when trying to classify this experienced day historically, I only knew that Masaryk, the president of the country to which I belonged ever since the ceding of my father's hometown to Slovakia, had now been buried in Lány near Prague, and that simultaneously with the anti-aircraft exercises in Berlin, grand maneuvers were taking place in Mecklenburg. I had always wanted to pick up as much as possible of the events that gave the days their outer stamp, and once again all that remained was whatever could be gleaned from cursory newspaper columns. We lived amid such tremendous simplifications while our thoughts moved nonstop in overabundance, and if it was escape that drove us from intricate connections, then it was a forced flight, we sank away in exhaustion, nor could a whole day between news broadcasts and press bulletins have contributed more to our knowledge of the situation. Yet when turning away from the information that covered none of the actual events and seeking ourselves in our special area, which could not be falsified, and in which our investigation could have free rein, we were again compelled to act according to the methodical givens that we had chosen. The only possible way of coping with the conditions of daily reality was to keep our resolves and courses of action utterly terse. The facts contradicted our belief that all events could be elucidated, explained. The retreat to the inability to grasp events left the world as is. For our progress, we prepared models in black and white, and we reached our decisions by limiting ourselves to a pro and con, a yes or no. The party we had chosen and on whose behalf we exerted ourselves was a definite stable concept, despite its constant internal shiftings. We countered the uncertainty factors with the absoluteness of a political standpoint. When learning about the disagreements, the quarrels within the leadership, we told ourselves that at bottom the Party remained the same. While we could not test the facts of many of the things with which our either/or opposed the complexity, there were nevertheless so many of us acting on the same viewpoint and standing up for the same impulse that our project, we said, would some day prove correct. It was by defining a front line and thereby making our activities meaningful that we were able to put out the illegal leaflet, transmit the directive to the cell, shelter a hunted comrade, travel to Spain. Staring into the kitchen, where the scraped wall paint, cracked all the way up to the ceiling, reflected the lamplight, I recalled what Heilmann had said about the filter covering our senses, allowing us to take in only what our brains could process. We made do, he had said, with a tiny strip of the spectrum, in which we understood only what we needed and in which the simplest explanation was always the true one. We picked over, he had said, the things that broke in on us chaotically and selected whatever could be integrated into our chain of experience. In and of itself, that was obvious, he had said, but in their reactions other people often insisted that what we had apprehended could not be within our grasp. Even at night school, where we in turn laid claim to increasing our knowledge, some of us voiced doubts as to whether we had really comprehended the given topic. All we were granted was a fixed, limited realm of thought. What was cheap for the university student was forbidden fruit for us. Hatred, as a driving force for learning, had never been so plain to me as one evening at a discussion after a guided tour through the Kaiser Friedrich Museum, when an art historian, upon finding out that Coppi and I were workers, was flabbergasted by our knowledge and kept reminding his audience of our background. The corner to my left had contained the wall rack with the books, above the sleeping bench, I also tried to conjure up the round table in the center of the kitchen, the diversely shaped chairs, the hutch with the dishes and silverware and the laundry, and from next door the radio voice penetrated once again, now with shrill clarity, announcing the High Treason Law, providing death by the executioner's blade, for every one of the despicable creatures, it said, that earned their filthy blood money through espionage and sabotage. In Assisi there was a chariot of fire, in which St. Francis, drawn by two red horses, rode from the roof of the thinly boxed house into a green sky, and when viewing this painting I was uncertain whether the link between the sleeping monks, huddling below in brown cowls and me, crouching in my leather jacket, was a mark of clear-sightedness or distress. But then my attention was diverted by a soft creaking in the floor and by a hint of stirring in the linoleum covering. There, where the table had once stood, right in the wavelike circling reflection of the lamp, one of the boards squeezed against the mat, and as it was raised, the sharpened notch burst, with a grinding screech the linoleum ripped nearly all the way to my feet, and I pushed back up the wall to the window, my hands propped on the sill, my shoulders leaning halfway out. What was happening in front of me was arduous but I could offer no assistance, for I was too paralyzed to move forward, whenever I tried to stretch out my arms I merely backed up further to the window. With the very first cracking I already knew that someone lay buried there, and when the loosened plank opened sideways, I promptly recognized my father's dust-coated hand with its broad wrist and powerful knuckles, his arm emerged from the grout, his face still lay in the tow stuffed between the boards, I wanted to help him, but I was hanging so far out the window that my very next stirring would hurl me out. What would he look like, I wondered, after such a long time under the floor, almost three years, how terribly he must have strained himself until he finally managed to burst the nailed plank and the linoleum glued on top of it. I pictured his face, barely noticing that I had glided across the windowsill and was now dangling high above the street, but what I saw was not his face, and I tried to find out why this gray loamy lump, with the grossly and crassly inserted nose, the crushed eye sockets, the hard-cut notch of the mouth refused to resemble the face of my father, who was, after all, lying there. This refers to the difficulty, I told myself, of imagining something, making something comprehensible. By kicking off from the windowsill and flying across the rail shaft, I thought of how peculiar it was that we had always lived among things with so much certainty as if they truly were what they claimed to be. I could still, briefly, feel the triumph of our having agreed on a reality, on our reaching this bold and unique accord to name and evaluate everything and lock it up in our minds, but then, stretched out and flying backwards, I saw that this was quite wrong, that the definite and the concrete were surrounded by a thronging, by a lurking and choking, and, immediately underneath it, all that was to be found of names and terms was a babbling. Since I had lost speech, nothing could be ascertained of what was bound to come. I had sunk away from knowing what sort of railroad station was down there, it was impossible for me to recollect all the minutiae producing this construction, all I knew was that I had seen it often, and now came a slightly rounded square with carriages and taxis, now came a perron, a portal, now came yellow clinker bricks, Moorish arch ornaments and rosettes, now came ticket halls, gates, platforms, buffers plowing into one another, people scurrying to and fro with suitcases, there was an entity that might be a train station, but there was no indication of where the station was or where a trip from there would go, not even the time of day could be determined, clothing and vehicles occasionally looked as if they stemmed from earlier decades. Existence between alternatives had been simple and persuasive, always leading to decisions, demonstrating consequences of causes, and swift and obvious was the transition to a state of imponderables, all that persisted was the feeling that what we were doing was right, that it could not be otherwise, I still had a sense of direction, turning around, grazing the blackened glass roof of the station, I knew that a broad avenue would be on the right, and already I was flying low over a dense stand of trees, past the colonnade of a museum full of primeval bones, petrified plants, and seashells, I peered into the dimness of the rooms through which I had walked on Sundays with my father, and burial sites resurfaced, I had to swing out my arms to soar up and not get caught on the stone monuments, and then, twisting to the right, I glided over stadiums with hurdles, sandboxes, sawhorses, and on the cinders of the track stood the black-clad men, molded into a compact row, arm in arm, and now they had started moving, very slowly, hooked tightly together, wheeling in cadence from the man at the extreme right, who was marching in place, and they swung clockwise across the parched stubbly grass of the meadow, and something stirred in front of them, limbs, bodies, they were driving prisoners who supported one another, pulled and dragged one another, for many were injured or already dead, no sound could be heard from them, and the hospital at the end of the field was also hushed behind the brightly lit windows, there they lay, mangled, blood-soaked, next to one another, atop one another, dumped on the ground, here and there a soldier was trudging through them, lashing them with an iron rod, and turning right once again, penetrating a narrow chasm, pitching down almost to the ground, I found my way back to the corner, the end of the block where I lived. I had flown around several neighborhoods, familiar things were close by, though separated from recognition by a tinge of exhaustion, as swift and imperceptible as the closing of an eyelid, the transition from one level to the other could be scarcely ascertained, and totally different from one another were the hierarchical orders, the prevailing laws, and because the habitual notion was preserved, the notion that everything concerns us, that everything is material, that we are at the life-and-death mercy of everything, the alien became the sole possibility, directly charged with all demands and dangers, any world other than this gray, leaden one was inconceivable, everything took place here, the buildings had to be so heavy and lackluster, the streets so full of blackness, the sky so low and smoldering, something different from this airborne swimming, from this groping along walls, posts, roof gutters was impossible, there was no denying the piles of corpses on the field, shoveled along by the endlessly slow-pushing rows of metal legs with their wound-up mechanism, and the hospital lay there, not moaning or wailing, just as the machinery outside moved without the slightest rattling or ticking, and there would have been no describing where this took place, in which streets, in which city, at which time, and yet every process was natural, it was only like this, feet first, on my back, through the window, that I could return to the kitchen, and it was the same kitchen that I had just left, the kitchen where the bulb was burning over the floor where my father lay between boards that were broken open. I only wanted, I said, now capable of speech, to check on what things looked like outside, on whether everything was still the same outside, because I could not accept that what was happening in the kitchen was true, and while looking around, I had convinced myself that the streets, the buildings, the squares and parks really were as they had to be, and that therefore nothing in the kitchen could be distorted. And because every doubt had vanished, the lump of clay could take on its assigned facial features. My father pulled himself up. His short bristly hair was full of plaster flakes, his lips were scabby, his nostrils and lashes were clogged, he was propped on his elbows, I waited for his eyes to open, his mouth to stir.

Do you remember what Pflugstrasse looked like, I asked my father, and can you describe the surrounding neighborhoods. First my father pictured our front door with the number seven on it. The door consisted of two heavy halves braced by two long iron hooks on the corridor wall and sporting barred glass panes. When he turned away from the carved wavy profiles of the outside surface, his eyes alighted on the detached red brick building across the street. It housed the elementary school, three floors, he believed, with ledges under the windows, and a couple of steps running up to the entrance. Next to it, on a stone pedestal, a cast-iron fence stretched along the narrow part of the courtyard, where a vegetable bed was planted between bushes. Adjacent to it was the larger, gravel-strewn courtyard, running toward the rear of the building. On the sides, fire walls towered, higher than the school, at the end of the courtyard lay workshops and small factories with chimneys and rows of sooty windows. If after crossing the pavement he turned toward our house, he would see the large block adjoining it on the left. The façade, with its sunken balconies, its broadly curving stucco decorations, stood out against the other tenements. That was where policemen and their families lived, chiefly mid-level officials who worked in the offices and barracks on Chausseestrasse. The house closed off our street at the corner of Wöhlertstrasse. Named May-Bug House after the green uniforms of its occupants, it provided us, said my father, with security, for it never occurred to anyone that, in the immediate proximity of such surveillance, comrades could be going in and out and, as of nineteen thirty-three, often hiding here for weeks on end. In the kitchen of the two-room apartment that my parents had rented in the basement of a private home on Niedergrunderstrasse in Warnsdorf, my father paced to and fro, trying to remember our apartment in Berlin. Down below, in the front hall, hung the small signs with the names of the tenants, handwritten, often changed, pasted over, left and right the stairs mounted to the side wings, in the courtyard the metal garbage cans stood in front of the wooden shed, which had contained outhouses when we had moved in, he barely recalled the steps he had gone up and down every day, but the view from the windows on the rear wall of the back wing was clear, four stories down to the ballast on the edge of the rails, across the widely ramified tracks, the switches and semaphores, the smoke-shrouded trains, and at night the A and E and G on the roof of the meter factory shone into our rooms. My goal was for him to confirm as precisely as possible the reality in which the few seconds of the absence of physical pains were followed by the direct perceptible action in which any freedom was conceivable, but from which there was no escape, in which we could be roused from any unconsciousness. The eyes had to be torn open, it was arduous bearing the consequences of experience. There was Invalidenstrasse, before reaching the museum, next to the Church of Grace, we saw a green taxi with black-and-white checkered stripes. Money dropped from the outstretched hand into the other, the slightly lifted hand. The stock market hung roaring from this money. Wheat, coal, oil likewise flowed into the flat, receiving hand over the steering wheel. The other hand was already flying away in an arch, vanishing amid cloaks, jackets, overcoats. We may have been accompanied by such a sight when, coming from Chausseestrasse, past the Geological Museum, we headed toward the Museum of Natural History, for this was the place we visited most on Sundays. On the square in front of the classical building, which was adorned with portal figures, rosettes, galleries, columns, stood huge trees, two beeches to the right of the central path, a beech and an oak to the left, and between each pair of trees a silicified trunk from the Mesozoic. Thus we had already glimpsed the iridescent, splintery primordial era before stepping from the portal into the vestibule and peering into the glass-covered hall where the saurians loomed. However, my father was unacquainted with the largest of these animals, seventy-six feet long, forty feet high. The skeleton had only been set up this year, shipped over from the Tendaguru Hills of Tanzania. The neck craned all the way up to the roof bars with that tiny head, which was really just a piece of vertebra equipped with eyes, nostrils, and thin staff teeth, its rudimentary brain barely sufficing to control the movements of the gigantic body. The brachiosaurus vegetated on the edges of lakes and rivers, a mountain of flesh sluggishly lumbering up from the swamp, plucking leaves and fruits off ferns, eucalyptus, and cycadean trees, sloshing back into the muddy water. We had studied these oversized waddling curs with their saurian mouths and chelonian claws, we had imagined them wheezing, rattling their teeth, striking no terror at all, but helplessly twisting their immense necks when, too late, they became aware of the pain urging up from the tip of the tail, the pain caused by the bite of the smaller, nimble carnivores hopping upright on hind legs. There was something grandiloquent about these peaceful mammals who, in the deserts a hundred million years ago, degenerated into a huge size that was never attained by anything, who were destroyed by this immoderate growth, at the mercy of springers and hunters, of quick, zealous, cunning predators. Now my father's hand pointed at a skeleton, traced the arching, prickly line of the back, circled around the hanging shoulder armor, and up came the landscape, where our own life had run through its preliminary stages. While the gigantic creatures could take shape amid reeds, steppe grass, myrtles, and mangrove palms, our imaginations focused on the hand-sized petrified archaeopteryx lying with fine bones and thin ribs, surrounded by the imprint of its outspread wings and tail feathers in the burst lime slab. The head with narrow, toothed jaws was tapered and reptilian, plumage grew from the long, skinny tail and from the arm joints, feathers as hatchwork, sketching a possibility of conquering gravity, of a new flying kind of locomotion, the claws were still tensed as after the launching from a branch, the body was held fast in flight, in the transitional stage from one form of life to the other, and always, when coming from the hurly-burly of the dinosaurs, we were drawn to this reptile bird, this Icarus of biological evolution. But then there was another museum, it arose with its smoke-blackened klinker walls, similar to a warehouse on Bremen's vast Railroad Station Square, on the street corner opposite the Hotel Columbus, its back adjacent to the area for unloading fruits and vegetables in the freight depot. The route to this museum ran across the Weser Bridge and the cathedral courtyard, past city hall, through the Schüsselkorb and the ramparts, on the left the park rose toward the arboretum, with the windmill above the Moat, from the Herd Gate, next to the Hillmann Hotel, the route passed through the throng of cars and trolleys, toward the already visible clouds of steam puffed out by the locomotives, and then we entered the hall in front of the rows of pillars that, under the high glass roof, led far into the depths of the continents. Carved poles, masts, and temple roofs towered behind the crowded tropical plants in buckets, I instantly pulled my father, who was holding my hand, to the right, and we veered toward the Pygmies abiding outside their low, rounded hut, the naked woman motionless, her left hand around the child sitting on her hip, bracing his foot on the waistband of her loincloth, raising his right hand to the necklace of leopard teeth, turning his face to the side, gazing through half-closed eyes, lost to the world, just like the man kneeling on the chaff and forgetting the chore in front of his hands, the smoothing and knotting of leaves. A monkey lay next to him, it had wanted to play, had gotten sleepy, its arm, still outstretched, had sunk down. Their home was the rain forests of Equatorial Africa, they wandered about as gatherers and hunters, the jungle permitted no settling down, the hut served them as a brief shelter, they owned very few tools, a bow and arrow, were on the verge of extinction. Their domed nest was built between roots and brushwood, propped on bent branches, covered with leaves, wrapped in slender lianas, a snail shell full of deep darkness. All around, the jungle stretched unendingly, alive with squawking, grunting, shrieking. Here the clearing-out of the tiny glade, the swift building before nightfall, the nomadizing along the river courses, the waterfalls, when the hut had long since merged back into the vegetation, had all turned into a single moment of waiting. No bigger than I, the six-year-old, the jungle dwellers lingered with bated breath, in crackling silence, not noticing when my fingertips touched the dull shine of their dark skin. There were also Bedouins here, in front of their tent, Australian aborigines with spears and boomerangs, tattooed inhabitants of houses on stilts from the Solomon Islands, artfully woven sentry huts from Samoa were to be seen, Japanese gardens, temples and ritual objects from Burma, Korea, Tibet, Eskimo igloos, totem poles of the prairie Indians, but the sight etched deepest in my memory was the family of the Pygmy people. I asked my father about our street in Bremen because I wanted to compare his impressions with my own recollections, which, stemming from the first few years of my life, were sharper, clearer than the image that Pflugstrasse had left in me. Now we were doubling back across the Weser Bridge, toward the Alte Neustadt [Old New Town], along the pontoons under St. Martin's Church lay the steamboats, including a side wheeler, which all went to Hemelingen and Delmenhorst, to the harbor and to Vegesack. Walking through the steepled bridge gateways from which the curving iron girders were suspended, we saw to our right, on the tongue of land in the middle of the river, the centuries-old district known as Herrlichkeit [Splendor], its storehouses and warehouses stretching all the way to the Teerhof's fortress-like buildings, which were connected to the Kaiser Bridge with its tremendous arches. Over on the narrow side-arm of the river, rowboats were moored on the sandy riverbank. A footbridge led from the peninsula over to the high, ashlared escarpment, where Brautstrasse branched off from Dike Way. This was where the rails of the single-track trolley ran, during the war it had been drawn by a horse, said my father, and at the corner of Westerstrasse stood the tavern where Ebert had become a barkeep after giving up saddlery. Later on, he said, the beer hall was renamed First President of the Republic. I tried to conjure up Grünenstrasse. Didn't it run up from Brautstrasse, I asked. It seemed to me that I had raced downhill from our house to Wempe's grocery, opposite the street lamp, next to the elementary school with the portico. My father could not recall that, for him Grünenstrasse was level, to the right Ziehm's butcher shop, Merten's dairy, the narrow street, called Short Street, veering off toward the dike, then a couple of taverns, warehouses, stables, Glazier Bachmann's workshop, and behind our house, number twenty-three, the walled-in courtyards of the slate factory and the coffee roasting firm, and the Office of Weights and Measures. Before we entered Grünenstrasse, I saw in front of me, beyond Westerstrasse, at the New Market, the watering place for horses, the worn lip of the well, the long pump handle, the stone posts to which the brewery draymen fastened their reins, and when they went into the saloon the draft horses in their copper-plated harnesses lowered their mouths into the water. The neighborhood living on inside me was different from the one my father now thought about. The skeleton of the streets could be laid out. We walked toward our house. The square was closed off by Häschenstrasse, with Bestenbostel's machine factory and Haake's brewery, further on was Grosse Allee, leading to the Kaiser Bridge and to Grünenkamp, where the free fair took place in the autumn, at the very end of the street lay the Neustadt Railroad Station, my father saw himself bicycling past the sites of the Kaiser Brewery, the tremendous Haake Beck Brewery, the rice mill, across the railroad bridge, on the wooden path along the freight trains, to the Weser shipyard. I remained behind in the house, where we occupied the top floor. A steep, narrow staircase led from the vestibule to the room with the kitchenette, through the window you could see the backyards, which were separated by walls and fences, and, above the roofs of the houses on the dike side, you could see the rows of gables in the Teerhof with their protruding tackle blocks on their skylights. What I possessed of my childhood resembled the preserve doled out to the Pygmies. Everything that had happened to me here had concentrated into a tiny space imbued with a feeling for directions, volumes, and with rebus-like allusions that came to life when my eyes were absorbed in them. Just as the gigantic jungles with their thickets, their gushing water, their wild beasts could be detected behind a heap of gathered-up foliage, so too did the yards and bridges, sheds and dikes, fair booths and street corners join into a warp and woof that hinted at a city, here there were no distances, everything was ruled by a sense of nearness and could be conceptualized through minor shifts of the vantage point. We were constantly surrounded by the aromas of malt and coffee blending with the vapors from the soap factory on the other side of the street. Evenings we would wrap the soap in paper, said my father, pack the cakes in cartons as homework, which was distributed to the residents of the street. Thus, my father's experiences enveloped the bounded, self-contained world in which the material of beginning accumulated. I was barely one year old when I heard the salvos of rifles and machine guns, the crashing of the mortars, but my impressions could only have become conscious through later stories. Early in the morning of the fourth of February nineteen nineteen my mother stood at the window, holding me in her arm, while the fighting raged in our neighborhoods. We did not know, said my father, whether the soldiers in the barracks at the New Town Wall were still on our side or had already joined the White Guards, who, as we heard from military runners, had occupied the inner city and were pouring into New Town by way of Buntentor. Our units had entrenched themselves on the Weser Bridge, we tried to fight our way through to the Workers' Council in the shipyard by heading across the Kaiser Bridge to the Lloyd's wharf, to the Schlachtpforte, a military train, we were told, was en route to the railroad bridge in order to block St. Stephen's Gate. During my father's account I saw the barracks in front of me, the red brick buildings around the parade grounds, the pruned black trees along the trellis fence, the gate with the sentry boxes, I saw Grosse Allee, with the promenade down the middle, the trolley tracks on the sides, I heard the factory sirens of the harbor district calling incessantly to encourage the fighting men. From the center of the city, divisions of the Freikorps [the volunteer groups], had pushed forward along Martinistrasse to the Kaiser Bridge. There was shooting by Sankt Pauli, in the New Market, on Johannis Strasse, the rebels, the cut-off revolutionaries came from the side streets, across the rooftops, over the garden walls, I saw it clearly now, I had already taken it in once from our apartment window without grasping it, my father was one of the men crawling over the shingles, through the snowy gusts, throwing themselves into the trees, climbing down to the Dike Way, and as he described the way they slowly forged ahead from the shore stronghold to Grosse Allee, the beginning of the bridge, the way they crept along the terrain, covered by gunfire from the Cuxhaven sailors, the riveted bridge arches hung over me with their dense crisscross of girders, mines exploded on the ground, a blue flame darted from a shattered gas line, the workers over on the Weser Bridge, said my father, had been overwhelmed, from their barricades, a patchwork of carts, crates, planks, mattresses, black smoke was rising, the cathedral bells were already ringing in the victory of the counterrevolution while we still lay in the middle of the Kaiser Bridge, there at the foot of the iron arch, where the road to the Teerhof branched off. The very instant, he said, that I was hit, I saw a sailor throwing himself on the burst gas line, he held it together with his body, why, I wondered, his uniform was already blazing, he was burning up, a couple of men crawled toward him to pull him back, they could not pry him loose, he clung too hard, it was useless, and my father grimaced in disgust or in anger, the fighting, he said, lasted all that day and the following night. The group my father was in had succeeded in reaching the opposite shore and struggling through to the railroad underpass at St. Stephen's Gate, and the docks, where they knew every corner, every hiding place. The shipyard had been taken by the enemy troops, but the work force was already re-mustering to attack, while my father was carried to a makeshift dispensary in a shed on Gröpelinger Fährweg, there he lay together with other wounded men during the days when the provisional Social Democratic government dissolved the Deputies' Council, the Workers' Council and the Soldiers' Council. When my father, pacing to and fro in the kitchen, now put his hands on his ears, it was probably also the recurring uproar of the February fighting that he was trying to ward off, but more than anything else we were harassed by the booming from the loudspeakers in the street. It made every phase of the event in Berlin come alive for all of us whether or not we wanted to hear it. Incessantly the announcements cascaded in upon us from the neighborhood windows, interrupted by march music and yelling. Yesterday the man known as Il Duce, coming from the maneuvers in Mecklenburg, had been welcomed at the Heerstrasse station, and now, on the evening of September twenty-eighth, he was heading toward the May Field, behind the Olympia Stadium, where, we were told, he would stand next to the Führer and address the world. When my father thought about the February days in Bremen, one could infer the burden of a sorrow that he could not cope with. There was that shed, a cleared-out stable belonging to the Neukirch Moving Firm, there was the bandage sticky with blood on his shoulder, from which the military physician, the only one siding with the workers, had cut out the rifle bullet. The woman with the baby carriage was allowed through by the patrolmen, under the blanket, next to me, my mother had hidden a couple of turnips, a piece of bread, she came to my father every evening, and one week later he was back in the shipyard, which had been reconquered by the workers and sailors. Here their council held out for nearly two more months as the last revolutionary outpost in the city, where the bourgeoisie had reconsolidated its power. The whole dilemma of this unequal struggle was still alive in my father, was repeated in him over and over again. In November, in December, during the double regime, it had been like Saint Petersburg one year earlier, the cafés, the movie houses, and the theaters were crowded when the armed workers marched through the streets, people for whom the mere mention of revolution was an insult drove in coaches along Nevsky Prospekt. But we lacked, said my father, the shots of the Aurora, which tore the ground away under their feet. Next to our Red City, which was proclaimed an independent socialist republic on January tenth, there coexisted the city of burghers, businessmen, and international commerce. When the Seventy-fifth Infantry Regiment, returning from the front, arrived in Bremen on New Year's Day, its leader, Major Caspari, had already been ordered to crush the revolution and reinstall the municipal senate. Viewed from the windows of the Hotel Columbus and from the veranda of the Hillmann Hotel, where the festively garbed bourgeoisie was celebrating the start of the new year, the soldiers, accompanied by officers with drawn swords, came as rescuers. They were greeted with cheers from the railroad station square to beyond the ramparts. Just as the sons of the city had been sent with roses on their rifles into the empire's war of conquest, so too the survivors, now being led to protect the grand bourgeoisie, were inundated with flowers. But in the marketplace the soldiers, whose staff had demanded free entry into the barracks, were received by the other power, which could still make itself felt. Just draining the champagne flutes that had been handed them by the hotel guests, they now stood facing the Soldiers' Council, it was also possible that a sense of solidarity crossed over to them, that a brief moment of class consciousness emerged, so that before reaching the barracks they surrendered their weapons to the revolutionary units. This city, said my father, where the patricians promenaded in the parks, where the suppliers came to the heated villas on the Contrescarpe, on Schwachhauser Heerstrasse, and where the workers' neighborhoods were cold and hungry, this city, where the desperate determination to continue the revolution was confronted with the obstinacy of old tradition, now lay as an objective on the planning tables of cabinet ministers and generals. Ebert, who, recalling his time as a saddlery apprentice and tavern keeper, was particularly fond of Bremen, transmitted directives to Noske, a former wickerwork journeyman in a baby carriage factory, risen from the Wood Workers' Association to the billy club profession, summoned to Berlin after the victory over the Kiel sailors, to the German Minister of Defense, named commander-in-chief, detailed by him to the staff of the Ninth and Tenth Army Corps and to Lüttwitz's general command, where assignments were distributed to the pro-governmental civilian authorities and to Colonel Gerstenberg, who had to prepare the military encirclement. With the help of shop stewards in the labor unions Caspari recruited soldiers, and the latter, once again at the mercy of their officers' orders in the garrisons, demobilized but still trained and drilled, preferred joining a voluntary battalion to forging an uncertain alliance with the fighting workers. They assembled in Verden and were re-equipped for war, routinely they returned to the cannon, flamethrowers, and tanks that had been sent to them from Berlin. In mid-January, when the Social Democratic deputies had smashed the revolutionary forces in the Reich's capital, murdering their leaders, and Germany was facing elections to the National Assembly, in which the new administration wanted to be validated as the custodian of the bourgeois republic, the military also had to take Bremen, the last city where the system of councils was still holding its ground. But what can I tell you about it, said my father, agonized, there is no explaining what happened, everything whirled past us, it was all different from what the books then said, everything that concerned us was expunged, the newspapers and magazines always showed nothing but the troops, who made up for their defeat in the war by winning a victory over their own nation. And he again felt the thrust, which hurled him forward, it was as if someone were slapping the flat of his hand on your shoulder, he said, and as if your shoulder were naked, and yet I was wearing the thick jacket. It was all, he said, misperceptions, there were only conjectures, here in our corner, the historical events rolled over us, did not have the slightest interest in us. When they dragged him across the bridge, he saw the towers looming out of the dark masses of houses ahead, the twin towers of the cathedral, the leaning tower of the Church of Our Lady, the superimposed cupolas on the high, angular St. Ansgarius Tower, the round steeple of St. Stephen's, and, over the trees of the Schlachte, the merlons, balconies, and serrated gables of the business firms. The pain came only later, on the road through the suburb of Gröpeling. The miners in the Ruhr, he heard a comrade saying, had gone on strike, were demanding a termination of the attack on Bremen, a hundred thousand men, then came an icy wind and tore him away, and he did not reawaken until he found himself in the first-aid station. He again saw the red flag waving from the roof of the administrative building, munitions, weapons had been carried to the shipyard by the sailors, their minesweepers and requisitioned tugboats lay moored to the docks. If my father thought they had fooled themselves, thinking the Workers' Council could hold out for another two months in the Weser Shipyard, he was seeing it from his current vantage point of a country captured by fascism. Now it struck him as merely phantasmal the way they had stood their ground against the government, which, after all, knew that no one would come to help them, they would be slowly broken down, imperceptibly overcome. What use was the operation, he said, heroic as it may have been, by now others could not be spurred on by it, swept away by it, the population had lost its fighting energy in the cold spring. They had buried their dead amid snow flurries, isolated cries for vengeance still rang out, the careworn procession could move unmolested through the streets, the rulers of the city were sure of themselves. Yet even today, I said, there

are people who are holding out. Only small groups, he replied, twenty years later the groups are still small, and back then we were committed to the only right thing, we were fighting for the complete transformation of social conditions, we held out because we believed that the masses everywhere would strive toward the same goal. We did not see, he said, that the city was bristling with weapons, when we proclaimed a general strike on April fifteenth and demanded an end to the state of siege, the release of the prisoners, and equal rights for the delivery of food. To retaliate, the municipal senate closed all stores, restaurants, pharmacies, hospitals. The rich had laid in supplies ahead of time. For them there were private clinics, doctors, nurses, midwives. Then the waterworks were partially shut down, the inflow to our neighborhoods was cut off. While the nouveaux riches flaunted themselves across the river, the women on our riverbank drew water from the Weser, dirty oily water, and we traveled miles into the countryside, tracking down a couple of potatoes, a glass of milk for the children. When my father raised his fist, it was as if he wanted to curse himself for the helplessness, the powerlessness he had succumbed to on the day before the First of May nineteen nineteen, when the strike broke off. One big disdain, one big humiliation had fallen upon the proletariat of Bremen. That was my father's experience, at this moment it could not satisfy him that I saw the possibilities of starting all over again. In the Citizens' Park behind the railroad station and out at the Vahr Athletic Club, adolescents, some only sixteen, were armed by the city fathers, equipped with uniforms and steel helmets, and incorporated in the defense formations. A few years later they were in the Black Reichswehr, the illegal German army, the Kyffhaüser or Escherich organizations, the secret troops with which the general staff bypassed the disarmament edicts. They were quartered in the barracks at the New Town Wall for crash training. The shouted commands, the bawling of marching songs from back then could still be heard today. In the dim light falling through the street-level windows, I could see that my father had aged during the past three years, his face was weary, his hair gray, he was obsessed with the thought that the workers in Germany had let themselves be forced into submission by their own indecisiveness and handed over by their own blindness. His right leg dragging after being hit by the bullets of a Czarist machine gun, his left shoulder stiff from the injury on the Kaiser Bridge, rewarded for one wound with the Iron Cross Second Class, prosecuted for the other as a public enemy, my father wandered around in the kitchen and, raising his hand and peering out into the dusty street, he tried to understand why back then, when victory had seemed possible, they had been deprived of their weapons. And just as I was enclosed by my father's world, so too was he enveloped by the other world, the world of decision makers, liquidators. The war-weary soldiers, the workers ground down by hunger, rising prices, and pillage had risen up, untrained in politics, without a revolutionary leadership, a movement of discontent, of impatience had spread, for many people the Russian example, still barely grasped, offered hope, the burgeoning strike actions, the improvised forming of councils made it seem as if the reign of the proletariat were beginning here too. An analysis of the situation, they opined, was not required, History itself had called upon them, the majority, to assume leadership. It looked as if the mere uprising of the people would topple the monarchy established by the grace of God, and as if the state were merely waiting to be taken over by the workers. However, in the military collapse it was not the rebels but the general staff, the Junker squirearchy, high finance, that had abolished the monarchy in order to salvage their own positions. The representatives of army and diplomacy, of banking and heavy industry had acted faster than the insurgent workers, sailors, and soldiers, fathoming the situation they allowed a pseudo-upheaval to come about, thanks to their partnership with the heads of the largest workers' party. It was not through the assault by the masses of the population, through the transformation of the imperialist war into a civil war, through the decision of the Workers' and Soldiers' Council that the Social Democratic deputies had been raised to the offices of the revolutionary government, but through the field marshals and administrators of capital of the old order. While utopias and hazy ideals were still raising false hopes for a socialist democracy, the government had already reached agreements with all institutions of the ruling classes for suppressing the revolt. At that moment, when the working class needed its party as an instrument of struggle, its interests were sold out in a betrayal that had been prepared for over a decade by the party leadership. Now, with the emergence of a revolutionary situation, not only did they feel the effects of avoiding any educational work, any organizational activity aimed at a social transformation, they also saw that not even the illusion, nourished by Bernstein and Kautsky, of a peaceful reformist evolution into socialism was surviving; instead the Social Democratic majority party had made itself the center of the counterrevolution. The outbreak of the war, said my father, had already refuted Kautsky's and Hilferding's theories. True, they had provided us with a very apt explanation of the growth of capital into an imperialist financial force, but they had dismissed the notion of warlike consequences of this expansion. Just as we had been impressed by their analyses when we were growing up, so too had they, for their part, been impressed by the seemingly unbeatable vitality of the plutocracy and had reached the point of assuming that our material and mental development could took place only in the closest cooperation with monopolism. Even the Independent Party, which my father had joined, had, under the guise of radicality, no other goal than to entice the left-wing Social Democrats and neutralize them in regard to the Spartacus League, their leaders, as members of the cabinet, had long been ready to thwart any further initiative of the masses. While Ebert, Haase, and Noske entered into an alliance with the Supreme Army Command and police power, Legien reached an understanding with the representatives of business, and, unbeknownst to the workers, the labor union leaders and the industrial magnates forged a coalition that was guaranteed to be free of socializing tendencies. The link to international capitalism had likewise been restored as a premise for building up the republic. In the imperialistic war for markets, Germany had been beaten, but now it was needed to stamp out the new menace to the international economic system. Scheidemann persuaded yesterday's adversaries that the German government was of one mind with them since the goal was the struggle against Bolshevism. Healing through Work, that was the watchword given throughout the country. The crushing of the proletarian revolution spelled the lifting of the blockade and the importing of necessary food from President Wilson's America, food that, it was said, would have been denied to an undemocratic Germany. With this initial success, credited with providing for order and security, the members of the government hoodwinked a large portion of the people. Bourgeois-democratic was what they called the revolution, which now had to be terminated. It had been fought by the working class, but it had not paved the way for the progressive bourgeoisie, instead, in its hesitation, in its confusion, a bourgeoisie hardened and smartened in colonialism was given the opportunity to climb another level. Many people found the development incomprehensible. The deputies styled themselves defenders of the revolution. What reason, a doubter could be told, would they have to turn against the workers, after all, they had come out of their own movement. In November, said my father, it was still assumed that despite the restoration of the dynasties, the banks, the bureaucracy of the totalitarian state, the revolution could be brought to its proletarian stage. That was, he said, the wrong conclusion. In trusting our ideals, we considered ourselves invulnerable. We had started out from the momentum of a higher power that we called Truth, or Justice, and that we expected would storm across all falsehood and deceit. Our juvenile faith, taken over from priests and grandfathers, was something we had carried through the entire war, notwithstanding the strenuous efforts of our intellects. We had not seen to it that we would stand united and consolidated at the historic moment or that our leaders would be protected. The Russian revolutionaries had eluded capture, had gone abroad, had spent years preparing the attack, had carefully set up a network of coherency and consistency, they knew exactly how the forces were distributed, but in Germany the best people ran headlong to their doom, and, when we needed concentration, construction, they let themselves be rendered harmless, and we watched, aghast. By the time Liebknecht and Luxemburg emerged from the prisons, the turmoil was in full swing, from the balcony of the Castle of Berlin Liebknecht proclaimed the Free Socialist Republic, and Scheidemann on the Reichstag ramp simultaneously proclaimed the German Republic, the masses surged to and fro, believing that the rupture could be overcome by joint actions in the streets. In our struggle for a workers' government, said my father, we saw nothing strict or constraining about belonging to a party, the field of theories and actions was open for us, it was the foundation of our debates, we shared principles with one another, principles that could not be marred by different readings of details. As a member of the left wing of the Independent Party, my father worked for the newspaper of the Bremen Communists, which in its focus on the politics of the Bolsheviks did not always agree with the Spartacists. But my father did commit himself to the program championed by Luxemburg, especially in his essays on the cultural revolution. In our quest for a form, a means of expression that could settle the ideological contradictions, we put up with a multiplicity of voices, he said, convinced that the violent events would bring about the unity that we were all striving for. The people who consciously followed a revolutionary line were a minority in the workers' parties, and the people active in the Councils had grown up with the majority party's thesis that the premise of a socialist development lay in conquering the parliamentary republic. Even the most active among them were marked by ideals nourished in the Social Democratic educational groups, they aimed not at a polarizing of forces but at conciliation, cooperation between the classes, not revolutionary discipline, but discipline in a given work relationship. It was only through the Marxist opposition in the Spartacus League that my father had encountered the necessity of breaking with the revisionist majority. Now he was able to give new meaning to Social Democracy's historical slogan, Knowledge Is Power. Nor could the cultural work that he pictured be implemented without a revolutionary upheaval. I began to understand how greatly my father's political path was dependent on such trains of thought, I also now recalled how he had aroused my own cultural interest by pointing out the connection between revolutionary theory and creative development. The workers, he said, should always be given the material and the themes by their parties, they should always be the recipients in case of seemingly fallow consciousness, the functionaries never turned to them with questions, ready to hear what the workers felt and thought. It was only in Luxemburg that he had found this openness and lack of qualms, this actual sense of democratic conduct. She, he felt, knew that although not in possession of conventional cultural goods, they did have a wealth of experience that, once called upon, would help the intelligentsia in widening its expression. She was always intent, he said, on listening to workers in order to glean what was going on in them, on getting to know them, for the renewal would be carried out by them, they alone were capable of overthrowing the system of class rule. That was why all political work had to focus on arousing their self-confidence, appreciating their knowledge and letting it be articulated. Over and over again, before we realized, said my father, how cynically, how unscrupulously the right-wing leaders of Social Democracy had turned into the defenders of reactionism and chauvinism, we kept stressing that the creation of peace, and also any agreement with the bourgeois strata, would have to take place on the soil of the working class and according to its stipulations. And yet in December, not understanding its own organizational form, the first Congress of Councils in Berlin voluntarily transferred all its power to the Council of Deputies and decreed that the weapons should be handed over to the officers infiltrating the commissions everywhere. No more prerequisites, we were told, now existed for the social revolution, and anyone who at this hour still insisted on continuing the struggle had to be viewed as an enemy of the nation.

Again my father covered his ears. The howling from the May Field invaded our space. The site of the mass meeting had been named for the date chosen half a century ago as the day of the workers' struggle, and the hundreds of thousands of participants gathered there were, by raising their hands, consenting to their own humiliation. The man with the moustache glued under his nose, with the strand of hair falling over his flat forehead had let his welcoming words resonate, he was cooing now, in a voice that could be hoarse, bawling, that could shrilly break, it was restrained, as it were, by the solemnity of the historic occasion, a lone sentence emerged from the guttural seething, loomed out in the room, the axis, it said, was now consummated. For several minutes the streets of this town and of the other places in Bohemia, and all streets, homes, offices, taverns, railroad stations, workshops, factories in the cities and villages of the Reich were swept by the hurricane of self-oblivion, the roaring of dazzlement, and then the other one made himself noticeable, the short man rising on his toes, crossing his arms, shoving out his chin and lower lip, rolling his eyes, for a few seconds the bated breath could be sensed all around the two shamans, then the bald man launched into his hacked-up squawking, in which the multiple call for a revolution, with an *r* like a rattling machine gun, could be identified. Revolution was the topic on the May Field, an Italian revolution, a German one, and a sibilance also resounded, as in socialism, and this could happen because the workers, soldiers, sailors in November nineteen eighteen had let themselves be hoodwinked. Not that they had given up their demands, they fought for the establishment of a rule by Councils, for the immediate nationalizing of all capitalist enterprises, for the dispossessing of all large estates, for an annexing to Bolshevist Russia, with which the German Foreign Office had broken off diplomatic relations. But they never dreamed that the men who called themselves the deputies of the people would resort to mass murder, to devastating the country rather than letting revolutionary rallying cries imperil their position, which they had gained through the uprising of the working class. This gullibility, this reverence for the Word, as expressed in the Erfurt Program and intensified in the statutes of the Independent Social Democratic Party, this confidence that a high leadership would do what was best for the workers made it impossible for them to recognize the enemy in their own camp. And that was what my father was trying to verbalize, how remote they, the fighters, were from the machinations of the leaders, how the fighters, on their level, were crushed and drained by the political game, how greatly their strenuous efforts differed from the movements that flooded over them. He kept touching on the incongruity between the events that were visible to him and the goals of the ruling powers. Yet it had been he and people like him who had lost their sense of proportion, they themselves, the majority, because of their peculiar tractability, were to blame for the deformations now spreading about them. They could not grasp that the elite groups, the Republican Soldiers' Defense, the reinforced police troops, had been summoned by the leaders of their party and labor unions to mow down the workers, even in the January days, when Noske, the self-appointed bloodhound of the new order, had ordered the killings of Liebknecht and Luxemburg and hundreds of workers in Berlin, the workers still refused to abandon the notion that the party with the largest segment of the proletariat could be won over for the revolution. On January tenth, in order to relieve their Berlin companions, the fighters in Bremen had proclaimed the Republic of Councils. We continued negotiating with the Social Democrats, said my father, until the very last day. They convened in City Hall, behind the bull's-eye panes, while our gathering place was the Stock Exchange. By February third we were still trying to bring about a fusion with the majority party in order to fight off the troops, who we thought were merely misguided by the old military spirit, we were so blinded that the comrades, whom we reminded of the Bebel traditions, could start strangling us unhindered. There was that Waigand, who emphasized that he was a Socialist, a proletarian, who championed the merger, who stressed the things that Ebert had accomplished for the welfare of the Bremen workers, and who, while praising his party's good will and his own honesty, kept running to the telephone to talk to Gerstenberg and Caspari in Verden and fix the time when the troops should march in. We had cried when Liebknecht and Luxemburg had been slaughtered, when all conceptions of our future had been smashed by a few blows with a rifle butt. However, we did not yet think our cause was lost, we believed it would go on, everywhere, here as in Russia, we felt that our struggle would bring the Russian Revolution the help it needed, we shared Lenin's conviction that October had only been the start, that the next decisive step would take place in Germany, we were conscious of the reciprocity between the Russian Revolution and ours, we were so preoccupied with our immediate tasks and already so isolated that we failed to perceive the discouragement and exhaustion all around us. Our impotence, he said, turning back to the window, became this mass subjugation. For him the May Field was the selling-out of all the values for which he had fought and for which so many of his near and dear had fallen. He knew there were very few people left in Germany who still clung to their conviction, who were not yet tainted by the poison, he shuddered when recalling how from one day to the next a procession of his union with a jingling Johnny and a chalumeau band had switched over to the columns of the brownshirts, he knew he could not remain for long here in Warnsdorf either, here too the pressure to be constrained and to conform ruled, they marched out there along the sandy road, keeping good time, with their polished boots, their sharpened daggers, and in the factory the comrades no longer dared to show their political affiliation, here too they met in secret, for it had been said aloud that the Sudetenland was German soil, its inhabitants had to be liberated from foreign rule, so now at the age of fifty-two he had to look around for places to emigrate to, Mexico perhaps, Australia, Canada, or Scandinavia, but he had no influential connections, nor could he show he had secure economic means, he was only a skillful workman, an engineer, but accustomed to applying his knowledge as a worker, who would take him at his age and give him a job. By the spring of nineteen nineteen, he said, brooding, his shoulders hunched, we began to recognize what had happened during the revolutionary winter. We learned about Luxemburg's objections to the armed struggle, it became clear to us that we ourselves had encountered qualms back in November, but had ignored them, swept away as we were by the actions. In a tremendous intellectual effort, the Spartacus leaders, exposed to the accomplished facts after their incarceration, tried to save whatever could be saved of the revolutionary energy. Their proclamation of the Socialist republic was a final cry for courage, they knew there was no longer any possibility of deciding against the bourgeois republic in whose National Assembly the counterrevolution had now constituted itself. They knew what we still refused to see, namely, that the energies of the people had been sold to the bourgeoisie, which would spare no crime to retain its power. Hunted from one hiding place to the next, Luxemburg, Liebknecht, Jogiches, and Radek fought against the panic that was sure to come when the defeat became a certainty. Now there was no holding back the forward charge, the sole concern was to avoid the bloodbath being prepared by the trustees of the bankruptcy of Social Democracy. This was not the revolution pictured by Luxemburg, the majority's struggle for the majority, a struggle needing no terror to achieve its goals, a struggle that would succeed because the time for it was ripe. The formation of Councils had been premature, only a small part of the working class backed the Spartacus demands, the majority was bamboozled by the slogans claiming that the resuming of production would also ensure its development. There was too little time for enlightenment to reach them. Their party press inundated them with propaganda, defaming the fighters as revolution romantics, as anarchist putschists, and mocking the Russian revolutionaries as social dilettantes. The old admonition spread over them, the reminder to stay calm, keep a level head, to return to hard work and efficiency. Justice based on class had struck roots again, styling itself the protector of the constitutional state, warning about the reign of terror such as was emerging in Soviet Russia. And now Luxemburg's own critique of the post-October measures was turned against her and the German revolution. The reactionary side asked her if she herself planned to carry out a minority's violent coup and set up the party's dictatorship over the proletariat. Precisely because there was no party capable of leading the German proletariat, Luxemburg had spoken against a revolution that was bound to lead to civil war. From their adversarial position, the leaders of Social Democracy likewise called for resistance against civil war, only to have their own civil war erupt since they had the superior force of arms. It was a war of the bourgeoisie against the working class, a war of the minority against the vanguard of the blinded, weakened majority, and we, said my father, did the same thing that Luxemburg had done, we did it half unconsciously, she did it with all her wits about her, she remained on the side of those who were taking the wrong path, yet who were right all the same. On December twenty-fourth my father and Knief, the editor of *Die Arbeiterpolitik* [Workers' Politics] and the leader of Bremen's radical left wing, were in Berlin to visit Radek in his secret quarters and obtain his directions for continuing the struggle. I wondered about all the experience, all the historical concentration contained in such a terse indication, but I received no answer. Could Radek actually be found, I asked. My father merely nodded. His eyes were dull, turned inward. Radek had said that all further action would proceed outside of Marxist rules, that it would include an element of chance, irrationality, he had called for a termination of the struggle, a return to political work, but Luxemburg, on the verge of physical collapse, still nurtured some hope of a final, instinctive advance of energy, driven by the pent-up revolutionary tension, it was this vision, said my father, that she, like the rest of us, kept alive, and a few weeks later we were fighting only to avenge her death, pushing any other thoughts from our minds, in the desperate satisfaction that the courage to perform revolutionary acts was preferable to submission. We were trapped in wishful thinking, the desire to set an example for others. Then we were forced to realize that this was wrong. Wrong not objectively but in the timing. For it was only the choice of the right time, he said, that revealed an understanding of Historical Materialism.

And why, I asked, did you rejoin the party that had come out against the revolution forever. His search for explanations showed me that however present the February days of the year nineteen nineteen were, they had left an amnesia, a blind spot in him. Naturally the period of the party struggles during the early nineteen twenties had often been talked about in our home, but only now did I realize how little I knew about that prehistory since my desire for a clarification of the most obvious circumstances had prevailed, monopolizing my attention. Even now that the night had finally grown still over Warnsdorf's streets, since the trains had freighted the May Field masses back to their neighborhoods, and since not another sound came from the resonators in the Berlin districts of Reinickendorf and Wedding, Friedrichshain and Neukölln, and the people lay stretched out under blankets, just a few more hours till early shift, there was something bizarre about my father's stories, his hesitation implied that he sensed how hard it was even for me to tackle this material, these thoughts that contained the roots for grasping the events of today. He saw the figures of Ebert, Haase, and Noske, Scheidemann and Severing, Legien, Landsberg, and Wissel rising over the cadaver of Bebel's social democracy. They had melting faces, puffy cheeks, bull necks, potbellies. They were flanked by Kautsky and Hilferding, Bernstein and Wels. A murmuring emerged from them, if he listened he could hear them trying to conjure up an image of the intactness of the world, interrupting one another, outwhispering one another, they denied the collapse of bourgeois society and challenged the theory of impoverishment, they kept bringing up imperialism, the maturation process of the financial system, until, in transfigured inflections, they lauded the unification of all factions under the power of highly developed capitalism. The gravediggers of the Second International were joined by the younger ones, who carried the bankruptcy of the workers' movement into the present, and a dull, pale cluster had grown in all around them, Groener, Hindenburg, and Seeckt could be identified among the ugly mugs with dueling scars, mustaches, and crooked mouths, and Stinnes and Hugenberg, and Kapp, Slarz, and Tamschik, and Lüttwitz, Epp, and Escherich, and Erhard, Lettow Vorbeck, and Hülsen, and all the other racketeers and lynchers, the leaders of the Volunteer Corps and veterans' groups, the Defense Units, the combat organs of the capitalist state machinery, the Steel Helmet trekked up and the Young German Order, and then came the forests of flags and standards, with the twitching, hacking crooked crosses in white circles, the armies of yellers marched up, and protective, surrounded by smoke, hovered over everyone else Thyssen and Krupp, Blessing and Blohm, Ambros and Flick, Haniels, Pferdmenges, and Bütefisch, Schwerin Krosig and Messerschmitt, and whatever they were called, my father knew their names precisely. He thought of the other names, the names of men who had precipitated the violent break in the block, in the mass of the party. The memory alone should have sufficed to remind my father of how final the separation was. These names had risen up as signs from the anonymity of the fighters, with them appeared all the others who had been resurrected when my father wondered what they looked like, Frölich, Knief, and Flieg, Liebknecht, Luxemburg, and Jogiches, Levi and Leviné, Brandler, Pieck, and Zetkin, Eberlein, Enderle, and Remmele, Duncker and Thalheimer, Eisner or Landauer, the faces of his companions thronged about him, his fellow workers at the lathes, at the forges, in the assembly halls. Mehring, sick, feeble from wartime imprisonment, was the last of the Socialist Party leaders to die, immediately after the murderous days of January, and then Knief and Leviné, Eisner and Landauer also joined the dead, and most of the Spartacus people who had founded the Communist Party had been expelled sooner or later, only Zetkin had died while still a member, shortly before the establishment of fascist power, Flieg and Eberlein had been executed by their own people in Moscow, all this dragged on right into the Warnsdorf kitchen, the breaks, the splits had multiplied, during the past few years my father kept hearing about this man or that man who had belonged to the pioneers and was now hunted, damned. Since the upheaval, in which he himself had been buffeted to and fro, had now been stretching on for over two decades, he had never managed to gain a perspective, an overview, only today, he said, was it possible for him to find some confirmation for decisions he had once made, for steps he had taken, often not knowing where they would lead. Back then, he said, we defended the Russian Revolution unreservedly. As for the setbacks, the emerging incongruities, we ascribed them not only to the difficulties caused by the intervention and strangulation efforts of the Entente, by the civil war, we blamed them chiefly on the failure of the German working class. None of us, he said, could now share Luxemburg's grievances. She too, had she lived, would have been willing to revise her critique, to put off issues like public control, freedom of assembly, freedom of the press, and universal free elections so long as they had to fight against the counterrevolution, the imperialist encirclement. Just what had we accomplished, he asked. We had not even gotten the eight-hour day. The revolution had given us back the old power apparatus, had guaranteed the sacred right to property, exploitation, and profit. If open government by the people had not yet been achieved in Russia, if force and violence had to be used, then it was partially our fault. Our goal was to safeguard the revolutionary conquests by doing all we could to defend and support Russia, we were, after all, fighting for our own future. We feared for this country, which after the devastations of the world war, the destructions and sacrifices of the civil war, had been subjected to attacks by Poland and the German militarists, and had also aroused the sympathy of leading Social Democrats. When the Polish invasion was accompanied by the Kapp/Lüttwitz putsch in a conspiracy with Ebert and Noske, the German proletariat briefly managed to unite, with the general strike it triumphed over the first fascist attempt to seize power. Nothing, said my father, at that time could turn us against the strict authority and discipline demanded by wartime Communism, after all, compared with the restrictions of democratic rights on the Russian council basis, every right here was not only threadbare but worn down. We regarded centralism as the supreme level of the collective, we viewed the command power of the top, the obedience of all subdivisions as necessary, precisely because our uprising had been thwarted by the absence of a centralized organization, of a strategy planned and steered down to every last detail, had been wrecked by federalism, by faith in spontaneity. Until the end of nineteen twenty we discussed our merger with the Communist Party, I was ready to cross over too, I could not imagine a return to Social Democracy. We strove to expand the Communist Party, to set up a broad proletarian front, it was the first effort to unite the forces set in motion by the revolution. The revolutionary leaders who had stood next to Liebknecht, Luxemburg, and Jogiches formed the young, still open party, adjusting it to the special conditions in this country. After his many years of working here, Radek, who transmitted the Russian directives, likewise counted himself among the German Communists. The world revolution had become very remote, it would no longer be a unique act, it would now be a long-lasting process of class struggles, crowded with victories and defeats. The workers had to be prepared for that, their real struggle was only just starting. The Social Democratic government officials crushed every single disturbance, every strike, every demonstration. The prisons were packed with workers. But while the nationalist associations were developing, the socialist forces were also forming, many workers were beginning to understand their situation and to recognize the Communist Party as the sole champion of their interests. The majority, however, remained in the old party, this was due not so much to ignorance and indolence as to exhaustion, which prevented resorting to a changeover. At times, said my father, we were so ground down by being poor, out of work, looking for odd jobs, that we lost all political initiative. And with the drive to consolidate a unity of action, the conflict of opinions was aggravated between the parties and within the factions. Yet the United Front did not wish to gloss over or settle the arguments, all it wanted was to find unification in a single, necessary, rational point, this was the only area for appealing for a common cause, otherwise the field remained open for ideological disagreements. The masses would have been willing, but the extremely different opinions of the party leaderships clashed with one another, and internally they also splintered into further antagonisms. It was not only the attitude of the Social Democratic Party, which made any approach impossible only because the demand for unity had come from the Communists before the putsch movement, before the perils of a military dictatorship and later of a rising fascism, it was also the radicalism of the leftists, who stuck to the revolutionary offensive, rejecting any alliance with Social Democracy as an expression of opportunism. The Social Democrats too fought, in their way, for unity, which they understood as involving a pull of the struggle toward the right, while we, who found ourselves in the middle between them and the Communists, were tried to the breaking point, until December nineteen twenty when one-half ran over to the Communist Party and the other half gave itself up to the mother party. Now, he said, the conscious, socialist proletariat stood on the left, while the people who clung to the petty bourgeoisie, to the middle classes, gathered on the right. And why, I asked once again, and this was on the morning of the next day, didn't you join the Communist Party. My father stood under the window, the light lay whitish gray on the left half of his face, emphasizing the weighty bone arches over the eye and making the eyebrow, the stubbly hair shine out. A deep shadow lay in the temple recess and in the hollow between the zygoma and the lower jaw, the right side of his face was black, perforated only by the tiny gleaming speck in his eye. Because I was no longer able to meet the criteria for admission, he replied. They set up doctrines to which I could not submit, to which I could not offer the absolute self-sacrifice they demanded. They revealed a Darwinist principle that I disapproved of, a selection of the fittest, a scorn of the deviators, the outsiders, this did not tally with my views. Back then I could not pinpoint my doubts, he said, but I was repelled by the way one group of leaders was replaced by the next in constant dissension, amid a terminology more hateful than that used by the Social Democrats, the most active, the most devoted people, without whom the Party and the International would never have existed, were suddenly cast out by their own comrades, who branded them as sectarians and renegades for not going along with the correct line of the moment. Ultra-leftists were those who endorsed only the catchwords aiming at the dictatorship of the proletariat, Maslow, Ruth Fischer were among them. The term "rightists" was applied to those people who warned against militant actions, who wanted to use party education to establish a party base in the general populace. Levi favored this, he and Zetkin were the only deputies representing the Communist Party in the Reichstag. With a new revolutionary step, as demanded by Fischer and Maslow, the Party, which had only just gained parliamentary legality, might have easily been pushed back underground by the opponent's superior strength. In the concept of internationalism, rightists and leftists were bound together, but this internationalism was interpreted in different ways. Behind it loomed a set of problems that had also led to difficult decisions in Soviet Russia, decisions necessitated by the cordon. The international proletarian solidarity was a joint guiding principle, but in its present-day brittleness it could only be a long-term objective for Levi, whereas for the left wing it constituted something that could be attained immediately. Parallel to the Soviet policies, which were starting to focus on the isolated building of socialism in one country, the Party headquarters spotlighted the national tasks, clashing constantly with the leftist forces they wanted to advance in stages, with partial demands, and, as a rapprochement with the ideas of broad segments of the people, propagate the struggle for the rescue of the nation. Levi, as chairman of the Party, as Luxemburg's successor, agreed only somewhat with this tactic, he did not want the dominance of the national question to allow any ideological hampering, any blocking of internationalism. Just as he rejected the leftists' appeal for a realization of revolutionary power, so too did he oppose the direction of a national Bolshevism. Prior to his ousting in March nineteen twenty-one, we still believed, said my father, that the relentlessness of the disputes was bound to produce a catharsis, a mutual understanding, we found links between all discussion points, they could complement one another in a politics without being opinionated, without dogmatic thinking. But then all we saw was deepened breaks, discharges of irreconcilability, while the backgrounds of controversies and power shifts remained, as usual, concealed from us. In March, right after the crushing of the Russian workers' opposition, the fighting had broken out in central Germany, it began as strikes against the military regime that had been established, the melees were provoked by the army and the police, thousands of workers were shot, wounded, jailed. A final desperate attempt was made to stir up the world revolution after all in order to help Soviet Russia. Everything was staked on the vaguest possibility of a revolutionary situation, the left wing of the Communist Party, the Comintern, was pressing for it, the right wing warned against it, urging them to stop. It was hoped that the masses would coalesce in the combat, that all the organizations anchored in the proletariat would push forward in a joint resistance, but that hope was blasted. After the defeat, the Social Democracy, mocking and maligning, said that for lack of detectable revolutionary conditions the Communist Party no longer had the right to resist. Levi, we found out later, had wanted the Party to stay out of the fighting so long as there was no guarantee that the majority of the population would participate. Above all, however, his falling-out with party headquarters was due to his criticism of the dependency on the Soviet guidelines. That month had been crucial for my father's decision to rejoin the Social Democratic Party. In his eyes the Red Army's attack on the workers and sailors of Kronstadt had spelled the abandonment of the goals of the revolution. Nevertheless, he said, I let myself be convinced by the arguments that the revolt of the social revolutionaries had been fomented by Mensheviks and White Guardists. Supposedly the revolutionary forces were at the front, politically inexperienced replacements, starved, dissatisfied, had let themselves be exploited by petty bourgeois, counterrevolutionary forces. They shouted, All power to the Soviets, not the Party. That had to be high treason at a time when survival was at stake. What else was the Party if not the supreme organ of the Soviets. And the Party wanted to achieve nothing else than what the workers and sailors of Kronstadt also wanted, peace, the building-up of the country, of the economy, of production. They called for control by the workers. Yet the power of the state was in the hands of the working class. The change to the new economic policy, the struggle for industrialization required the same energies that had helped the Revolution to victory. Now that everyone had to give his utmost, there could be no tolerance of groups whose deviating opinions hampered the planning. Anyone who rebelled was supporting reactionism, which still lurked, ready to pounce and destroy what had been achieved. Only years later, said my father, did we find our way back to our original idea that Kronstadt represented not so much an attempt to restore bourgeois hegemony as a desire for democratic rights. Despite his realization that the opposition at that moment in time was objectively helping the enemy, he could no longer understand the necessity of the countermeasures. But still, his doubts, he once again pointed out, would never have driven him to take a negative attitude toward the Soviet state. In the organization of the workers' aid, he endorsed assistance to Russia, and in all discussions he underscored the significance of Russian endurance. I rejoined the old party, he said, because I could take the critical position that would have been refused me in the Communist Party. It was also still the biggest party, we stood there together with the majority of workers. I did not see that as capitulating, he said, I was not deceiving myself, the Party had unambiguously enough declared where it stood, what it advocated. I opposed its policies, but as a union member I exerted an influence on the professional events and I could, more emphatically than from the outside, be active in developing a socialist unity. I had previously conferred with Radek. He too felt it was necessary to build up positions inside the Social Democratic Party in order to advance the idea of the United Front. For him, as later for Merker, Wehner, Münzenberg, it was important to have contacts with cadres in our party, our trade unions, cadres that would champion cooperation. But then, mentally hurdling one and a half decades, he no longer saw his party's insurmountable, compact rejection of all Communist overtures, he saw only the boundary drawn by the Comintern, the definitive incorporation of the entire Social Democracy into the camp of the class enemy. He forgot what he had just explained, his generation's responsibility for isolating the First Workers' State, for condemning it to build up socialism in a single country. He had experienced the disorganization and powerlessness of the German rebellion, its degrading collapse when the revolutionary leaders, defenseless, could be seized, dragged away, and murdered by a handful of thugs, and now he accentuated only the deformations in the state produced by the October Revolution, the degenerations, which, he said, left not only their own country but the whole workers' movement numb and dazed. The dismantling of the collective leadership stipulated by Lenin, the transfer of omnipotent executive powers to a lone man, showed, said my father, the final point of a development in which the proletarian democracy, the free exchange of opinions, the direct active involvement by the people in all matters of social and productional life had been banished, nor did he view it as a sign of strength that the domestic crisis had been dealt with so openly despite the perilous situation. Suddenly an antithesis emerged between us, and I wondered whether now, after our long separation, my father and I had wound up in different camps. And if discord could ensue between us even though we had always been understanding of one another, then how was it possible for the parties, after twenty years of enmity, to find some way of working together. For us, said my father, the first goal is to have a clear conscience. Nothing achieved through distortion can be fruitful for us. It is one thing to strike down traitors who jeopardize our political work, it is another thing to hold a trial in which a totality of power executes any other will. The Communist International, which knows more than we, I replied, backed the verdicts. My father, whom I had always known to be calm and collected, erupted indignantly. They say, he cried, you cannot make an omelet without breaking eggs, and this applies to the revolutionary struggle against classes that want to deny us our rights, but here the pioneers of the new social system are being annihilated in the name of the Party. We, who are hoodwinked by school, press, and diplomacy, who are pronounced incompetent by the higher party levels, have to hold fast to our own standards. It is not only our sole remaining ability, it is also our task to pit our paltry reality against the demonic political machinery. We have to guard against taking over ready-made opinions and passing them on, the stupidest reactionism is better than dutifully parroting litanies that command respect or remaining silent about deeds that we cannot put up with. For what do we have, he asked, but our intellectual plight, after all, our ignorance has to be fought, what else is our stammering and stuttering but a sign of inveighing against lies. I tried to remind him that he had always argued against the people who carried on about morality and humanity while doing everything in their power to debase any progress in the socialist country, the people who, while ruthlessly conducting their business, cunningly wiping out their competitors, developed an idealistic solidarity in regard to preserving the joint predatory system, the people who praised civilization and human dignity while mocking the socialist upheaval. I recalled conversations we had had in Berlin at a time when all the newspapers had again waxed indignant about the lack of rights in the Soviet state, and he had stressed how the judicial proceedings there stood in relation to the injustice practiced in the capitalist countries. Was the execution of Sacco and Vanzetti an expression of rights guaranteed by the legal system, he had asked, and I still remembered the way he had talked about the hundred thousand people murdered in Europe, in America, in the colonial and semicolonial countries, in the breakups of demonstrations, in the crushings of revolts, the way he had described the conditions in prisons throughout the Western world, in the Indo-Chinese dungeons, where for years on end each prisoner had been chained and, at night, fastened to a pole by an iron ring around his neck. Other things lingered in my mind, in debates with fellow workers he had talked about the billions of marks embezzled in all municipal and national agencies, laundered and then spent on bribes. But never, he had pointed this out, was this corruption linked to the society in which it occurred, the scandals were treated as isolated incidents and forgotten, while the vast racketeering that involved the entire imperialistic world remained intact amid smug, unctuous tolerance. But my father barely listened to my protests. He thought about Radek, about the last time he had seen him, again in a hiding place, in Berlin, in late October nineteen twenty-three, after the collapse of the Hamburg revolt. I will be blamed, he said in his soft drawl, his Austrian accent, I will be made the scapegoat for the failure of the German working class even though I tried to stop the operations because of the lack of revolutionary strength. Once again the left-wing forces in the party had favored an armed attack. Radek, however, dispatched by the executive committee of the Comintern, wanted to limit the actions to demonstrations, to a general strike, wanted to first press the tactics for creating the United Front. But the uprising could not be held back and was smashed by the Reichswehr, the German army. Lenin is deathly ill, said Radek in his melodious voice, I can expect no help from him if the Politburo calls me to account. Then he had added something that my father did not understand until years later, namely, that you have to dig in your teeth, dig in your claws, be prepared to try all dodges and disguises if you want to see this work through, and then he had lost his leading position in the Party and the International, had been deported, had broken with Trotsky and finally made himself available to the secretary-general, jeering at everything he had previously advocated he had built up the cult of the highest person in the Party and propagated heroic realism as the only valid socialist art form. And now, said my father, he has been condemned as a saboteur and capitulator, as a traitor and enemy of the people because his intelligence was not sufficiently adaptable after all. He saw Radek's and Piatakov's unbelievable trial testimonies as the final attempt at pointing out a delusional system that was spreading through the land. But while he may have been right in saying that there were deformations, that in retaliating against the adversaries of the Party leadership they had also felled innocent victims, it was certainly no delusion that the imperialist side was striving incessantly to undermine and destroy the hard-won achievements of a few brief decades. To England, France, and America, Bolshevism still represented a far greater peril than fascism. Unanimously the governments of the Western countries rejected all Soviet efforts at creating a defensive alliance, instead they condoned Germany's, Italy's, and Japan's extortions and aggressions and wormed their way into the dictators' good graces, waiting for the defeat of the Spanish Republic and the revolution in China. If the Soviet Union saw itself in mortal danger, it had good reason, the workers' state had been blockaded and cut off, and anyone who focused solely on the results rather than constantly reemphasizing the causes of the raging defense was treading on thin ice and serving the interests of the enemy.

For there, on the other side, capital reigned supreme, there the power of suppression and exploitation kept increasing, there new wars were being prepared to maintain colonial ownership. But with every word the alienation, the distrust between us grew deeper, soon spreading to any theme that we had agreed on earlier. Thus my father also felt that the concept of the progressive working class, historically called on for leadership, had become invalid for the next few decades. In the workers' struggle, the proletariat had barely gained any insights, he said, the actions with which it responded to any emergency were always inadequate, it had achieved none of the knowledge mandatory for cultural advancement. The workers had lost all independent strength, they would integrate themselves in the imminent campaigns without so much as a peep even if these campaigns led them against Russia. The majority of workers, he said, had come to terms with their existence as slaves under fascist pomp, consoling themselves with petty bourgeois promises rather than upholding the idea of internationalism. I argued against these views by citing my experiences in Berlin, saying it was presumptuous to belittle the unremitting work being done there, on the contrary, given the situation, the still surviving actions could not be valued highly enough. While the number of activists secretly holding together might be small, we nevertheless had to see them as the people laying the groundwork for the future renewal of the country. My father said that the illegal work could barely make itself noticeable in Germany and that the rearmament was proceeding under high pressure in the factories with the help of our former comrades. An impact on the German conditions, he opined, could come only from abroad. Once again, he said, we have to start from scratch, from where Luxemburg's plans broke off, where all the people who wanted to carry her ideas further were ostracized, where the conception of a free proletariat taking action with self-awareness was lost, where the Party did not operate to develop the individual's faculty of judgment but instead became a church in which the self could dissolve. I replied that I viewed the Party as neither a mystical organization nor the ruler of my will. Instead, the step that would lead me to the Party and to my solidarity with it was, as a matter of principle, absolutely voluntary. I could never see the Party as a coercive system, but only as an institution of rationality. If I joined the Party, my doing so would be the result of sober, practical consideration, free of any irrationalism, an action with an underpinning of insight and knowledge, and with the goal of putting my own political aims in a larger context, thereby strengthening them. But my father had once again covered his ears against a deluge of fanfares and choral singing. This terrible national anthem was now assaulting an entire continent, washing away everything that tried to stand in its path, and when, stomping around, he again murmured something about the Kaiser Bridge, I realized that it had been arrogant of me to reproach him for his inner disintegration, his unclarities, for he had done his best, and suddenly I saw him, with the trimmed beard he wore back then, the dark-blue felt jacket, the upturned collar, pushing the bicycle from the garden into the hall and out into the street, saw him pedaling over the paved road, out to Grosse Allee, looking back one last time, waving, before he vanished around the corner and sped along the bald, smoothly cut Dike Way to the railroad bridge, over to St. Stephen's Gate, then farther, past the cranes, tracks, and warehouses, past the overseas harbor, the wood harbor, the grain harbor, all the way to his workshop, there below the gigantic walls and bars of the shipyard, with the blaring of the riveting hammers, the bellowing of the welding flames, and the shrieking of the metal saws. And then we could again talk to one another, it was again clear that we were in the same camp, and just as the misunderstandings between us could be cleared up, so too would the parties, I felt, transcend their ideological differences and, because it was necessary, form the United Front.

It was by fighting out conflicts, contradictions that we found what we had in common. There had been rejections, difficulties, and always the striving to pass through thesis and antithesis in order to achieve a condition that was valid for both of us. Just as divergences, disagreements gave rise to new ideas, so too did every action emerge from the clash of antagonisms. The understanding and articulation of these processes made it possible for us to live together and appreciate each other. However, no hint of agreement could be found in the confrontations between the parties' negotiators. A broad coalition had crystallized only in Spain, its tenability not yet evident, so far, according to whatever we could learn, the efforts of German Social Democratic and Communist functionaries to agree on positions and objectives appeared to have foundered. Only now did I perceive how limited the region was in which we had lived. We had always been confronted with only one and the same foe, who dictated our actions. In the underground we found ourselves in a specific circle, and all orientations emanating from it were bound to its dimensions. We had not dwelt on the fact that contact with superior cadres was broken, that the Party was surviving only in the tiniest of cells, it was enough for us to get directives, reports every so often, to keep receiving the newspaper printed abroad. The least signs of activity continuing on the outside encouraged us, made us feel secure. Now the field suddenly opened, and we had an inkling of the complicated picture of the power structures, which constantly had to be dissected and pondered. For us there were the direct, obvious measures that tied us together no matter what group we belonged to, but for every undertaking the leaders had to gain an idea of the total situation in all its shifts and calculable future phases. But now I also realized how greatly our project, in the middle of enemy territory, had contributed to the other, comprehensive, ramified investigations, how much of our experiences at work sites, in residential areas had been transmitted by messengers to the range of tactics. Our chief task had been to keep from being discovered, and carrying it out often consumed most of our energy, whatever we could find struck us as trivial, but when suddenly seen from a free place, the mere fact that some people were holding out, remaining in their places, making themselves available when needed proved meaningful enough. Remaining in illegality, which was dominated by conspiratorial lawfulness, no one had felt cut off, even a protracted solitude had nothing to do with oblivion or isolation. And how could anyone even imagine standing alone since tens of thousands of us were in the prisons and camps. Never had we seen ourselves, as my father saw himself, far below the decisions, with no influence, no connection to those who steered the events on the levels of actions. What appeared there as a frail scaffolding demanded knowledge, insights to which I was not yet entitled. I was familiar with only a few main policies, the strenuous effort to produce broader and stronger positions against fascism, to win the support of all progressive forces for a Popular Front, to get volunteers and military assistance to Spain, to widen the campaign to release Thälmann, who was threatened with the same fate as André, murdered in a Hamburg prison, and then there were the constantly repeated overtures that the Communist Party made to the executive committee of the Social Democrats. For my father the difficulties in getting to understand the conflicts in party politics were due to principles. When we seek an explanation for historical events, he said, we are always thrown back upon second- or third-hand intelligence. The causes of the events we are entangled in remain veiled, we have to interpret them by our own lights. Mostly we possess no facts other than fragments gleaned by comrades. We have never been satisfied with what has been doled out to us in protocols and communiqués, things that were external and tailored to a certain effect, we have always resisted letting others feel it was good for them to know more than we did. In our discussions we often got closer to the facts by relying on our instincts than by reading an official announcement, news from a fellow worker could tell us more than the Party program that was handed out. And just what is that, the correct line, said my mother, she always has something of the preacher about her as if trying to inveigle us into believing that there is only one sole truth. I replied that a specific line of action was necessary now just as it was necessary to cover up, encode important strategies. Perhaps, said my mother, since the participants in the course of events are so accustomed to hiding something, they are just as baffled, just as badly informed as we. Then again they want to put on airs. The reason everything is so muddled, so lacking in perspective is that anyone who has a minor function wants to make it more important, so he puffs himself up and creates secrets with his peers in order to ascend to the higher ranks of the mysteries. We see this flair for conspiracy everywhere, the advocates of scientific socialism cluster into circles, cliques, centers, wings, and platforms, following an ancient proclivity for forming clans. We can break this pattern only by gaining insight, discernment, by having an impact on every administrative issue, by refusing to accept these groupings and concentrations, which lock us in, by rejecting them because it is their nature to proliferate and develop a rule by offices. We, on our side, never have anything to conceal. Our conduct is always completely open. We take to the streets, shout out our demands. We are vulnerable at every step. It is only self-interest that keeps up its guard, that needs feints, masks, pitfalls. But because we have not yet succeeded, said my father, in exerting any influence on affairs of state, we have to obtain news as well as we can on our own. We cannot as yet prevail against the system that wants to make us pliable and keep us in ignorance and dilettantism. Actually everything that is devised, prepared for, resolved ought to originate with us, we have been conscious of that for a century now. Our achievements ought to be at the center everywhere. But we have allowed our decision-making power to be wrested from us. We remain wage slaves instead of steering production processes. The visions of liberation, of renewal come from our side, but the powers that be are superior to us in their lack of ideology, their absence of ethics. They need no philosophy for plundering, on the contrary, the more brutal, the more mindless they are, the higher their profits. Proletarian internationalism is a grand idea, but the international of capital owners has a more forceful clout. And yet my parents knew that the changes would penetrate the old, dogged patterns. Imperialism could still murder and devastate, but the rebellion against its violent power went on and on in the most diverse centers. The arrogated right to exploit all natural resources, the distribution of all wares met with resistance, in Indochina revolts broke out against colonialism, China and

Spain entered into armed combat. Whatever solidarity could be mobilized coalesced in the International Brigades. The worldwide insight into the dynamics of the suppressive system did not yet exist, and how could that comprehension have emerged given the disablement, the terrorism inflicted on the nations by the literates, the opinion spreaders. The scientific alternative, pitted for the first time against the anarchistic drive for enrichment, was young. The people who wanted to translate knowledge into deeds had themselves emerged from the old order and were corrupted by the feelings and features that belonged to it. Minds were engaged in a relentless struggle against the brutality, even the people we trusted in political organizing were marked by existing in concealment, equivocation, dissembling, and lies, which were necessary in the fight against the foe. Often they themselves did not know what they might dare to say, their situation was infinitely more difficult than ours, they could never be certain where treason and deception lurked at meetings, to what extent the man they were seeking as an ally had sold himself to the adversary, they had to constantly censor themselves, never relax their alertness, their suspicion for even an instant, take nothing for granted, secure every step in all directions. How could all this be depicted, I wondered, now torn from the simplifications that had enabled me to endure. How could what we were experiencing, I asked myself, be delineated in such a way that we could recognize ourselves in it. The form would be monstrous, would cause dizziness. It would let people sense how inadequate the description of the shortest stretch of road would be by opening the multivalence of every direction taken. Our further conversations revealed the way my father found his bearings among the phenomena and obtained information on the backgrounds of the political complexes. He showed with what attentiveness, what need for signs of life he devoted himself after all to the situation of the working class, the way he kept trying to procure contacts, indications, news, all of which dispelled his fits of resignation. He had had several meetings with Wehner, who was now a member of the Central Committee and a candidate for the Politburo. They knew each other from joint union and agitation projects since the early thirties. Their last encounter had taken place in Paris during the previous year, but when trying to report on it he kept getting distracted by memories of other meetings and events. In nineteen thirty-one, after the electoral victories of the National Socialists, when the Communists had instituted the Red Front League for their own protection, the Social Democrats likewise pulled together a combat organization, the Iron Front, consisting of the Reich Banner and formations of athletic clubs and labor unions. In a merger both workers' parties would have possessed a strong resistance alliance, but the Social Democratic leaders were not ready for any united action. They preferred letting the so-called hammer groups of the trade union associations smash down the Communist workers rather than siccing them on the fascists. The latter had no numerical superiority as yet, a coalition could have defeated them. Once again rudimentary efforts to establish a United Front were possible only on the lowest level. When National Socialist Storm Troopers set up quarters in a beer hall on Schwartzkopfstrasse in order to guard the area at the approach to Wedding, the local inhabitants spontaneously banded together, championed their concurring interests, and made a political issue of their demand that the assembly place be shut down. My mother, who through her work in the meter factory had close relations with the Communist shop groups and street cells, tried to remember that time. It had once been important, all deliberations circled around it, the enemy had not yet launched his regime, suddenly there was a possibility of breaking his influence and through personal initiative urging the party leaderships to conclude a pact. But the energy of those days was soon dissipated, indolence spread out over it. The want of unified strategy, then a premature reaction destroyed any further advance. The protest movement, abruptly reaching all around in the spring of thirty-two, already contained the paralysis that struck down the working class one year later. Only scattered Communist functionaries, Merker, Wehner, Peuke, Dittbender, supported the undertaking of the residents of that street. There they stood, the implementers of the action, on Schwartzkopfstrasse, Pflugstrasse. They had come from the plants, the workshops. They wore masks of soot, dust, black oil. They rallied outside the windows of the Brown House, which were draped with small flags. Sentries stood at the door, their thumbs in their belts, the straps of their caps slung under their chins, the murderous songs ringing out behind them. My mother pondered what had happened that day when she had left the building on Ackerstrasse at five in the afternoon. She sat in the corner of the plush sofa, with the brown-green pattern of ferns, her elbow propped on the arm of the sofa, her heavy face in her hand, she gazed out into the street, where the din had now stopped. From Schwartzkopfstrasse she saw, next to the slate tower of St. Sebastian's Church, the broad arched windows, behind which she had assembled electrical devices for eight hours. She stood in the throng of male and female workers, she was still silent like the others. We had believed, she said, that we could get rid of the fascists by waiting, persevering. We were the majority here. It was our neighborhood. Then isolated threats were hollered. The voices swelled up, the crowd pushed toward the tavern. And suddenly the clatter of glass could be heard, stones flew through the windows, fistfights broke out inside, the gunfire began. But the shots came from all around, police troops had marched over from Chausseestrasse, had only been waiting for the signal, the shattering of the window. Now that my mother was talking about it, I remembered the agitated debates about whether the shoot-out, which left several dead and wounded, had been caused by police provocation or by the impatience of the Red Front Leaguers. The policemen, standing ready with their dogs and vehicles, pounced upon the workers in the street. They acted as defenders of the Brown House, after the local inhabitants had been demanding its clearance for a week. Now the moment had come for showing that the tavern was open for everyone, that nobody had the right to entrench himself there. Do not commit any violence, they shouted. But even if we had not stormed the tavern, said my mother, there would have been a clash with the police. Neumann's slogan, Beat the Fascists wherever you meet them, was frowned upon by the leadership of the Communist Party. We should have followed that appeal, said many proletarians when it was too late. The Communist street protection was necessary when the National Socialist echelons invaded the red districts. The Front League had courageous, reliable people, who knew why they were switching to the offensive. We considered the other tactic better, said my mother, the tactic of workers' solidarity to overcome the conflicts between parties. But immediately after the event they sharpened the fiats against fraternizing. Hate propaganda turned us against one another, she said, when we crossed paths in the same hallway, we who had only just acted in unison were embarrassed. And after our retreat the Storm Troopers could open their meeting places everywhere, under police protection. And so they rose, disguised as a workers' party, pretending to combine nationalism and socialism, and using deception and dazzlement to draw along the faint of heart, the eternal pushovers, the ignorant hopers. At first shyly, then blatantly, said my mother, tenants on our street also joined them, lifting an outstretched hand instead of a clenched fist. How would I picture my mother, I thought, if I had not seen her since the day she stood with me at the window on Grünenstrasse. A darkness belonged to her. Her eyes, her hair dark, similar to the deep resonance of her voice. I would have imagined her forehead as wide, her cheekbones too, her eyebrows energetic, but her narrow mouth and her nose, which ran straight, with almost no notch at the edge of the forehead, were all too clear before me, I could not have looked for their shapes, familiar things covered what I wanted to put at a distance in order to rediscover it. Would her hair have been so smooth and short if I had had to conjure it up, and was it parted on the side, I asked myself. She sat there, slanting forward, her hand under her chin, her mouth barely stirring when she spoke. Her voice still had an Alsatian tinge, recognizable perhaps only by us, more than two decades of northern German, the Berlin idiom, lay upon it. In Strasbourg she had been a nanny for a German family, accompanying it to Bremen shortly before the war. Actually she had wanted to work in her father's business on a side street of the cathedral square, which was lined with rows of trees, I knew the house from a photograph, he had been a sign painter, making signs for guilds, stores, he had also done coats-of-arms and doorway decorations. There would have been a lot to tell about the house in which my mother had grown up and which I had never entered, about her parents, who were buried in Strasbourg, about her meeting my father while working as an assistant nurse at the Delmenhorst Convalescent Home outside Bremen, about my father's ancestors, who had been peasants, farm laborers, about his progression as apprentice in a smithy, as locksmith in an engineering workshop, as machinist on a Danube Shipping steamboat, studying in his spare moments, obtaining his high school diploma at a night school in Budapest, then his conscription in the Pioneer Troops in Galicia, but these things had never been talked about at home, no other meaning than that of the given job was attached to the road he had traveled, the changing places of residence. Here in the apartment in Warnsdorf, the difference became insistently clear between our life and bourgeois existence, which had a lavish atmospheric coloring, which had solid and heavily traditional relationships to furnishings and ornaments, to suites of rooms and gardens, while we found ourselves in a waiting room here, a transitional room, which could easily and quickly be forsaken and forgotten. The narrow two-story house in Strasbourg, with the worn front stoop, the lead-mounted panes in the street-floor windows, the crossed brushes and the palette on the wooden board hanging on a chain, I could have viewed them, back then, wrapped in thought, with a flair for escapism, as a fifteen-year-old, when I learned that my schooling in Scharfenberg was to be terminated. Neither my mother nor any chronicler had ever set about depicting the old-fashioned fairy-tale quality of this milieu, there had been no trace of homeyness, of security, my mother and her sisters had begun earning their livelihood as young girls, they drifted apart, never got together again, the changing places, the travels, the arrivals in strange cities were linked not to epic impressions but to the question of whether a job could be found here. Since from *Wilhelm Meister* to *Buddenbrooks* the world that set the tone in literature was seen through the eyes of those who owned it, the household could be captured with such love for details, as could the personality in the richness of all stages of development. Ownership molded the attitude that was taken toward things, while for us, to whom the living room never belonged and for whom the place of residence was a matter of chance, the only elements that carried weight were absence, deficiency, lack of property. There was no wasting any breath about it, at that moment I could not have mentioned anything but the iron can opener that I saw lying on the buffet, shaped like a herring, the lower jaw protruding as a bayonet-like cutter, it had already existed in Bremen, I had played with it, no doubt, and my mother had taken it out of my mouth. Otherwise we had no time to think about the frugality, our life story consisted more of figuring out how to get through the next few days and weeks, how to pay the rent, than of registering objects among which we were barely tolerated. If the house in Strasbourg did cross my mind, it was because I had often looked at the photo of this house and its small painter's sign, everything that I subsequently got to know in art seemed to derive from that house, and in this way, in overcoming poverty and alienation, a family history could be conceived, a history in which the intrinsic ensued from a lack of connection. People appeared, they were tangible, evident, they were spoken about, they were judged, they belonged to the unpropertied class, this was captured, who had helped and mediated here, who had participated there in a project, the people, independent of landscapes and cities, molded by political insights and decisions, formed the milieu in which our development occurred, and their statements, their questions and answers, were joined by books, they were as detached from their origin as the people, constituted, like them, nothing but what they had opted for. Books, people, pictures, those were the solidities in a life that otherwise knew only unsteadiness. The work in the underground, the travels with a forged passport, the anonymous sojourns in foreign countries, the exile, these were the final results of a condition that had always been nomadic. The room in Warnsdorf, below in the house of the sedentary, served as a secret meeting place for the vagabonds, the proletarians, who were used to wandering around, hawking their labor, a meeting place for those who were given nothing, who had to queue up, wait on line to obtain the barest necessities for surviving. Here, from rough hints, from perceptions conveyed by other people, from comparisons and associations, here, where we were vulnerable to disturbances, to the risk of a raid, our minds caught something of the web being spun around us. My father's words were faltering, seeking, and he struggled to overcome our differences of opinion.

The threads he followed had begun in September of thirty-six, when he, as part of a Czechoslovakian delegation, met Wehner at a function of the World Peace Movement in Paris. Before he attempted to describe something of this encounter, the threads moved to and fro between other stations, conversations with Taub, one of the heads of the Czechoslovakian Social Democratic Party, with Peuke, who had come into the country across the mountains near Bodenbach and was hiding out with friends in Prague, and the threads now began in November of thirty-five, when the first meeting between top German Social Democrats and Communists took place in Prague.

And how should writing even be possible for us, I asked myself during my father's account. If we could grasp anything of the political reality we lived in, how might this flimsy, dwindling material, which could be obtained only in dribs and drabs, ever be converted into a written page with a claim to continuity. Tranquil and persistent research and reflection were beyond our reach. The events thronging in on us forced us to gain insights that became fierce reactions. They could lead to actions, but they could not be rounded off, could not yield an overall view. They always had to remain fragmentary, had to be torn apart, wiped away by newly surfacing demands. But should I ever succeed in outfoxing the forces that kept trying to distract me from my trains of thought, should I ever manage to grant free scope to the stimuli and brain waves, to the emerging contemplations, then I would not accept the view that a writer must belong to a specific country, a precisely outlined sphere of existence, a national culture for his writings to sound convincing. The issues given priority in the magazines concerning realistic art, concerning workers' literature, the elucidation of an everyday milieu, the linkage with its inhabitants and the exchange of ideas with them, these elements would apply to me only in a limited sense. Just as this room we were talking in was accidental and could be located in any country whatsoever, so too would my writings address people who might be found anywhere, whatever their background, internationalism would be the criterion of my affiliation. For though I was only at the beginning of my journey it had become obvious to me that we were at home nowhere but in our partisanship. Granted, I could see the advantages of belonging to a country, a city, but for my purposes there was no such point of departure, I would have to start with the shapeless, the unattached and seek connections beyond the borders of states and tongues. Perhaps we had meant something along these lines when calling our discussions of art and literature political. If ever we became implementers in that area, our activities would be steered by our intention to bridge gaps, to find something that might be common to us, who were cut off from being at home anywhere. Thus, to me, the national question, however urgent and acute a problem, had always seemed merely part of a transitional stage, serving its purpose only when joined to a comprehensive development. We tied what was happening in Germany to the events in France, in Spain, in China, and whenever I thought of people in places whose addresses could no longer be determined, had been wiped from my memory so that they would not be blurted out under an extorting interrogation, under torture, people in a small circle, planning the future development of their country, then this global net would always settle on their words, what they said was recorded by a whirring, was indissolubly hitched to what was being blueprinted and carried out in Africa, in Asia, on the American continents. We were individually scattered and simultaneously embraced in a totality, our mission was to make ourselves as conscious as possible of whatsoever was happening around us, including whoever, as my father put it, patronized and penalized us, whoever did not ask for our comments, whoever tried to keep us mute and pliable. But in contrast to my father, who started off more from the dazzlements and whitewashes, I perceived an unflagging tension when I looked around. While I did not need to limit myself, the politicians had to focus on a precise topic, I had a wide variety at my disposal, they had to research, excerpt, had to delve into partial tasks, I did not have to reach a goal, they had to demonstrate results, were responsible for details, made history by patching together, each in his own location, tiny parts into a whole. It was this laboring with details, this tireless rummaging and scrutinizing, that was expressed in the declarations of the World Congress of the Comintern during July and August of nineteen thirty-five. All attempts at creating a unified action formed the basis of the policy resolution for the Popular Front. The new guidelines revised the notion of the past few years that Social Democracy constituted a single reactionary mass. Now a precise distinction was to be made between the rightist leaders and the huge segments of workers in the Social Democratic Party. But before this directive could be driven toward reality, the divergences had to be removed, and whoever wished to fathom any of the references to the talks held in Prague that November was again forced to transfer his own research to the harsh exterior work and establish an order himself. In the underground we had faced an unambiguous foe who could be precisely identified, no words had to be wasted on him, fighting him was all that mattered. For us fascism was the open dictatorship of high-finance capital, it was the weapon of the most reactionary forces, serving their plan to redivide Europe. But that formula, said my father, did not explain why a large portion of the working class had cast their ballots for the National Socialists as far back as nineteen thirty or why the number of pro-fascist voters could have increased to seventeen million by the spring of nineteen thirty-three. It was not enough, he said, to blame it solely on the years of crisis, on the splintering of the working class, we had to seek the true reasons why the unification could not crystallize. All that came to light were tactical rivalries, and they covered up the deeper motives for the indecisiveness or for the catastrophic misreading of the situation. Even after the fascist takeover the Communist Party leaders still insisted on viewing Social Democracy as the main enemy because of its constant efforts to achieve a compromise with the bourgeois center. The thesis of social fascism failed to bring about any joint actions in the struggle. With the Reichstag elections in March nineteen thirty-three, Communists and Social Democrats, had they been capable of rethinking their opinions, could have mobilized a proletarian front of twelve million. But the Communist Party waited for the revolutionary upheaval, while the Social Democratic leadership favored a policy of accommodation and noninterference and felt that its task was to assume the role of fair critic of a lawful administration. While the Communists believed that National Socialism was already toppling, the Social Democrats, in the spring of thirty-three, were of the opinion that Germany was being governed according to the letter and the spirit of the Constitution. So without hindrance the government could smash the Communist organizations as well as disband the Social Democratic Party and the Federations of Trade Unions. When those Communists who were not overtaken by the fascist terror went underground in order to build up a resistance, the fleeing executive committee of the Social Democratic Party was still reeling from the shock. Confusion and paralysis were all it could respond with when the Communists suggested that the situation be reevaluated. In France during February of nineteen thirty-four, five million Socialists and Communists went on strike to protest fascist putsch attempts, thereby sparking the first creation of a Popular Front, in Austria that same month the workers fought an armed four-day battle against fascism, but the German Social Democrats remained inactive. And yet it could not have been only the quarrel of the party chiefs, said my father, that deprived the working class of its power to act. Though it was deeply immured for two decades, it should have kept its eyes open to its own capabilities, had they existed. Its lack of instinct for the mortal danger, its self-deceptions, the fruitless mutual reproaches that we indulged in as far back as during our revolutionary winter, he said, were problems we did not know how to solve despite all our experiences in the later years. Leaders of the caliber of the Russian revolutionaries had been eliminated at the decisive moment, compared with the minds now being lost by the Soviet state, most of our people had a more limited, more petty bourgeois character, were anything but farsighted or skillful in regard to bold innovations. Above all, however, he said, he wanted to ascribe this feature to the leaders of his own party. What he had seen twenty years earlier as the greatest negligence of Social Democracy had subsequently become crucial for the collapse, namely, the failure to exploit the vast educational possibilities within the unions. Countless Social Democratic workers, he said, would have been capable of expanding their consciousness, had they only had the necessary incentive and support. But then, again, he said, the functionaries were not alone to blame for the lack of initiative, for we have to ask ourselves why the workers did not insist on schooling, on betterment. The economic plight, he added, hampered all of us, yet it too could not be held responsible for the passivity, the fatalism, the inability to intervene. And thus my father had asked the core question as to why the workers remained in the party whose central planks were anti-Communism, the fight against the revolution, and the fostering of the reactionary society. He avoided answering. He viewed as mechanistic the notion that fascism was nothing but the extreme, offensive, brutalized form of the monopoly rule. We also have to count the deformation long prepared by the powers that be, the destruction of self-determination. But those very things belonged to the system of exploitation, I replied. It was the institutions of bourgeois society that subjugated the worker, they alone were intent on producing a body of ruined followers, who, if suddenly foddered, could be used as a fighting unit. It seemed as if that were the source of fascism, but the flushed-out devotees had no idea of what was what, they had nothing but their emptiness, were as feeble as before, could only pretend to be bursting with vigor while they hollered out the power cravings of their superiors. One-third of this army, said my father, consisted of workers, there were not just the philistines, the low-level officials, the bewildered housewives, all the underpaid, the unemployed, the impoverished, there were also our fellow workers, they too were broken, they too were ruled by a readiness to submit when the crisis recurred. This, he said, ought to be examined by the leaders of the workers' parties, why the beginnings of a belief in freedom, an anti-imperialistic attitude, turned into chauvinism, why the desire to transform society changed into mystical devotion, why they had failed to make the proletariat aware of the lie. And so the tremendous façade of fascism rose up, and everything still had to be done to clear away the disorder of ideas, the rubbish of platitudes and specious explanations behind the confusion, and to seek an orientation for advancement. But were the leaders, my father asked, really eager for insights that exposed their own mistakes, were they even capable of undergoing self-criticism, of dealing with the causes of the collapse. So long as things remained unresolved, no reconstruction of the workers' movement could succeed, and the call for a Popular Front had to sound hollow. And so, out here in exile, we had to keep watch for signs of who would first manage to overcome inner disintegration. While the old Social Democratic school with its teachers, Wels, Vogel, Ollenhauer, Stampfer, or Hilferding, still rejected any joint action, younger Social Democrats and members of splinter groups made contact with the Communist Party. There was the Red Combat Patrol, composed of erstwhile members of the Socialist Workers Youth, the Reich Banner, and various student organizations, whose agenda was to create a movement without a party membership book. There were the Red Fighters, the Work Team of Revolutionary Socialists, the Socialist Front, the International Socialist Combat Alliance, and New Beginning. The ideological goals of these small groups were as ambitious as their names, their often sectarian insulation was joined by their notion of becoming an elite that would be able to lead the working class. United actions with them were scarcely possible, and they were interested only in limited agreements. Clinging to their revolutionary ideals they were bound to be driven more and more into a corner and eventually annihilated by the State Police. The Communists could form ties only with groups in the Socialist Workers' Party. This had drawn my father's special attention, for there was Frölich, his earlier companion in Bremen, co-founder of and outcast from the Communist Party. The mere mention of such a name could reveal all the difficulties of making overtures. In many ways Frölich's position resembled the stance of the left-wing Communists, who saw the efforts at cooperation with Social Democracy as an expression of falsehood and treason. It had been thought that instead of being vanquished by the fascist takeover the proletariat had merely beaten a temporary retreat and that a revolutionary situation could still emerge, but that prevalent notion had been revised. In August of nineteen thirty-four, when the Central Committee called for the establishment of a front to combat fascism, the Social Democratic Party was still described as the mainstay of the bourgeoisie. It was only one year later, at the World Congress of the Comintern and the subsequent Brussels Conference, that new evaluations came to the fore. Now a sharp line was drawn between the right-wing leaders of Social Democracy and the masses of workers who were members. In practice, the tactic of the Popular Front and the United Socialist Front had long since been tested by Communist and Social Democratic cadres in their work in businesses, factories, and organizations. There, in the underground, mutual support had been a matter of course. For the workers the remnants of a union tradition still existed, and they could advance from fundamentally wanting cooperation to understanding that the now needed front had to encompass all levels of labor as well as progressive bourgeois circles. No single group or party could topple the fascist regime. It was made clear that the most urgent objective was to stave off the danger of war. This was the joint concern of a Popular Front made up of wide segments of the population. Such a Popular Front would not exclude the proletariat anchored in the United Front. The class hierarchy still existed, nor could even a temporary coalition obscure the need to continue the struggle against the reign of capitalism. The leading Social Democrats justified their refusal by pointing out that in the fall of nineteen thirty-five the Communist International still tied the notion of victory over fascism to the slogan of the proletarian dictatorship. Yet at every point, even during the time of the Popular Front, the goal of Communism was the classless society. Although the Communist Party now emphasized that this development did not have to emerge from a socialist revolution, the Social Democratic leaders refused to participate in negotiations, thereby clinging to the splintering of forces. Foremost for them was the future society and not the immediate necessity of the antifascist struggle. They did not wish to override the basic ideological differences in favor of a shared point of departure. The continuation of efforts toward unity demanded energy, patience, discipline, and strength of mind from the initiators. And there were several Communist functionaries who could not immediately manage to switch over to the new guidelines. Things that could emerge on the bottom would often run into doubts and protests when translated into governing principles on a higher level. The spontaneous secret overtures were to be organized and incorporated into a comprehensive policy, the directives caused tensions before a lucid pattern of action could be discerned. The labor movement, they now said, had to devise new forms and methods of struggle, new transitional stages corresponding to the realities of each country. The conspirators included Wehner, Merker, Ackermann, and other Communists along with unionists like Brass, Michaelis, Kleinspehn, Petrich, Brill, and Künstler, and we who were trying to learn something about the historical processes could not tell whether that conspiratorial front was already linked to the Popular Front as prepared by an initial committee in Paris during the summer of nineteen thirty-five. The overall tableau was dominated by the contrast between the actions determined by socialist motives and the demonstrations marked by the liberality of the left-wing bourgeoisie. Behind the former activity stood, undemanding, silent, concealed, the anonymous workers, the other activity was pushed into the limelight, subsisting entirely on the names of the participants. However, the struggle was not to be waged only sub rosa, it had to reach the general public in order to spread the message. Nevertheless the contradictory makeup of this planned fellowship was obtrusive. Down there, the activists, the practitioners of unity, who risked their lives hour by hour, isolated in their conviction, up there, unhindered, openly presenting themselves, the theoreticians, fine-tuning every word of their edicts. Once again, the entire undertaking is being carried by the workers, said my father, supposedly they are not so skilled in making formulations, yet the best appeals, with the greatest clout, always came from them during the revolutionary struggles, the strike actions, but now what counts is diplomacy, a realm from which they are traditionally excluded. Nevertheless it was significant that several leading Social Democrats had accepted the Communist Party's invitation and, by joining the committee founded by Koenen and Münzenberg, had taken a position against their own party leaders. In October nineteen thirty-five, when Dahlem, Merker, Ulbricht, Ackermann, and Wehner were assigned the operative foreign leadership of the Party, they found partners in Paris who agreed to form a Popular Front but had no power of decision. Here they tried to find out how cooperative the Social Democratic executive committee would be in its exile in Prague.

Often, in Taub's opinion, they acted rashly, under pressure. The Communist comrades always want instant results, he had said. The first goal should be to get to know one another, inform one another about intentions, about future paths. But what else should they wait for, they asked, did they not know one another well enough. There was no time to lose. Wehner said, in regard to the Prague meeting, that here at least the barrier of total inaccessibility had been slightly lifted. Perhaps, on the twenty-third of November, during the three-and-a-half-hour conversation between the Communist plenipotentiaries Ulbricht and Dahlem and the Social Democratic Party leaders Vogel and Stampfer, there was a moment of remembering the conferences of Zimmerwald and Kienthal. In such a second they could recall Liebknecht, who had sent his best wishes from prison, many of the comrades, who now belonged to two different Internationals, were in the same prisons in Germany. However, the fate of the activists could not bring about an alliance, instead there was a recurrence of vestigial bitterness. For the Social Democrats the Communists were still the splinterers, the people who had broken away from the movement, and for the Communists the leaders of the other workers' party were still the betrayers of the Revolution. The enemy remained the same, but his strength had greatly multiplied, and once again they faced him in isolated positions, the Communists urged immediate intervention, the Social Democrats looked for evasions, delays. The compromise of nineteen fifteen, nineteen sixteen, was used up, a joint condemnation of imperialism was no longer possible. The statement that an antifascist coalition as suggested by Ulbricht and Dahlem was necessary was rejected by the Social Democratic executive committee. Later statements by Vogel and Stampfer hinted at their fear that a public declaration would drive many of the sympathizers toward the right on the assumption that the Social Democrats had now gone over to the Communists. They accused the Communists of exploiting the front merely as a way of ousting the Social Democrats while they themselves tried to pull Communist workers over into their own camp. In announcing that the Communist Party was intent not on restoring democracy but on creating the prerequisites for the proletarian dictatorship, the Social Democrats were expressing the fear that in a sanctioned solidarity of interests the Communist influence might grow too strong. While the Communists demanded steps toward immediately supporting the antifascist actions inside Germany, the Social Democrats wanted to first work out a government program. They kept admonishing the Communist Party for only temporarily shelving their plans for revolution. Like the one-time advocates of the offensive theory, certain Communists, my father named Schubert and Schulte, Dengel, Leininger, and Maslowski, stuck fast to the goal of a soviet Germany and decried the rapprochement with the Social Democrats as appeasement, and when these critics were censured and threatened with expulsion from the Party, the Communists were once again rebuked by Taub and Peuke for following undemocratic procedures. As a sign of the strife between the parties the measures were named for dealing with comrades who did not go along with the change of position, they were to be singled out by the administrative machinery, and then struck and felled. Granted, the Social Democrats likewise cast out a few members, said my father, but these expulsions were not personal in the same total and definitive manner. Because, one might answer, the Social Democratic Party did not require definitive actions, because the total overhaul of society was not a crucial issue for them. The Social Democratic leaders, as was clear from the sparse information about the meetings, were more concerned about their prestige than opposing the advance of fascism. They preferred waiting, abiding in inextricable problems, to jeopardizing their earlier alliances by taking a step that could be interpreted as yielding. Even if the Front slogans of the Communists with their nonpartisan viewpoint were a tactic adjusted to a particular situation and if, after a successful fight, the ideological divorce would again come to the fore, they nevertheless had no more to lose in the alliance than their fellow participant. He too embarked on the experiment of cooperation, risking a test of strength. What guarantees can you give us, the Social Democrats asked, that after the reconquering of democratic freedoms the population itself will decide whether it wants a soviet regime or a national assembly. They simultaneously negotiated with representatives of capitalism, the grand bourgeoisie, the military, with circles that now saw their own interests endangered by a development that was growing more and more extreme, threatening to turn self-destructive, and with the help of those representatives they hoped to restore a republic of the old style. They pursued the same line that they had started with in nineteen eighteen, they did it somewhat hesitantly, but knew from the outset that they would never put up with any possibility of an alternative. In all probings the two poles, socialistic democracy and democratic socialism, stood out sharply. In the one social system, as the preliminary stage of communism, the power of the propertied classes would be eliminated and government by the people would be established, in the other social system violent revolution was out of the question, the hegemony of capitalism would gradually be superseded by way of parliamentary decision in the liberal struggle of the parties. But for two decades my father had seen what Social Democratic reformism was capable of, and any future collaboration with the bourgeoisie would be hemmed in by a limit beyond which nothing could be attained. For even if the workers were ready to take the peaceful route to social justice, the owners of the means of production would never be willing. Sooner or later the reforms would recede and turn against themselves because they preserved the existing conditions. Reactionism would supplant progressiveness, whereby the working class would be debilitated and demoralized by unfulfilled hopes, by endless waiting, and people would lose their powers of discernment. Appeals were constantly made to the patience, the readiness of the proletariat, while such reserve was always confronted by armed might. Should the workers attempt to take even the tiniest step beyond the permissible boundary should they voice their requests in a tone that was not docile, that sounded menacing, then the rulers' troops would already be lining up in front of them, and they never spared the salvos. Even if the Social Democratic leadership was moved by idealistic conviction and not bent on dissolving an ideology, one nevertheless had to ask once again why these leaders, whose party had numerous militant members, were unable to see that they were fooling themselves with their pacifism. Democratic rule, said my father, meant allowing all opinions. But what good were the demands of the working population, I asked, so long as army and police, education and mass media were in the service of the ruling classes. Political enlightenment, strengthening of the union organizations would some day, he said, shift the balance of power toward those who did the producing. The language of strikes, of unarmed means of pressure was bound to ultimately show its superiority to guns. And whenever our arguing came up against a wall, and I insisted that a flash flood of lies and slander would render any protest, any progressive action harmless, that the slightest attempt at socialist thinking would be undone by imprisonment, by liquidation, he retorted by pointing out that in their efforts toward a Popular Front the Social Democrats had to prefer joining with bourgeois-democratic forces since they regarded the Communist Party as discredited by the events in the Soviet Union. Did such a thesis, I asked myself, conceal not only personal discouragement and paralysis in regard to action. Or was the hesitation shored up by the hope of a war between Germany and the Soviet Union, a war in which both fascism and communism would bleed to death so that the Western powers could eventually step in, bringing victory not only for themselves but also for Social Democracy. And indeed, the highlighting of so-called Western values, the diplomatic activities in the capitalist centers, the constant denunciation of the Soviet Union revealed the Social Democratic design to expose Germany to an internecine war rather than to form an alliance with the Communist Party. The consequences of such thinking were inconceivable for my father. If they came true, he said, they would destroy the Party down to its very foundations. The task that the Communists kept highlighting was the fight against the imminent danger of war, but the Social Democratic executive committee could not be won over to any participation. The antifascist groups still existed in the armaments industry, the Labor Front, the air-raid protection network, the athletic clubs, the youth organizations, but the Social Democratic leaders let it be known that the working class was incapable of rising up against the dictatorship, and that any attempt at strengthening and expanding the fight was irresponsible since these efforts would merely claim new victims. The mass strikes, the coalition of the various French trade unions during spring of thirty-six, had imbued the German opposition with new confidence. If a program of action had been decided on abroad, it would have had an immediate impact on morale. Since the Social Democratic leadership clung to its hesitation, its rejection, there could be no doubt that it not only had given up activity in Germany, but was trying hard to isolate such activity and have it destroyed. Peuke likewise did not believe, said my father, in any underground activity. After leaving the Communist Party, he had joined the New Beginning group. According to Peuke's statement, it was wrong to even maintain the Communist Party in Germany in the current situation. Today any resolute Marxist had to work in a broad mass party along the lines of the British Labour Party or the French Socialist Party. Like many left-wing Social Democrats he was thereby going along with Trotsky, who rejected the idea of the Popular Front and recommended that his supporters in France disappear among the Socialists. Ultimately all these maneuvers were aimed at preventing the antifascist alliance that the Soviet Union was striving for with the Western powers. Powerlessness was emerging in regard to splintering, which, as a difference of opinions, brought no clarifying of ideological positions, rather it led to disorientation vis-à-vis the growing solidarity of the enemy. But then the Communist Party again showed its strength, for, as the only party with an organizational machinery, it pitted its staying power against the waffling and despondency of the other groupings. Starting in the summer of thirty-six, the Social Democratic leaders now really wanted to wait. First, lessons had to be learned from the Spanish Civil War. They felt that the balance in the French Popular Front was guaranteed by the policies of Blum, who knew how to push the conservative forces against the pressure of the Communist Party and to avoid any interference with the struggle of republican Spain. The volunteers may have gathered in France, but they could only sneak across the Pyrenees as individuals or in small groups. The Social Democratic camp maintained a close watch on the development in the government of the Spanish Republic. Within a short time the Communist Party had gained the leading position there. Like Blum, who waxed grandiloquent about the power of the people and protected his country's bourgeois system, the German Social Democrats joined Western efforts to ward off the emergence of a soviet Spain and to prepare a diplomacy that would enable the Spanish Social Democratic Party to conclude a future peace treaty. In their focus on their conception of a new development in Germany the word "socialism" now had the significance of a mere fossil, they stressed that the working class must never again be set off against the other classes in the country, that anything smacking of class struggle must be avoided. If the stance of the right-wing Social Democratic leaders was dictated by the decision they had long since reached to work inside the capitalist economy, one nevertheless had to ask again why the masses of workers in many countries were still following the traditional reformist ideals, the concept of peaceful evolution. This could be due only to an elementary insecurity, a fear of the disintegration of the familiar. They knew all too well the injustice, the violence inflicted on them. But the greater the oppression in daily life, the stronger the urge to cleave to the scrap they had gained over the years. They stuck to the unions as a surrogate for their own influence on society, comforting themselves with the thought that they possessed an organization that defended their minimal demands. The unions were no longer an instrument in the struggle for independence, instead they were hogtied here, kept down, diverted from their true concern. The unions had become a weapon that the rulers employed to pacify the workers. An attitude was being cultivated. The Social Democratic syndrome undermined the sense of belonging to a class, it built upon the anxieties of the union members, made their inculcated timidity constitutional, drew them into the strata of the petty bourgeoisie, where they, belonging to neither the proletariat nor the middle classes, let themselves be exploited as a reservoir for reactionary purposes. However, my father's behavior was incomprehensible. At best it could be explained by his disappointment at the development of the Communist Party. Adjusting to the Social Democratic struggle to recuperate was the furthest thing from his mind. He obstinately remained on the lower level, which was still marked by a solidarity among his fellow workers. He would never have followed those who for the sake of some minor climbing became dependent on shop stewards, foremen, and managers. He saw the way his party had separated from the interests of the working class. It was this upward thinking that gave the functionaries at work and in the Party their faces. Down on the job level the worker thought horizontally, he saw the next man, but at the very first contact with a superior the obsequiousness began, and the further he climbed, the more familiar he became with the views and notions of the higher-ups, and when, flattered by associating with them, he then brought their arguments down below, it easily happened that he appeared as their spokesman. If adhering to the Social Democratic system blocked a consistent social analysis, then, in my father's opinion, the Communist standpoint could no longer be advocated after August nineteen thirty-six at the latest. Toward the end of the second five-year plan, he said, with the triumphs of industrialization, the successful buildup of the collective economy, the First Workers' State, for all its violent measures, constituted a model for many people. When the trials then began, there were qualms. But they could no longer be talked about. The presence of repulsive things on both sides did not free us from reaching a decision as to which path offered possibilities of advancing. Passivity, pessimism were the external features of the leading Social Democrats, but in secret they recommended themselves in the administrative centers of the monopolies. The decimated Communists, anxious, distressed by the uncertainties in the Party, kept on with the work that had to be done so as not to abandon Europe entirely to fascism. Between mystical concepts, like fascist obfuscation and rapacity, and the personality cult practiced by Communism they had to mobilize their faith in socialist scientific rigor, entangled in rumors they had to stick to practical thinking, and, at the risk of being recalled or interdicted, they had to carry out the tasks that were nearest at hand. So, given this pressure, they could not be reproached for developing a hardness that might stay with them for the rest of their lives. And this hardness, this nonstop exertion were premises for continuing to negotiate with the representatives of the party, whose executive committee had prohibited the Social Democratic workers in the German firms from cooperating in any way with the Communist cadres. Prey to informers and provocateurs on not only the fascist but also the Social Democratic side, and unconditionally committed to toeing the party line, the Communist cells had to safeguard themselves doubly and triply, which at times almost crippled the domestic German efforts. Everyone in the center was forced to be prudent, yet on the outside they were supposed to work toward eliminating distrust while still trying to form a Popular Front. The Communist deputies had confronted Breitscheid, the former chairman of the Social Democratic faction in the Reichstag, Braun, the former head of the Social Democratic Party in the Saar region, and Grzesinksi, once Prussian minister of the interior, and perhaps, we told ourselves, that encounter was actually an attempt to cause an upheaval in the Social Democrats' top echelon and replace the right wing with the leftist forces. But just as the Social Democrats gathered in Paris were ruled by the elite that enjoyed the trust of the Western powers and without which the party would instantly lose its support by international finance, so too the Communist functionaries were hindered from ever moving by their own lights. A mere conversation between a Communist and a Social Democrat outside a specific body could arouse suspicions and lead to lengthy interrogations. Thus because of his personal relationship with Breitscheid, Wehner had been threatened with expulsion from the Party, and he had jeopardized himself again by meeting with my father in Paris. As was reported by comrades arriving in Prague from the Soviet Union, he now had to stand trial before the Party leadership in Moscow. Once more, the picture, which was still shadowy, conveyed this vulnerability, this tremendous uncertainty. Each person, even if the thought of him flashed through my mind for only seconds, gave an impression of utmost concentration. The feverish encounters of this time, the steady growth of the enemy's offensive weapons were bound to have an impact in our own camp as a war of nerves leading to quarrels and schisms. Often, the delegates, while traveling through the fascist-occupied country, were cut off for many weeks from the political development, they then found themselves in a different situation, which demanded a shift of tactics. To transmit a brief report, they had to take labyrinthine routes. On the basis of meager information, conspiratorial processes had to be fused into something that could be seen, identified. Perspectives were to be drafted, and the participants in the investigations were often vulnerable to the same enigmas and conjectures, the same fortuities and fallacies as we. Wehner had been in Prague several times, the go-betweens had never shown up at any of his visits, so that the accommodations failed to materialize. In the spring of thirty-five, while staying at a hotel, he was captured in a raid. Though he was equipped with papers from a hideaway in the Treptow Observatory, the best existing forgery center, the Czechoslovakian police, who were probably informed by some émigré, ferreted out his true identity, put him in solitary confinement for two weeks, then kept him in prison for another five weeks, threatened to deport him to Germany like other Communists, and finally, with no advance explanation, freighted him to Morask Ostrava (Mährisch Ostrau), where Germany, Czechoslovakia, and Poland came together, and there they handed him over to the Polish police, who transported him in a sealed railroad car to the Soviet border station in Negoreloye, where he had to spend several days in a windowless shed until the Comintern's secretariat for German affairs sent him his visa. There was always something casual about mentioning such journeys and odysseys. Weeks, months of incarceration, sometimes with no cot, blanket, or washing facility, were part of everyday life. It was normal to get your bearings blindly, to wangle every bit of information on the sly. Taking the railroad, after a lengthy absence, through the country whose citizen he had once been, the traveler would listen with sharpened ears to conversations, trying to gain a picture of fluctuations in mood, signs of fatigue and surfeit, of anger or rebelliousness. He surfaced at a gathering on the Hamburg waterfront, at a workers' meeting in the Ruhr, he joined the throng of mass assemblies, but now and then, sitting at a restaurant table or in a train compartment, as the landscape glided by outside, he could be overcome by a feeling of foreignness. These were the most threatening moments, when his mimicry became threadbare, when he forgot his false name. And while many, because of a second's carelessness, because of betrayal, may have wound up in the prisons and torture cellars, others nevertheless reached their destinations. The messengers came through the Ore Mountains every day. Comrades who had to be brought to safety were kept hidden in the forests and mountain villages, then guided on to Prague. There the Social Democratic refugees were given help, food, asylum by their party, by committees. They were tolerated here by the thousands after promising to refrain from any political activity. However, when Czechoslovakia was told to improve its relationship with Germany, Communists, tracked down by the immigration police, were intermittently deported and handed over to the German border guards. Such hints provided by infinitely complicated events had to be acted on, and yet only shadowy things could be attained, and they were promptly wiped away. It was as if there were no language as yet for this grubbing and rooting, for the hours of lying with bated breath, the slow groping forward, the searching for nameless middlemen, for encoded addresses, for the sudden confrontation with the murderer. If, as happened to Wehner, someone failed to make contact with the nearest place of the opposition, then this meant that a group had vanished from one moment to the next, and new decisions had to be made. Everyone, even if involved in a sweeping action, was on his own, thrown back on himself, and, bearing responsibility for all the others, had to, if necessary, perish alone with this responsibility. In Prague, in Paris, in specific places, specific people constantly took part in dialogues, agreements, arguments, which were also meaningful for us, who were the people helping to determine our future, how did they move, what went on in them, which spaces surrounded them, which streets. I wanted to know these things, and my father brooded over what could actually be said about the fleeting encounters in Paris a year ago and about this city, which, as he now realized, he had barely gotten to know.

My image of Paris was composed of photographs of well-known buildings, book illustrations, color prints, a few movie scenes. I could see the river before me, the bridges and quais, I could hear the echoes of praises and temptations. Paris was the metropolis of literature, of painting, of philosophy. Paris was the masses who with sticks, hoes, and crowbars stormed the smoke-shrouded Bastille, it was the triumph of hands over stony tyranny, it was the teeming of tiny people amid tremendous and towering things. Paris was the toppling of Napoleon's victory column on Place Vendôme. This was a party, over on Rue de la Paix people who had never been invited to the opera were now performing their own folksy songfest with accordions and brasses. Paris was a satirical ditty about the potentates who had fled to Versailles. The ropes of the winches were pulled to the sounds of four orchestras. The direction in which the column would fall was calculated, the notch was cut deep into its foot, the incision was made on the opposite side. Barricades had been set up all around. On May sixteenth eighteen seventy-one, at five thirty P.M., amid the clatter of the breaking bronze plates that had been cast from twelve hundred conquered cannon, the column hurtled down, lit up by the sun setting over the Tuileries. Amid the debris, in a cloud of dust, the imperator lay with his toga and laurel wreath. His swindling of the Revolution was expiated. Courbet was standing among the Communards. He wore a visored cap and a thick dark beard, he looked as if he were in disguise, ready to flee, go underground. As plenipotentiary for artistic matters, he was responsible for the demonstration that day. Anything useful to the people was to be preserved, anything exposing their humiliation was to be demolished. But, as in a film running backward, the column was already rising anew, the bronze plates spiraling up, the emperor's fragments fitting together high up into a Trajanian figure. Courbet had to pay for the restoration, five hundred thousand francs in gold, prison, garnishment, exile. Paris was that hopeful rampage, that intoxication, all-too-quickly terminated, shattered, Paris was the firing from the rifle muzzles of the defenders of wealth, it was the dying who had neglected to take possession of the Bank of France, who had been too kindhearted, too peace loving to cut the bankers' throats. Paris was the workers and artisans who were mowed down on the walls they themselves had built, it was the eleven who were shot to death, squeezed into tiny crates, with number tags on their necks, two with the number four, father and son, bloody, half-naked, or shrouded in sacks, some with open eyes, the eleven from the ranks of the twenty thousand, of the thirty thousand men, women, and children who, after the seventy-two days of a people's government, had fallen victim to the restrengthened bourgeoisie. Paris was a strolling amid the temples, obelisks, and fortified towers of might, past radiant white Sacré Coeur surmounting the hill where the cannon of the National Guards had once stood. Paris was a wretched death on the curbstone grill, in raggedy sewage-soaked clothes, Paris was an endless freedom of the imagination. In September nineteen thirty-six my father and Wehner were walking along Boulevard Raspail, under the shade of the leaves, Piscator, just returning from Moscow, had joined up with them, his face gray, his hand running over his eyes, he described the suspicions confronting the actress Carola Neher, who had fled from Germany overnight, and he described the fruitless efforts to reach her as well as other antifascists who were being questioned by the investigating authorities. The trial of Kamenev, Zinoviev, and other Bolsheviks had begun in August, and Wehner saw it as a one-time demonstration, meant as a warning, a deterrent. It would have been incompatible with his political position to articulate any doubts regarding the legality of the verdicts. And yet he had been unable to conceal his bewilderment when he then reported on Dittbender's arrest. Dittbender, a former district representative of Wilmersdorf, Berlin, a member of the board of the Red Aid, where my father had worked with him, was one of the first to be arrested in February nineteen thirty-three, during the Reichstag Fire Trial he had been hauled out of the penitentiary along with other imprisoned Communists, and had been promised his release in exchange for testifying against Dimitrov. But instead of incriminating him, Dittbender defended him, which earned him ruthless tortures. Three years later, after surviving his heavy internal injuries, he reached the Soviet Union, where he was charged with buying his freedom by promising to serve the German State Police. Dittbender, whom Dimitrov had called one of the finest members of the German working class, who had been devoted to his Communist convictions since his teens, whom nobody could reproach for cowardice, was now indicted for agreeing to conspire against the state that he had always defended. Uneasiness, inner conflict emerged during the listing of the names of those who had participated in founding and building the Party and the International and who were now accused of treason, of collaborating with the enemy. In the fall of nineteen thirty-six everyone saw the imminent danger of falling into disgrace, of being expelled, apprehended, nobody was now certain of his position, everyone was fighting for his existence in the Party, for his life, yet not knowing what he had to account for. One year later, in September of thirty-seven, they had all been drawn into the chain with no end in sight. Carola Neher had been arrested as an agent, a spy, her two-year-old son, born in Moscow, was taken away from her, Neumann, Schulte, Remmele, Kippenberger, Flieg were detained and never heard from again. One year earlier Wehner had likewise felt he was in danger, and many people prophesied that Münzenberg, who was one of the Party notables, would soon topple. Wehner had worked with him and Beimler in putting together the first squad of volunteers, who were to join the Centuria Thälmann formed in Spain and who, led by Beimler, had seen action near Huesca that autumn. My father tried to recall Wehner's qualms about the Spanish struggle. He wondered what he could repeat of his conversation with Wehner, what was not subject to the dictates of secrecy, what could be underscored for like-minded people. Wehner had drawn him into his confidence, for him too discretion had its limits when one had to gather material for understanding a situation. Everything that could be handed on despite its confidentiality was a matter of our life and death, however taciturn with the enemy, we had to know about the things that could sweep us away if we had no purchase on the overall context. The two men were close to one another, as members of different parties they had been able to count on each other. So it had been possible for them to cooperate down on the job sites, in the residential neighborhoods, on the street. But now Wehner was being questioned by the investigation commission of the Comintern. My father could not say anything that might incriminate him. I sensed that once again he was uncertain about me. For an instant he seemed to be wondering whether I had come solely to pump him. I respected him for his caution. When he then spoke, his terse, hesitant words betrayed the fact that he was hiding things from me. He held back the reasons why Wehner had insisted on being transferred to Spain. Although familiar with the difficulties, the intrigues and quarrels, which were also linked to organizing the voluntary troops, he would certainly have preferred joining the armed units to enduring the doubts and controversies that emerged in Party work. But even there perhaps, as Wehner had hinted, he would not have entered into the direct, open struggle against an identifiable enemy, instead he would again have been dragged into mistrust, slander, accusations. Marty, who had once gotten the French fleet intervening in the Black Sea to side with the Russian revolutionaries, was ordered to build up the voluntary troops in Spain and be their political leader, and whenever a German wanted to join, Marty viewed him as a spy, a saboteur and Trotskyite. It was due to his malevolence that the first German centuria was sent into battle with defective equipment and without reinforcements. Wehner had told my father something about starting the formation of the brigades, further accounts had come later. The Thälmann Centuria, called together during the July days by Schreiner at the behest of the Central Committee and assigned to the Carlos Marx Spanish workers' militia, originally consisted of some sixty men, more than half of them socialist athletes who had come to Barcelona for the counter-Olympics. In early August, Beimler, coming from Paris, likewise assembled a group. Different figures were now cited, the centuria had grown to eighty or ninety members. It was only in October that they spoke about a unified centuria containing one hundred forty-three men. The first time they saw action in Tardienta, Beimler was their political commissar, Geisen their commander, with Wille and Schindler as next in command. This counting and mulling, which was my father's characteristic way of homing in on events, now seemed influenced by Wehner's viewpoint. Wehner had talked about the inadequate preparations for fighting, the lack of munitions, rations, and orderlies. On October twenty-fourth, one month after my father's return to Warnsdorf, the heights of Santa Quiteria, which were occupied by Falangists, were stormed by the centuria. In conquering the fortified monastery, said my father, thirty-four members were killed and one hundred forty were wounded, including Commander Geisen. However, these figures too were unreliable, all in all they were only summed up in the statement that the centuria had lost over half its men. Something vague, unsettling was concealed in my father's hints. I wondered if he was trying to warn me, keep me from leaving for Spain. But his delving and reckoning clarified chiefly his own insecurity and non-belonging. I had never heard anything about a rejection of or discrimination against the Thälmann Centuria, from which the Thälmann Battalion eventually emerged, rather the centuria was famous for its courage at Tardienta, and it had been decorated with an honorary banner by the government of Catalonia. The losses were due to the inadequate military training, the improvised form of fighting during the first few months, and the absence of a centralized staff. My father spoke evasively, distractively about Spain in order to avoid touching on the real problems. During their meeting he had felt that Wehner was involved in a pitched conflict with leading Party members. And when he then lapsed into silence, he visualized the interrogations that Wehner endured. These negotiations were so confusing and nerve-wracking because one could never pinpoint where the suspicions came from. One could presume only that Münzenberg, now himself an object of investigation, had handed the commission a portion of the incriminating evidence. My father was afraid that the Party machinery had already started implementing Wehner's removal, just as Münzenberg had been robbed of his rights, his reality bit by bit. In Paris my father had had no inkling that this process was beginning. Outwardly, Münzenberg, co-founder of the Communist Party of Germany, one of the few German Communists who had been close to Lenin during his Swiss exile, still enjoyed great prestige as a propagandist and journalist, people knew only about his friction with the Party group led by Ulbricht, but no one was exempt from such disagreements about the tactics for continuing the struggle against fascism. Only now, in the fall of thirty-seven, could my father see that a revision of the Münzenberg concept was setting in, that occasional hints were changing Münzenberg's past, that his merits were being denied. Not only was his significance for the history of the Party downgraded, distorted, but his countless projects, from the construction of the International Workers' Aid for Soviet Russia and the founding of his publishing house to the Anti-Fascist Writers' Conference in Paris, the Popular Front Committee, the World Peace Movement were detached from him, robbed of his name. These things indicated the fierce and dogged determination to snuff him out. In nineteen fifteen, while working for *Volkswille* [Popular Will], the newspaper of Hungarian Social Democracy, my father had made contact with Münzenberg, who belonged to the Zimmerwald leftists. Then, while on the editorial board of *Arbeiterpolitik* [Workers' Politics] in Bremen, he corresponded with Münzenberg, who was now head of the Socialist Youth International. Later, in Berlin, my father had had dealings with him in the organization of the Workers' Aid, and for a time he also wrote for *Arbeiter Illustrierte* [Worker's Illustrated], published by Münzenberg. This newspaper, said my father, was crucial in helping to shape our opinions. Every week it supplied material for the most important debates, and it guided many of us to problems of art, literature, scholarship, science. Pictures fleshed out the discussions stimulated by the great films of Eisenstein, Pudovkin, Ekk, Vertov, brought to Germany by Münzenberg. And now, said my father, I hear that even this effort has been depreciated. Earlier, Münzenberg, who had succeeded in smashing through the bourgeois monopoly on the press and putting mass media in the service of the Party, could already be denigrated as the Red Hugenberg, and now it was claimed that he had only wanted to enrich himself and had been ordered to report to Moscow for embezzling the Comintern funds entrusted to him. In September nineteen thirty-six Wehner likewise seemed to have turned away from Münzenberg. He had made comments suggesting that he regarded Münzenberg as a bluffer. That Münzenberg had been unprincipled, had all too often changed his tactical positions. My father defended him. His refusal to be pinned down, he said, was part of his style, his journalistic exaggerations, his polemical method. He wanted to explain contemporary phenomena, and he could do so only by constantly shifting his point of view. His versatility matched the art of photomontage, promoted by him, and the experimental political cinema. The current editors of the newspaper in Prague maintained that Münzenberg had played no role in shaping the periodical, that he had, in fact, tried to prevent them from publishing Heartfield's impressive montages. The only thing Münzenberg cared about, said Wehner, was developing his personal power. Granted, he had come up with lots of ideas, but others had had to do the work. My father saw nothing wrong in this capacity of inspirer. He called it strength that Münzenberg, as a member of the Central Committee, had always appeared to be totally independent. Münzenberg was the last holdout, said my father, to favor Luxemburg's demand for open discussion in the Party. Anxious in a period when any utterance, any enterprise could arouse suspicion, he registered the fact that now it was Münzenberg's turn to be condemned, and nobody was able to stay free of such encroachments on one's neighbor even while realizing that you yourself could be the very next victim. Irrationalism overshadowed logic. Science was replaced by chimera. In traveling to Paris, my father had hoped to see Münzenberg again, but he did not manage to speak to him during the congressional session. He had not seen him since nineteen thirty-three, but had kept abreast of his activities. The calls for resistance against the anti-Soviet smear campaign, for the struggle against fascism, for support of the Chinese Revolution, for assistance to rebellious colonial nations, whom he called the damned of the earth, were all linked to his name. He had succeeded in winning over many people who were still undecided about socialism, many of the sympathizers, people in the humanistically oriented bourgeois intelligentsia, he had managed to draw them to his side and to politicize their progressive stance. His appeals were signed by all the people who gave a face to the art and literature, the stage and screen of an era, even now, as often in the conversations of those days, names associated with works resounded, people who headed the political movements, initially I wanted to push them away, who cares about these names, I thought, why should I bother with them, since all the other people, those who really matter, are not named, but then they were there again, urging themselves on me as road signs, as monuments, Brecht, Piscator, Dudow, Ihering, Jessner and Busch, Grosz, Dix, Kollwitz and Heartfield, Feuchtwanger, Döblin, Toller, Tucholsky, Ossietzky, Kisch, Becher, Seghers and Renn, Gorky, Gladkov, and Ehrenburg, Dreiser, Shaw, Sinclair, Nexö, Barbusse and Rolland, Gropius, Taut, and van der Rohe, Kerr and Jacobsohn, Pechstein, Muche, Hofer, and Klee, Einstein and Freud. And what a gathering of authorities had been invited by Münzenberg to the Hôtel Lutétia on Boulevard Raspail in September nineteen thirty-five, first fifty-one of them, then one hundred eighteen, to set up a committee, named after the hotel, for preparing the German Popular Front. The writers and journalists included Heinrich Mann, Klaus Mann, Feuchtwanger, Arnold Zweig, Toller, Leonhard, Olden, Ludwig Marcuse, and Schwarzschild, and the representatives of Social Democracy included Breitscheid and Braun, Grzesinksi and Kuttner, Schiff, Hertz, and Schifrin, who had held high-level positions in the Weimar government. By then it must have been questionable whether this heterogeneous circle of politicians and leading cultural figures could produce the leadership of a Popular Front. But at first it was seen as advantageous that leading Social Democrats sat down with Koenen, Münzenberg, Dahlem, Matern, and Abusch, the Communist envoys, that it was even possible for them to reach an oral agreement, that earlier opponents, trying to relearn, issued the joint appeal now, for the first time, an appeal that had not yet materialized within the party leaderships. Even though it was merely a general condemnation of fascism and a demand for restoring the most elementary human rights, it nevertheless revealed the need for a coalition. The tasks and goals of the committee were not yet on the agenda, and the domestic German opposition remained in the dark as to how a collaboration with it could be established. Rather than actual effectiveness, said Wehner, Münzenberg was thinking in terms of an effective charisma of the group. He envisaged a sort of intellectual counter-government consisting of celebrities, who would issue memoranda and pen exalted speeches to the survivors in the German underground. However, this noncommittal plan was incongruent with the designs of the Central Committee, which wanted to use the Lutétia group to gain influence on the bourgeois oppositional currents in the country. The Communists were accused of planning to refashion the cross-bench group into an executive organ of their Party leadership. But in contrast to the committee's Social Democratic and liberal members, who wanted to remain on the outside when dealing with the conditions inside Germany and hoped to avoid any participation in militant actions, the Communists were striving for an activation within Germany. They could only view the loose alliance with more or less progressive people as a means of getting further, reaching an accord with the Social Democratic executive board. It was only by coming to terms on a party level that they could find their way to practical cooperation. No sooner did the preparatory circle start focusing on ideas for the structure of a future government than the differences of opinion grew deeper. In appealing for help for the victims of fascism, demanding amnesty for the incarcerated, and protesting against war preparations, an agreement could be reached, but what kind of state, they asked, should some day emerge from the antifascist struggle. It was not enough to declare that peace, democracy, freedom of speech, of scholarship, of teaching, of religion should prevail. Who would exercise the power, they asked, what were the foundations of that state. In June of thirty-six, after a text was worked out by the Central Committee, the Communists spoke about a democratic republic, in which the people would freely decide on all matters of economy, policy, and culture, and the government would be elected by a universal secret and direct vote, one per person. But how broad, they asked, was the word "people," at what point would some persons be called enemies of the people, and according to what standards would the bourgeoisie be subdivided. There would be equal privileges for all those offering their services to the front against fascism. This front, assembling for their rights, would demand the nationalization of landed estates, heavy industry, and banks. The democratic republic would not yet be a socialist state, but it would bring an end to fascism and prevent any reemergence of private finance. However, the representatives of the Socialist Workers' Party rejected any cooperation with free trade-union groups and left-wing bourgeois circles. While Seydewitz switched over to the Communist line, Frölich and Wolfstein retreated. They regarded the United Socialist Front as more important than the conglomerate of the Popular Front, which would only preserve the class society. They, like Maslowski, refused to grasp that one front did not exclude the other, that the struggle to unify the working class was no less crucial than the effort to get as many segments of the population as possible to join the progressive side. But Hertz and Schwarzschild tried to blast the conferences from right-wing positions. A Popular Front with a crucial place for the Communist Party, said Hertz, might strengthen fascism, not weaken it. On the outside, Hertz, together with Hilferding and Ollenhauer, began calling for the liquidation of the Communist Parties in Europe, and their appeal was supported by Schwarzschild in his *Neues Tagebuch* [New Journal]. A tremendous readjustment, a tremendous effort to overcome earlier mistakes were demanded of the people attending the meetings, and the huge extent of those expectations was shown when Communists sat across from Social Democrats, who once, as high government officials, had given orders to shoot them, had declared martial law against them, and had banned their combat units, party organizations, and newspapers. Extreme self-control and insight into historical necessities were the premises for creating this coalition, it showed the rallying power of a party that was free of resentment and stronger than the combined abilities of all individuals. Hard as it was for the Communist functionaries who were acting on behalf of their party, it was harder still for Breitscheid, Braun, Kuttner, Grzesinski to sign the committee's declarations, thereby opposing the rejection by the party's executive board. But how long, I wondered, might their signatures remain valid and what impact would they have on the cells in the German underground. I could see Coppi's family before me, in the green kitchen, reading the leaflet that Grzesinski had helped to write, Grzesinski, who as Prussian minister of the interior had been responsible for the homicide committed by Zörgiebel, his police commissioner, on the First of May nineteen twenty-nine, the murder of the workers of Wedding. That date had also been meaningful for me. According to my only indirect memory of the Bremen uprising, the street fighting around Nettelbeckplatz had spurred me to take my first political position. We were living on Brunnenstrasse, and when the events occurred, they did not yet

penetrate my consciousness sharply, I did not comprehend the full scope until two years later, when, as a thirteen-year-old, residing now on Pflugstrasse, I read Neukrantz's book, *Barricades in Wedding*. Earlier I had heard about other people, I had listened to my parents' accounts, but now I spent days in tremendous agitation, in a fury that became conviction. Here a book described a street, it was Kösliner Strasse, which, short, narrow, cut off by Wiesenstrasse, resembled our own abutted street, a book described how human strength had risen up against mechanized violence and had managed to hold out for a few days behind piles of stones, without weapons, barraged by machine guns, sharpshooters, armored cars. As I read about how the bourgeoisie had smashed the proletariat's right to demonstrate on the First of May, the brutality took my breath away. The crudely plastered bullet holes in the building walls along Kösliner Strasse could still be seen. Here the red flags always waved densely from the windows. There had been resoluteness and rebellion on our street too. On weekends, when, coming home from the Scharfenberg School, I walked along Pflugstrasse, I would always imagine the possibility of new fighting. Initially by instinct, then bolstered by theoretical insights, I started to grasp the mechanism that was cornering us more and more, that wanted to rob us of our voices, and that on the First of May nineteen twenty-nine had led to a discharge that could only be a priming for further, more violent blows. I saw the contradiction between the Social Democracy's alleged loyalty to the constitution, the workers' hope of achieving liberation in the existing system, and the building of the fortress from which the attacks could be mounted against the working class. I remembered running to and fro in the kitchen, in this kitchen, where the soot from the train station seeped in through the window cracks, where, if we had to keep the windows open in the summer, the floor and the table were coated within the hour by a layer of black dust, and I remembered wondering how my parents could still see their party as a guarantee for improving their situation, for transforming the means of production. Why hadn't the workers in May nineteen twenty-nine finally shattered the rotary presses of the newspapers that insulted them daily, not only the bourgeois gazettes but also the Social Democratic ones, which spewed out all those lies, claiming that the workers themselves had caused the butchery by challenging the police, why did they merely curse and keep going to the plant, why did they give in, knuckle under, and now, in Warnsdorf, my father repeated his earlier response, saying we had no choice, we had to work in order to pay the rent, buy our daily grub. What good did it do that in nineteen thirty-six Breitscheid was trying to bring about a united action with the Communists, that he approved of the Soviet policy for establishing European security, that Grzesinksi and Kuttner wanted to repudiate their earlier measures, what use was it if their party leadership stuck to the alliance with the forces that would always oppose the interests of the working class. The rejection of a common front in the German underground merely showed the last phase of decades of obstruction. It was now the Communist Party that was pushing for an agreement, just as at the start of the nineteen thirties it had called for unity, even though its goal had been hazy and it had not distinguished sharply enough between the Social Democratic leadership and the masses of party members. In nineteen twenty-nine, when the National Socialists still had few seats in parliament, the Communist Party may have failed to calculate the rapid progress of fascism, but it nevertheless kept urging a proletarian solidarity as resistance, while the Social Democratic central committee with its supposed liberalism offered its services to the bourgeoisie, and, in courting the votes of the middle classes, it accepted any use of violence against the revolution-minded workers. Though some Social Democratic leaders may have been against this policy, they did not extricate themselves from their contract with the power-wielders in business and in the army, when taking office they had to distinguish themselves through a special rapport with patriotic traditions. And yet, my father told Wehner, he did not really understand what Münzenberg was being charged with. Münzenberg had succeeded in establishing friendly relations with high-level functionaries in the labor unions and the Social Democratic Party and setting up the conditions to start creating a Popular Front, he had achieved what Communist policies were basically striving for, and he had supplied a spectacular framework for this rapprochement in order to gain wide attention. Hadn't Münzenberg, asked my father, pointed out the significance attached to the committee by the name Lutétia. Hints, charades, concealed mockery were part of Münzenberg's work method, so that Lutétia was not only the name of the city of Paris during the Roman period, the Celtic water dwelling on the Île de la Cité in the Seine, it was also the title of Heine's Paris journal, in which he committed himself to communism. This was one of Münzenberg's favorite books, it may have dealt with the years eighteen forty to eighteen forty-three, as the author wrote in his preface to the French edition, but it was to be viewed as a primer for the outbreak of the February Revolution in eighteen forty-eight. If the participants at the hotel, said my father, had read the introduction to this work, then Münzenberg's plan would have been clear, which, of course, might have discouraged some of them from joining the committee. Under the sign of Lutétia, bourgeois freethinkers had linked up with Communists, and the poet Heinrich Heine, whom they venerated, gave them a lesson about who the real hero of the moment was, the Social Movement. Gathering with the best intentions, these people, had they pricked up their ears, would have heard what Heine had to tell them, primarily about the mendacious farce of parliamentarism and its supernumeraries, and about the only doctrine capable of shaking the power of high finance, the idea of communism. And my father went over to the hutch, opened the upper glass door, and removed one of the books kept on the shelf. It was the burgundy-colored volume number thirteen through fifteen of Heine's works, put out by the Bong publishing house. He opened the marked page and read aloud, conveying how Heine with the self-irony that was also characteristic of Münzenberg segued into the epoch in which the dark iconoclasts, the Communists, would come to power, smash all the marble statues of beauty, shatter all the frippery of art, chop down the poet's laurel groves, plant potatoes there, and use the pages of his books of poems to make bags for coffee and snuff. Ah, Heine had exclaimed, I foresee all this, and I am overcome with unspeakable sadness when I think of the doom with which the victorious proletariat menaces my verses, which will sink into the grave with the rest of the romantic world. My father said he could imagine Münzenberg's laughter when he thought about the meaning he had given to the assembly of late-bourgeois intellectuals at the Hôtel Lutétia. However, there was nothing to be felt of such gaiety when Münzenberg in September of that year invited Wehner and Dahlem over, shortly before leaving for Moscow, to read to them a study that he was planning to submit to the Comintern. Katz, who had collaborated on the text, and who had also coauthored the *Brown Book on the Reichstag Fire*

Trial, did not join the conversation. Münzenberg was intent on getting to know the comrades' reactions, their judgments, he was tense, nervous, anxious about his imminent visit to the executive committee of the International, he, who had usually been superior, self-confident, appeared unsure of himself, he must have gotten warnings, he wondered if he should not put off his trip, citing his urgent activities on behalf of Spain. It was not obvious who was flimflamming whom, who was playing whom off against whom. Katz may have already withdrawn from Münzenberg, trying to cover his losses, waiting for the results of the confrontations in Moscow, Wehner and Dahlem were cool, reserved, they already viewed Münzenberg as a turncoat. Nor did Wehner feel any sympathy with Katz. When my father now thought back to those days, it struck him that he had found fault with Wehner's arrogance and vanity. Katz had been a member of the Communist Party since nineteen twenty-seven, had worked as Piscator's administrative director for a time, had then been active in the Soviet film industry, was known as an extreme hardliner and was something of a spendthrift, which had repelled Wehner, who was accustomed to the Spartan lifestyle of the underground. He felt queasy about Katz with his puzzling character, although Katz's abilities were respected Wehner saw him as a snob who claimed to be the spokesman for the proletariat and whom Wehner, who came from a working-class background, had to watch out for. However, Wehner added, given our camouflaged existence nowadays, such an impression could be unjustified and would have to be attributed to the overall atmosphere of distrust and irritability. My father again wondered what could really be retained of his conversation with Wehner. He had caught only meager, wary hints. They had met at the headquarters of the Peace Committee. The declarations aimed at the public had been issued the previous week, at the great congress in Brussels, now only plenary sessions were being held. The delegates from the parties and unions withdrew into committee meetings. In Brussels, the major issues, the antifascist struggle, the Spanish Civil War, had been avoided. All they wanted to emphasize was the role of the League of Nations in preserving world peace. After the Soviet Union had failed to recruit the Western powers for an alliance against fascism, the goal in Geneva now was to win support for the Soviet policies. But in Paris, instead of debates on common interests, more intense disagreements emerged between the factions. The Communist delegation was accused of trying to gain control of the congress and furthering Party politics instead of working toward a Popular Front. My father, being an unknown union representative from Czechoslovakia, remained in the background of the hectic goings-on. He was not allowed to attend Münzenberg's report to party leaders and parliamentarians. He then only saw Münzenberg vanishing in the hurly-burly of French and English diplomats. And where did he get a chance to speak to Wehner, I asked. My father was at the mercy of an overwhelming Paris, and this was in the governmental cauldron of the city, here between the Chamber of Deputies, the Ministries of Foreign Affairs, Army, Industry, Labor, Education, the métro dragged him back and forth between his hotel at Gare de l'Est and the Invalides station, always beneath the Place de la Concorde, the Champs Élysées, the Tuileries, he did not see Notre Dame, or, as he had always wanted to, the Louvre, every evening and morning he saw only the Eiffel Tower, though never riding up to its improbable top. However, there was a tiny park in the midst of this intensifying activity, he remembered that its name was Square Rousseau, Samuel, not Jean-Jacques, right before the pseudo-Gothic church of St. Clotilde on Rue Casimir Périer, where the guests from abroad were offered the house of the Swedish banker Aschberg with the rooms of the Cercles des nations. Coming from a meeting there, my father and Wehner had walked toward the Ministry of the Army and stepped into the park garden, into this eye of silence in the middle of the hurricane, and their sitting here on a bench, that was at least something tangible, I could picture the bushes, the pigeons, the surrounding buildings, the conversation itself was barely concrete. What my father learned was already filtered, and what he told me was a faint echo. Münzenberg had written a paper on a strategy for crushing German fascism, but today, one year later, given the vastly altered conditions, that was no longer a secret. However, my father was likewise unfamiliar with the contents of the piece, which Münzenberg, a blusterer according to Wehner, presented as his credo and as a model and guideline on which the Communist International and the Soviet Politburo should take a position. Wehner only said that Münzenberg had not managed to come up with a true analysis of the German situation, he had, said Wehner, sidestepped the existing problems and conflicts, blaming the triumph of National Socialism chiefly on its propaganda, agitation, and mythology, and demanding a greater amount of enlightenment. The Party refused to acknowledge the importance of fascist demagoguery. As usual, said Wehner, Münzenberg was merely trying to show off in his own field. He was sticking to the exterior, Wehner went on, he had erected a dazzling façade in which the German émigrés could be self-complacently reflected. Katz had repelled him with his elegance, his dexterity, and likewise it had been Münzenberg's claim of infallibility to which Wehner had to close his mind. Where did Wehner stand, my father had wondered, as Wehner, still casually waving, had vanished around a corner. He could no longer, my father mused, concur with the policies of the Central Committee, if anything happened to him the likely reason was that he was making too great an effort to compromise with the Social Democratic functionaries, that he refused to allow the sharp lines to be drawn. But then why did he oppose Münzenberg, my father wondered, since Münzenberg was pursuing the same goal as Wehner. Münzenberg had not been allowed to see the Soviet Party leadership. When, immediately upon arriving in Moscow, he tried to see Radek, he learned that the latter, together with Piatakov, Sokolnikov, and Muralov, had been arrested. Instead of being allowed to read and explicate his memorandum in the Comintern, he was ordered to appear before the International Control Commission, where, they said, he would be prepared to be tried for circulating internal Party information, lack of revolutionary attentiveness, ideological deviation, and oppositional impulses. From the comrades who had reported on Wehner's whereabouts, my father learned that Togliatti, who was now representing Dimitrov in the International, had succeeded in obtaining Münzenberg's release. After the Soviet arms deliveries to the Spanish Communist Party were announced on October fifteenth, Togliatti could confirm that Münzenberg's presence in Paris was indispensable. But Münzenberg was no longer empowered to continue helping Spain. A Czechoslovakian functionary named Smeral took over his duties. Now, in September of thirty-seven, the Party initiated the procedure to oust Münzenberg. And who, I asked, is left of the Lutétia circle? No one, said my father. The group's last united appeal had been published in December of thirty-six with a strong Communist representation by Florin, Dahlem, Merker, Ackermann, Dengel, Koenen, Ulbricht, and Pieck, then one Social Democrat after another dropped out, until May of thirty-seven, when Braun and Breitscheid resigned after accusing the Communists of trying to take things into their own hands and monopolizing the committee, which was now on the verge of disbanding. At the actions for Spain, occasional joint speeches of solidarity were given, but just as the Social Democratic executive board took no stand on the Spanish struggle, it likewise uttered nothing about the further development of a German Popular Front. Wels expressed the position of the party leaders most unequivocally when he asserted that the fascist dictatorship could be wiped out only by an opposition within the Wehrmacht and within German commerce and industry, and that he desired a conservative military regime as a transitional stage. Thus, Noske's voice could again be heard. Münzenberg, maintaining his Communist convictions but torn from the field of Party activity, joined the leftist bourgeois liberal German Freedom Party, which was formed in Paris at the start of nineteen thirty-seven. It was to continue the Lutétia front without ideological watch-words or partisan politics and bring that front to Germany by a conspiratorial route. With its idealistic humanistic stance and its effort to rebuild a constitutional state, this party had the practical goal of making contact with antifascist circles in the army and the business world. Sending out its freedom letters addressed to the so-called decent Germans, this organization had its limits, which could not fit in with Münzenberg's modus operandi, yet it was on the side of the fighters and it lost some of its members to concentration camps and execution sites. As for Wehner, my father believed that this man, who had spent years deploying his abilities in the underground, would stand firm against the interrogations he now had to endure. Dimitrov and Manuilski were favorably inclined toward him, furthermore he had a knack for spending months stubbornly advocating a viewpoint while maintaining a vast overview. I noticed how deeply afflicted my father was by all these arduous efforts and sacrifices for a cause, how affected he was by the knowledge of these sufferings in which personal tragedy was subordinated to higher ends, and how unnerved he was by the thought that, after a quarter century of political labor, all actions may have been useless and that he no longer had the strength to start all over again. I accompanied him to the factory, Fröhlich's Textile Prints, located on the Mandau, the feeble stream that crossed the town and trickled toward the Görlitz Neisse River, and we discussed my imminent trip to Spain, thereby restoring our old rapport. Despite the dangers awaiting me, he preferred my resolution to my obligation to report for military service in Trencin, my official place of residence in Slovakia. He was certain, he said, and a red leaf dropped upon him from the acacias along the shore, that if he were younger, he would be in the brigade, on the main front, where they were now fighting for a verdict.

Before the Spain Committee in Prague notified me that Hodann was expecting me at the Cueva la Potita Hospital near Albacete, I spent a few days in a state of mind that had already developed in Berlin during the final hours in our apartment. I waited, and this waiting was neither calm nor idle. If, sitting on the floor of the kitchen on Pflugstrasse, I was absorbed in a kind of hermitage, a contemplation, it was because everything that had gathered inside me was overpowering, demanding an examination, a clarification. Everything that had been thrashed out since our encounter with the Pergamum Altar concentrated into a basic image, a thesis, a way of living, from which my impending steps derived. Now, one week later, I still knew nothing about my tasks in Spain, all that lay ahead of me were the trip to Perpignan, a border crossing that was called illegal but that we associated with supreme lawfulness, and a trek to Figueras, where, upon arriving, I would belong to the organizational machinery that would decide my further actions. My anticipation of the future was built on a foundation created by constant anonymous cooperation. Like my kin, my friends, I had long since been involved in this secret priming for actions that would change our situation. Thus my activity, paltry, infinitesimal in the gigantic network of forces, led me from the underground into the stage of national war, which the class struggle had now entered. Here, in a secluded Warnsdorf, I was already mentally participating in the armed conflict. The enemy had to be defeated before the development imagined by us could be realized. The motive force behind this focus had been an incessant hatred, a hatred of greed and selfishness, of exploitation, subjugation, and torture. At first, this hatred had expressed itself subjectively, it had targeted a diffused and total superior force, a society that wanted to prevent us from studying, from advancing. Later, after we achieved political understanding, our hatred grew more intense, we began purposefully fighting those who tried to hold us down, annihilate us. We were guided by a cold, homicidal repulsion. Very seldom did we find this sensation articulated in art, in literature, rudiments surfaced in pictures by Grosz and Dix, Heartfield's collages came closest to it, we then found it clear-cut in Lenin's April Theses. For us fascism contained all that was inimical. Whatever we learned in daily work, in social life, in our investigations of painting and writing, of science and scholarship, it was drawn into the chief task of overcoming the enemy world. Every theme that we assigned ourselves, every project actualized the clash between rapacity, monstrous destructivity, and the scale of values that gave meaning to our lives. At times the hatred was suffocating in its overpressure, it wanted to burn itself up when faced with the gigantic power of those who, plundering and murdering, wanted to pull the world to its doom. There were periods when all reason abandoned me, when there was nothing but the hammering in my temples, when my brains were made of lead, and only rage, blind fury could be mobilized against the forces that were thoroughly obliterating us. But then another impetus broke through, our integrity was at stake, our ability to hold our ground. Tied to the wish for achieving a fundamental transformation, for building a new existence was the sense of togetherness with the country that had toppled the rule of capitalism and established the power of the workers. Our indignation and rebellion would have been hopeless if that country had not spelled something indestructible for us, something that had to withstand all insult, all malevolence, all anxiety. Out of our own despair, we understood that fits of derangement, of frenzy could occur there too. We approved of the intolerance that was deployed there. There could be no waiting-and-seeing. A reconciliation, a compromise were unthinkable. While people might speak of aberrations, blunders, panic, we felt that any hitting, any violence were justified. The country stood alone, just as we stood alone, and in standing alone we were bound to one another. This bonding offered the only conceivable endurance, and this endurance contained the unique and thrilling images of October. No doubts, no qualms could dim these images. They overrode everything, wiped away everything aimed at plunging us into darkness. They prompted each of our actions, each of our references, those that were marked by emotions and dreams as well as those that were precisely weighed, calculated, constructive. It was this main thought, this maxim that lent a rationality to fleeting things, things that seemed inexplicable, and this reasonableness was a feature that enabled us to get through the period of tribulations. We therefore never got rid of the skepticism, the uncertainty that might overcome us, anything dubious merely impelled us to initiate new attempts at explanations, and if something we recognized was outmoded, then we went on to new interpretations. Despite the certainty and unanimity that we had given it, the thesis of our choice was composed of many things, it had developed in a process of assertions and counterarguments, of assumptions, findings, and conclusions. The fight against fascism, the solidarity with the Soviet state, these were the absolute necessities resulting from our experiences. Like Coppi and Heilman and countless others who remained in their places, I too was ready to carry out any orders I received in Spain, and since this was correct, conceivable, tenable for us, these days that suddenly emerged without responsibilities did not become untenable. Again they conveyed the assurance that we were inside a totality, that nothing could guide us but that which we had justified ourselves. It had often happened to me that our consciousness, that every concentration on a specific field of interest ran into things that were connected, that were vital at that very point. Our consciousness guided us to books and pictures, it triggered conversations for which we had become ready only at this moment. This too showed in what universality we were at home, nothing took shape if its premises had not yet been created, we recognized the things already preformed in us, and we incessantly relied on the totality for our subject matter, storing it, enriching it, often unawares, until it became perceptible, concrete. The sensation of hatred always hovered nearby, for the openness that was intrinsic to us, acting as the basis of our autonomy, was to be ground down, and how many had already fallen by the wayside, so utterly destroyed that they did not even recognize the disfigurements to which they fell victim, this had been described in very sharp detail by someone whose work, *The Castle*, I found in the bookshop on Market Square. But before I opened it, began reading it, purchased it, and took it along, I perused another volume, which the proprietor brought over, it contained color reproductions of Brueghel's paintings, a volume published by Schroll and meant for people who were safe and settled, not for travelers with light baggage. He placed the wide-format book on a standing desk, and the small town of Warnsdorf in an autumnal Bohemia melted into the Flemish landscapes of the sixteenth century, just as during the next few days, when I read Kafka, the hamlet and the castle he depicted belonged to the dismal, petty bourgeois rustic isolation of my surroundings. Brueghel and Kafka had painted world landscapes, thin, transparent, yet in earth tones, their images were both shiny and dark, they seemed massive, heavy on the whole, glowing, overly distinct in their minutiae. Their realism was placed in villages and regions that were instantly recognizable yet eluded anything previously seen, everything was full of the sensibility, full of the gestures, feelings, actions of everyday life, everything was typical, demonstrating important, central things, only to seem exotic, bizarre at the very same moment. Through the bookshop window one could see the stands of the produce vendors and the poultry dealers, one could hear the rolling of wagon wheels on the cobblestones, the people, in hard contours, stood alone, in groups on the bluish-gray pavement of the square or in front of the brownish, reddish façades of the houses, they moved around one another, dressed darkly, the women in lots of black and umbra, the men clayey, leathery, bright spots among them, the green, the white of a kerchief, the red and yellow in a child's frock, and the distances they covered resembled a ceremonial, a solemnly measured obeisance. I took in this circling around one another, this passing, but it was no playacting, it was reality, it served specific ends, the search for food, the hawking of wares, assessing and selecting, buying and selling, there was nothing special about this hustle and bustle, these noises and voices, they were the same on every market day, but the ritual with its rattling and jingling, rumbling and scraping turned into a different, an exemplary and didactic procession, the struggle between Carnival and Lent. The shreds of a marching song, the stamping-by of feet were the final racket, the processions that followed, led by clappers and bagpipes, fifes and drums, were soundless, only the memory of the resonance persisted, only the colors and figurations were hallucinatory. Draped in brown cowls the heavy shapes trudged up the street, past stakes and dancers, and they poured from the side exit of the church, several wearing three-legged pews on their heads. With prayer books and rosaries, bent over, castigating themselves with clusters of leaves, the penitents slogged toward the revelers, children followed the groups everywhere, they belonged to the ranks of their fathers and mothers, breaking out here and there, forming their own mummers' parade, scuffling with one another, whipping tops, but they were always hauled back to do as they were told, in a semicircle, twisting rattles like prayer mills, behind the emaciated crone, who, sporting a beehive on her head and rolling along on her dray, led the sanctimonious throng, disguised in the other, masked, accompanying the procession of Prince Carnival riding a barrel, amid the gorgers and guzzlers streaming out from the Blue Ship Tavern. The crippled beggars, hopping after them on crutches and rummaging for the crumbs of bread and cake like the swine at the well, got nothing from the merrymakers. It was only on the other side, from the people who had to practice mercy, that the beggars extorted a few alms by flaunting their rags, their illness and blindness, their leg stumps and handless arms, their careworn babies wailing in baskets and their dying people drawn along in plank carts. Nor was much to be expected here, the people in noble garb were marked by avarice, the thin pretzels, the dry patties, the scrawny herrings on the old hag's battledore were meant to feed them during the castigation, they concealed the loaves of bread under their gorgets, and the jugs of wine that they had filled at the Sign of the Dragon were empty. It was all ruled by a shabby dream of greediness. Eggs from the market stand lay smashed next to gnawed bones and thrown-away playing cards, wooden ladles were admonishingly stirred in empty pots or tucked into caps and belts, waiting for meals that would never come, pewter mugs rotated on sticks, knives were sharpened on metal scraps, dangled from bellies and between thighs, sliced through rolls and, up front, at the bow of the carnival cask, obscenely skewered the epitome of all gluttony, a flat, smoked ham. The women at the draw well had only meager wares to peddle, a basket of cabbages, a couple of fish for the fasters, and the adjacent peasant woman, at the brushwood heap, was frying a last crepe for the tired participants of the final feast, and yet for the paupers, for male and female farmhands, drifters and wandering buskers, this tiny morsel became a vision. Here, in the middle of the marketplace, encompassed by the closing circle of the parade, something, fat or lean, could be obtained for money and was demanded by customers, otherwise the commerce paid no heed to what was happening all about. And in the middle of the painting, scornfully turning their backs to the viewer, a middle-class couple was walking, he under a gigantic hat, she with a farmyard lantern swinging on her behind, and their clothes were stuffed to the hilt, they had planned ahead. There was no trace of pleasure or conviviality in the paintings that depicted folk-life. The farm laborers, the draymen and porters, the woodcutters and cattle whackers, the craftsmen and peasants, they all were often stamped with an almost stupid dullness, whether cutting switches from the willow trees under a stormy sky or building the tremendous structure of the Tower of Babel around the rocky peaks, whether leading Jesus to the crucifixion or dancing a round at the kermis, they always remained trapped in their unchangeable fate. The expression of intoxication was indistinguishable from that of pain. There was only the gaping mouth, never laughter. No plow halted for a living person, said the bookseller, pointing to the skull of the old man who, stretched out, barely visible, lay under the bushes at the edge of the field being plowed by the peasant, and the shepherd boy, leaning on his staff by the sheep, gazed up into the empty sky, from which Icarus, unnoticed by anyone, had fallen. The inwoven motif of the proverb focused on the unshakability of earthly labor, but it also captured its heaviness and bleakness, what was done was done under the yoke, there was no such thing as renewal, distant, tiny, incidental, the son of Daedalus, the wax having melted from his wings, splashed into the ocean, only his kicking legs could still be seen, the waves would close over them right away. The eyes that saw such things were pitiless, unerring, I imagined the painter's squinting eyes, his clenched lips, he rendered exactly what was happening, he could find no relief, no help. And then the peaceful hamlet spread before me, with bare trees, snowy roofs, a frozen brook. Someone came, in iron armor, riding across the bridge, accompanied by his squire, a petrified woman stood at her front door, her hands clamped together, a soldier was dashing away with her baby. From this vanishing point the event widened into mass murder, the armed cavalry stood crowded together, blocking the way for each fleer, on the sides the lansquenets stormed the houses, in dreadful graphicness the children were torn from their parents, dragged away by a shirttail, an arm, run through by swords, by spears, and aghast parents crouched over the corpses. The hamlet, a self-contained place of the ordinary and traditional if seen from afar, became the site of nameless despair when the viewer drew closer. The choreographic pattern, occupied by the figures and rhythmically interspersed with the red jackets and trousers of the Walloon killers and with the leaps of the dogs, made the terror inescapable. The things occurring between the villagers and the mercenaries, who were their own kind, who were merely, as usual, carrying out their superiors' orders, were unbearable, and yet in their lasting gesticulation of horror, of cold slaughter they were stamped forever in the iconic white surface. This ambush in a supposed shelter, this sudden irruption by the unimaginable had also become something permanent in the tale of the land surveyor. Here there was no thought of a realm in which the individual will had any power. The village to which the surveyor came was the home of those who questioned nothing. Even though the Castle was visible with its flat, far-stretching buildings, its round, ivy-shrouded turrets, its swarms of crows, it was nevertheless situated utterly beyond any possibility of approach. The agonizing thing was that this separation was determined from the very start, that nobody wondered why the law of inaccessibility had to apply to the Castle. All the people living down here in the hamlet, even the surveyor, a newcomer, put up with the forced gap between their world and the world of the lords and masters, accepted it as an absolute. During the days on which I read the book, in the Lausitz Mountains and on the Schöber Line, a pass that, fortified with bunkers, constituted the border, I got to know my own traits and features and those of my people, characteristics that I had previously kept at arm's length or had dealt with only casually. The surveyor spoke about his being a worker, about his being a subordinate, he based it on his contractual arrangement with the Castle, he had no interest in moving up, in gaining something outside his class, he only wanted to be recognized in his work. Rather than bucking the system that made him a servant and the employer an autocrat, he simply wanted to be appreciated as what he was, an attitude recalling how greatly people like us were always under the duress of frugality and how many people there are who, for self-preservation and with no approval, actually defended the situation they were in. Often, fearing that protesting, rebelling, striking would cost them their jobs, they said they ought to be grateful for the work given them by the owner of the plant, the workshop, their entire consciousness was shaped by the fact that they could never cope with the greater force, that they always had to be below, trodden, knuckling under, that there was no justice for them, only a kick for acting up. We condemned the resignation to such a state of affairs, but there had been little we could do to repudiate it. Our superiors and also the Castle let it be known that they wanted satisfied workers. But in no way did they advocate oppression, rather they practiced supreme justice, though beyond our influence. A heavy responsibility lay on the authorities, they were incessantly given to pondering in order to keep the economy of the village going. And when I thought about the wretched living conditions of workers during the two decades of my growing-up, then life in the miserable dwellings that the villagers made the best of was even more undisturbed than in the cities. Only the resignation that we repeatedly broke through was absolute here. Since the poverty, the humiliation were even greater for us than here, amid the eternal petitioners and laborers, the whole, seemingly incredible prostration had to strike us too and perhaps even more powerfully than in the village. The coercion to work at the mercy of this system, to perform labor that was far below our abilities, characterized the lifestyle in the village as well as our own experiences. Not only I myself, my parents, Coppi's parents, but also all the people next to whom I had worked in various jobs, were constantly exposed to this degradation. But since production offered them nothing but the chance to perform a few minor flicks of the wrist, they had to deny their qualifications from dawn till dusk while sinking deeper and deeper into torpor and apathy. This state of defeat, together with the widespread illusion that our subsistence was a matter of grace, formed the basis of Kafka's book, and it unnerved, oppressed the reader because it actualized the full range of our problems. We could cite our political measures, we could talk about perspectives that would lead us out of captivity, and yet we felt the same constriction as the surveyor. We could reproach the author of the book for not more clearly specifying who lived in this Castle, who it was who cultivated his perfection there, we could criticize him for shrouding our rulers in a mystical, almost religious darkness, for not exposing the interior of the Castle or showing the preparations for its fall, but these objections, which, as I now recalled, I had heard earlier, were meaningless, for the principle described by the writer was sufficiently insightful, and the consistency in the manner of depiction evoked an even stronger mental involvement. The Castle was shabby, after all, brittle, old-fashioned, there was nothing imposing about it, there were no fortifications, it could have easily been taken, and the officials, if they ever appeared, were frail, feeble, woebegone people. That was how the structure of capitalism had shown itself to us, as on the verge of collapse, bizarre and despicable, and yet it remained erect, doling out its mean little strokes, its frauds, its nasty tricks, keeping us at bay with its unreliable messengers, customs officers, and sentries. In the debate on realism, Kafka had been written off as decadent. But his detractors had thus closed themselves off to his intensified image of reality, in which the lack of rebellion, the sedulous circling around trivia, the dreadful absence of insights confronted us with the question of why we ourselves had still not taken action to eliminate the deplorable state of affairs once and for all. What I read in Kafka's book did not leave me hopeless, it made me feel ashamed. I had often enough faced one of the engineers or overseers at Alfa Laval, just as was the case between the Castle envoy and a villager in Kafka's spaces, and at such moments the same artificially veiled gap opened between us. I remembered the glib friendliness displayed by the inspector, though it was also obvious that he did not see me, that I did not even exist for him, making his morning rounds of the assembly hall he was well rested, well fed, freshly bathed, while we, after four hours of assembling cream separators, were sweaty and weary. Glancing around, nodding our way, exchanging a few words with the foreman, he made it clear to us, with not a single one of us waxing indignant, that it was the shareholders who provided our work, and so we were unexpectedly reconciled and may even have felt praised and honored because the inspector had brought us closer to the factory management and for an instant we felt safe from dismissal to the poorhouse. It was always touch and go whether the decision makers still found us acceptable, nor could the unions offer any security during the crisis years, the middlemen of the higher consortia always said well-meaning things about the reforms and rights we gained, but these achievements were wiped away with a casual, deferring hand if they did not suit them. It was this definitive gap in power and privilege that was expressed in Kafka's book. We had constantly put up with the way our principals sat so high above us that we never set eyes on them, the thought of visiting them in their shells, simply opening the doors to their offices, standing in front of them, speaking our mind was as unthinkable for us as the road to the Castle was for the surveyor. The ruler's least messenger was worth more than we, nothing ruffled him, he could strut in front of us, take any liberty. It was entirely consistent with the events around us that the commanders stayed hidden in their regions, that their diligence grew into a chiming, a singing, a roaring just as the surveyor heard when he, worn out, worn down, picked up the receiver in order to place a call to the Castle. And naturally, what he heard gave him no information about the machinations up there, he merely got the impression that something important, momentous was happening, tremendous, worldwide doings, which we, as tiny components of the machinery, had to serve. That was how the voice of imperialism sounded to the person who had previously been too weak to obtain knowledge about the dynamics of the economic processes. But even if we gained understanding, we remained equally far from this humming though participating in it as stokers, mechanics, luggers, cart pushers, all we possessed as a result of our self-education was a power that the surveyor's village had not yet discovered, the power to go on strike. Nor could Kafka be faulted for not pointing this out, for we had been all too timid about using even the weapon of work stoppage, and, upon resolving to go ahead with it, we had constantly returned to the old invariable high-spirited singing that had faded only temporarily in our insignificant circle but had continued elsewhere merely all the louder. The deeper I got into this book, the more it touched upon the world we lived in. After all, it dealt not only with our lack of connection to work but with our entire relationship to the ubiquitously active establishment. We could have no impact on the plans of the concerns and monopolies, and likewise we had realized that the transactions of exchanging goods had grown more brutal, that exploitation had been joined by homicidal robbery, even in our political cells we were still closer to the village's ignorance than to the state of knowledge promised us by social science. Never had my parents, my friends been able to choose their places themselves, we had to let ourselves be moved willy-nilly, glad just to have a place at all. I could see my mother, sitting crooked on the sofa, her hips, her back rheumatic after years of standing on the stone floor of the factory, I could see Coppi's mother, her swollen feet in the basin of water, I could see my father in the steam of the textile plant, see him in the kitchen in Warnsdorf, with a bare torso, scrubbing away the red, bluish-violet spots left by the block printing, just like the evenings in Bremen, when he had cleansed the sprayed tar and metal dust from his skin, and all the people I knew resembled these villagers, large groups of them always crowded into a room, men, women, children, one person sleeping here, the blanket pulled over his head, others sitting at the table, washing themselves in the trough, everything happened in the same room, here some people were conversing, there someone, his hands on his temples, was huddling over a book, and anyone over forty was already an invalid, the oldsters crouched like refuse in a corner. There was no possibility of retreating, of being alone with someone. The encounter with a woman took place behind a bar, on the floor, amid beer puddles, and even Frieda, the surveyor's companion, who had something special about her because she had been the lover of a Castle official, was scrawny, sickly, with yellow skin, sparse hair, any sexual temptations, any intimacy offered in literature, in movies was inconceivable for us. What Kafka had written was a proletarian novel. Love was never talked about, it never even struck us that we were lacking anything, missing anything, and the young working girls, the unemployed girls were subject to the same humiliation as the women in the village, clerks and secretaries from the Castle could grab them, summon them, use them up, and toss them away, they were at the mercy of those people, and yet they talked themselves into believing that their value increased whenever they caught the eye of some brute and surrendered to him. Many of the female packers, the errand girls hoped to be discovered by a pen pusher, just as the female secretaries, above us, in the offices, spruced themselves up for the dandies in the administration building. Frieda had stepped back to someone in her own class and had promptly been disciplined for her dissidence, her resolve to no longer be abused made her an outcast. In the society ruled by the law that demanded she sell herself, Frieda, trying to plead for her independence, was doomed. Standing on the Lausche, the highest peak in the mountain chain, peering over at Germany and at the town my parents lived in, behind the autumn-colored forests under the Spitzberg, I wondered if these devastations and desolations, these areas of defeat that Kafka described might not make us brood unproductively, render us apathetic, if these torturous memories of the filth, the misery, the baseness of all the things that were close to us might not rob us of the strength to rebel against what seemed beyond change. But then again I saw that my resistance was linked to my bewilderment, I had recognized my neighbors, myself, in these crooked, damaged, used-up villagers, there was this mustiness between us, this stunting, this philistine moroseness, and even when the issue was ideals, getting ahead, many of us shared the surveyor's striving to be finally appreciated by the authorities in the Castle. Granted, one could repeatedly tell oneself that over there, behind the border barriers of Seifhennersdorf, a reality began that did not brook the slightest weakness, slightest inattentiveness, a reality in which any sign of lethargy had to be fought, and yet Kafka's book retained its validity for our social and political world. Not only the Castle with its hierarchic structure, where everyone had his assigned precinct and knew no more than what he happened to be allowed, always carrying out only what others demanded, not only the Castle but also the things occurring on our own level possessed a kind of strength in which concrete experience passes into the images of dreams.

And whenever I compared the book about the Castle with *Barricades in Wedding*, there was another clash of the two opposites that were decisive for me, on the one side the difficult, intricate, constantly evasive reality, and on the other side realness, tangible, massive, a squared block.

Kafka's work, in earth-brown binding, was filled with endlessly ramified trains of thought, with connections and intersections of moral, ethical, philosophical notions, with constant questions about the meanings of manifestations, the intentions of activities, Neukrantz's small battle-book, from the Red Novels series, priced at one mark, did not ask, it only supplied an answer, called upon its readers to forestall nihilism, to throw up a practical defense against suffering, it spurred us on to direct intervention and could be understood by all the people who lived on our streets. There was no time for sidestepping, for reflecting, the thing that had to be tackled was clear and complete, the thing that towered, fateful, fraught with doom, over Kafka's village was, for the inhabitants of Wedding, easy to grasp as a class-determined process of oppression to which they showed a bold front. The one book consisted of flowing material that could slowly take shape in the imagination, the other book was an object that you bumped into. It had no intricate conversations, no dissections of the psyche, no guilt-fraught, doubt-ridden investigations of a cosmology in which the reader's self was entangled, it had only the concrete stone that was joined to the other stones on the street, the beam that blocked the front door, the cloth that bound the wound. Everything that was discussion of the nature of the Castle in Kafka was an accomplished fact here. The workers did not shrink back from entering the building that the surveyor found questionable, for them it was the police headquarters on Alexanderplatz, they headed there straight-away in stained trousers and smocks, coming from their scaffoldings, strode along the corridors to the rooms of the potentates, marched into the anteroom of the supreme boss, refused to be put off by the secretaries, and stood in front of the representative to state their demands. This mannequin was straight out of Kafka. His custom-made clothes, useless for any physical labor, snugly enveloping the wretched figure, his prattling, his pomposity were suitable for the Castle official, except that the delegation paid him no respect whatsoever, the workers did not approach him as petitioners, they demanded their rights. And even though he courteously ushered them out with a vacuous verbal stew, they had nevertheless shown that they could push into the heart of the enemy fortress. This was exemplary, under the prevailing conditions it was the highest possible achievement. And the subsequent fight waged in the streets was likewise proof of utmost courage, for there was only one escape from death and destruction. The Castle was still invincible, and the desire for a dignified life, for eliminating the cheating of workers, encountered only people who said that this was outside their jurisdiction and who referred them to people who were beyond reach. The paralysis that wore down the villagers could no longer be endured, it was more dreadful than the approach of the tanks, the booming of cannon, it had to be demonstrated that people were still determined to rise up, to hit back, the mere fact that the workers held out for two or three days was their victory. Henceforth the lords of the Castle would know that the workers on the outside refrained from making demands only because they had no choice, and that they might start in again at any moment. Kafka had circled around the theme, he kept returning to the same point of departure, he brooded, tried new possibilities of moving, lay in wait, lurking, roused himself, let himself be fooled, rejected, thrown down, could never achieve any result, yet he never even considered giving up. His book had no end, and his project was likewise endless, he dealt not with an individual case but with all existence, which contained no hope, yet did contain action. His hero was anonymous, a cipher, it was only thoughts that developed their images, that were tortured by the limits imposed on them, and that wanted nothing other than to expand these limits, burst through them. Neukrantz dove right into a specific historical situation, matter-of-factly, with the help of documents he explained how to get at the root of what had happened. His language was not finely chiseled, people spoke as they would speak at work. The obvious thing would have been to emphasize the world of the intellect over the world of labor, but then the aims of either book would have been falsified. In the past, I had sometimes felt that dealing with art and literature as opposed to practical tasks was an evasion, a self-isolation, just as other people distrusted and disparaged intellectual products. However, both books, which I now compared with one another, showed clearly that the differences were interdependent, that they complemented one another and could not get along without each other. While reading Kafka's book I never removed myself from our daily schedule, from the packing rooms, the assembly halls, from the commute in the jam-packed train at four-thirty A.M. and after the shift, and the material force in Neukrantz's book would have been useless had it not been backed up by ideas. The labyrinth and the parable were as close to us as our coping with the things that were immediately tangible before us. Investigation and defensive combat were two sides of one and the same position. Here in Warnsdorf, during the days of roaming, the criteria of art, which had previously seemed encumbered with the reaction of retreat, now became more graspable and self-evident; while reading, while examining images I no longer entered a secluded special area accessible only to initiates, instead everything that was shown was integrated into my daily experiences. When reading

Neukrantz's account I had already managed to think of the activity of writing as a handiwork, a vocation. Earlier I had read James Fenimore Cooper, Daniel Defoe, Charles Dickens, Frederick Marryat, Herman Melville, Jonathan Swift, Edgar Allen Poe, Joseph Conrad, and Jack London, but *Barricades in Wedding* was the first work that made me wish to set down something myself, make something visible. I wanted to tackle it with the same bluntness, the same openness and partisanship, and I tried to do so when composing my essays in Scharfenberg. The book about the Castle then settled upon a long pent-up disquiet and an incipient craving for knowledge. It evoked anxiety, forced me to view my weaknesses and omissions. Back then, six years earlier, nothing had been insurmountable, I sat in the branches of the linden grove, on the reed bay opposite Baumwerder, and I wrote in the blue notebook, never changing a single word, swift, unhindered, following my inner dictation, then I entered the work world, and easily as my creations could be rendered, it was arduous capturing anything that had actually happened to me. While seeking expression I first had to overcome the smashed things, the ripped things burdening us. We asked ourselves what was true in art, and we found that it must be the material that has passed through our own senses and nerves. Yet when we applied the weighing and judging entirely to ourselves, when we said they were part of existing and they had to connect with one another and imbue our self-determination, then we again felt that our tools, machines, and time clocks, our overcrowded rooms depended on all libraries and museums, all science and scholarship, and, amid erupting scorn, amid mutual ridicule, we saw no continuity, no expanded field of vision, just the blinders on our functionless minds. There, on the edge of the School Island, in a primordial era, I led the strikers, I had memorized the *Manifesto* and now I blared it through the loudspeaker across the square in front of Stettin Railroad Station, or else, behind the studio windows that I had seen on the roof of a house on Dresdener Strasse, on Oranienplatz, I painted gigantic allegories of liberation. Afterwards, on Pflugstrasse, the visions had evanesced, no wishful thinking led us out of the social insecurity, the economic plight, the political rape, and it was only in September of thirty-seven that I began to understand that in trying to gain insights, we always had to share the burden of the muteness and weariness of our fellow workers and that anything we found was also acquired on their behalf. For our efforts to conquer art and literature could have no other purpose than to strengthen the togetherness of people who had so far sensed only their isolation. If we wanted to flee to the intrinsic value of an artwork, we risked winding up in a vacuum, our learning, our studying could be fruitful only by interacting with the conditions, peculiarities, and behaviors in the territory of our life. We had long since determined that a day was unfulfilled if we had not spent at least one hour with a book, a scholarly or scientific problem. In our struggle against the normal obstacles to thinking we had obtained subject matter from the political and sociological manuals, from the night-school courses, but we had to rely on ourselves to discuss the topic that particularly attracted us in those years and that contributed toward expanding our consciousness, it was the theme of ambivalence, of controversy, of contradiction under which we lived. Here, where the issue was the sensory absorption of reality, it was mostly stimuli from poems, novels, paintings that we linked to our experiences and ideas, this was the best method of achieving harmony with ourselves. Our reflections dashed to and fro between the antitheses. We were to be ground down, against that we pitted our endurance. Our imagination held its own against the system forced on us. Our initiative was our response to the systematic undermining of our freedom to act. There was no way we could gain an absolutely correct, accurate view of current affairs, but we resisted this impossibility with our fundamental decisions. After Zola, Gorki, Barbusse, Nexö we had read the proletarian writers of our day. What was new about them was, first of all, the depiction of our existence in the back courts and tenements, in the dark, filthy workshops and storage basements, at the lathes, machines, and loading docks, the reporting on shop-floor meetings, strike preparations, and political clashes. In the books by Kläber, Gotsche, Hoelz, Bredel, Marchwitza, or Neukrantz, we were confronted with the proletarian reality, between drab, gray exhaustion and open fighting, between living in a hideout and being locked up in a prison cell. Often we heard the opinion, and advocated it ourselves, that only these works had any validity for us because they described our practical experiences, our tasks, because they provided the instructions that everyone could comprehend, the directives for transcending the oppressive monotony and developing our own strength. We found that their linearity, their plain, reportage-like style chimed with our efforts to get the condition of oppression clear in our own minds. A deepening of every character, every artistic technique in rendering the mental world or the changing spaces struck us as deviating from the actual topic. We felt it was right to lend expression not to the personal but to the interest of the class. In this compactness, we figured, the writers had to stand up against the individualized novel, which, superior, rich in associations, rose up, opposite us, tower by tower, in the rampart of bourgeois culture. Yet Rolland,

Trakl, Heym, Hauptmann, and Wedekind already made our attitude totter, to the extent that we had worked our way out of ignorance we had also become more open to accounts of experiences that were beyond our immediate sphere of life, the language tied to our everyday practices had expanded, suddenly we understood poems that seemed to have nothing to do with our timecards, our inventory lists, our wage negotiations and union meetings. And within a short time we had come so far that during lunch breaks, in a corner between crates, we read *Jean-Christophe*, van Gogh's letters, Gauguin's journals, Gide's *Counterfeiters*, or Hamsun's *Hunger*, wrapped in wax cloth. Weinert, Becher, Renn, Plivier, Döblin, Seghers, Kisch, Weiskopf, Friedrich Wolf, and Brecht had emerged from the bourgeoisie, the petty bourgeoisie, reorienting their thinking and thereby becoming spokesmen for the working class, and likewise, without our changing our position, it was possible for us to gain insights into the problems of the other part of society. Thrust into the contradictions of a transitional phase, we absorbed the things that bourgeois authors, with the detailed precision they had taken over from classical security, knew how to say about the crumbling, the rate drops, the fiascoes of their era. Occasionally our dealings with their disclosures had given us bad consciences when we were rebuked for meeting them halfway, reconciling with them, or preparing to become turncoats, but when I looked around, any activity in this area was justified. The system of exploitation ran straight across all social strata, we were all trapped in the chains of command, sharing responsibility for the rampant growth of the hierarchies. The more unreservedly we received the testimonies from the most diverse directions of entanglement and seething, of destruction and authoritarian uprisings, the more nuanced became our image of the world and our appreciation for the richness of language. Stammering we had begun, and, when reading, when trying to write, we kept returning to square one, where our own life had started, with every understanding of an intricate context we visualized the impoverishment in which we and our fellow workers were to be detained. Though books were building blocks for us, Professor Kien, Canetti's book man, perished amid literature. For us the works still had sparsity, were laboriously acquired, Kien had an abundance, all his gathered wisdom blazed up in the auto-da-fé, instead of drawing conclusions from his knowledge he went under in hectic madness. Céline, who, in *Journey to the End of Night*, moved through a morass of poverty and misery, did not brook a single glimmer of possibilities of improvement, in lieu of resistance he offered cynicism, cursing, instead of a burgeoning political underground he showed us an underworld of despair and hopelessness. However, such drastic antitheses sharpened our own retorts. The books had recorded the state of disease, it was our job to expose the causes of the infestations. When artists from a middle-class background expressed their disgust, their non-belonging, they remained stuck in their background by digging in individual pain; but by writing they got closer to the people who viewed their activity as an unnecessary, luxurious extravagance. Perhaps they themselves did not yet comprehend, perhaps they would never transcend their desperateness, their powerlessness, never be able to transfer their disquiet to a search for political insights, would despise their origins only generally and not manage to join the forces of upheaval. However, the movement they found themselves in, whether mournful or frenzied, single-minded or uncertain, was large enough to make it clear to us that the struggle to advance was being waged everywhere, that the rules, the methods of expression were going through a metamorphosis, that they were disintegrating in some places, being renewed in others. Full of misunderstandings, the members of the middle strata, of the petty bourgeoisie, were pressing for a change in the conditions, many were enticed by fascism, with their half-baked ideas they wound up with the teachings of the reactionaries, others began to understand their dependence on capitalism, they too were wage earners, producers of surplus value, bled white, none of them, whether in an office, a bureau, a university, or a research center, owned the means of production. If they dared to see through their situation, they all made contact with people in the industries, the workshops, thereby broadening their concept of the working class, more and more of these people, who had once had to be counted as part of the bourgeoisie, made the path of the proletariat their own, often even adding weightiness to it with theoretical and practical contributions. These reflections were very seldom to be gleaned directly from books on the era of crisis, outwardly most works were still reserved for the educated elite, the definitive step was not taken, was guessed at only as impatience, as dislike of the status quo, as something in the future. New progressive forces that had freed themselves from earlier bonds drove us to make others more conscious of our own position. The students and academics, the artists and writers who joined us had not seen their background as definitive, and we likewise had to overcome the arrogance of assuming that we alone, on the basis of certain social and economic conditions, were at home in the proletariat. Rather, by precise differentiation, we had to once again choose and define our standpoint. A person belonged to the working class if he acted on its behalf no matter where he came from. This was particularly important now that large segments of labor had gone astray and were being shoved away from their point of departure. The broad unity of proletarian action had failed to materialize. The workers had not known how to define themselves against fascism. A defense was now possible only if they became a Popular Front that included organizations, parties, social strata that were not counted as part of the proletariat but shared its interest in defensive combat. While the working class had not yet serried its ranks, cooperation with other political groupings should not mean abandoning the goal of the leading role that it would have to take some day and that it already had in the Soviet Union, in Spain, in China. Despite all tactical alliances, the conflicts between the classes had to be continued and, if necessary, exacerbated. My father described the restructuring inside the social forces as a historic block, he spoke about Gramsci, who had died that April after ten years in the prisons of the Italian fascists. Gramsci, on the basis of the historical realities, had pointed out the route that the intelligentsia, freed of the bourgeois obsessions, would take together with the workers. Yet this could never mean simply taking over cultural values from the hands of people who with their privileges had formerly served the rulers, for that would have involved adopting the depoliticization of culture, the rejection of the class struggle. Instead, there had to be a reciprocity between the things that had been shaped and the quest for an expression of their own. While we acquired culture, that overall mechanism, of which culture had been a component, had to be destroyed. That which could continue educating us had as yet to be created. Once they were put on the ground of the proletariat and interpreted there, the works of literature, art, philosophy would gain a new meaning. From deep down, our eyes focused on a scientific age. We were still in the phases of terror and persecution. In the narrow window above my father's head, we again saw the marching legs, in lace boots and white stockings, behind them, on a taut leash, an Alsatian with an open maw, whistles could be heard and the thunderous shouts that demanded submission to the empire of violence. But how can we sure, I asked, that there will not be new fraud when the trained academics begin having an impact on our fragmentary knowledge. In his response my father combined Luxemburg's notions of a school of free initiative, an education in creative activity, with Gramsci's negation of mechanistics, of authoritarian learning. Ahead of us, said my father, we still have the cultural revolution that was talked about in the early twenties. This would transform not just us but all the people who were receptive to the pressure of history. The common intent to take possession of work would drive us to a mutual understanding. And if we stopped handing over our basic production and started using it ourselves, he said, who would then deny that, once their organizational and pedagogical capacities for planning and guiding were liberated from suppression, all our former suppliers and subalterns are intellectual workers. His indulging in such reflections showed that time had not yet worn him down, that he was still ready to begin afresh. Indeed, as he had often done in Berlin, he had now turned the kitchen into a workshop and was occupied with a series of improvements for block printing. On his workbench he had one of the wooden frames on which he was strengthening the fortification arrangement for the printing table, just as he was trying to provide a more stable shape for the spatula that squeezed the pigment through the master of fine-meshed wire cloth. Resettlement had been harder on my mother than on him. She, who was accustomed to working, who had always contributed to supporting the family, was now condemned to inactivity, no office or factory hired her, and in her restlessness she, who had always done her part of the housework quickly, now spent hours polishing the sideboard, the table, the chairs, the silver, and, occasionally lost in thought, she would stare into space, oblivious of her surroundings. Once, when we had sat down on the bench in the front yard of the house, the landlady, Frau Goldberg, came and asked us to leave the yard, because first of all, she said, we were paying only for the apartment and not for the garden, and secondly the bench was not meant for Jews. When I indignantly tried to reply, my mother held me back and, standing up, pressed my arm hard against her body. While pulling me into the house, she said that after being called a Jew several times because of her dark hair, she had now declared herself a Jew, which, however, made it difficult for her and Father to find another apartment in Warnsdorf. So she had to knuckle under to the owner of the house, who made it clear to her at every chance she got that she was allowing her to stay here as a favor and that soon, the day was just around the corner, she would get what was coming to her. During one of my last days in Warnsdorf I saw what that could mean. On the edge of town, coming from Saint George's Valley, near a gravel pit, where the road passed through the so-called Kirchenbusch, I heard the shrieks and laughter of a group of children and adolescents. At first I thought they were playing a war game and I slowly walked on, but then I noticed that in their midst a man was lying in the shingle, uttering rattling sounds, and as I came closer, I saw that it was Eger Franz, who was being called names, village idiot or Yid, a harmless, mentally retarded day laborer. His face covered with blood, his mouth foaming, he rolled around convulsively amid the teenagers, who kept kicking him and smashing sticks into his head. Driving his tormentors away, I picked him up and carried him to the Fiala Nursery in Niedergrund, where help soon came. I later heard that he had died as a result of his injuries. His young murderers, whose identities were known, were never called to account, it was announced that the vagabonding Jew had fallen during an epileptic fit and fractured his skull.

HERE I am in the right place, here in the landscape of Don Quixote, these words from Hodann's letter, which had been forwarded to me in Warnsdorf by the Spain Committee in Prague, flashed into my mind when we, crowded together on the truck, drove into the high mesa of La Mancha, under the heaps of clouds, which were colored red and violet by the setting sun. One week earlier we had left the French border guards behind us, had crept through the detritus between Céret and Junquera, through shrubs and olive groves, and bumped into the first Republican sentries. Lumbering through Gerona and Calella, the train had brought us to Barcelona, to the black, smoky terminal, but our impressions of the day in this city were constantly overshadowed by the images of the ruinous, jagged structure that we had suddenly reached, emerging from the ravine of an avenue. Turtles carried the columns of the dust-wind-blasted portal with its high-twisting, riddled campaniles and the lateral vaults embracing the dream of a cathedral from an unknown world of forms. Throwing our heads way back, we stared up at the proliferating stone, saw a Gothic that bore reminiscences of Egypt and Babylon, that had passed through citadels, Baroque castles, and Indian temples, through art nouveau and cubism, studded with stalactites, with petrified plants budding very high, blossoming into red, blue, golden wicks, cones, spheres, and cubes, further down, between the pillars, in the niches and gables, around the glassless windows with their entwined frame branches, human shapes in the heroic style of the nineteenth century, baked into the pegs and clubs, into the patterns of mosses and ferns, algae and corals. Turkeys and chickens, peacocks and geese, mules and oxen rallied around the Holy Family, which, on a vine-clad tablet over the central entrance, gave its name to the fragmentary temple. Ayschmann, four years my senior, the son of Jewish refugees, having come from London via Paris, having met me in Perpignan, asked in what manner the compound of kitsch and architectural vision had been carried out, and it seemed to us as if the disinterested way of treating all artistic directions, the lack of a specific, so-called sure taste, had been the prerequisites for creating this monstrous and completely free-standing formation. Mary, under the tent of her kerchief, shielded the crèche, and Joseph's worshipful gesture in holding up his hands and bowing sideways to her was flat, epigonal, while the angels blowing into realistically inserted metal trumpets were bombastic. The saints and apostles, in and of themselves, could likewise derive from some trivial monument or other, but their location in between the geometrically hewn yellowish-gray blocks, their contrasting with an unrestrained ornamentation, their balancing on grooved and fluted globes, on sharply jutting edges, made their naturalism look exotic, in the immediate vicinity of frozen mud and filth, of coagulated ocean foam there was something bizarre, insane about their pious gestures, and it was like that everywhere, the armored warrior holding the cast-iron sword in one hand, hurling the stolen child aloft with the other hand, the woman begging him to stop next to the child's corpse dangling down to the hissing geese, the patriarchs and divines, in their shelters, all of them, objects to be viewed at school, gained a new expression in a totality whose essence was mixture. Buttressed by rotational bodies hugging and clasping each other, the sculptural associations thronged into and over one another, inundating every recess, every cupola, and always lightness emerged above them, in unfolded palm fronds, in tapering mountain peaks, and any downward heaviness dissolved in the lines of waves, lianas, and roots. Jumble and hodgepodge were ruled by the logic of the hyperbolic, paraboloidal system of architecture, eruptive superabundance was flanked by unadorned ashlars in fortress-like walls, a grandiloquently illustrative detail collided with a gush of lava and slag, a hand stretched out in blessing, an expectation of a divine mission found a response in the widespread pinions, the heads of long-necked birds. Chain links, weights hung from the tortured, bursting stone, and a surf bristling with huge, listening ear conches spewed transfigured faces, their eyes and mouths closed, bodies, amid seaweed and algae, starfish and cuttlefish, worked their way out of the flakes of the stony foam, taking on weightlessness, flying into the afterlife, here the instant of death was depicted, the transition from one state to another. The central portal, praising brotherly love, was full of wound areas, curlicued serpents were stuck above the clusters of blood and pus, ready to drop, giant snails, extending their feelers, monsters of sea urchins inched down the sides of the gates of faith, of hope. Behind the loopholes of the apse lay the emptiness of the unbuilt naves, a draft swept through the hollows of the frontal mass, where the philosophers sat conversing in the lowest alcoves, and a worker shoved his chisel into the slab on the workbench. Through the entrance arches we peered at the harshly sunlit courtyard, where the granite shards, abandoned by the stonecutters, lay in heaps, with their incipient faces, their rawly indicated skulls of reptilia, and we perceived this structure of antitheses, bare and overburdened, seeking itself from hardness to softness, from roughness to smoothness, fragmentary and with completed details, coming from ancient times and guessing the future, unclassifiable, and now it was as if those that were single or grouped in the fossil vegetation were bearers of tidings, as if they wanted to report about wonders, break out into shrieks, dance, ecstasy instead of prayers, and the donkeys, the bulls, the dragons laughed at it all, there was a yowling, a whinnying, the iron swords flashed up, harsh sounds came from the long trumpets, the dents, knots, and clumps began to vibrate, to flow, the incised letters turned into mouths, the stone began to speak, to call, scab trickled down upon us, cannonades could be heard far away. The mountain of the front structure rested on turtles, the patient keratinous backs carried the scenario of Biblical history, they would imperceptibly move forward with their tremendous backdrop, pushed from behind by a few mastodontic snails that found no room in the towers. On the inside everything was made of mighty Constructivism, with hard-jagged stairs, semicircular, echeloned overhangs, slanting displacements, the walls rose around the ground of the basilica. What choruses, said Ayschmann, would ring from the singing sites that ran in series of steps along the side walls and in the transverse gallery of the triforium in a nonexistent edifice, what antiphonal choruses, sung by thousands, and what songs they would sing, and he squinted, listening, in a cloud of dust. There, on these tracks, he said, pointing to the place in the middle of La Gran Via, that was where the architect was killed, under an electric trolley, he was wrapped around the wheels, shredded, rolled up, in June nineteen twenty-six, the swift, jingling, and roaring thing ran over Gaudí's private world, we again encountered its billows, its sandbanks and hollowed cliffs on Paseo de Gracia, around the Casa Battló, the Casa Milá, and once more, shortly before continuing our journey, we returned to the split grotto of the Sagrada Familia. Scaffoldings, ladders leaned against the walls as if the construction were to go on. Peering through the cracks of boarded-up sheds we could make out plaster shapes, busts, entangled bodies, legs and arms stretching out from bars, in the junk, amid fluttering pages covered with mathematical formulas, stood models of construction elements, perforated, resembling ribs, arm bones, thigh bones, showing the basis of the structural bearing capacity, if we turned around, we recognized, under the tumultuous external forms, the skeleton, the organism with its sinews and muscles. Children, in long gray smocks, played in the courtyard among the mountains of stones, they came running out of straw huts next to a low house with a corrugated roof, there were classrooms inside, this had been the architect's wish, they were to grow up and study under the growing structure, were to train their imagination through the variety of this creation. On this day, walking through Barcelona, we found allusions to the cathedral everywhere, references that concentrated all the agitated things, transforming them into monumentality. All along the boulevards, which were so lengthy that usually a mere glance sufficed to make the thought of overcoming them impossible, figures of marble, of greenish bronze stood on pedestals and columns, staring into the distance. Strings of stuccoes ran along the building fronts, shoulders heaved up the entrance arches, the cornices, here and there the ornamentation of the palaces was hung with posters, placards. Going out for meals, we left our quarters at the Hotel Victoria, veered through Plaza de Cataluna with its stone benches, its mythological heroes around dried-out fountains, and reached the Hotel Colón, its portal flanked by banners on which an angry Lenin glared at his smiling secretary-general, we walked up Avenida Pi y Margall, past the House of the Party, far ahead of us, on a lofty capital, a naked female figure, across us strode the goddess of freedom, we went to the endless Avenue of the Fourteenth of April, where, at the office of the International Brigades, we received our papers and travel instructions, walked again through the crisscross of streets to the main square, to the telephone headquarters, in whose façades bullet holes were still visible from the fighting in May, when the anarchist opposition, we learned, had been crushed by police troops and army units, and then on to Las Ramblas, the broad tree-lined promenade, we walked between the vendors' stands, here flowers, wreaths and garlands, there parakeets, pheasants in cages, goldfish in glass pitchers, here clay things, woven things, enameled fans, combs, mantillas, there red-and-black kerchiefs, red-and-black caps, blue overalls, and on the sides of the thoroughfare the trams rattling by, they too painted with the diagonally divided red and black of the Iberian Federation, until we came to the column that was ringed by roaring lions and on whose top Columbus, standing on the globe, gazed across the harbor at the ocean. Amid swarms of pigeons we waited for the picture that the cannon photographer pulled from the box on his small red three-wheeled cart, and then, immortalized on sticky, yellowish paper, we turned into the streets of the Old City, where martyrs, vultures, lizards protruded from the walls and where the reverberating Plaza Real welcomed us after we stepped into its sole entrance. Closed in by the square of galleries, sitting on a bench under palms, stretching our feet out after walking and walking, we again discussed the vegetal architecture that had risen before us, and now, three days later, shaken by the truck, Ayschmann said that the work may not have been carried through because the ecclesiastic and religious motives for the construction had lost all meaning, this devotional place had been erected around a drained idea, and that was why such a cathedral could only remain incomplete, could survive only as a fragment, find its value in a hyperreal omni-art opus. If other people, he said, were ever to continue building in order to have masses sung inside, they were sure to produce something retrograde, the edifice could retain its authenticity solely as a ruin, but as a house of God it was bound to become something artificial. And the clouds now hung over us like gigantic bodies, stretching knots of arms down, tremendous clenched fists, bloated faces, they drifted, bluish red, over us, with smoldering hair, faded wings. Leaving Barcelona, we took a train to Valencia, from dawn till dusk of the next day, riding in a wooden car. Toward noon, near Vinaroz, as we once more reached the edge of the sea, the reality that we were here for came thronging in on us, out there, as indicated by hands, lay the German fleet, blockading the Spanish coast, the enemy was fleshed out, he spoke the same language we had grown up with, his emissaries had sat next to us in school, had run into us on our home streets, had worked the same machines in the factories as we, but now that we met again, we no longer had anything in common, we had separated for good, only that gray impersonal might lay in front of us, and it had to be annihilated. Santander and Gijón had fallen into enemy hands, hundreds of thousands of refugees jammed the roads, the fascist troops were pushing forward along the Ebro, twenty thousand Italians had just been shipped off to Cádiz to strengthen the expeditionary force, and our own front had to be solidified after the armed clashes that summer. We heard that during our presence in Barcelona over a hundred anarchists had been arrested in the city. We heard conflicting, confusing things about the anarchistic, syndicalistic bands that opposed the government directives, about the United Marxist Workers' Party, whose abbreviated name, like a dull shot, we would often get to hear, and we learned about the actions against the anarcho-syndicalists in Aragón. Right after the fighting near Brunete, when the battle of Belchite was already being prepared, when the bombs of the Condor Legion were dropping on Saragossa, General Líster with the eleventh division of the people's army had pushed ahead into Caspe in order to smash the headquarters of the independence movement. The council committees surrendered, supposedly without resisting, the revolutionary worker-soldiers were disarmed, after a period of re-schooling many of them went over to the regular army, so that the main forces of the splintering had been rendered harmless, and the Popular Front government had demonstrated its sovereignty. With no grasp of the internal controversies that paralleled the antifascist struggle, but warding off any disquiet and sticking to the thought that unity had to be manifested here at any price, we passed through the orange forests along the Costa del Azahar, past hamlets, through small towns, which seemed unaware of the war, stretches of beach emerged, waiting for their guests, perhaps the fight being fought in the interior of the country made up only one part of this reality, in a die-hard everyday life in which selfishness and faintheartedness kept operating alongside our ideals, our faith in the emergence of justice. Perhaps beach life would soon recommence behind the slopes, making people forget the rides and marches, the strains and sacrifices of these months and years. We felt hatred of the traitors in our own ranks, this helped us to bond all the more strongly, we knew that nothing could shred our togetherness, but, because of our inklings of contradictions, we had henceforth become alert to and suspicious of anyone who tried to distract us from focusing on the enemy's war machine, which was built up broadly in front of us. Then there was an evening in Valencia, a city where the Baroque swung up into the highest balustrades, where gods and angels hovered over the gigantic blocks of houses, where one entwined balcony grill joined the next, and the tiniest chamber nevertheless had room for faiences, blossoming festoons, and putti. One night in the tents on the trampled field of the arena, next to North Terminal, and by dawn on Plaza Castelar, where the open trucks were standing by in front of city hall. We had to wait and wait there for a unit belonging to our transport, we loafed on the benches amid the flower stalls, squinting up at the wingspans of the angels, of the enraptured saints in wafting garments, and once again it was as if the citizens, who had now awoken and were all around, entering the portals guarded by Cyclopes, had nothing to do with our war, we were curious about the kind of business they were attending to, there behind the windows, behind the iron filigree, and whom this business was useful to. Through the gaps of the lace curtains they peered down at us, adventurers, guerrillas camping at the feet of their building colossi, and a sigh of relief accompanied our departure. And yet we had been nothing more than flaneurs, tourists in Valencia, in Barcelona. We had examined what artistic perfection, what values of beauty could be read into the stone, now, riding through the fields, hills, mountains we no longer asked what the formations were meant to represent, we now asked what intrinsic worth they had. Here the clay was cut from the ruddy earth and baked into bricks in the fiery kilns, the pantiles of the houses were of the same earthen red, the masonry shimmered rosy through the whitewash. On the slopes, on the terraces, supported by low stone walls, the grapes, ready for harvesting, hung from the vines, the rows of trees in between, growing up from the ferruginous soil, bore fat green and violet-black olives, cypress hedges protected the orange plantations against the winds sweeping up from the ocean, across the rice paddies on Lake Albufera. Tree-high reeds, thick, dusty agaves grew along the roadside, the heights behind Chiva were gray, here, on the excavations, the cement factories lay in smoke. The clouds gathered above the mountain chains, concentrating higher and higher, endless was the wealth of grapes, of olives, but the mule was pathetic, driven through the narrow strip of farmland by the terse shouts of the peasant behind the wooden plow, and the shepherd with the crook, wearing a leather pouch on his back, squeezed into a shadow, in the parched grass between the sheep, which resembled the round rocks, came from a different time than ours. The shepherd and the peasant with their primitive tools, said Ayschmann, are related to the masons of the Sagrada Familia, the frugality of their workaday life corresponds to this craft, in which, for the lowest wages, one sculpted stone is arduously heaved up to another by the tackle block attached to the scaffolding, as was done in the camps by the Gothic cathedrals, where generations patiently served the hierarchies. In the afternoon, as we came from Requena to Casas Ibañez, the landscape began to change, here we found huge processions of harvesters in the fields, their movements, their faces had a new expression, they acted not singly or in small groups, instead their activities were coordinated with one another, they showed an eagerness, a momentum that grew more emphatic because many of the workers carried weapons or had left their rifles together within reach. Youth brigades helped with the vintage, with picking the olives, they banged poles on the branches of the low trees with thick trunks, the fruits were gathered up or plucked from the twigs by hands gliding loosely through foliage, the grapes, deep green, filled the willow baskets that were carried on backs, the baskets with the loads of olives were broad, shaped like dishes, they were swung up on the carts, feet shoved into the spokes of the high wheels to make the pulling easier for the mule. Shouted commands and the rattling of gunfire could be heard from behind sandy hills, the camps, the training grounds of the International Brigades stretched in a wide semicircle all the way from Casas Ibañez to Madrigueras and Tarazona and all the way to Villenueva de la Jara. Earlier features, almost medieval, could still be found, in the village of Mahora the rough quarry stones in the house walls were plastered with clay, the doors were made of gray rotten boards, the oldsters sang in the gateways, the men with scarves wound deep around their necks, the black caps drawn low on their foreheads, the women in black, fringed kerchiefs, chickens scratched in the sand between the thyme bushes, just one year ago everything here had been isolated, lost in oblivion, and would have remained forgotten if the change had not violently broken in and not entrenched itself here. The innovation was the tie between labor and weaponry, production and alertness, here the Republic was being defended at its center, and suddenly all doubt and uncertainty retreated, a security was established, a trust in the tenability of the northern and western fronts. The towns on the eastern coast lay behind the open conflict, there, in the rock masses, there were many people who neither believed in nor wished for the victory of the Republic, there the strength to hold out was undermined, there the fifth columns were at work, and goods were hustled on the black market while people lined up at the food distribution points. There, where the plutocracy was waiting for the distribution of commodities to resume, where international relations served not solidarity but profit, where much secret planning was targeted at the Popular Front government, to exacerbate the differences between political directions and make them incompatible, to foment confusion, promote breach of promise, where many people were seeking their own way and their way out, there was no possibility of fostering the sense of community that had developed here on the high plain. So far everything had been an arrival, an initial tracking-down, now we were deep inside a land that, while not yet knowing its language, we saw as our own, for by now we had no other country but this. We found ourselves in a new kind of army, an army that wanted to conquer nothing but the liberation from suppression, an army that wanted to help no one get rich, an army that was meant to bring about the end of all exploitation. We had not been drafted into this army, we were not forced to fight, each person had volunteered of his own free will. For the first time we stood outside the realm of the superior power that had always affected our moves, our actions. Never had we so sharply felt our right to make our own decisions and also our need to take arms against the forces that had previously kept us down. Thus we turned into the tremendous openness of the plateau, on a dead-straight road, toward Albacete, through the parallel wheat fields, vineyards, stretches of deep-red soil, and strips of violet thyme, above which scattered pines rose with straight smooth trunks, round crowns. A half-decrepit stone bridge led across the Jucar, a narrow stream in a broad bed of detritus. The nearness of the military center was shown by the ambulances, the troop transports that came toward us, the higher number of sentries at the various crossroads. In the swift onset of twilight, Albacete stood out as a white line on the yellow horizon, under the clouds, which discolored, inky, leaden, the city, as its Moorish name El Basiti, promised, was the plain itself, the heart of the plain, it lay there flat, squeezed into the pattern of rolled lineups, a component of the worn hatchwork of geological strata. In the darkness the trucks rattled across train rails, through one of the roads that plunged like rays into the rocky tissue, the trucks then reached a gate under merlons and circular turrets, the gate of the barracks of the Guardia Civil.

Originally a Roman settlement and a rest stop for Arab caravans, ruled by caliphs, changing royal dynasties and conquistadors, by the landed gentry, the provincial town, already too small for its twenty thousand inhabitants, had now become an army camp for the International Brigades. The new, the revolutionary upheaval expressed itself as a shapeless teeming, as an inundation penetrating every nook, every space in the chains of low, impoverished houses with only a few pompous edifices towering above them at the center of town. The financial institutions, the insurance companies, the commercial firms, established for the benefit of the owners of the latifundia, decorated with the borders that blossoming capitalism had used as an ornament for its profit margins, served mainly the supreme command, the staffs, and the administrative authorities, while the homes and shops, the sheds and cellars took in all kinds of matériel together with their echelons of suppliers and distributors. However, the replenishment of the city was not systematized in an intelligible way, instead everything was interlocked, lapping into everything else, clerks huddled over makeshift tables next to piles of crates and barrels, a workshop where a blacksmith was hammering at a fire doubled as a bedroom for truckers, pointers moved across maps of theaters of war, next door mechanics repaired machine guns and undercarriages, while sandbags, flower sacks, cartridge boxes were unloaded in a courtyard, from which a field mess came with a steaming cauldron of soup. At Plaza Altozano, behind the sculpted façade of the Gran Hotel, a wall bedecked with balcony railings, with gables and turrets, two stories had been rigged up as apartments for officers, overhead there was a depot for clothing and laundry, while on the top floor seriously wounded men lay in forty beds. Catty-corner across the square, in the Banco de España, Barrio, the head of the recruiting office, was headquartered, while in the other rooms, amid card catalogues, file cabinets, and safes, newly arriving troops were put up. The Café Central, with its marble columns, its broad stairway and polished wooden banisters, was reserved for the higher military ranks, through the vaulted window you could catch a glimmer of famous patrons, Hemingway, Ehrenburg, Louis Fischer sat here at the round tables, and now, next to Koltsov, the Soviet adviser, you could recognize Antonov Ovseyenko, the consul of the Soviet Union, I wanted to wave at that man, who had led the storming of the Winter Palace on the seventh of November, nineteen seventeen, but he was surrounded by uniformed men, whose stars, stripes, and lapels shone out from the thicket of potted plants, suitcases were carried over, attack guardists blockaded the street, a car drove up, he was supposedly leaving, he had been called back to Moscow together with Rosenberg, the envoy. History flared up in tiny hectic hearths on Plaza Altozano, in the middle of which a few dusty scrubby palms surrounded a pool of water, meanwhile, at the casino, between the bank and the town hall, the brigade members sat in olive-green felt, in wide breeches with puttees, and they likewise thronged together at the wooden tables across the way, in the former Circulo Mercantil. It could be conjectured that this square, where the Palace of Justice and the Capitol Theater were also located, was the hub of all planning and activity, however, the only boulevard, Paseo de la República, flanked by pruned plantains, led to the train station, and there, in the old Dominican monastery, lived Marty, the governor of the garrison, with his household and his domestics, this was the nexus of power, of authority, but next to this man, whose name was pronounced with a blend of awe for his legendary fame and repugnance at his arrogance and thirst for power, there were other commanders, Italians and especially Germans, and once again on this first day in the military, we were confronted with the disagreements, tensions, and ruptures that seemed indissolubly tied up with the organizational setup of the international army. Upon reaching the city, we had entered a totality that had to encompass all conflicts and in which the solution was always armed action at the front. No longer as individuals, we perceived the phenomena, what we saw was complemented by many other eyes, each of our steps was movement in an organic whole. In Albacete we received our first impressions of the force that would be steering us. Before we were directed to our destinations, formations, training grounds, our concept of a popular army's fighting was put to the test. For many of us, who knew no grand words, but only sober resoluteness, the image of war, under the impact of manifold judgment, was bound to suddenly take on new, almost hectically flickering aspects. Most people insisted on joining their units as soon as possible, away from the cauldron of polemics, where jealousy and hostility fermented and brotherhood ran the risk of being forgotten. But it was already part of the experience we had gained that we had to keep aloof from any moral temptation. For us, we insisted, and we heard the confirmation from men returning from the front lines, the international solidarity against fascism had begun in Spain. This answer was one of absolute certainty. Here, in this city, where the wind swept through the bare, monotonous streets, eddying at the corners, we had only one day in Barcelona before we had to report, Ayschmann at the training camp near Posonubio and I, five kilometers farther north, in Cueva la Potita, on the Jucar. We were components of a collective, but the disorderly, multivocal reality bearing in on us had to be harmonized through personal investigation. It would be part of our mission to constantly mobilize our consciousness. Our volunteerism, which was inseparable from our fundamental position, would demand an understanding of the contradictory impressions, not in order to nourish doubts, but in order to cope with the lurking defeatism. We saw a necessity in the struggle between the leaders, in arguments that hammered away at one another. The whole of Europe was a field of antagonisms, different kinds of independent energies had to flow together in Spain and look for a synthesis. Each of us had the task of fusing divergences into a unity. Earlier we had often tried to imagine what it was like gathering for an attack on the enemy, facing him openly, while otherwise encountering him only in secret. The time of our arrival was still marked by the summer's events when a major segment of the extensive opposition had been eliminated and the government had been reshuffled. It was decisive, and plausible for us, that all energy now had to focus on the security of the army, only through the military could the war, provoked by revolutionary hopes, bring victory over an adversary who from the very beginning had preened himself on his excess of weapons. The establishment of authority and discipline, the reintroduction of ranks had dampened some of the original élan, which, however, in its spontaneity, had led to swift defeats, and people realized, even among the anarchists, that experienced strategists were needed to confront the armies of professional soldiers. Some people saw it as contradictory that the fight for renewal should take place with the help of antiquated institutions that did not meet the desire for equality. And yet a steered, tamed violence was the only possible procedure for dealing with the battles of matériel. Although inferior in our equipment, we could never expose any gap in our ideological self-confidence, our commitment to social change was huge, but could be sustained only if it resulted in an unbreakable consolidation. We tested one another and ourselves before the dualism that was evident in our tasks, we tried to weigh the discordances against one another in order to answer for the whole. All the men who had headed for Spain were filled with pride, with the sense of doing the right thing. They came from countries that styled themselves democratic yet had done everything they could to prevent the departure of the volunteers in order to wipe out the emerging United Front and isolate the people's war in Spain. The volunteers had come out of conviction, surmounting their governments' deception, extortion, their policies of evasion. The readiness to risk their lives involved the demand to be recognized and appreciated as having equal rights. Their resoluteness was carried by a class standpoint, which initially found agreement throughout their own ranks, but then required a sophisticated interpretation. Since their presence here made them all equal in value, they did not wish to be distinguished from superiors. Now they had to integrate themselves into a system against which they might have rebelled earlier when doing their military service in their own countries. At the front lines, according to numerous reports, the distribution of functions had become a matter of course, in closest cooperation the soldiers trusted the officers' abilities. But here, in the headquarters of the brigades, the hierarchic machinery had developed an atavism that contrasted sharply with the goal of the struggle. People were bound to be dismayed by the supreme political leader, who, like a prince, from his cloisters and stone halls, maintained a regime of personal autocracy and arrogance bordering on paranoia. One heard bitter remarks that the proletarian army left room for patronage, squabbling, and cunning. Yet it was possible that Marty's ill fame, which poisoned every conversation, was deliberately fostered by a subversive intention. It struck us as possible that his despotic features could be traced back to the responsibility he bore. We needed only to see photographs of his face, pale and puffy, with dark rings around his eyes, to understand the panic he had to contend with. The Republic had lost the important industrial provinces of Asturia, Vizcaya, Santander. The naval embargo prevented the delivery of huge supplies of matériel. There was a constant threat that the Pyrenees border would shut down. Marty's face reflected the emergency in which he had to form effective units for a new offensive. At the slightest objection to his planning, he lost his temper. He sniffed treason in every derogatory remark. We tried to explain his harshness with the fact that he, put in his office by the Soviet Party leaders, was responsible for the implementation of all directives regarded as crucial to strategy and tactics. Other people, however, saw only the warpings of his character and said he was inflicted with the delusion of potentates and could hold on only because he was supported by his supreme patron, who placed him beyond all criticism. People also said what Wehner had already hinted to my father in Paris, that Marty wanted to keep his distance from the German brigade leaders who had attained influence and prestige on the basis of their accomplishments. He had persecuted Beimler before the latter had fallen in action near Madrid in December of thirty-six, then Marty had opposed Regler and Renn, Kahle and Zaisser as well as political functionaries like Dahlem and Mewis. One man pointed at the perron of the Jesuit church on Calle de la Concepción, here Marty had supposedly shot a few alleged saboteurs, prisoners whom he had dragged from the rooms in the wing of the military police building. Passing the church, we glanced into its nave, where rows of crowded cots stood left and right on the red tiles; in back, on the dais, from which the altar had been torn down, soldiers were warming up at an open fire. In the flashing tableau, the soldiers, wrapped in gray blankets, were the same size as the group in front, at the portal, where a flask of wine in a bast weave and with a long spout was passing from hand to hand, their faces, lit up by the lofty windows, the stream of wine that was guided into the open mouths, the round of gestures, the standing in the reflections of the flames, all these things were of equal significance, looming against a single plane with a light-gray grounding. The self-enclosed stances, the hard-cut lines of the columns and corbelings spoke of coldness and ill humor, only a low narrow door separated the refuge from the prison, from the interrogation rooms, the Inquisition, which had applied its tongs there, may have dragged along the tale of torturous judicial proceedings. Supposedly, however, Marty had personally carried out death sentences in other places too, at a pond in the city park, in a gulch near Los Yesares on the Jucar, and even if these stories were slander, they nevertheless expressed rebellion, indignation at the fact that top ranks in the international army were inadequately filled, that injustice was tolerated and nothing was done to clarify matters. It was also wrong, said one of the men, to let political loyalty inveigle us into concealing abuses in our own camp. The anarchists had been fought, he said, because they refused to put up with constraint, with the oppression of free will. But with their sense of freedom, said another, they had been in a fair way of losing the war. They had been thwarted by the issue of power, the power of the state had to be taken over, but they were against the state, they relied too heavily on individual initiative, their concept of government had failed for lack of central planning, production went down, the crop perished. They had collapsed, the first man rejoined, because the land, the factories had been restored to the former owners. When the people's army had marched into Aragón, the fields of the collective farmers had been devastated. It was not inability, he said, but the violent disbanding of the councils' government, the disarming of the farm workers that caused the disintegration of the resistance force. Yet most of the people we conversed with favored discipline, adjustment to a uniformly led army. A rigidly guided organization, they said, had nothing to do with suppression. The enemy's strength, they said, demanded our total obedience. Ruthlessness, even brutality, said Ayschmann, could sometimes be advocated, but a counterforce had to be maintained, otherwise a cynicism would pass into our blood, and someday it would hinder us from helping to build the new order. The problem, albeit just hinted at and seldom articulated, was to what extent an authoritarian model, a depleted system that was recognized as wrong, had to demand validity under circumstances in which people asked only who the stronger was. People ridiculed the paternalistic banners that ubiquitously held their precepts before our eyes. Homilies, adages were to be hammered into our minds, drilling us in simplified thoughts, though we ourselves knew best why we were here. And yet these mottoes had their truth. They touched only on externals, but stood for essentials. They were slogans, the actions came from us. We thought of the ribbon over the door of the House of the Party on Avenida Pi y Margall. The political commissar, it said, always goes first, ahead, at the lead, we could not remember the exact wording, and now, reaching La Feria, an outdoor space set up to house troops, we saw another inscription, over the round entranceway, shouting a truism at us. However, it did not hurt to be reminded again that command of military technology was decisive for the outcome of the war, every movement needed its simplifications and summaries, even the lyrics of the Marseillaise, of the Internationale had words that the people involved had memorized long since and yet wanted to hear over and over. That was why Gaudí, for himself and his fellow believers, had carved, in eternal remembrance, a Gloria, Gloria, a Sanctus Sanctus, a hosanna in excelcis all around in the brickwork. But then again, this could be proof that we were being kept down by a superior leadership, that we accepted out prerequisite lack of independence, that we clung to being patronized, that the watchwords of our allegiance were marked by a false consciousness, that we were far from mastering scientific thinking, and that we were still stuck in petty bourgeois idealism. We were en route to our own values, but overhead we carried flags, banners, coats-of-arms, insignia deriving from times that had nothing to do with us. No, we needed them in this era of war, for us they spoke about future things, about the defeat of war, about liberation, peace. Here we were, on the former fairground, a circle stretching out into a tree-lined covered walk on the edge of town, where the fields joined the meager workers' settlements, where the cattle market took place and the peasant carts brought in wares during the early morning hours, here we were, between the arcades, where, before the war, stands had been put up for the popular festivals, and in the labyrinthine paths around the band mall, which was hung with gaudy lamps and artificial flowers, people gathered from all European countries, southern and northern America, they had set their emblems and epigrams in front of themselves, as during the preparations for the march on the First of May, these areas were now thronged with the members of the battalions, which covered universal concepts with their names: Thälmann, André, Beimler or Vuillemin, Lincoln, Garibaldi, Dombrowski or Chapayev, or the Austrian Twelfth of February, the Commune de Paris. For several moments it seemed like a holiday, a touch of relaxation, of lightness could be felt, as if the imminent efforts were behind us, as if the victory had already been won, laughter, applause resounded, there, in the open arbor, in the middle of the boulevard, we saw the Knight of La Mancha hopping and fencing on stilts, his squire, puffed out with pillows, was apparently trying to bring him to his senses. The nobleman embodied all naiveté, all irrationality, while Sancho Panza incarnated the calm, the shrewdness of the people, this was again an explication, simple-minded perhaps, but plausible, the pantomime showed that all it takes is a slight nudge to eliminate a fallacy, the hero was certain to find his way out of his phantasmagorias, grasp the situation, and hit on an effective resistance. Earlier he had been led astray, his actions had been triggered by disguises, ominous pranks, ironic machinations, now he was exposed to unconcealed mockery from his audience, decrepit, as tall as a tree, he wandered about, all pathos and tragedy left him, amid the heckling he already began to doubt, he had been violently wrenched from the time of wandering buskers and dreamers into the warlike present. Theater groups at fairs may have often danced the drama of the heroic fool, this epic of a Spain that had frantically sought to overcome evil, to discover justice, human dignity, and that had always been undone by falseness, malevolence, deception, but here the players on the platform had no awe of tradition, of classical grandeur, as the ghost of an old-fashioned upbringing Don Quixote had wandered into the circle of new conquerors, who had no pity for his lame excuses, his miscarried ideals, who pulled him down to their level, forcing him to croak out the doctrine of his about-face. Just as labor, by being armed, had thoroughly changed its essence, so too had the notion of culture been taken out of its isolation and placed in the very midst of guerrilla warfare. Small mobile troops of the Batallion de Talento brought fragments of art and literature to the military camps, the dugouts and villages. Crude beginnings could be erected from the shattered monuments, some wastelands were initially penetrated only by letters of the alphabet, with which people arduously learned how to read. Something of what we had pictured in a long-ago past, this triumphal entry into learning, took place here, becoming part of the perseverance. On the square of the Feria a reporter offered us a different image of Marty, contributing to a better grasp of who he was. Standing on a chair in the Arena de Toros, amid the Islamic towers and arches, he had given a welcoming speech to a thousand volunteers, and the aftereffect made any scorn of the quartermaster impossible. When asked about the contents of the address, the witness was unable to repeat anything, all he knew was that it had radiated encouragement. Such charisma also belonged to the heraldry that made up for our lack of overview. A wealth of symbols, ciphers, appeals overlay the blend of impulses that had led to our participation, our commitment, but in our togetherness with others no one asked for subtle analyses, we needed signs for quick communication. If we gathered under those signs, we knew we were bonded with one another, there was no time for individual explanations. This morning we had already stumbled on that kind of symbol when, emerging from the quadrangular barracks courtyard surrounded by wooden galleries, we had entered the mess hall on the other side of the street. In the lengthy, stall-like building, whose roof beams were carried by a row of pillars, there was a mural on the narrow left side. In the dim light slanting in through the high vaulted window, we could at first recognize only the red color plane of the flag that rose to the middle of the picture, it was only when we drew closer that the details of the composition became visible. A man with a cartridge belt over his shoulder and a rifle slung across it, a woman, and a worker, all of them in blue-gray overalls, gazed, as a rigidly stylized, echeloned group, toward a future city, a silvery-gray metropolis, the huge M over the metro entrance recalling Moscow, the structure peaking in the star with the hammer and sickle on the pointed tower. The right hand of the armed man clutched the flagpole, his left arm veered across the section of a harbor with silhouette-like hulls, emphasizing the diagonal of a bridge supported by airy arches, over which, blurring in its speed, a train with a smoking locomotive zoomed by. The artist was unknown, but the stances of the figures, joining together into a bulwark, the look of tense concentration in their faces, the perspective lines of the façades running toward their line of sight, the rhythmically staggered verticals of the towers, the almost monochrome coloring, with the red of the flag as the sole contrast, were indicative of an extremely effective concentration. On a crude lime-washed wall in a stable furnished with the barest necessities, someone had painted a picture that gave no heed whatsoever to the provisional arrangement, it had been put into the haze of onion soup and black tobacco, staunchly it rose, with utter equanimity about the fact that cracks were already running through the plaster, that the thin layer of pigment would soon be scraped up and scratched up, would burst because of the humidity and the settling of the clumsily laid fieldstones, it defied its ephemeralness, it devoted the utmost of its abilities like the fighter in the field, it presented itself as if painted for a long duration, for the cosmic length of time we would be spending here in Spain, in an enormous concentration of energy, the picture stuck fast to the wall until with our victory or our defeat only flecks would survive, and it clung most obstinately where the strokes were most densely combined, in the faces, the hands. That evening, before I was to report to the city's medical center for the next leg of my journey, we took in some more of the dichotomy that was becoming a Spanish leitmotif. Up beyond the market hall on Plaza Major, by the water tower, in the former Arabian quarter, we found a remnant of what had been left behind, pauperized. Next to the tavern counters, narrow recesses in crumbling brickwork, the women stood at the trapdoors of their hutches, selling their bodies, retaining nothing for themselves in the commerce, abandoning themselves to the total liquidation of what was theirs, behind them, in the glow of a miserable kerosene lamp, a piece of wallpaper shone, hanging on the clay wall above their degradation. Soldiers who fought for the liberation of the exploited slunk through the penumbra of the alleys, bent as if trudging on sloshing ground, surreptitiously glanced about before letting themselves be drawn into the system of sharing in the human plundering of humans. The modern age, said Ayschmann, is a prophecy, we ourselves still live in the Middle Ages, there may be a second or two of illumination, it takes our breath away, makes us euphoric, then we slump back again. His statement could be refuted, for it was also indisputable that we were part of the most advanced leap of the present, our knowledge about those who went ahead without looking back, without fearing their downfall, demanded our relentless and strenuous effort to protect and consolidate their achievements. Now we were surrounded by the dirty tiles of the toilet below the market square, I caught only a brief glimpse of Ayschmann's profile with the sharply curving nose, the jutting chin, before he turned off and headed back toward the barracks. I steered toward Calle Major, the city's main commercial street, narrow, without sidewalks, covered with quadrangular stone slabs that gently bore down toward the middle gutter. The medical building was located between the pharmacy and the textile warehouse. Behind the heavy, profiled wooden door with the number seventeen on it and the year eighteen hundred ninety-six forged in iron, a marble staircase led up to a hall, where, as a patio, a cube with glass walls rose in the middle, circled by a corridor on whose outer walls glass doors led to the other rooms. The stuccoes on the ceilings, the floral patterns of the mosaics on the floor were reflected and refracted in the panes, while the boxes and bottles, the surgical instruments and hypodermic needles on the tables were doubled, forming rows, there was no telling in which glass chamber they actually lay, the medics, the soldiers on temporary duty were multiplied as they walked in and out of the proliferating rooms, holding written orders, carrying bundles and pouches, and the kaleidoscope of a face, full of curvatures and shiny spots, full of small black beards, pushed toward me until it became a single face, it belonged to Feingold, a member of the administration of Cueva la Potita, who was waiting to usher me into his fully loaded car and drive me to the hospital on the Jucar.

This too was a square where something was to be compressed. At times cloudlets drifted in, buzzing, humming, they brought no drizzle, just swarms of tiny black mosquitoes, otherwise a hush settled around the hospital ward under the pines, up by the edge of the steeply falling riverbank with its densely growing poplars. Only the anti-aircraft gun on the stone bridge leading across the ravine with the detritus grotto signaled the presence of a military facility. Under the high trees, their crowns blocking the tower of the main building, sat the patients, the furloughed soldiers, in the ring of the tiled benches and around the concrete fountains and basins. The frog in the middle of such a container resembled a primordial monster, a blessing Christ rose from another receptacle, on the socle in a third pool stood a boy and a girl, who, with arms around each other's shoulders, were hunched, daydreaming, over an open book.

In an urge for activity someone had lined the paths with round yellow stones that were to be found below in the caverns, and with the same dour patience, the backs and arms of the benches in the terrace walls over the riverbank had been baked out of loam and shaped like knotted branches, clay pots with cactuses and dwarf palms had been set up, the bars and iron arches had been erected for the tendrils of ivy and wild roses, and the wires had been pleated into the high dome of a cage with a sleepily ogling peacock. The rattling of machine guns, the clattering of maneuvering tanks in the drill camps near Posonubio had long since faded behind the slopes, anything that stirred here merely circled lazily to kill time, between staked-off boundaries. The winged lions on the porcelain slabs, the Virgin of Llanos on the house wall, the patron saint of Albacete, each with a halo, a white doll face, and a gold-embroidered violet mantle, the chiseled grilles on the windows, the Doric columns on the front steps, all these things were the sediment of a civilization that had nothing left to do but attend its own funeral. In nineteen twenty, the big landowner Nieto had given the country house to his wife as a wedding present, the ashlars from a torn-down bank that the padron had owned in the city, its columns, cornices, and window grilles had been used in the construction, and likewise its oaken doors, panels, beams, and stairs. Visited only for hunting by the family, one of the wealthiest in the province, flaunting its half-dozen similar properties, the mansion presented itself as idyllic on the outside, but its inside revealed a somber forlornness that could not be expelled even by the new administrators. For the soldiers gathering around the gigantic open fireplace in the hall, it was no consolation in their inactivity that the final owner, Baron Núñez de Balboa, now faced a Republican prison as an enemy of the people. The newness we had encountered out in the countryside could gain no foothold in this twilit feudalistic refuge. Since, contrary to my plans and expectations, I was assigned to the hospital, the architectural details kept forcing themselves upon me, and their peculiarities were bound up with the events in this closed precinct. So my theater of war was not, as it was for the others, the changing landscape, which had to be defended, clod by clod, both in an advance and in a retreat, my battleground was a sequence of rooms, chambers, stairways, and corridors, a line of spaces arranged specifically around an obsessively filled grove of pines. The unchangingness of the region, amid ravine, river valley, fields, and vegetable patches, marked the topography of the inhabitants' movements and interrelations. New arrivals had an impression of peacefulness, but soon, imperceptibly, everyday life manifested constraint, inevitability. Sitting across from Hodann, in his workroom on the corridor between the staircase and the administrative wing, I assumed that, after conferring with him, I would be directed to a training camp, but instead he talked about needing an assistant for administration and hospital care. He felt I had the right stuff because several years ago I had completed a medical course in Berlin. The police headquarters on Chausseestrasse had called upon the teenagers in our neighborhood to undergo this semi-military training during the summer. This was chiefly an attempt to recruit young men for the army, the police handled everything, the courses were given at the barracks of Döberitz. I joined the participants, thinking that the knowledge I acquired might eventually be used against my teachers. The following year, adding to the practical experiences I had gained during those weeks, I attended medical lectures at night school, and so Hodann had good cause to ask the leaders in Albacete to have me stay here. The impact of Cueva la Potita must have already made itself felt by now, for I did not protest, I was already trapped in the square of the settlement, albeit still imagining myself in a transitional phase. Hodann sat with his back to the window, beyond it the front yard was visible, almost entirely filled by a cistern with a high-curved handle on the pump head. Hodann's broad face, slightly wall-eyed, his high brow passing into the bald front of his skull, remained in a dull, gray-blue shadow. His voice was strained, hindered by his difficult breathing, but his calm, his pleasurable equanimity when showing the document that rescinded his medical degree let me only suspect a hoarse throat, a cold. His diction strongly colored by the Berlin dialect, he read the announcement published in the *Deutscher Reichsanzeiger* of October eleventh nineteen thirty-seven, the resolution passed by the University of Berlin, where he had graduated from the School of Medicine in December nineteen nineteen. He put the notice, supplied by the press service, into the folder, which, he said, contained another honorable document, the revocation of his German citizenship, July fourteenth, nineteen thirty-three. Now, after he turned to the side in his swivel chair, half his face revealed a yellowish pallor, his skin was moist, his forehead beaded with sweat. No sooner had he closed the folder than he started gasping, struggling against a fit of choking. I had not known that he was asthmatic, I had never seen him sick in Berlin, when I jumped up to support him, turning toward the door in order to shout for help, he vehemently pointed at the black leather case on the desk, I opened it and removed a syringe and an ampoule. Sitting there crumpled up, he squeezed mucus from his throat with a bellowing cough and spat into the bowl on the floor, with his trembling hands he simultaneously undid the seal of the adrenaline capsule, filled the syringe, held it up between his thumb, index, and middle finger, he tested the jet with bulging eyes, and stuck the needle through the cloth of his military trousers into his upper thigh. The ampoule contained two milligrams, but, he said later on, he had already taken as much as four or five milligrams and he had to try to get away from the interior and live by the ocean, where he hoped the climate would bring relief. For another minute his bronchia were paralyzed, torturously he leaned forward and backward to relax the cramp in his windpipe, spit dribbled from his mouth, and, after I took the syringe away from him, his white-knuckled hands clutched the arms of his chair. Outside, soldiers were huddled around a stone table with griffin feet, rhythmically picking up cards and slamming them down. With a tremendous moan, Hodann succeeded in catching his breath, and for a while he sat, hunched over, inhaling arduously, exhaling with long, drawn-out rattles, then he mopped his face and forehead with a handkerchief and started smiling again. Formerly a municipal physician and head of the health office in Reinickendorf, Berlin, a member of the Chamber of Physicians and of the city's Social Hygiene Commission, a member of the Socialist Physicians' Association, since July of this year head of the Convalescent Home of Cueva la Potita, which was assigned to the Thälmann Battalion, Hodann had left Germany on May tenth, nineteen thirty-three, the day when, for the first time, on the square between St. Hedwig's Church and the monument to Frederick the Second, a flautist and military taskmaster, a friend of Voltaire's, the books of heretical authors were burned on the National Socialist pyres. Since the late twenties and early thirties, Hodann, a cofounder, along with Hirschfeld, Forel, Havelock Ellis, and Kollontai, of the International League for Scientific Sexual Reform, had been famous, controversial, and libeled because of his candid enlightenment about sex. He had been close to the Communist Party, and, on the basis of several visits to the Soviet Union, he had written articles and books depicting it as exemplary, so that after the burning of the Reichstag, he had been arrested and taken to Moabit prison. One month later, while in the yard where he was walking his daily round between Ossietzky and Mühsam, he was summoned to the commandant, who handed him a piece of paper on which the inmate was to confirm that he had been well treated. Convinced they were going to shoot him for supposedly trying to escape, he was led to the gates after the announcement of his release, but then he reached the street unhindered. In recounting such stories, Hodann had the roguish, derisive manner of a teller of fairy tales. He could turn a matter of life and death into a humoresque. He had to report to the National Police Building on Alexanderplatz, and there, under the eagle's outspread wings, an SS officer in dark glasses popped up, and Hodann recognized his voice. As a forensic medical expert, he had once gotten the court to throw out a rape charge against the then-unemployed defendant, who now returned the favor by slipping Hodann into a male chorus that crossed the border into Switzerland at Schaffhausen. In Geneva, he worked at the International Bureau for Health Issues at the League of Nations, and there, in nineteen thirty-six, he met a Norwegian journalist and historian named Lindbaek and moved to Oslo with her. Here, in the raw cold on Karl Johan Gate, he suffered for the first time since childhood a bout of asthma, which would never relinquish its hold on him again. An unnecessary complaint was what he called it, nothing worth talking about, but the latest attack had patently worn him out, his face was still waxen, his shirt soaked on his chest and back, he had to make an effort to stay calm. His work in Cueva, as I learned on the very first day, was done under pressure to guarantee confidence despite the shortage of food and medical equipment, despite exhaustion and uncertainty. Recently he had had to treat almost the same number of mental cases as patients hospitalized with physical injuries. He had to cope with the conflicts assailing the soldiers who were idle, and he was responsible not only for food and advice but also for checking out minor incidents that might occur in situations of overcrowding, of waiting in isolation. Although not worth more than Hodann's gesture of dismissing them, the numerous infractions of house rules, the thefts, embezzlements, and denunciations, created a disquiet, a poisoning of the atmosphere, and from time to time, when the offenses increased in number, requiring an especially thorough investigation, his health deteriorated. Thus, today, after the delivery of poultry as dietary fare for the seriously ill, staff members had reported the absence of the best pieces of the meat and innards. So far the inquiry had established that the chickens slaughtered in the courtyard had been brought to the kitchen, where they had been distributed by helpers named Koelln and Hochkeppler. Still utterly preoccupied by the vastness of the land and the greatness of the imminent tasks, I accompanied Hodann through the corridor and into the kitchen, the stone room next door, leading to a square inner courtyard. The room had a counter at its center, two hearths under the chimney hood, a sink, and tables heaped with pots and cauldrons. The cook's helpers were not willing to make any further statements, they pushed bundles of wood into the fire, barely turned to us, hurried back out to the cart, which was groaning with branches. On the threshold of a door inserted deep into the brickwork sat a couple of oldsters, shrouded in black, staring motionlessly at the man who stood by the saw horse, violently shoving the saw into the wood. The wide, vaulted courtyard gate was open, outside, in an earthen area, men were running, leaping, one stormed past and kicked the soccer ball high into the air. Shouts, whistles could be heard from there. Mikhel, the porter, of Ukrainian origins, emerged from behind a pile of dried towels, from his room across from Hodann's came Feingold, his fingers on his moustache, Koelln and Hochkeppler had to follow, they were ordered to open the lockers in their room on the courtyard side. Here, in the old staff room of the manor, they discovered traces of spit-out bones and gristle, the helpers said they could not find the key, but clay bowls containing the leftovers of the missing chickens were hidden under the beds. The two helpers stood there sheepishly, their aprons snugly tied around their baggy trousers, Feingold inserted a chisel into the crack of the thin closet door, broke open the board, pulled out a sack of coffee beans, a carton of cans of condensed milk, plus a few more crates and packages. In the hinterland of the war I had participated in reconnoitering a house, it was a place of rest for soldiers carried away from the front, upstairs the rooms lined the second-floor corridor above the dark hall, treatment rooms, supply rooms, rooms for the physician, the medical orderly, the administrator, I was still unfamiliar with those higher regions, but the corridor downstairs, the kitchen, the cobbled courtyard, the surrounding rooms took shape, there, under low ceilings, lived staff members and the peasant family that had earlier tilled the soil of the baron of Balboa. I had not come here to see Hochkeppler's haggard face sullen with shame, Koelln's disintegrating features, and yet, Hodann explained to me, such investigations were part of the vast interconnected work of defense. The kitchen helpers, both of them members of the Party cell, had to be removed from their jobs and handed over to the brigade leadership in Albacete for punishment. Returning to Hodann's office, I instantly had to take part in registering the case, recording the facts, and, on the list, marking the misappropriated forty-eight cans of Dutch condensed milk and twenty-one lightbulbs in their original packaging as well as the weight of the located coffee and sugar. How, I asked, did such minute itemizing tally with the war of liberation now shaking Europe, and Hodann merely smiled, pointing out once again that we had to view ourselves as a general staff even here. The erroneous kitchen ledgers, the disappearance of medications, the settling of hostilities among the patients or between Diaz, who was in charge of political issues, and the German troops, whose language he did not know, the clashes between the staff and the administrator, Feingold, who always felt his authority was in jeopardy, the summoning of the military police, the humiliating good-byes of comrades who had not set out for Spain with impure motives, but here, in some forgetfulness, in some weakness, had lost their direction, the ceaseless confrontation with the dark side of a great historic achievement, all these things belonged to the daily routine of a doctor who had to muster his tenacity and helpfulness, his knowledge of human beings and his powers of persuasion even against a sudden wave of fatigue. It was solely the lack of time, the military laws that forced him to take measures that did not fit the perpetrated offenses. Now once again a group burst in, straining for self-control, but the rigid earnestness of their faces could not hold for long, they broke into confusedly overlapping arguments. Private Hornung, pale, bloody around his mouth, with the others clutching his arms, was shoved forward and accused of a crime, a murder perhaps. But then the issue seemed to be incitement, mutiny, the arrested man, they said, was imperiling the unity of work with his temper tantrums. Hodann wanted a detailed account of what had happened, and the reason for the tumult was already turning into something ordinary, having to do with roof tiles, the speakers themselves felt how embarrassing the scene they had made was, and faltering, using words that could not possibly explain the fury they had demonstrated, they mentioned, more and more casually, that Feingold had called them away from building a shed and told them to repair the kitchen roof, whereupon Hornung, as always at the slightest disturbance, had yelled out, demanding that they drop everything, stop working, not touch another stone. Now they had released the accused, who pressed his hands into his belly. Hodann, sitting there lost in thought, his shoulders hunched, spoke a few propitiatory words, blaming all the excessive irritability on abstinence. On the shortage of cigarettes. As soon as tobacco comes, he said, things will calm down again. And besides, he added, they ought to remember that Hornung was especially bristly because of his stomach ulcer. The eruption of anger had blown over. The men, who knew how to use their weapons, who had held their ground against overpowering attacks, turned away, humbled by their incomprehensible weakness. This too, said Hodann when we were alone again, is part of the etiology. The soldiers had suddenly been pulled from fire into idleness. At the front they had bonded closely because of the nonstop tension, the danger, the necessity for mutual trust. The sole task out there was to defeat the adversary. Now that they were separated from their units and left to their own devices, their shock-like experiences were making themselves felt and had to be overcome. When they had faced the enemy, there had been no doubts, no vaguenesses. The antifascist struggle in Spain was the touchstone for a generation of workers and intellectuals. By joining the battalions, they had taken an unequivocal stand. In their partisanship they had been able to transcend any imbalance in their personal lives. It was only here, in this banal seclusion that they felt their own needs reasserting themselves. Not only was the sexual abstinence disquieting, but ambivalences, antagonisms in the political picture haunted them, evoking questions that they, however, did not dare to ask. And so they were assailed by gloom, by brooding. They, whose sincerity was beyond the shadow of a doubt, revealed anxious, unworthy characteristics, they grew quarrelsome, often, to their own surprise, indulging in outbursts, which may have been merely signs of a desire to be brought back to their senses by objections, rebukes. With more than a hundred patients, only one assistant doctor, and few trained people, it was impossible for Hodann to fulfill every single wish for conversation and support. One of my tasks would be to aid him in trying to activate the convalescents, say, by forming study groups or publishing a news sheet, a wall newspaper. Under Hodann's gaze, I realized what the decision of this hour would mean to me. I wondered whether I was capable of performing the administrative job demanded of me and whether I was not about to retreat. Hodann's eyes were nearly black, his right eye was bigger, the brow pulled up. I had counted on joining the military units. There were three front lines in this war, the military, the political, and the cultural front. Although they formed an inseparable whole, the military front was the most tangible, here the actions led to an immediate outcome, were carried out by and on one's own self. This front was simple, clear-cut. It fitted in with the intentions of most of the people who had set out for Spain. Now, after I saw the marked faces of the men who had returned from the front lines, it became clear to me that during my preparations I had never weighed the possibility of losing my life there. Had I instantly joined the armed units, then this fearlessness might have continued. But now, held back here, I became aware of the tremendous risk of participating in a war, I became conscious of how terrible and indeed unnatural this conflict was. If I was evading Hodann's demand, it was because I was intent on denying a stirring of cowardice or showing that such fearfulness was part of my decision to face combat. Fighting on the front-most line was not necessarily more heroic, said Hodann, than protecting the fighting troops. The greatest sacrifices, I protested, were being made at the front, and no work as organizer or first-aid volunteer could replace that service. And yet, said Hodann, you are where you are needed most, and now we had walked through the pine grove, over to the whitewashed bar-rack with its twenty double bunks, where apathetic patients were lying here and there.

A row of rough-hewn stakes, rammed into the stamped clayey soil, carried the crossbeams under the gable of the corrugated metal roof, in the side wall the wide leaves of the door were open, low stalls could be seen outside, with plank fences, troughs, a haystack, sheep were driven by the Spanish farm workers, and sometimes chickens passed by, clucking, scratching the sparse, burned grass. It was only in the evening, after a ray of the setting sun had fallen through the door, casually lighting the heads of several beds, that for anyone who cared to view it, a colorful interplay of red and gold flashed along behind the pine trunks, narrowing down until it evanesced in the rising fog. They had to begin with the men who suffered most from being inactive, who were tied to no language, who could now communicate only by showing their wounds, but otherwise held their tongues. The promise of communality had to be demonstrated to them, a few Danes, Swedes, Yugoslavs; the daily athletic hours, the soccer matches, the games of pinochle, of chess, the gatherings at the electric piano in the hall of the main building were of no help. One had to start with the men who felt the most alien, yet that touched on something that applied to all the others too, the fundamental difficulty of expressing oneself. If it was a matter of standing up for a cause, each man could muster all his energy and generosity, but when asked about his experiences, his leanings, he had to grope for words, and he was beset with the inhibitions imposed on him since his youth. Coming from all kinds of trades, they might have shared their opinions on vocational problems, but their modesty prevented them from voicing theoretical statements. Hodann's goal was to make sure that they experienced their stint in the sick ward not as a weakness, a failure, but as a new concrete task, to be performed as matter-of-factly as when they had chosen their side in the struggle. Just as they could rely on one another at the front, so too they now had to fortify one another with organized conversations, discussions. Lecturers, training leaders had been requested, but instead of waiting for them, said Hodann, they could start the instruction themselves, in their own group, for everyone who had learned something ought to be able to impart his knowledge, everyone was a potential teacher, and by sharing what he knew he would not only gain in self-confirmation, he would also inspire his listeners to have faith in their own knowledge. But Hodann's suggestions, in the barracks or at meetings in the manor hall with its wooden paneling and high ceiling, were greeted with embarrassment. All these men certainly wanted to learn, to continue their education, but they could find nothing that they felt was worth passing on. English translations and Hodann's familiarity with Norwegian drew the foreign comrades into the deliberations, and the laboriousness of this procedure matched the arduousness of the overall project initiated by Hodann and was then thwarted by the remark that it made no sense thrashing out issues of wage labor that they were all acquainted with. What interested them, they said, was information about the military and political developments. The news reaching us twice a week from Albacete was not enough to supply a picture of the situation, these men wanted precise facts about the fight with the anarchists and the Marxist opposition, about the intentions of the Popular Front government and the Socialist Party, about the background of the war, about countless details that had always required elucidation by an expert. As long as the experts had not yet arrived, Hodann again wondered whether each man's image of the International Brigades might not be deepened if they presented the motives that had brought them all here. Perhaps it was a proof of strength that nothing could be said about this, that they had all come simply because this was the only thing possible for them to do. But Hodann was not satisfied with that, and it was only when it came to a conflict between him and Diaz that some of the men began to understand what he was after. Diaz, the deputy from Marty's staff, had to watch out for any deviation from the correct line. To him, probing the possibilities of self-studies was questionable. He opposed the idea of assigning a group to listen to and elaborate on radio reports. You see your job, said Hodann, as goading the troops on with speeches buoyed by sloganizing optimism. You believe you can maintain Party discipline only with the principle of orders and obedience. You build on the authoritarian models to which many of the volunteers feel close by force of habit, and you thereby prevent them from freely speaking their minds. When fighting, they did not ask one another about party membership, they judged one another purely by their military abilities, by how reliable they were. The Popular Front was put into practice there. Here, the cooperation that prevailed in a combat sector has to be practiced in a different way. The responsibility that each man bore in the field is still the same, but it has less to do with immediate adjustment and integration than with a self-reliance that has as yet to be formulated. Since according to the statutes it is the political commissar's obligation to look after the person, not the soldier, you have to do all you can to foster the initiative, the inventiveness of each individual. After the vehement retorts from the man responsible for political matters, the only decision reached was to authorize a news service, but now more and more of the men became active. Since my main function was nursing, which brought me into contact with all the patients in the home, I could take in some of the deliberations emerging all around me. A few men still balked at dealing with their situation, reflection could be disconcerting, the men lacked any direct guidance for overcoming their ill humor. Others, albeit undecided, voiced the notion that the goals in Spain were not just military and political, their task was to change human beings and all their living conditions, and such a change would succeed only if it were implemented in each person's consciousness. Yet such ideas also revealed how shaky, how unlikely they were, for the things we were mainly confronted with in this seclusion were distress and scarcity, were the unspeakable difficulties in procuring even the most makeshift necessities, the constant search for surrogates for whatever we lacked. We had no medications for calming the mentally disturbed, nor could we use pain-killing injections since many of the patients had dysentery, and the hygienic equipment was inadequate, so the issue of the importance of one's own personhood sounded almost ludicrous. But that was precisely where Hodann's arguments began, each man, he said, was part of the forces working on the future. No one must lag behind the decision-makers and let himself be patronized. Having evinced courage and steadfastness at the front, they should now practice mental endurance. However, the contradiction still existed between Hodann's demand for sincerity, questioning, criticism and Diaz's emphasis on the necessity for unconditional agreement with the proclaimed policy, and this gap elicited a reaction of caution and distrust at every larger meeting. When Diaz called for ideological firmness, Hodann declared that our allegiance could never be damaged by the demand for constantly examining the politics that we had chosen as our own. If anyone ventured to speak, he performed a balancing act between the desire to gain clarity in an issue and the striving to say nothing that might flout the official resolutions. We know, cried Hodann, the integrity of your stance, so you do not have to look for the correctness of every single word, you do not have to make an effort to repeat what you have learned, instead you ought to tackle things that are still vague, imprecise. But there was no way of eliminating their inner tension, their fear of being reported by the commissar. Heightened alertness was law. The man whose views did not conform to the specific model was bound to face mistrust. Each man was intent on proving that he was doing his duty, that he was rigorously following the current catchphrases. No matter how convinced he was of his own loyalty, the fear of sounding suspect could sometimes almost tear him apart. Amid all these unresolved matters only the news service found a continuous form. This was something regulated, iron-clad. Technicians had supplied a roof antenna for the radio receiver, a Telefunken, the six members of the editorial committee spelled one another, monitoring the loudspeaker. At night, however, the summing-up of the bulletins triggered the dichotomy inherent in every utterance. What should we select, we wondered, how could the enemy's announcements be set off most urgently against the Republican reports, how could omissions, obscure presentations be translated into comprehensible facts, just what, in the roaring profusion of voices, was important, tenable, showed the way. The reports we received from the transmitter of the brigades, short-wave frequency twenty-nine point eight, constituted a norm for the pages we tacked on the hallway bulletin board every morning. Here, from Madrid, we heard whatever concerned all of us in the same measure, about the status of the international aid, about the further efforts at unity, about the situation in Germany. And again we caught the names of those who supported the Spanish struggle, who were here, like Renn, Uhse, Weinert, Bredel, Regler, Busch, Marchwitza, Seghers, Kisch, Alfred Neumann, Alberti, Hemingway, Ivens, Ehrenburg, Malraux, Saint-Exupéry, Branting, Toller, Spender, Dos Passos, Neruda, Siqueiros, or those who addressed the public from abroad, people like Heinrich Mann, Thomas Mann, Arnold Zweig, Feuchtwanger, Brecht, Wolf, Piscator, Rolland, Shaw. What we did not write was that the circle of solidarity was very small, compared with the enormous concentration of forces steering toward a world war, and that it was always the same voices warning, calling for common sense. In France, in the British labor movement, in Scandinavia, in the United States, in Indochina, and especially in China, we looked for any hint of socialist development, every demonstration, every agitation, every strike helped our cause. And then along came Diaz, first he complained about the radio reporting, the many sides of which simply made it confusing, and as for the wall newspaper, which appealed to most of the men, Diaz called it an adequate outlet that made further discussion extraneous. No, replied Hodann, the wall newspaper only reproduced something, and while it was informative and useful, the real benefits were the conclusions drawn from this review and the comments it provoked. In late October, he had ordered a meeting in the hall. The winter was early, with storms and rain squalls, the bats, one of which was preserved in Albacete's municipal coat of arms, threw themselves against the house, emblems torn loose, blindly fluttering around the symbiosis of banking and latifundia, we heard them thumping against the colorful panes of the windows above the stairs, and the dull thuds mingled with the crackling of the wood burning in the fireplace. The red flag, hanging from the very lofty glass roof down to the second-floor gallery, lightly fluttering in the breeze over the wooden hoop of the candelabrum, was part of the effort to transform the nature of the confiscated building, but the perforated rolls, inserted into the piano case at the outset of the discussion and emitting the *Tannhäuser* overture, *Cavalleria Rusticana*, and Sibelius's *Tristesse*, had actually hammered the ghostliness in. The winged lions pulled here too, on small slabs, around the walls, and angels, with worn naked chests, hoisted themselves out of the door frames. Security was simulated by the seething distillation apparatus and by the mugs filled with a few drops and handed around, but, freezing, we huddled together on the wall benches and around the tremendous boardroom table, and our breath rose in clouds from our mouths. Most of us were still silent, and how could we even think of a discussion, someone asked, if every utterance was to be recorded and, should the occasion arise, be laid at the speaker's door. Hodann designated himself as liable for all statements, he alone, as head, as officer, could be called to account by superiors. This was rejected, it was paradoxical, they said, that people who, conscious of their responsibility, had joined the defense, should agree to be patronized. Each man, they said, had to answer for his own words because they were all under the same flag. Hodann's remark may have been deliberately provocative. He turned to Diaz and said that the power of dogmatism had to be countered by increased historical, scholarly, scientific, and philosophical education, voicing opinions was unavoidable precisely in a critical situation. That, Diaz replied through his interpreter, would bring about anarchism at a time when the working class needed the tightest possible organization to resist the irruption of chaos. Actually the restraint effected by Diaz and his group of followers was consistent with our situation, for the desire to explore was bound to trigger protests from men advocating the commandment of unconditional allegiance. This was the case not only in this circle but also wherever the Party of the Proletariat fought to maintain and expand its positions. We were in a state of war, no latitude could be given for doubts and deviations, the orders of the higher Party organs were binding and brooked no contradiction. Hence Hodann's project was dangerous, and it could awaken the suspicion that he indeed had anarchistic or bourgeois-liberal motives for trying to pilot the discussion. The question of whether an open debate was at all possible could theoretically widen into the pronouncement that, given the enemy's watchfulness, the slightest mistake on our part could have devastating consequences. But that would mean, said the first speaker, whose powerful face, deformed by a scar, was squeezed out even more broadly by his supportive fist, that we too were assuming there were traitors in our own ranks, but I refuse to acknowledge such a thing, rather any scruples about participating in the dispute reveal our entire undemocratic upbringing. Münzer was a typesetter, he came from Hemelingen near Bremen, his speech, flavored with Low German, had aroused a sense of familiarity in me. The soldiers, he went on, who are committing their self-assurance, their energy and generosity, hold their tongues whenever they have to freely speak their minds. All of us trained ourselves—I personally lost an eye, and one of my ears was busted—for the main thing, for the crucial actions, now we have the right and we have the leisure to think about these actions. They are to lead to liberation, and our class has the task of initiating it. Liberation cannot be handed to us, we have to conquer it ourselves. If we fail to conquer it ourselves, then it will have no consequences for us. We cannot liberate ourselves if we do not eliminate the system that suppresses us, and the conditions that produce the system. But how can *we* bring about liberation, how are the upheavals to be carried out, if we have always learned only to submit, acquiesce, and wait for mandates. Even Lenin felt we were capable only of thinking in trade-union terms and he had the Party vanguard make decisions in our stead. That may have fitted the historical givens back then. The Party executed politically what the proletariat set in motion spontaneously. But should our tasks forever be restricted to trade unions, he asked, should we be allowed a certain mobility on the lowest level while the decisions are made by an elite. The delegates are elected from bottom to top, but orders are issued from top to bottom. We have no influence beyond our jobs and cells, we cannot exercise control, we produce under directives. Such is our working life, our political life. Letting ourselves be reprimanded, humiliated is in our nature. Out of that was rationalized a useful characteristic. We had to be proud of being industrious, proficient, and obedient. Our humility became the ideal of discipline, of Party loyalty. I want, he said amid incipient agitation, to point out the following. All our efforts toward liberation were dictated by the attempt to cast off the hegemony of the authorities and finally reach a place where we ourselves could judge and decide. Yet we kept encountering the people on the top, who kept explaining to us that we did not know what was right for us and that therefore the leadership had to act on our behalf. When I try to figure out my position in the workers' movement, I feel as if I first have to start digging, have to burrow my way, claw my way out of a mass of debris that covers us. Our organizations are like geological strata, which we have to lift off so that we can find ourselves. That is what I wanted to say. That no equality exists. That no matter how hard we strive for independence, we always bump into someone who prescribes what we have to do. That we are incessantly regimented. That no matter how right the things presented to us are, they are nevertheless wrong so long as they do not come from ourselves, from myself. But the Party, someone else threw in, it stands for us, we are the Party. That is what they say, replied Münzer. But the people who say that usually come from the upper regions. And when they say it, they have a transcendental aura. They rely on their decision-making privilege and on our compliancy, they remain unapproachable by dint of their rank. Diaz leapt up, for a while only an excited tangle of voices could be heard, but then Hodann likewise got to his feet and shouted with unexpected sharpness that Münzer still had the floor. In the ensuing hush, Münzer said that there was a lot of talk about the future man in the future society, but that we absolutely had to think about today's people, for if they were fearful and humiliated, crooked and crippled, then they would be of little use to the people of the future. The so-called policy of freedom, aimed as in Spain at the authoritative, centralist model, said Hodann, basically belonged to a bourgeois revolution. In their rejection of political actions and in their striving for independent production collectives, the anarcho-syndicalists were following a populistic direction, in stressing individualistic values they did not want to get beyond small natural work groups. Just as they were against the mass organizations, the bureaucratic Party machine, the state machinery, so too they opposed technological development, the planned economy. In this way they steered the struggle of the working class backward, toward a romantic, nostalgic artisanship, instead of impelling it forward toward a socialist economy. Münzer for his part recurred to the conscious personal limitation, the discipline bordering on self-surrender, that threatened to stiffen, to harden the Communists. The greatest freedom, he was answered, was precisely to be found in this resolve to step back as an individual for the good of the cause, which was the best for the many. Settling the conflict, Hodann insisted that we focus on the Spanish problems, especially since tonight a member of the Socialist Youth Alliance was to join our discussion.

Gomez and Hodann now tackled our frequent questions about the antagonisms in Spain, by going back to the underlying conflict. From the uprisings of the slaves against Roman rule, the revolts of the serfs against the feudal lords, the struggle of the landless peasants against the oligarchies of the big landowners, to the guerrilla warfare against the Napoleonic occupiers and the dynasty of the Carlists, this country had gone through rebellions aimed at finding solutions consistent with the characteristics, the lifestyle of the people. With sticks, scythes, and pitchforks or with shooting irons, whatever happened to be available, constantly with weapons inferior to the enemy's, yet always imbued with an almost death-defying will to fight, the workers charged against the oppressors, their pride, their indignation were enough for them and were never shattered by the mercenary armies of the grandees. The revolt always came from below, flared up spontaneously, it was never orderly, serried, even the guerrilla wars were made up of crews, bands, gangs, and alongside the partisans, who served the poor, there were adventurers and prowlers. In eighteen sixty-eight, when Bakunin, belonging to the First International, wanted to extend the Workers' Association to Spain according to his lights, he had Fanelli, his Italian deputy, introduce the teachings of the secret anarchist society. Not only had the groundwork been laid by generations of attacks against the establishment, it was also underpinned by Proudhon's theories. The rural populace, which would have to be called upon for setting up anarchist communes, was beyond reach because of its poverty and illiteracy, but craftsmen and factory workers listened to Fanelli. A time of ferment came, since an army revolt had just broken out against the royal house, and the soldiers' appeals for the overthrow of church, state, and capital were bound to have a favorable reception. From the very start, Fanelli's name was linked to something like hero worship, people were willing to build up his persona, give it a mythical nimbus, which affected all subsequent descriptions. He was depicted as tall, with a thick, black beard, dark, fiery eyes, and a voice that took on a metallic timbre during violent emotional outbursts. He was not only a revolutionary, but also a wandering preacher, an Anabaptist, a conjurer. He did not master the Spanish language, his rolling diction was not always understandable, but his statements, bolstered by his sweeping gestures, that the land should belong to those who farmed it, that all workshops and factories should be taken over by those who labored there, required no translation or more detailed explication. The ideas of a socialist state could not be spread, but the demand for self-help found resonance in the workers' own experiences, any directive from a higher level was not to be trusted, there was no counting on the leadership strata, the upheaval had to come from small groups, and no actions should result in forming a party. The workers were to gain power through neither a program nor a dictatorship, any hegemony and authority were to be banished, the federative communities foreseen by anarchism could emerge only on a voluntary and equal basis. In eighteen seventy-one, in London, the dispute over the participation in the political struggle led to Bakunin's rupture with Marx and Engels, through his Alliance Bakunin pitted libertarian communism against the rigorously structured system, and during the next few years he tried to test his model in Spain. In this country, where there were no major industries and where the workers in the traditional family businesses were in physical contact with the owners, experiencing their subjugation directly, each man was geared to an immediate reaction to resistance. In his notions of collectivism, Bakunin may have included an elite that would draft a new life together, but this concept was dominated by his idealistic faith in the instinct and togetherness of the people, and he hoped that the dominion of freedom would spontaneously develop from their obscure, yet elemental strength. And within two years it already seemed as if the path to the brotherhoods had gotten through thanks to constant pressure, zealous subversion. The forces of freedom had brought the monarchy to its knees, the king abdicated, the Republic was proclaimed, its first president, Pi y Margall, lauded Proudhon and the beginning of the federalist era and condemned order, which had always served as camouflage for injustice and violence, he initiated the total decentralizing of the country into municipal subdivisions. For many people, it was as if the dream of the Paris Commune, which had just been smashed, were coming true. The role of the revolutionary national guards was taken over by the Republican militia, here and there workshops, land holdings were communized, mayors were removed, priests lost their parishes, officials were dismissed, the rich had punitive taxes inflicted on them, several members of the nobility, of the royal family were exiled, the struggle against clergy and aristocracy, against capital and state order aroused enthusiasm in Europe's radical youth, in Spain the Revolution had truly commenced, permanently, as people said, with the goal of completely and definitively wiping out the state, that principle of evil, and all oppressive institutions and replacing them with free cooperatives. But the leaders of scientific socialism turned against such actions, which led to individual terrorism, to burning down factories, castles, and churches, to looting and killing. The socialists recommended strikes in lieu of bombs, training and schooling in lieu of cutting throats, educating workers in the consciousness of their class in lieu of improvising. Isolated measures, declarations of independence by village communities, clusters of sects, avengers, and secret societies would be useless for freeing the landless peasants, the impoverished workers, they could be liberated only by joining forces in a party that safeguarded the interests of the proletariat. And yet the riots occurred precisely where no class consciousness had as yet developed, where the lack of knowledge, the emotions of hatred were greatest, the upheaval was initiated by destitute and starving farm workers, with no tactics, no coordination. And according to the anarchist principle, this was the only way to achieve any real transformation, for no change could survive if it were not brought about by everyone of his own free will. The personal decision, the recognition of the individual's mental strength had to come first, the worker would be able to liberate himself only when he no longer felt like a dependent. Marx sent Lafargue to Madrid, hoping to stumble on the rudiments of socialist thinking among the Libertarios and to prevent the Anarchist Alliance from splitting from the International. But a further feature of the underground movement was that no one proved to be in charge, that no leadership was to be identified, and so all the emissary could do was to roam the country, from one godforsaken hamlet to the next, he could watch when, in sudden flarings of anger, local representatives of exploitation, a manor lord, a home owner, a padre were taken prisoner and executed, and when many tiny victories were passed off as a great victory, while the pillars of the old state, the middle classes and the oligarchies above them, were scarcely affected in their system and were as intent as ever on preserving their property, waiting for a favorable moment to strike back. As surprising as the breakthrough to a voluntaristic structure was the disintegration of the units, for lack of planning and organizing they had ignored the fact that the indestructible opponent was gearing up to attack, that the fostering of regionalism played the initiative into the hands of the generals. And the generals, for their part, deploying thoroughly cohesive troops, cleaned out one nest of rebels after another in order to recentralize the country as a new stronghold of the monarchist bourgeoisie. Despite their rationality the founders of historical and dialectical materialism had made no impact on the antagonists of the workers' movement, but then history itself came to their rescue, and Engels expressed his relief when the anarchist Republic showed its weakness vis-à-vis his and Marx's theses and suddenly collapsed. Nevertheless the federalist tradition remained as powerful as ever. During the next half century little changed in Spanish society. Aside from the Asturian coal mines and the Basque steelworks and shipyards, there were virtually no major industries in which a unified proletariat might have developed. Furthermore, ninety out of a hundred businesses had fewer than five employees, closely tied to the owner. While workers had by now realized the necessity of forming unions, the tendency toward individual action still predominated, even in the Communist Party, which had only a few hundred members by April of nineteen thirty-one, when the Republic was reconstituted after the fall of the monarchy and the military dictatorship. The meetings of the sixty Communists in Madrid, Gomez reported, included one comrade who always showed up with a huge, handmade bomb that he placed under his seat. When asked why he carried it around with him, he replied that if a bomb were suddenly needed, there would be one here. At this time, the Party was against parliamentarism, against cooperating with the Socialists, who had affiliated themselves with the bourgeois groups. For us, said Gomez, the Republic could only be a transition to a soviet government. The members of the Central Committee rode a few rented coaches to Plaza Major in Madrid in order to join the fifty comrades reporting there and to call for strike actions, armed combat, and preparations for a rule by commissars. Part of the audacity of this notion was that the gathering took place on a square that was completely hemmed in by buildings and accessible only via a few narrow alleys, and in the pushing and shoving hardly an escape route was available, so that in the end almost the entire Party group was imprisoned. It was only after such experiences that the Party, driven out of politics for a year, tried to tailor its tactics to the concrete reality. Still extremely tiny in size, it nevertheless gained influence in the harbor areas and mining districts and also in the rural populace, which felt the plundering most intensely. But behind the uprisings of the farm workers in Andalusia and Catalonia stood the anarchist and syndicalist associations. Given the absence of reforms, these groups supported dispossessing the big landowners and giving their land to the farm workers, and they proclaimed a general strike in Valencia and Barcelona. The differences between Communists and anarchists were hard to pinpoint for the unenlightened proletarians. Since their aim was an elementary improvement of their situation, the makeup of an organization and the participation in a government were issues that meant little to them. Even he himself, said Gomez, had barely noticed how he had moved from the bloc of revolutionary farm workers to the Communist Youth League. The only clear line was the one dividing them from the Socialist Party, there stood reactionism and the petty bourgeoisie, and behind them feudalism. On this side of the front there were the anarcho-syndicalist and Communist forces, until the rebellion of the Asturian miners in the autumn of thirty-four. It was this turning point that first revealed the contradictions within the widely ramified ideological policies. The unity of the working class, which everyone had been striving for, was not to be achieved. Instead, there were swings, changes of goals and viewpoints, from which the Communist Party developed its new policies, a program that, two years later, in a specific historical situation, would put the Party in the lead position. A socialist left wing, under Caballero, the union chairman, had sided with the rebellious proletariat. The Communists and the regional syndicalist groups joined the appeal for a common action. But the Iberian anarchists, who saw themselves as a revolutionary elite, and the leadership of the major workers' confederation refused to participate in the fighting, which they viewed purely as an expression of the partisan power game. And power was the objective again, a power that was to keep its internal antagonism. The passivity of half of the Spanish working class, as dictated by the anarchists, contributed to the defeat of the Asturian insurrection. The establishment of the United Socialist Front shattered on the antithesis between the communist and the anarchist principle. The idea of a rigorous party structure was incompatible with the freedom of improvisation. In October of thirty-four, one year before the reorientation of the Comintern's policies, the foundation of the Popular Front was laid in Spain. This strategy alone, it was acknowledged, had the potential for overcoming the future conflicts. Though Caballero remained hostile to the Soviet Union and the Communist International, the Communist Party nevertheless allied itself with him, realizing that the forces in the middle would have to be won over for the struggle against a growing fascism. However, the anarchists demanded a shift in focus toward the left. Yet during the revolt in the autumn of thirty-four, said Gomez, the Communist Party's tendency toward reducing collectivist intentions was not yet recognizable, the rebellious miners formed their own soldiers' councils and revolutionary committees, and their appeals for unity were aimed at creating a strong socialist basis, deemed necessary for the imminent coalition in a broader front. The ruling strata of the country, frightened by the hint of unification within the workers' movement, sent out their military to strike at the isolated rebels with a violence and brutality that were harbingers of the Falangist counterrevolution. The workers' regiments had to drum up pistols and shotguns to defend themselves against three army corps with tanks, heavy artillery, and air squadrons, and when this was called a bloodbath, the word was to be understood literally, as a frenzy with all conceivable cruelties. Trained to inflict torture and slaughter, the troops of the Foreign Legion and the Moors shipped in from Morocco went after the survivors of the bombings. In Asturia the era of torture was ushered in. If anyone fell into the clutches of the killers, they used tongs and red-hot pokers on him, they crushed his hands, his genitals, they hammered his knees, his feet to pulp, he had to suffer multiple deaths, he was led to the wall, to the gallows, to the grave that he himself had dug, he was tied to the chair to be executed in front of the wives and mothers before he was finally hanged, garroted, shot, or driven into the sharpened stake. With three thousand deaths, seven thousand wounded, forty thousand prisoners, the Asturian population had to pay for the attempt to oppose despotism with a rule by workers. And yet the atrocities could not stifle the insurgence. A revolutionary process had begun, the political consciousness of the working class grew stronger, and in little less than a year, by February of thirty-six, the Popular Front government, striven for by the Socialists and Communists, had become a reality. In everything emerging from now on, Hodann remarked, we would have to side with whatever came closest to our own idea of truth. An objective appraisal was not yet possible, he said, we could use our faculties to decide between two directions only by determining which of the two involved a fitting assessment of the situation, a sure tactic for proceeding. Both the anarcho-syndicalists and the Republic's Popular Front were pursuing the same goal, he said, to liberate the country from fascism, but the means they employed and their methods in pursuing their goals were irreconcilable. The tug-of-war already started with the elections. The anarcho-syndicalist groups, loyal to their traditions, refused to participate in order to maintain their sovereignty vis-à-vis the parties and the parliament. These groups included huge segments of the masses, who saw the syndicates and not the political organizations as the mouthpiece for their interests. Nonetheless many workers voted for the Popular Front, not only because it promised the release of political prisoners, there were still thirty thousand, but also because the projected agrarian reform and industrialization guaranteed an improvement in their living conditions. The conformist solutions, the anarchists claimed, would lead at most to a socializing of poverty, only a violent overthrow could carry out the workers' demands. The Communist Party was accused of betraying the revolution. However, the Communists pointed out, the balance of power in this country did not permit any overthrow, and the patience and restraint they propagated were convincingly validated by the election results, in which barely five million votes for the Popular Front were juxtaposed with four a half million for the right and the center. For us, said Gomez, the true Realpolitik actions now began. We were the smallest party. Next to the eighty-nine Socialist and the eighty-four bourgeois deputies, the Communist Party now occupied sixteen seats in the Cortes, which, compared with the single parliamentary representative in nineteen thirty-three was already a victory. We have to compute with a different yardstick than the immediately obvious one, he said. By July of thirty-six, our Party membership had increased to thirty thousand, but there were over a million in the anarcho-syndicalist association and one and a half million in the Socialist trade union. So it was significant when our campaigns succeeded in fusing the Communist Youth and the Socialist Youth into one organization, which brought the Party two hundred thousand new allies. During the first few days of the war, thirty-five thousand of them joined the armed combat. In the brief years of building the Party, said Gomez, we first had to overcome our lack of theoretical knowledge and our propensity for boastful and individualistic heroism, and then we had to learn not to be fooled by the swift triumphs of the anarchists and to substitute sober actions for our revolutionary exuberance despite the opinion of the proletarian majority. At the outset of the antifascist war, it was said that power was up for grabs and that the party of the proletariat had to seize this power. But power was not up for grabs, to be snatched like a pack of cigarettes, it was out front in the combat zone, and if it could be found there in wracking battles, it first had to be supported by political efforts. In the first storm, the will to set up a Popular Front had scampered away from any deliberation. The fantasy was spreading that for the first time since the October Revolution, in the Europe of aborted uprisings, a government by councils could be established, and we ourselves had once helped to create this image. We had to get over not only our qualms about the Social Democrats, said Gomez, but also our entire loathing for the shopkeepers, the petty bourgeois, the middle classes, whose tightly knit animosity we had felt while growing up and with whom we now had to collaborate. We greatly sympathized with the arguments that this time, in fighting the enemies of the Republic, we must not stop halfway, that we had to drive forward the social revolution together with the military actions, and we needed all our newly gained discipline to adjust to the Party guidelines. But soon we were won over by their assessments of the situation and their organizational know-how in building up the defense. Within a short time the Party was involved in all measures pertaining to politics and war. We were still opposed by the great mass of Spaniards who did not understand why the Communist Party had brought the revolution to a standstill, who refused to cooperate with the liberals, the center, who charged us with hypocrisy and deceptive maneuvers and accused us of wanting only to put through the Comintern's directives against the interests of the country. In overestimating the achievements of the first few months the anarcho-syndicalists believed that the dictatorship of the proletariat was already a fact. After the power of the landed gentry, high finance, and the church had been broken, and the committees of workers and peasants had taken over a number of factories and estates, they fantasized that Spain would now be the birthplace of the world revolution. They failed to see that they were confronted by armies that would wipe their collectives away like chaff, that it was too early to think about a radical reshaping of society so long as the great fascist powers were in Spain, planning to turn this country into a test site. In the spirit of Don Quixote, with the same blind enthusiasm that used to be ours too, said Gomez, they threw themselves, in programmatic disorder, against the enemy fire. And anyone who was not left for dead, but got away instead, carried along with him his utopian notion that if only everyone firmly believed in an anarchist community, it would drive out the enemy forces. We were not, he said, against taking over banks, industries, and major land holdings, how could we as Communists have been against that, we were only against radicalization. What we had attained was a temporarily noncapitalist state that could introduce a limited land reform and lay the foundation for an educational system, all other energy was to be concentrated on resisting the foe, who was intent on destroying the extant bastion of socialism in western Europe, thereby also gaining experience for the decisive battle against the Soviet Union. The prerequisite for our defense was the unity of the people. That was why the small landowners, the tradesmen, the bourgeois center had to be reassured. The Party had to assume the role of keeping order, of maintaining a conservative element. It advocated moderation, parliamentarism, the fulfillment of government obligations in order to guarantee a revolutionary development over the long haul. During this stage of the conversation Münzer expressed the anarchist view that deviating from the revolution had debilitated the people's war, that the unity aspired to by the Communists could not come about because the militant workers felt cheated, because they could place no trust in an alliance with the bourgeoisie. A war of liberation could have succeeded only on a proletarian basis, such as had been established in July of nineteen thirty-six, but now the workers were disoriented, they no longer knew what to fight for since so much energy was turned around and used up in the internal quarreling. For the attack against fascism the workers were willing to make any sacrifices, but they refused to give their lives in order to preserve the bourgeois state. However, the call for continuing the revolution, the desire for further expropriations, replied Gomez, would have brought the war into the very midst of the Republic. The Party was forced to risk losses in its own camp in order to keep the Popular Front from crumbling, to prevent the center from defecting to the other side. With rational arguments, and then, when it became necessary, with violence, the Party moved against the left wing of the anarcho-syndicalists and against Nin, Gorkin, Andrade, the leaders of the United Marxist Workers' Party, which, despite a name feigning a large enrollment, had scarcely over three thousand followers, albeit extremely active ones. While here the Communists came up against an irreconcilability aimed at splitting the Republic, the Party nevertheless kept gaining more and more ears, and its growth to over half a million members by the spring of thirty-seven showed that it had won its mass basis. But now the newcomers were recruited less from the working class, said Münzer, and more from business, officialdom, academic circles, the corps of officers, whom the Party offered possibilities of career advancement. It had been shown that you had to be a member if you wanted to obtain influential positions. The large number of people coming to us from the middle class, retorted Gomez, was due to Party tactics. With those words, he stood up in order to launch into an excursus on statecraft. The reflections of the fire billowed on the flag, hands, and faces, as if carved black and red, moved forward over the tables. The central column of the hall cast a heavy shadow straight across the men sitting on the side. Cunning, cold blood were necessary for preserving the Popular Front. This policy had to win over forces that, by their nature, were close to reactionism, that, ever accessible to enemy propaganda, were trying to hinder progress and champion the revival of the old ruling system. They had to be wooed, given incentives, for there were many among them who were needed, whose knowledge could be utilized. And once the middle strata were drawn in and appreciated, the Party could then influence the strong rightist peripheral groups, whose bases were in the Spain of the Falangist generals and all around in a lurking Europe. Careful distinctions had to be drawn among them all, the interests they represented kept shifting incessantly, depending on which prospects of advancement offered themselves. This activity had suddenly brought the once unsightly Communist Party to the fore. The point had come when the Party became the center of social solidification. It became the mouthpiece of reason, it interceded in order to prevent energies from chaotically flowing apart. The militias' first disorderly resistance had lost its strength, the Popular Front was on the verge of collapse. The fear of fascism had penetrated even the petty bourgeoisie, which, for all its selfishness, had nevertheless taken over something from the country's generations-long strivings for independence. With the embargo by the Western powers, with France and England clearly waiting for the destruction of the Republic, a panicky willingness had emerged to surrender to the foe, but then the self-assured demeanor of the Communist Party indicated new possibilities of defense. The patriotic achievement of the resistance was not yet worn out, only the military means had dried up, and the effusively inflicted social changes revealed how unstable they were. The fighters would have to strengthen their vitality, in the hinterland the shock of violent actions had to be softened. This required a position of power, and such a position could be won only by the side that could show it had an arsenal large enough to supply whatever was needed at any time. Ships sailed from Odessa in order to run the blockade and bring the Communist Party weapons, without which the fronts would have fallen. The goal was to preserve the Spanish Republic, that was what the Communists, as well as the Socialists and anarcho-syndicalists, had fought for from the very first day. The Republic, the popular bloc, and not a specific party, were to benefit from the help. The sign of the new action was heroic, but its effect relied not on wishful thinking but on practical abilities. Communism as an objective was not abandoned, even though it looked as if the Party were expelling all efforts at upheaval, at revolutionary transformation. Bourgeois assistance was needed only for smoothing the path, on which the middle class itself would eventually be disempowered. Now, after the confiscation of all property had been revoked, the bourgeoisie could still consider itself a partner of the Communists, defying the people who had openly threatened to wipe them out. The task that the Party set for itself was to issue such a revocation and yet gain the sympathy, the support of the workers. A government had to be established, with the kind of makeup that could overcome the antagonism. In nineteen thirty-four Caballero had broken with his Party's view that all socialist forces had to be put at the disposal of a coming bourgeois revolution, since the uprising in Asturia he had stopped endorsing reformism and was now advocating the elimination of capitalism, and Caballero had a strong influence on the working class. Switching to a libertarian communism that was not taken seriously by the center, but which guaranteed him the respect of the anarchists and syndicalists, he let himself be maneuvered into a position in which he retained proletarian approval but did not yet frighten off the liberal side. During the first month of war he had regarded the Communist demand for rebuilding the army as counter-revolutionary, but then, with the exacerbated military situation and the collapsing of the supply system, he soon realized that they needed not only a centralized army leadership but also a stabilized governing power. Flattered by Communist diplomacy, Caballero, known as Spain's Lenin, let himself be pushed upstairs into the office of prime minister and war minister. The responsibility conferred upon him as chief of the Popular Front led him, in line with the Communist Party's reckonings, to a moderate attitude that also gained him the cautious trust of the bourgeois side. His position was consolidated by the inflow of military equipment from the Soviet Union, the display of international solidarity by the arrivals of the brigades. The Communist Party, on whose planning he depended and which took over the leadership of the general staff, assured the population's right-wing segments that, rather than veering toward the workers' government demanded by him, he would stand and fall with the Popular Front. The Party had initially drawn close to the Socialists, and now, expanding and safeguarding the coalition, it aimed to establish beachheads among the forces that, by their very stances were bound to feel distrust and hostility toward the Communists. The anarcho-syndicalists might be swayed by the courage, the strategic abilities that the Communists had shown in battle, but in order to convince officers, specialists in economy and administration, they had to promise, cajole, appeal to ambition. Any rewards paid to them had functioned simultaneously to put them under the control of the Party. The peasants were likewise more open to delivering food if the Communists promoted their wish for owning a bit of land instead of being forced to accept a production method for which they were not prepared. Such an approach was not a cynical calculation, it expressed realistic thinking. Many farm workers, said Gomez, had been anarchists so long as they owned nothing, but once they were granted fields, they preferred replacing anarchism with rational organizations. The protection of private property, the concern for the national budget—in the eyes of many people who still preferred disorder and crisis as accumulators for an overthrow, this was a procedure the Party was using to seize the hegemony, and if it provided the military struggle with rules suitable for the enemy, then the Party was accused of relying purely on Soviet support for gaining power for actions. As the Communist Party it belonged to the Communist International, that was its strength. It had attained its decision-making position because it was part of a worldwide movement that was now having an impact here, in Spain. The weapons were paid for with gold from the salvaged bullion reserves of the Spanish National Bank, he said, and that was appropriate, Soviet industry had to work to make those weapons despite its strenuous production for its own defense. In our vaults the money is useless, but this way it can be allocated for gaining the victory and later for rebuilding the country. Suddenly one could feel the dimension of death opening up behind the attendees. It was as if not only Münzer's face, with the one shining eye and the adjacent black cavity, but all faces turned toward the speaker, were revealing a yearning for different words, explanations, for a language more suitable to the events they were involved in. With no questions being asked, it was difficult to make out what they wanted to hear, only the silence, the motionlessness of the gazes, the way arms and legs were being held implied that they were waiting for something. This abiding was marked by the knowledge that they could immediately be snuffed out. Yet there was nothing tragic about this comprehension, death had after all been present in every second, it was taken for granted, it was part of the deal. However, the willingness to be overtaken by its definitiveness had sharpened the claim to responsibility, the sensitivity to truth in every direction. It was not that they distrusted the reporter, but at this moment politics appeared detached from what was of the essence for the fighters. They were not frightened by the sacrifices that had to be made for the triumph of the political line, they wasted no words on that. Nor did they object that the decisions were made on a higher level, that they were the implementers. They had come to Spain to fight, it went without saying that a staff should pilot their movements. But in the emerging hush, in the sudden awareness that they were divorced from any influence on the development, they were afflicted by all the unresolved issues concealed under the clear, smooth surface of strategy. The house they were in made them feel something of the isolation. They thought about their fellow workers, their relatives, the might of reactionism enveloping the countries they came from. They wished they were back at their sectors, where their strength had always been present even in the tiniest unit. What is happening now in France, in Scandinavia, they wanted to know, what is heard from the working class in those places. They had stumbled from simple, direct actions into intricate diplomacy. They were overwhelmed by powerlessness. Why has no one yet managed, they could ask, to settle the conflicts in the antifascist war, why could the upper echelons not forge unity such as had been attained under fire at the front. Durruti, the hero of the first offensive, the embodiment of the untamed popular will undisturbed by any Party quarrels, had fallen in November nineteen thirty-six, during the battle of the university town of Madrid, just in time, said many, to avoid being eliminated like the leaders of the Marxist Association, too early, said others, for he may have been the only man capable of joining the ideals of the revolution, the rousing solidarity of the initial period with the centralized government, the effective military machine. Durruti, Hodann said, had known that his militia troops were no match for the enemy, prior to his death he had demanded a unified military administration and had welcomed the Soviet arms supplies even though he remained an inveterate anarchist. Then, with his inquiries into Nin's organization, a barrier sprang up in our thinking. The Partido Obrero de Unificación Marxista was viewed as an instrument of Trotskyism. Even Hodann hesitated to break the taboo linked to that name. In the side room, which had its glass doors wide open toward the hall, I saw the rows of small, awkwardly painted pictures inserted into the wooden walls, the tiles depicting scenes from the life of Don Quixote. The fireplace, with its projecting structure, towered up to the black ceiling joists of the former baronial dining room, and here, in the glow from the hearth, one could recognize stations of the narrative, the hero being knighted, setting out with his squire, battling the terrible windmills and wineskins, emerging victorious from all subsequent exploits, until, abandoned even by his Dulcinea, he returned to his village after a bad omen and there, not without drawing up his will, the confession of his follies, he gave up the ghost amid moaning and weeping. As heads of the Confederation of Workers, Nin and Maurin, Hodann then said, originally favored joining the Communist International. They co-founded the Communist Party, but disassociated themselves from the Soviet line after the events in Kronstadt. Later on, as oppositional left-wing Communists, they were close to Trotsky, adopting some of his orientations, but then they repudiated him too since he told them, as he told his allies in France, to sign on with the Socialist Party in order to establish a revolutionary platform there. Trotsky could only jeer when the group around Nin hitched up with members of the bloc of revolutionary farm workers. Never, he said, for all its gushing about the ability of the amorphous and illiterate masses to act on their own, would this coalition succeed in building the political organization necessary for pulling off a revolution. In Trotsky's eyes, it had been an unforgivable mistake to talk about the dictatorship of the proletariat without first having vigorous workers' councils or to call for a deepening of the revolution when the revolutionary situation was a thing of the past. From Trotsky's vantage point, a revolutionary development was impeded by the so-called Marxist Workers' Party and left-wing anarcho-syndicalism as much as by a Communist Party dependent on Soviet directives. But what alternative, asked Gomez, was offered by his own International, which was distributed in small cells around the world. By fighting the Soviet Party's leadership he was fighting the Soviet Union. Any attack on the power that shields us is an attack on us, an attack on the struggle of the Spanish Republic. Nevertheless, he said, it was correct to deal with Trotsky. In order to beat the adversary we had to be familiar with his concepts, his ideas and plans. Suppressing his name did us no good. And it was even possible that, in our urge to increase our knowledge, we might learn a thing or two from him. But of course, said Gomez, this puts us in a quandary. We cannot escape measuring with two different yardsticks. We ask for a sophisticated analysis, but the lack of time, the life-and-death struggle force us to take a simplified, summary approach. If we want to contend with the evolution of Lenin's erstwhile colleague, the co-planner of the Russian Revolution, then we instantly have to face the fact that his antagonism toward the Soviet state places him in the fascist camp even though his motives are not fascistic. The nature of the enemy can be measured in degrees, but in a crucial moment we are confronted with only a single foe. That was why Nin, Gorkin, Bonet, Andrade, Gironella, Arquer, and other spokesmen for the opposition had to be arrested. They were indicted, said Münzer, for profiteering, arms smuggling, espionage, sabotage and for preparing to hand the country over to the Falangists. Those charges cannot be compatible with their stance. We are fighting for the truth, for a better future, said Gomez. On our path we need deeper insights into the historical dynamics, incessant training in the issues of the proletarian movement. At the same time, the enemy conspiracy is sneaking in from all sides. Distortions, misrepresentations, conflicting slogans mix in with our statements and directives. In order to distinguish between what is useful to us and what is harmful to us, we have to agree on specific concepts. Later on, when our tasks have been carried out, we will expand the present black-and-white drawing into its full color spectrum, today any accusation against one of our foes must also be applied to all other foes. That is why the people who resist the government's decisions have to be court-martialed and, if necessary, liquidated. This, said Münzer, was not in tune with the conception that large groups in the syndicates and labor unions had. There, Nin and his companions still enjoyed great prestige, and more and more people were concerned about their whereabouts. Perhaps we can blame them for nothing more, said Hodann, than dedication to an atavistic heroism, to a dream of utter freedom, doomed to be pulverized under the Italian tanks and under the bombs from German planes, but we must nevertheless agree to their elimination because, with their enthusiasm for ideas that they have not reasoned out they are hampering the emancipation of the working class. Münzer, however, disagreed.

For he had fought alongside them in the field, said Münzer, and he could talk about their valor. Their degradation, he said, was determined by ideology and Party politics. At the front the fighting comes first, all attention focuses on the enemy's movements, all energy concentrates on striking him. But in the interior a lot of strength and means are applied to probing the troops and monitoring them, submitting them to *Gleichschaltung*, making them toe the political line. The police have grown into an army within the people's army. The secret service, the interrogation authorities are expanding. More and more places of detention, prisons, examination commissions, and special courts are being made use of. Our consciousness, he said, is in danger of breaking under the steady pressure of directives that do not jibe with our own insights, but that we are disciplined enough to follow. Ayschmann, who, pending further assignment, had been transferred from the northern front to the camp near Albacete and who had visited us in Cueva, responded to Münzer's reflections. This effort toward conformity, he said, is being made not only in the political and military headquarters but also inside ourselves, it is the very condition for carrying out our struggle. No one can wage this war on his own, we are forced to recognize the principles of the leadership. He, for his part, he said, had to go along with eliminating anyone trying to cling to free speech and promote factionalism. For him the only security at the front lines, he said, had been the solid and unified strategy that backed him up and that he knew would, if necessary, be maintained by violent means. Not just reliable comrades had come to Spain, there were also adventurers, swindlers, informers. So it was better, he said, to act on the least suspicion than to let any sabotaging force operate unhindered. After all, he said, we stood alone, here in the southern fortress of Europe, spied on by a reactionism that was constantly gaining strength, and it would be devastating for the morale of the troops if they got to sense a disintegration of the country's law and order. In the struggle, said Münzer, we can see no distinction between our goal and the government's goal. At the front, men and officers are bound together in absolute trust and mutually dependent at every step of the way. There is no such thing as ignoring an order. But now, in our forced rest, antitheses are evoked, cultivated. Dissidents, heretics, turncoats among us are to be tracked down. Suddenly we have to account for the motives that brought us to Spain. The suspicions demean us, degrade us. Who, he asked, has mandated the leaders to compromise us and disempower us in that way. When I claim that the conflict we are involved in is creating dichotomous people, he went on, I am referring to the pattern that has always tried to push us into a subordinate position. Ever since we began thinking for ourselves, we have looked for the things that are intrinsic to us, to our class, we have tried to criticize and reject the things that were to be inflicted upon us. I understood Marx as wanting to teach us to view our relationship to work in a new light, rather than adjusting we had to smash the mechanisms that made us dependent. But instead of getting our hands on the means of production, we were asked to make do with half-measures. A different force kept advancing simultaneously with us, a force of containment. Whenever we thought we had found relief, regression began, whenever we formulated things that applied to us directly, they were declared obsolete. Ayschmann replied that many of the people who had received confidential posts, leadership missions were as unfree as we and vulnerable to the same difficulties in seeking what was right. They too could bring about no more than temporary solutions, transitional forms, compromises, and that was a lot, for the enemy was advancing more and more strongly at the same time that we were moving forward and he was trying to compel us to stand still, become passive. We are engaged, said Münzer, in an open struggle with the enemy, but our appreciation of the working conditions of our superiors always makes us put up with unsatisfactory things, stopgap measures, aberrations, obvious miscarriages. And if we were in their place, said Ayschmann, we could attain no better results. That was not true, said Münzer as we walked down the slope to the river, past the grotto, through the detritus in the ruins of a stable, for by using a division of labor, that is, constantly doing the basic tasks and leaving the administration to others, we were getting further and further away from the original objective of scrapping the apparatus of control. By now two decades have passed since October, he said, and we are given countless reasons why the patriarchal state, the tutelage by officials and functionaries, the officers' castes, blind obedience, the ranks of supreme commanders have to continue, more reasons than the steps separating us from the power for workers. I came to Spain because I believed that people here were not fatalistically reckoning with the gradual perishing of the old, but were overthrowing it, with both fists, as is necessary, blow by blow. But I was forced to realize that they too are following the narrow path and that anyone who tries to stretch beyond it is cut away. Now I am struggling for my self-preservation to avoid exposing the fact that what I have committed to does not tally with what the leadership is projecting for me. Quails fluttered up from the opposite bank, whose lowest strata were deeply leached out by the water. There was that rustling of leaves on the poplars, their trunks densely entwined with ivy, there was that swelling, sinking noise in the breeze, never entirely stopping, I could hear it even at night in my room off on the tower stairs, we walked along the thicket, in the softened earth, grayish-violet mossy plants blossomed here, as late as November, were called romero, wild asparagus grew between the roots of trees, it tasted bitter, the swarms of tiny mosquitoes smoldered up, hung motionless overhead for a while, then, with a sudden swerve, fled across the river and then back again into the overgrown woodland. We dashed from stone to stone across the narrow vehement flow of icy water, walked along the steeply looming, whitish-yellow sand formations, and Münzer, said Ayschmann, had better hold back, for after Caballero had been dismissed and now also detained, criticism was high treason. After hearing the broadcast we were to report the news of the former prime minister's arrest with the sole comment that he had joined the anti-Republican forces. During the discussion in the hall the removal of the co-founder of the Popular Front had been concealed. He had done his duty in the Alliance politics. He had been moldable, cooperative only to a certain degree, when differences of opinion came up the Party had been strong enough to topple him and, along with him, the government's anarchist ministers. Such a fellowship did not have to lead to a reconciliation of the camps, it could also bring a subjugation of wavering minds through superior, discerning action. This was a victory of historical strength. Anyone who did not go along with the government had to be tossed aside, regardless of what functions he may have previously performed. Only one line could be valid in the people's war, the strategy could run in only one direction. The concept of morality had to be measured differently in politics than in interpersonal dealings, politics was determined by a sense of reality that asked only about utilitarian values, not feelings. The sole possible distinction was between friend and foe. Caballero was irresolute, incapable, according to the official explanation. He was responsible for military failures. In May he openly showed his disloyalty when he refused to advance against Nin's unit. Because he found it incompatible with his position as leader of the workers, said Münzer, to disband a workers' organization, because he still saw patriots in the oppositionals. And they do help fascism, said Ayschmann, by working against our policies. Our goal was to prove that the Communist Party knew how to maintain a Popular Front. This was necessary not only for Spain, but also for the continuation of Soviet efforts to achieve an antifascist defense alliance with England and France. The Spanish Republic had to gain the respect and trust of the Western powers, if it aroused so much as the slightest suspicion that it approved of a revolutionary development there, then this would have wiped out the frail negotiations in Geneva and in the diplomatic centers of the West. Simultaneously with the fight for Spain, the Soviet Union had to be defended, jeopardizing it would lead to our defeat. It is not, said Münzer, that I refuse to recognize the Party's policies, I am after something fundamental that is linked to our existence in the Party. It is one thing to hold your tongue because you are facing an enemy who is so vile as to make all mistakes and defects of the Party irrelevant, it is another thing to practice a silence that is a sign of inferiority. We built our organizations around us for our protection. They are meant to strengthen us in our consciousness. They are not supposed to promote our docility. They were created by our will to join together, to act in unison. Anything we may imagine about our road to progress, to liberation stems from the thought of this solidarity. But participating in such a fusion would be worthless if we also brought along our habitual weakness, if we entered into this bond out of passivity, if we were merely seeking help, if we merely wanted to be driven along by the collective. Perhaps, he said, the organization ought to incessantly ask each person to make a difference, to help lead. In battling the falsifications that have been trying to capture us since childhood, we picked our standpoint, we did not expose ourselves to the reformist opinions that flatten everything, to the depoliticizing in the labor unions, which were now interested purely in achieving higher salaries. Rather, we demanded that we ourselves gain an understanding of the social, economic, and cultural totality. We are here, he said, because we grasped the basic issues, and the same strenuous effort that drove us is now resisting the attempt to block our urge to know more. The submissiveness that is asked of us should always be viewed in connection with a stance of utter solidarity. I accept the fact that the struggle in all its harshness can be waged only with full unanimity, but it must be made clear that nothing holds us fast in vaguenesses, dissimulations, and mystifications. If we were willing to give in to all that, then we would have no response for the millions of people back home who let themselves be driven into the illusions of fascist demagoguery, who, in their self-delusion, allow themselves to be crammed with nationalistic, chauvinistic, racist trash, who credulously parrot any slogans they are served, about bringing territories back to the Fatherland, about blood and soil, about strength through joy, about motherly women, strong men, and grateful children, who, in the whirlpool of tastelessness, enthusiastically bedizen themselves with chamois tufts and hunting knives, with uniform pipings and iron-tipped boots. These things, he said, his hand sweeping across the sandy slope, could come about because the soil lay fallow, because the workers' movement failed to assert its own values, because it all too easily let itself be impressed by canaries and garden dwarfs, embroidered cushions and wall maxims about peace and calm and security, and so the bedazzled got their false security, their false peace, and their false prosperity, their false work for all, their new order. How can we effectively tackle all that if we ourselves are unable to stand behind each of our actions, if we too are bogged down in self-delusion, between vaguenesses and restraints. Authoritarian domination was necessary, said Ayschmann, for coping with the enemy, who, in this period of extortion and blindness, so intensely represented absolutism, extreme constraint. I do not wish to be convinced, replied Münzer, that the confrontation with the reign of terror exempts me from continuously providing information about the means that I myself employ. It would be deadly for us, who are fighting for a future goal, to take a stance that the people coming after us would have to renounce. Mayakovsky, he said, and he uttered the name so loudly that it reverberated between the riverbanks, Mayakovsky gave form to our vision, for him there was only the sense of justice in the masses, we could discover our own thoughts and feelings in his words, much of his writing sounded euphoric, utopian, but it was quite harmonious with October, which, after all, stretched out into an indiscernible distance, that was the starting point, when I was a trainee in the late nineteen twenties that was the beginning of the development that Lenin had striven for, and I always saw this evolution in terms of our own sphere of activity, in the workshop, in our streets, this was the only place for finding what was valid for us, we always kept going back to Mayakovsky, his was a name that was identical with a specific person and that drew others, a name that said that we too were capable of expression, that we all had the possibility of speaking, of creating, that we, who usually sat in the midst of the crap, were deemed worthy of achieving something. I hate, he said, now across from the water mill of Los Yesares, anything decked out with supremacy, anything sporting the privilege of perfection, of inviolability, and if Mayakovsky was the epitome of our protection, then his death, his self-destruction, was also our fall, suddenly we saw that we had as yet barely begun with what lay before us as a promise, suddenly we again sensed that work was shattering us, that anxiety about our livelihood was leaching us out, that we were incapable of marshaling the strength to shape ourselves. At this point a dam made the river branch off toward the mill, but the paddle wheels were still, the water lay grayish green, motionless in the basin, it kept flowing only in the narrow branch canal, between concrete fragments and burst beams under the wooden footbridge, and the buildings we reached on the other bank had collapsed, exploded, and were now deserted. Perhaps it was the ruins of the stable, of the adjacent hayrick, the desolate home, with a bit of surviving furniture, the walls damp, mildewed, that reminded Münzer of his own frustrated life, for, having only one eye, he said, he was no longer fit to be a typesetter, and his wife must have given in to pressure by now and initiated divorce proceedings for the sake of their two children and to avoiding losing her teaching job. This too was part of the people's war, bygones, disruptions were close at every moment that was claimed by the fighting. Uneasiness about your family's whereabouts came up, but the same steadfastness demanded at the front was to be practiced in your personal life, and actually the courage, the self-sacrifice in Spain could be gauged correctly only if we factored in the self-control and strength of mind that an individual mustered on a daily basis. The major part of heroism remained invisible, all we could see was the troops surging forward in one or another sector. Any life contained in those movements found no place in the reports, and even in private groups it was joked about, laughed at, waved off. Nor should we waste our breath discussing whether it was true, and how could it have been otherwise in this concentration of human contingents, in this collision of social forces. They had arrived here with their personal lives, but their sole task was to form a chain that held together. Each man could think about himself, but he was seen purely as a part of the whole, if he left, the breach would have to be closed, and he would have to remain as unknown as his grave. There could at most be a hint that he had once existed, like now, when Münzer pointed at the empty, fog-bound house and mentioned the Italian brigade member who had been shot dead here by the peasant with whose wife he was having an affair. This was said casually, nothing was left of the misery, the terror, the despair. And if the crack of the shot had ever been heard, it may, perhaps, in a twisted, far-fetched way, have turned into the rumor about Marty's court-martial in the river valley of Los Yesares. We were already climbing the path, Münzer walked along the dunes, back to the medical building, I accompanied Ayschmann for a stretch. He may have assumed that he would never see me again, for he confided something that should have been one of the unsaid things in this war. He spoke about a face, he asked me whether I remembered the dark, narrow face with the shiny eyes in one of the doors in the alley behind the water tower, and I vaguely saw the woman, to whom he had gone again. He wanted to explain something to me as if I could safeguard it for him. To be done with the price issue once and for all, he had given her everything he had on him, and she had instantly caught his drift. She was not selling herself. Both of them were there for one another of their own free will. When he told me this, it was already evening, hazy, we were standing at some distance from the sentinel's bunker, the trucks drove up between the barracks in order to ship the company that night to the embattled mountains near Teruel. At first his conscience had stirred, after the slamming of the door, walking toward the low bed under the loose tatter of dangling wall paper he had almost hoped his betrayal would be punished with all diseases. But then he forgot all that, he said, when he removed the black rag from her bony hips and shoulders. He spoke about a wound closed with cellulose, about the reflection of the kerosene lamp on the golden pattern of the wall paper, about the rustling and crackling of the paper, about a sea of paper, and his hands moved through gold dust, through foam, through powdering ice. For a moment it was as if he had been describing a dream, but then, as he turned away and disappeared, I took along a piece of his reality.

The date that we had gathered in the hall to celebrate had a special meaning for me, because twenty years ago, at eight P.M., when Lenin had started out toward Smolny, accompanied by Rakhya, a worker, and disguised in a wig and glasses, with an old hat pulled low on his forehead, a scarf around his neck, my mother had been in labor at the women's hospital on the bank of the Weser, and at midnight, when Lenin discarded his masquerade in the room at the end of the corridor, up in the institute for aristocratic girls, right next to the auditorium, where the delegates of the Soviet Congress sat crowded together, in ragged army coats, and when the shots from the six-inch cannon of the *Aurora* could be heard, my father was still nervously pacing up and down the waiting room, and at ten minutes after two, on the morning of November eighth, when Antonov Ovseyenko, with narrow shoulders, in a trilby and rimless spectacles—just as I had seen this man, whom I called my godfather, through the café window in Albacete—declared that the members of the Provisional Government in the Winter Palace were arrested, I came into the world, and I lay washed and diapered during the proclamation that all power was now transferred to the soviets of the workers, soldiers, and peasants, who would guarantee a true revolutionary system. There were shortages of everything, said Hodann during his speech, in the young Soviet state just as in today's Republican Spain. And if there was no food, no equipment, there were all the more quarrels and fierce rivalries. Along with starvation and deprivation, he said, every people's war or revolutionary movement is bound to have antagonisms, vehement conflicts, they are a natural component of the struggle, for no social upheaval ever has two classes facing one another with precisely defined interests, on the contrary, the fighting camps themselves are assaulted by internal hostility, which constitutes the driving force of the whole violent clash. The momentum of the attack, in which we all look for unity, for joint action, for understanding and solidarity, is accompanied by the ferment of the various kinds of conceptions, aspirations, directions, the wish to agree on the policies, to cooperate against the common enemy is always confronted with the urge to carry out the ideas that are recognized by some people as absolutely right and true, while others see them as deviating from their truth. All this can appear so minor in the first forward thrust as to be forgotten, such instants produce genuine revolution, the new start, the beginning of the new human being, this is the moment when Idea becomes a material force, when all people are carried by a force that creates a previously unknown value, but this condition can never hold, it requires immediate underpinning, otherwise it degenerates, disintegrates into thin air, and that is why theory dashes toward actions and tries to gain acceptance in degrees, with its claims to being well reasoned, and because theory always triggers more discussion than practice, the crisis occurs right after the opening steps, discord mixes in with unreflected conviction, the simplicity of action is destroyed by the complication of thoughts, which attempt to cancel each other out. And this precipitates a paradoxical situation, in which all the people striving toward a common objective are divided by the sharpest lines, even to the point of mangling themselves. Only the craftiest and most tenacious leadership with the broadest historical overview can produce a synthesis out of the wealth of tendencies. After the hard-won peace of Brest-Litovsk, he said, the next task was to preserve the revolution, and, he asked, did they not have to crush the uprising of the social revolutionaries and, after the end of the civil war and the victory over the intervention, the Kronstadt revolt, and then, during the buildup of the Soviet state, didn't the oppositional groups, the various platforms hold out, thereby forcing violent counteractions in the trials. We must not, he said, apply our tiny personal measuring stick to the complicated and interminable political developments, we are inconspicuous next to the locomotive of history, even if we ourselves are the ones who, with our unique and singular actions, made it start moving. Hodann told about his first visit to the Soviet Union, when that pauperized country, with its backward economy and industry, was still suffering the impact of the civil war, and the people were going to work, carrying out the first Five-Year Plan. With no means of transportation, with no adequate tools, they tackled the excavating, the building of scaffoldings, the laying of foundation walls. Many people belonged to a new generation, they were the sons and daughters of people who had carried out the October Revolution, and all of them, the younger and the older, were now putting up their dams, factories, and technological plants, arduously deciphering the workshop drawings, wracking their brains about how to assemble the delivered machines, mastering the laws of mathematics, statics, hydraulics, and electrodynamics through everyday experience. The faith, confidence, and perseverance of those years infected us when, in the middle of the steppe in the southeastern Urals, in front of Mount Magnitogorsk, we saw the procession of horse-drawn carts driving up with the American components for the new collective metallurgic combine, we saw the construction crew, the former barge towers and nomadic herders, coming with hoes, shovels, and wheelbarrows, digging, and, in the support structure of knotty planks, laying the foundation of the first blast furnace, we saw them spending two years in tents, camping at the foot of the mountain, gradually bringing forth a city next to the growing iron-and-steel mills, placing stone upon stone for an industry that should eventually produce tractors, turbines, and excavators. The names Magnitogorsk and Dniepropetrovsk, where the huge hydropower station arose at the same time, had the effect of signals, they spelled renewal, they cast light on the ability of human beings to transcend any and all deprivations when pursuing a specific goal. Of course, the construction could not compare with what had long existed in Western countries. The photo-reportages in Münzenberg's *Workers Illustrated* had triggered mockery from the higher classes. Those were illiterates playing civilization there, who cared about a factory, a power station in the wasteland when, in Europe and North America, the chimneys were towering from gigantic areas, electric works were humming everywhere, and conveyor belts were spewing out cars and farm machines. People looked down on the workers, a bit unsettling were only their masses, so persistent, so inventive. For us, the things created there were superior to Detroit and the Ruhr, for this was the first kind of production meant to benefit the producers and not the owners of capital. The wealthy countries could strut and sneer at the shortages afflicting Russian workers, but we reminded them of the millions of their own people who lived in a poverty ten times worse, we pointed to the looting on which they grounded their prosperity. Indeed, they had gathered riches, monopolized resources such as were not to be found in the Soviet state, they played themselves up with booty, while concealing the fact that the acclaimed superiority of their own system was borne by wretched nations and continents. In suspense, we watched the roads stretching out, the railroad tracks being laid. Even when everything was still in an inchoate state, defective, imperfect, the scorn of the West turned into annoyance, and when the turbines on the Dnieper began running and, one year before the outbreak of fascism in Germany, the fires in the blast furnaces of Magnitogorsk blazed up, and the surrounding city had over one hundred thousand inhabitants, and when the convoys of tractors came from Kharkov, and the trucks from Gorky, and the stream of coal from the Kuznetsk basin, the bearers of Western civilization voiced their indignation, for the workers and peasants must not oppose them with an industrial state of their own, a state that likewise now knew how to arm itself in order to fend off the aggression that the West was always willing to engage in and would have preferred to hush up. The entire personnel, including a few seriously ill patients, who had been carried here, was in the hall and in the side room, the steps of the staircase were occupied, and so were the window seats under the red and blue panes, and from the upstairs corridor legs dangled between the banister posts. In moments of silence we heard the ticking of the tall grandfather clock that stood in the stairway corner and that Feingold wound with a key each morning, and every quarter hour the grinding clockwork expelled the strokes of a bell, the echoes underscoring the meaning of words that someone had just spoken. When we thought about the creation out of destruction, something of the pride of the pioneers stirred in us. The heroism, the grandiloquence in Soviet art fitted in precisely with the epic achievements. Most of us were as unschooled as the Russian construction workers and for us the things that might appear sentimental, idealistic to outsiders were glimpses of the realization of a century-old utopia. Münzer at best may have believed that the utopia had not yet come, that the builders of the workers' state had not yet received the reward for their strenuous efforts, and then what we imagined would, for him, have been a mere tearjerker. But then I saw him, next to me, as he listened to a miner expanding on technological details by talking about the mill trains and open-hearth furnaces of the iron-and-steel mill, and then explaining by himself how the dammed-up water spurted through the shaft, the narrowness of the shaft making it plunge faster, into the spiral feed-pipe, setting into motion the paddle wheels of the turbines, and he told of how water power produced energy, adding electricity to the Soviet Union, and one could tell how completely Münzer too agreed with the motive and goal of these actions, and how important he felt it was to preserve the achievements. It was only his need to attain absolute clarification of every issue that made him cite all aspects and mention especially the mistakes, the fallacies, the failures. When asked why his book on the Soviet Union also contained negative statements, Hodann said that such a critical approach shows greater appreciation for the object than does unconditional acceptance. Total compliance, he said, is always proof of weakness. We tackled the problems faced by the Russians, and we reconstructed their solutions. This was a process that stretched out through the following weeks after our meeting was adjourned to the clattering strains of the march from *Aida* rolling out of the piano. For many of us this was our first scientific demonstration of physical laws. We had taken it for granted that we could stay in balance, that things constructed with a plumb line, a T-square, and a spirit level would stay in place. But now, conversations gave us facts that helped us to understand the conditions of the stability and motion of bodies. We had all handled tools, tightened screws, pressed down levels, we had cut, twisted, riveted, we had assembled engines, hauled coal, bedded roads, completed building projects similar to those on the mural in the Albacete canteen, erected into high, rectilinear blocks, and yet we could never have communicated anything about the forces causing something to abide or change or about the elementary knowledge that the size and motion of an object were based purely on their relationship to those of another object. The October Revolution was not a past event, it was something immediately present, it reached into the far-flung estate of Cueva de la tia Potita, driving out the weariness, the recent paralyses, and when we headed for the meetings in the farmhouse, on the dirt road, between barn and stable, it was as if the ghost of the former owner were being conjured up, the deceased Aunt Potita and, in the low, cavernous rooms of old Spain, being confronted with utterances about a different life. In the course of the discussion it became obvious that we had a mathematician and an astronomer among us, one a construction worker, the other a Swedish seaman. Both had pursued their studies alongside their regular jobs, the mathematician led us out of the confused notions of space and time, demonstrating the calculability of all entities and processes and their relations to one another. Rogeby, the Swedish comrade, informed us about Galileo's view of the world. For nights on end, in the room I shared with Feingold, I thought about the proposition that all bodies try to keep their situation or speed and that they can be restrained from doing so only under the effect of another force. Hodann's coughing boomed from next door, I was ready to hurry over if he knocked on the wall, his bed, with the brass bars, with the huge spheres at the head and at the foot, slid to and fro, grinding, the naked angels stretched out here too, on the upper corridor, over the door frame between the mirror-smooth surfaces of the plaster walls. Hodann, unable to sleep, kept going down the creaking steps, to the room off the hall, where the table was cluttered with his papers, notebooks, books, wrapped in a coat and a blanket he would sit down, in the black wooden armchair, whose back towered hugely over his head. If he was not working on essays or making entries in his journals, he would read Hölderlin on these nights. After a choking fit, when I had gone down to him, he showed me the notes on his readings, it was not Hölderlin's insights, his Hellenism, that costuming of the spirit of the French Revolution, said Hodann, that had taken effect in the character of the Germans, it was Fichte's Germanizing chauvinism, just as the rational, enlightened Hutten had been upstaged by a populist Luther, the sober, scientific, and scholarly Herder by an emotionally idealistic Goethe, the dry Kant, limiting himself to the realm of human experience, by the metaphysical Hegel. He did not want to deny the significant features of these stronger men, said Hodann, but they had always served the rulers, for all their progressiveness they had always advocated the preservation of a system of government, on which the genuinely democratic forces were bound to shatter. This discrepancy between the titans, those pillars of authority, who denied the right of the people to have reason and independence, who told the people to be devoted and obedient, while the development of humanism in Germany had kept down revolutionary outcasts and outlaws, figures like Forster, Kleist, Grabbe, Büchner, Heine. Those, he said, were the reasons for fascism's mass psychosis, which wrapped itself in Wagner's notes and misused Beethoven. Then scraps of paper were to be seen, inserted into the lists, bulletins, medical reports, peace volunteers instead of war volunteers were demanded by his small, neat, flowing script. The feeling of being a master had to be transformed into a healthy sense of self that was capable of integrating into the international necessities, and the war hero had to be opposed by the ideal of a peace hero. But how, his words asked on the crumpled slip of paper, could we attain the required reorientation and stabilization. These were hidden sequences of thoughts, to which he yielded, encircled by the scenes from the imaginary life of Don Quixote, and those ideas were instantly covered up by the protocols, no one needed to go into that during the wee hours, there was no time to implement them, I thought about them for just a little longer, as I lay on the cot, next to Feingold, who snored as he tossed and turned. I also saw the other rooms in the surrounding buildings, they were filled with bodies on straw pallets, and when they slept pictures awoke in them, some of the men lay stretched out, helplessly afflicted by a firestorm. They were mute, but their lips stirred, they wanted to let the shriek in them erupt, they did not sense that they were lying in safety, they were crawling somewhere or running, they had to shriek, shriek out, against the storm of projectiles, all they knew was that they had to shriek against that elemental violence and yet they did not emit a sound. Then again others merely lay there, listening, they lay in the earth, and they heard those shrieks from far and near, and those were the shocking shrieks for the woman who had once born and fed and raised them, the shrieks before the end of the circulation, before the return to the source. Perhaps Hodann had meant something of that when he had reflected on the soldiers of peace. Perhaps he had been thinking about the insanity of war, about that total annihilation, that terrible, premature breaking off of all possibilities of life. Yet could one not claim, I wondered, that the soldiers of war, the mercenaries of destruction were only on the other side, while the ones that Hodann meant could already be found here, for there was no other heroism here than the self-sacrifice for peace. I saw that Hodann was in jeopardy. I felt anxious about him, but could not explain it to him. Toward three A.M., if we had failed to drop off or were suddenly awoken, that was always the time when we were defenseless, and that was why now, with the sun still hanging far below the curvature of the earth, the condemned men were taken to their execution, Feingold moaned, Hodann's numbed breathing penetrated the plasterwork, and most of the sounds that could still be grasped were detached, unconnected, belonged more to the emotions than to reason. Things were being pondered that were not part of a waking condition, and that was why they seemed bizarre, growing banal in daytime and evanescing, the notion, say, that there were more things binding people together than keeping them apart, more understanding than brutality, and yet everything was ruled by destructiveness. Nor were such things articulated when Hodann was put through a kind of test, by no means with any air of distrust, just casually, in response to some sort of accusations that were not to be taken seriously, and no one made clear what they wanted to know about him.

Only the stress and strain of the drive to Cueva indicated the urgency of the visit. The road in front of the car was cleared by a snowplow driven by Hodann's companion, Lindbaek. Amid swirling flakes, dressed in her boots, a fur cap, and the gray-green felt of the army uniform, she was the first to enter, with the muffled-up retinue behind her, all of which lent the visit a touch of familial mythology. She blew her nose on her fingers and, after tearing off her cap, shook the deluge of her black kinky hair. Hodann looked small, frail next to her, and, as he said, he felt pretty beat this morning, he had just injected himself with five milligrams of adrenaline for a serious asthma attack. Arms burrowed out of the coats, which slid back like clouds, Lindbaek, who had just spent another two months reporting from the various fronts, pulled Hodann over, then Ehrenburg, swinging his Siberian wolf fur over a chair, strode up to his friend of many years and nearly squeezed the life out of him. Bredel, stocky, dark-haired, grabbed his hand. I would have liked to call over Coppi, Heilmann, for Bredel had been our ideal, he had shown us that it was possible to find expression for our situation, to break through the blockade, hurl one's own books into the preserve of culture. A Spartacist, a member of the Party since its founding, imprisoned for two years in the penitentiaries of the Weimar Republic, escaped the concentration camps of the fascists after one year, this thirty-six-year-old embodied proletarian endurance and superiority for us. Mewis and Stahlmann, the representatives of the political and the military staffs, stood off to the side. Ehrenburg, we were told, wanted to view the army hospitals in the surroundings of Albacete, this made the project seem like an outing, guests, not a commission, had arrived, we settled down around the brass basin, which was filled with glowing charcoals. But then Mewis promptly brought up Hodann's request for a transfer to the coast, given Hodann's state of health, asked Mewis, could he even take over as head physician of the facility near Denia. There appeared to be a certain resemblance between the two men, whose eyes now met. Mewis sat hunched forward, his left iris was greenish gray, the other bluish gray. One of Hodann's eyes was larger than the other, and now the pupils narrowed, the right brow arched up. Aside from the peculiarities of their eyes, nothing else was congruent about them. He had not requested resignation or retirement, said Hodann, huddling on a footstool, rather he felt that his abilities could be put to better use in a more favorable climate. But any hint of controversy was instantly wiped away, Ehrenburg praised the Cueva hospital, he had heard, he said, a lot about the effectiveness of the study groups, the outlets for the patients' energies. But reservations, said Stahlmann, had to be voiced about certain projects. He had brought along the magazine *La Voz de la Sanidad*, which had published an article by Hodann on sexual problems of the soldiers in the war. Such a discussion, said Stahlmann, was petty bourgeois; in a liberation struggle, such as was being waged in Spain, sexual needs had to be put last, and in a time like this it was not part of a physician's duties to deal with private matters. This was meant to be funny, nor did Stahlmann seem prudish, with his squat, powerful build, his broad, weighty forehead, slanting eyes, high cheekbones, cords of muscles bulging over his mouth. But Hodann did not join the laughter. With softly whistling breath he launched into an explanation, continuing even when Mewis and Stahlmann waved it off. Every war, he said, including a national people's war, constituted a pathological condition, with all the individual sequelae. No matter how politically aware the fighters were, their abstinence made them irritable, weakening their resistance. In the class system the state had set up brothels to satisfy the drives of the soldiers, but while this process might provide them with mental stability, it was degrading for women and therefore unacceptable for a people's army. The fascists had no qualms in that department, for them women were a commodity even in war, for sale according to demands and at various price levels. But in Republican Spain, he said, we are trying to wipe out prostitution, and, after the elimination of social and ecclesiastical dogmas, women are basically equal to men. In these terms, he added, the war had also triggered a process of recovery. However, there was still a tendency, especially among the Spanish comrades as the aftereffect of Catholic morality, to bypass the problems between the sexes. They still believed in the stupid doctrine that a woman must not be deflowered before marriage, and many men, who tenderly embraced their girlfriends during a furlough, had to then seek relief in a bordello. Now that we have to retrain prostitutes for a more dignified form of work, he said, men likewise had to learn a new attitude. Ehrenburg, recalling Kollontai's propagation of free love during the building of the Soviet state, pointed to the burgeoning propensity there to reassign women to kitchens and cradles. Supported by Ehrenburg, Hodann talked about the difficulties of changing the sexual notions in a country like Spain. The comradely togetherness of men and women in the liberation struggle was merely the beginning of a liberation from the cult of female purity. And as for masturbation, given the war and our ban on prostitution it had to be viewed as a natural prophylactic method. Stahlmann raised his leonine face, waved off those words, and burst into a peal of laughter, which had been brewing in his face all this time. But Hodann was already explaining that these issues, which for many people were tied to puritanical restraint and a sense of guilt and insecurity, had to be treated with the scientific clarity that was part and parcel of our political conviction. Lindbaek, stretching out her legs, leaning way back in the armchair, had put her arm around Hodann's back. It was as if she had him in custody and as if the others, after initial maneuvering, were now clustering around for the actual interrogation. But they remained just as they had blown in, for now, in a soft, vague fumbling, there was no determining whether the conversation was supposed to focus on Hodann's views on sexual hygiene, the others now tried to move on, but he was the one who would not let go. He disputed the idea that the working class was the master of its drives and had gained harmony from ideological discipline. Practical experience had shown him that malfunctions, anxieties, depressions linked to sexual problems were to be found more often in the proletariat than in other social strata, and treatment was as crucial as sociological enlightenment. In thrashing out contraception, abortion, and masturbation, he said, we are dealing with prejudices and constraints inflicted by the bourgeois moral code, and the people who were hit hardest by the system of exploitation also had the worst conflicts in their sexual life. Despite his circumspect reasoning, one could still feel the surrounding rejection. Physical toughening, as through sports, further military training, said Mewis, were more useful to the soldiers' well-being than any grubbing in their psyches. For Hodann, a man who could be called socially fit had to constitute a wholeness, and this wholeness was unthinkable without the involvement of the psychological reality. Replying to an objection from Mewis, Hodann said he was no advocate of individual psychoanalytical treatment. He had always preferred a direct and open dialogue with the patient or therapy in a group in order to decipher the social context within an individual problem. Hodann, Mewis rejoined, was treating working-class issues on a civilian level and thereby reducing them. Here too the Party had sole jurisdiction, for the individual could be strengthened only in political fellowship. Just what are you people doing here, asked Stahlmann, switching over to the attack, you probably want to establish a camarilla or an anarchist coffee klatch in Cueva, and he could afford to make fun of them, for the tasks he performed contrasted sharply with Hodann's psychiatric concern. In the enemy's hinterland he and his troops had blown up bridges and munitions dumps, advancing all the way to the Portuguese border. His remark hinted at the reports that Diaz must have supplied. Ehrenburg, in his answer, surprisingly enough opposed any kind of statutory severity and respectful caution. Slavish obedience, he said, belonged to a decaying era, and it would be an anachronism to go along with it. Rogeby, between several staff members who were present at the discussion, raised his hand. Quiet, reflective, nicknamed the Philosopher, he always commanded attention upon taking the floor. Prussianism, said this man, a one-time machine gunner in Jamara, Guadalajara, and Brunete, can nevertheless still be found in the German antifascist units, to the great regret of foreign comrades. Not that he was against the hard drilling in the training camps, he said, he was merely against a tradition that was useless for the fighting spirit of the soldiers in Spain. Scandinavians, returning from battles with great casualties, had been confronted by German commanders, who checked to see if their jackets were correctly buttoned, and a few men, who had been furious about being called on the carpet for not polishing their boots, had gotten several days in the guardhouse. We must, said Mewis, leave the definition of military duties to the officers, with their experiences in the World War and the Russian Civil War. If, said Stahlmann, we convened a debating club prior to every decision, we would bog down totally, and he could say this too precisely because there was no blind submission in his partisan column, only very close cooperation as a matter of course. Moreover, said Mewis, the army permitted all soldiers to speak their minds, thereby giving them the chance to make suggestions in a democratic way. The anarchists, Ehrenburg retorted, had not even asked if this was permitted, they took it for granted in their free communism. None of them would dream of speaking on behalf of a fellow fighter, and none of them would have had the nerve to claim a higher rank, greater privileges, together with higher pay. What was he after, we wondered in our rising astonishment, was he so sure of himself, did he feel so invulnerable that, after the elimination of the anarchist influence, he could stand up for anarchism, he who had been close friends with its leader, Durruti. But now he executed one of his characteristic dialectical turns. The anarchists were right in many of their revolutionary principles, he said, the morality they lived by was exemplary, their goals chimed with the hopes of a large segment of the populace, but in a certain situation what was right and true about them could become wrong and untrue. Their morality had been worth striving for, and great enough for self-sacrifice, but it was unable to prevail in the long run. Something that was morally right was wrong if it was doomed by the social and political circumstances, and something that initially seemed to contradict the ideal could, when logically reasoned and bolstered, eventually prove to be of superior quality. After the lentil dish was served, Bredel touched on the contrast between an antifascism that was general and was kept humanistic and a precisely worked-out position that was consistent with the Party line. If he cited Thomas Mann as an example, Bredel's intolerance was justified by his own militant activities, by the worker's constant struggle against the bourgeoisie's self-assured system of concepts. Mann's road from a liberal author to an out-and-out opponent of the fascist dictatorship was certainly admirable, he said, but it was nevertheless a comfortable road, on which daily hours of political obligations were accompanied by an independent artistic world. The writer did not burden his insights by taking the logical step of joining a party that knew how to act on those very insights, nor did he let the events of the crisis infringe on his creative freedom. Today the choice of a political side had to be demonstrated with one's entire person. Bredel challenged the right of art to occupy its own region outside the immediate present, its own time dimension next to our continuity. A writer, he said, was as ineluctably and directly tied to the concrete occurrences as a front-line soldier, as an organizer of illegal undertakings. Any attempt at confining artistic work to a narrow margin between the decisive actions not only was synonymous with sticking to the norms of an obsolete world, it actually constituted blatant service to the enemy. And once again it was Ehrenburg who played the devil's advocate. He did not unconditionally share Goethe's ideal, he said, that one could be creative only in perfect stillness and isolation, far from the bustle of the world, yet deep in the eye of the hurricane, where the artist was beleaguered though undisturbed by current events, he could have poetic visions that said more about their time than the most informative reports. If the author devoted his entire being, his essence to participating in the living world, reacting with his intrinsic means, then that was one of the most essential actions in politics, the politeia, the freedom of the city, and it had to be judged per se as having prime importance. Stahlmann, pushing back his chair, had gotten to his feet. We are en route to Teruel, he said. The decisive battle has begun there. And you people are conversing about the nature of poetry. Yes, said Ehrenburg, in a few days I will be there, and so will Lindbaek, and Bredel and Grieg, and many others who write. We fight there by reporting. And why are we fighting, he asked. Because we want the world, in which our literature too belongs, to be freed of disfigurement. We must not be discouraged by the assessment of the weapons employed in this fight. Some people may not be at the front, and yet the things that they see, that they describe, that they project for the future give us strength and support when we emerge safe and sound. We are no more courageous than those who unstintingly allocate their energies to their mental image, whose feelings are uninfluenced by the practical demands that are our top priority. Without us, cried Stahlmann, they are helpless, lost. And we, Ehrenburg countered, would be nothing without them. In several weeks, he went on, I may be back in my city, in Moscow, it gives me strength to know about all the people there who are laboring partly to make words permanent, keep them alive. I too knew whom he meant. Even though not mentioning the names, he put himself at risk. The inaudible naming of Babel, Meyerhold, Tairov, Tretiakov, Mandelstam, Akhmatova could spell his doom. Hodann's sudden question about Ovseyenko, Rosenberg, Koltsov, Ehrenburg's companions, who had already returned to Russia from Spain, showed me that Hodann too was stunned by Ehrenburg's statement. And Ehrenburg was already sitting up again, the man who cannot stand his ground goes under, this, he said, is what I mean by the threat of death to which we are all equally exposed, whether in the front-line fighting or somewhere in the rear, in some entrenchment. And now what was this visit all about, I wondered, was Hodann to be tested, provoked, warned, or merely primed because a new leadership would take over in Cueva at the new year, and Hodann would switch to a new post. His transfer to Denia, harmoniously worked out, was now definite. The hospital there was described not as a convalescent home but as a transit station, they expected a large influx of wounded men. Didn't Hodann's efforts to mentally activate his patients clash, as was hinted by Mewis, with his long-expressed wish to leave the hospital camp in Cueva, had he not, asked Mewis, from the very start conducted his initiative on a temporary basis. No, said Hodann, even if he had just a few weeks at his disposal he would use them to provide not only medical help for the sick but also intellectual stimulation, that was the only way to further the recovery process. Most of the patients, however, would be sent either back to their units or on to other rendezvous, they could already anticipate a new contingent of soldiers needing recuperation. From Hodann's gaze, which darkened by one shade, I could glean that he realized how suspect his activity was to the political leadership in Albacete. Though even if the visitors were intent on cleaning up in Cueva, they did not have to be accused of sharing Marty's views. They themselves disagreed with his high-handedness. When they transmitted directives, their approach was not irrational or inconsiderate. Hodann was granted the relief required by his illness. However, primarily because Ehrenburg was eager to become familiar with the institutions of the brigades, Hodann wanted to show what the responsible persons demanded in order to keep passivity and ossification from emerging in the silence and isolation. He insisted on it, perhaps precisely because of the unfavorable weather. I did not follow the group, which, wrapped again in their coats, plunged out into the blizzard, instead I climbed the steep narrow steps to the tower, to the covered belfry. Inhospitable as the hall downstairs was with its many doors, its brownish-black wooden walls, its excessively high ceiling, the tower was more of a sham, merely pretending to fulfill the demands of a country castle. Externally joined together out of big ashlars, provided with arched window hatches, with no light entering, it was cold and entirely walled in. There was only the slender gallery up above, blasted by the wind, nor was it inviting in summer with its narrow wooden bench that ran around the walls. Nevertheless, it provided a panoramic view that was already a farewell, the entire grounds offered themselves, embedded in the white surfaces, ringed by the black lines of the trunks and branches. Leaving a slanting trail, the visitors stomped toward the barracks with the corrugated-iron roof, their location joining the direction of the kitchen wing. Smoke rose from the flues of the hearths. In the courtyard inside the rectangle formed by the low side buildings, people, as usual, were sawing, were chopping up the branches. At a right angle to the barracks, the farmstead, lying on a road with dark furrows left by cartwheels, stretched out with roofs of various heights, behind it walls enclosed the square with the dung heap and the basin of liquid manure. All around in the depressions there were the smaller structures, the stalls and sheds, linked by a scrawl of fences. The wells, statues, and benches, assembled like an amphitheater, lay deserted under snow cushions, at the bridge, by the cannon, the sentry marched back and forth. Now the visitors stood inside, in the dormitory, where the floor of hard-stamped soil was decked with pine twigs, while across from the plank beds the longitudinal wall sported, in between flags, an astral chart painted on wrapping paper and a drawing studded with colored pins and showing the frontlines. The soldiers, the furloughers, the convalescents, having climbed off their beds, had blankets over their shoulders, for despite the fire in the iron stove, the huge room was cold. In between the posts under the roof beams, they stood, rallying in front of the rare, high-level guests. Perhaps they would be asked about their experiences, perhaps they would find attentive listeners, perhaps there would be heartening words, and so they optimistically pulled themselves up, pressing their hands rigidly into their trousers, perhaps they would also sit on the board benches, around the cannon stove, for a long discussion, for it always took time for people to get close to one another. But the procession already passed through the thrown-back door and trudged through the snow drifts, toward the farmhouse, where, recognizable in the illuminated windows, the participants in a course had gathered. Further off everything lay in a thickening whitish gray. Peering down over the frost-dusted poplars, over riverbank and ravine, I suddenly felt how cut off we still were from this country, how little we knew about its inhabitants. This country, in whose civil war we were entangled, was little more than a symbol, we had merely transplanted our own interests, our own activities. All we got to see were a couple of cities, a rear-area military hospital, we were present in a barracks, in a transport, we entered combat zones, tiny fragments showed themselves to us. We had been content with the work to be done here, our international task was oriented into the distance and we had spread it across all that was lacking. The most important thing had been that in this country, we, with our hodge-podge of languages, weapons, and equipment parts, were maintaining the idea of the survival of a worldwide movement. We had found what we belonged to in political decision, but this field of activity, this tactical image, this map of Spain had not yet been transformed into a living structure containing encounters with people, specific ways of seeing and expressing things. All I could perceive, leaning over the railing of the steep watch tower, was the stone table, ringed by stone seats, on a narrow terrace, amid artificial vases and columns.

Below, at the stone table, peering up at the top of the tower, with a suddenly clear sky on one of the first days in January, I caught something of the dimensions that I had entered. Tomorrow I was to follow Hodann to Denia, the time in Cueva was over, our comrades, including Münzer and Rogeby, had already set out for their destinations. On his final round Hodann checked with the farmworkers who supplied the convalescent home with meat and produce from the surrounding fields. Frequent conflicts likewise had to be settled among the peasants, who, according to a decree of the Ministry of Agriculture, had to donate their surpluses to the Brigade authorities and to the administration, which, with its monitoring and directing, interfered with farm management, so that the campesinos often threatened to go on strike. When handing in his reports, Hodann had made it clear to his successors that constant efforts at getting along with the populace were as important as the military struggle, and that no victory might be won if the soldier in the war of liberation could not, as the ancient Chinese saying put it, move through the people like a fish in water. At the last farm we visited, the seventeen-year-old son was about to set out for his military service, and we were invited to join the going-away party. This was also a celebration for Hodann, who they had heard was being transferred. Following the campesino past the draw well, with its slanting wooden pole and the pail on its chain, we reached the cellar, whose clay dome loomed out of the snow. Thus began a ceremony, which continued with the slow opening of the board door and the descent down steep, worn steps into the grotto dug deep into the soil. The glow of the kerosene lamp, held aloft by the peasant's son, revealed the rows of barrels and the quadrangular basin with the manual grape press. The peasant pulled out the bung from one of the barrels and filled a large carafe swathed in bast. The grapes for this wine had been harvested, and the wine closed up, the year of the son's birth, and according to custom the barrel could be opened only when the son would be leaving for the army. With the heavy carafe on his shoulder, the peasant climbed up the hardened clay stairs, the son closed the door wing, which lay flat in the dome, and we walked back to the low, whitewashed kitchen in order to drink the wine at the table. The cognac-like taste of the transparent, light-golden wine, which had been stored for a long time, lingered on our tongues and palates when we drove back from Albacete to Denia in the car lent to us by the staff. The farmhouse visit had not aroused any feeling of exoticism, rather it had evoked something familiar. The group around the table reminded me of the room I had been at home in since childhood, we too had always sat like that, on wooden chairs, near the hearth. In the farmer's country kitchen, my sense of togetherness with this land had grown more solid than during the months at the Cueva estate with the constant presence of another class. This enmity was smoked into the walls, it creaked at us from every opening door, from the trodden steps of every stairway. At the gigantic dining-room table, the children, girls with ribbons in their hair, boys in ties and white shirts, had had to sit without letting their backs touch the backs of the lofty chairs. Those, as the driver reported to us, had been the orders of the grandfather, who was now jailed in the fortress, under the castle mountain of Chinchilla, which was gliding past us. Since the afternoon with the farmers the Republic was no longer merely a theater of war, a survey map for retreating and advancing troop movements, it was a soil on which every footprint was tied to our own destiny. The pruned grape vines loomed from the thin snow like bony hands, the fallen soldiers seemed to be lying there in rows. And every encounter with a military transport, every sighting of a watched depot and camp, every cannon, every tank gave us hope that we would survive the struggle. What energy would be demanded of our men to ward off the threat to a division of the Republic from Teruel to Castillón, and how trivial were our own efforts during the past few days, when we had used insect powder and soft soap to cleanse the hospital of lice and cockroaches. Even though each of us, said Hodann, is performing historic actions and even though we, no matter where, are participating from dawn till dusk in a tremendous deployment of energy, our personal work often seems fruitless. Since summer, he said, I have been treating wounds and mental disorders, attacking insomnia, dealing with the shattered egos of the patients, I have refuted the opinion of Professor Tissot in Lausanne, who, in seventeen seventy-six, described the dreadful havoc wrought by masturbation, I have devoted a great deal of time to presenting the causes of sexual fear, and, along with such meaningless-sounding therapy against ignorance and distress, I have had to cope with innumerable minutiae, with procuring eggs and milk, bandages, gauze, cotton, salves, and soap, I have tried to turn this dilapidated estate into a passably functioning convalescent home, I have negotiated with the commissar over every detail and I have had to explain to the administrator that the farmers know more than he does about handling their tomatoes and mixing the fodder demanded by their pigs, and all the while I have battled with my bronchia and filled the bag with my sputum. And now I have handed my job over to successors, who are forced into an equally stubborn, meticulous, and draining activity, and I am about to begin the same endeavor in a different place, though under more favorable weather conditions. We must, he added, recognize some progress, for otherwise all these humdrum actions would be in vain. It was in these terms, I said, that this war would some day have to be depicted, Lindbaek, Ehrenburg, Bredel, and Grieg, and many others provide information about the visible occurrences, about the changes significant for the political development, they record the necessary things for a future contemplation of the events of these years. But who, I asked, logs the patience with which most of the people here live, since it is part of their very nature to view everything regarding their own condition as not worth communicating, to be self-effacing and hold their tongues about it all. Such an attitude, said Hodann, revealed a certain background. If you, he said, had had a bourgeois upbringing, you would come with the assurance that everything happening to you concerns you and challenges you to express your opinion. Wherever you wound up, you could, as a matter of course, claim any situation for yourself. Instead you still bear the weight of experiencing your inferiority, you believe that no one wants to listen to you, you are uncertain as to how your studies can be utilized, expressed. This is something, he said, that I have repeatedly found in conversations with young workers, they shy away from transmitting their knowledge because they are filled with the scorn shown by others, because they already sat on the sidelines in classrooms, allegedly with no calling for science, scholarship, art, for running a business, predestined to enter the machinery as soon as possible, at the very bottom. I wanted to disagree, I wanted to explain how much we had already gained, but then I had to admit that we managed to achieve anything only by stubbornly fighting against being educated for passivity, that nothing could be attained in a calm, natural fashion, that we could accomplish things only by rebelling, by violently hitting back, and that, despite everything, we would never succeed in leaping into the world of decisions. And yet, said Hodann, the power of the workers is superior to the power of the men who pass resolutions. The workers have simply not yet used their strength in society, but on another level their ethics and solidarity indicate the prospect that they will rule in the future. It is mainly workers, he said, who have come to Spain, and the men of a bourgeois background who join their side have broken with their class. There is something else, said Hodann, that points to the future of the working class, none of its members has to abandon his background in order to become aware of his worth, on the contrary, his entire potential lies in that background, while for us, with our middle-class burden, the achievement begins only with our rebelling against our background. In some ways, he said, the development of the person who has to deny his class is harder than the path of those who can affirm their class as the progressive one. And while we may have this advantage over the renegade bourgeois, I said, they nevertheless always possess a greater overview, in their apostasy they sometimes accomplish more than we in our togetherness. But we have never really been disheartened by their knowing a few thousand more words and concepts than we do. Whenever we debated literary, artistic, and scientific topics, we realized that we had all this on loan, that we were merely sketching things that would have to be carried out, redeemed later on. Everything had been a preparation. We were sure that our current verbal fumbling could some day be translated into consistent, continuous series of words. What we cannot express now, we concluded, we will formulate in ten, in twenty years. During such conversations we always asked for a long life, this was the premise for overcoming our handicap. But you should not delay, said Hodann, what you could record now, the sense of inferiority is, I think, bound up with discretion. We also have to assume that our life expectancy is shrinking more and more in this period. If you do not utter or actually jot down the thoughts that cross your mind, then you are clinging to the prejudices aimed at you. The workers' literature that we are demanding must, from the very outset, transcend any limitation, it must not wait for the level of education that we take for granted in regard to bourgeois literature. But then again I viewed it as a prejudice that the same standards obtaining for any other artwork should not be applied to a worker's writings. Until recently, all I knew about Spain was wrong and inaccurate, a few memories of Goya's *Caprichos* and *Desastres*, of poems by Lorca, of the images from a surrealist film by Buñuel. It was only after visiting the farmer's home, I said, that I began to grasp something of why I am here. At first I found Hodann's laughter incomprehensible. He spoke about the pharmacy near the central medical office, we had gone there before leaving Albacete. In the front room, which was lined with marble slabs, a granite table, resembling a catafalque or a dissection surface, stood between the opened wings of a richly ornamented triptych, the sentry behind the table either waved the visitor off or, if he knew him, motioned toward the room in back of him. At night, with the shutters down, said Hodann, one could end up on the altar in order to be dismembered. For me, he said, coughing with laughter, that back room is the epitome of my time in Spain, that chamber with its shelves rising to the ceiling like steps, which are full of vials, jars, and mugs, and with the master at the blending board, grinding together what I need to survive. It struck me that, while observing the artfully painted blossoms and spices on the porcelain pitchers and the rows of blue, green, and violet bottles, I had noticed a sweetish, slightly heady smell emerging from the receptacle under the pharmacist's pestle. Morphine, opium must have been in the small packages that Hodann had taken, along with the adrenaline capsules, from the store on Calle Major, number sixteen, and now that we had passed the Citadel of Almansa and were driving over mountain roads toward Denia, his laughter required no further discussion. Hodann had also started saying that people praise the exoticism of a country only if its social and economic background is to stay hidden. The stranger and more mysterious a country, the greater its injustice, poverty, misery, the glossier its tourist postcards, the more intense its state of ferment. On all continents, he said, my knowledge of the material factors constituted the tension in my encounter with a city, a landscape. I did not seek differences in manners and customs, in myths, dances, and music, I looked for similarities with things I was familiar with, for lines leading me to common origins. Nothing was unintelligible, and if someone claimed he had come upon a bizarre ethnic group, he was merely showing his own isolation and his intellectual arrogance. Once, he said, proletarian internationalism, by stating that there was no fatherland for the worker, had gone along with such a humanistic view. In October nineteen seventeen Lenin had a very close look at India, China, the Latin American countries, an Africa still in bondage, but for the next two decades the rampant power of imperialism had shattered the revolutionary continuity, and there had been only a few scattered uprisings. The dangerous thing about this development, he said, is that liberation struggles are limited to individual countries, that the idea of internationalism is being put on the back burner and disappearing, and that we are ultimately fighting one another because there is no agreement on the concept of revolution. Soviet military assistance to Spain, Hodann added, could be seen as an attempt to get back to common foundations, but we were not certain how feasible this effort was, or whether it was not bound to reach a final point, determined by the necessity of putting all forces in the service of defense within a single country. For Hodann his sojourn in Spain was a direct extension of his earlier activities. The concept of being uprooted, of being an émigré did not exist for him. He had been driven from Germany, he had left it behind, but not in order to lead the life of a refugee, a lost outsider. He had found tasks in Geneva, in Oslo and Paris, there were tasks in Spain, and there would be more and more tasks wherever he ran into friends, comrades. There is a difference between an émigré and a political exile, he said. The émigré feels he has been forced into an alien world, a vacuum, that he painfully lacks familiar things, the things of his homeland, that he often cannot or will not grasp what has happened to him, and that he tussles either with his personal sufferings or with the difficulties of reorienting himself and trying to adjust to the new country. On the other hand, the political exile never accepts his expulsion, he always keeps his eye on the reasons why he was driven out and he struggles for the change that will some day enable him to return. That is why, he said, we have to fight against the fatigue manifested in exile, against the first signs of psychoses caused by functionlessness, we must always view ourselves as activists who are merely assigned to different venues under the demands of historical events.

While Cueva may have been concealed, encapsulated in a wasteland, the hospital near Denia, surrounded by gardens and fields, country homes and olive groves, lay in a vast openness that, on the northeast, melted into the horizon of the sea and, in the southwest, merged into wooded hills and chains of bluish-hazy mountains. The destination could be reached not through chasms and taluses but through a pastoral gateway flanked by white stone posts, overarched by airy flourishes of wrought iron containing the name of the estate, Villa Candida. Running through the orange plantation with low-hanging branches full of ripe fruit, the path led to the well-proportioned, light-yellow building, whose external corners were lined with protruding red bricks, as were the windows with their balcony columns. The interior architecture resembled the mansion on the Jucar, but there was nothing tomblike about the huge rectangular hall, its top lights hung with draperies striped green and white, every ornament, every object, every piece of furniture was recherché, cultivated. The faiences inlaid in the reddish sandstone slabs, the dolphins, lions, eagles, lilies, and coats of arms on the floor were the products of sound craftsmanship, just like the ceramic friezes that depicted scenes of rural life on every step, all the way up to the next landing. East Indian and Chinese porcelain plates, swords, color prints hung in between the sconces on the wood-paneled walls, richly sculpted Renaissance chairs, chests with griffin claws, cupboards stuffed with pewter mugs, heavy tables with crossbeams and open sideboards filled the gigantic space, the banisters of the surrounding gallery were carried by helical pillars, and once we climbed past the women farmhands in the grape harvest, the donkey carts, musicians and dancing peasants, hunters and stags, we faced a family history arranged in groups, on framed daguerreotypes and photographs, spanning a century, children in laced clothes, top hats, and tuxedos, ladies in pearls and mantillas, gentlemen with all kinds of medals and beards. Merle, a banker, had been the last owner of the house. Stepping out to the seaside terrace along the row of bedrooms, we could survey the ornamental garden replete with palms, cedars, laurel trees, magnolias, and fronded jacaranda bushes. At the right the mountain of Denia rose, crowned by the castle, the hospital was across the bay, the convalescent homes had been set up all around, in five other villas, down under a steep brick roof the side building contained the kitchen, the poultry coops, the laboratory, the administration offices. However, the lab had neither a kiln nor a microscope nor a hydroextractor nor an electric water boiler, and there was no typewriter anywhere in the rooms of the officials. The car had been driven back to headquarters, in case of sudden illnesses or reported accidents the doctors and orderlies had to walk the several kilometers between the various houses. Beds, towels, soaps, wash basins were almost nonexistent in the manors, the patients lay on mattresses on the stone floor. And the hospitals lacked the most basic sanitary equipment, there was no possibility of inoculation, disinfectants were nowhere to be had. There were over four hundred wounded and sick, but for even the simplest prescription they had to send a written order to Albacete, a day's drive, and then wait for a week until an ambulance arrived with the required medications. During the battle of Teruel, we cleaned the rooms with sand and water, combed Denia for towels, blankets, pails, pots, stationery and telephoned for iodine, lysol, chlorine, for bromium, aspirin, and medical examination instruments. When the property was taken over, it was stipulated not only that the legal ownership would be protected but also that no changes would be made in the Villa Candida. The mansion could be inhabited at most by the head physician. Hodann refused to take advantage of this offer, he strove to gain authority over the building in order to use it as a headquarters. The infirmary had been set up without a plan. A couple of doctors had thrown together a staff and filled the cleared houses with patients sent from the overcrowded hospitals in Alicante, Benidorm, Alcoy. Isolated mansions and estates all the way up to Olíva, Gandia, were used to house people, some of them sick and orphaned children. The subdivided facility had not been organized since most of the doctors and orderlies had been called to the front near Teruel. At the La Bosque estate there was only a nurse guarding forty-eight children, no one could be dispatched to Olíva, where a children's home was to be fixed up with Scandinavian assistance. First they had to gain an overview, obtain self-help, and look among the admitted patients for volunteers capable of performing some kind of medical service. Most of the soldiers, disheartened, had participated in the defeat and been content with staying alive. It was only Hodann, weakened by disease, who had given them the impetus for activity. It was as if they had all been waiting only for Hodann's arrival in order to do what was necessary. In his case, that questionable, often misunderstood, and misused quality known as leadership was expressed as self-sufficiency, as an ability to listen and let others sense their own worth. They began with the simplest chores, taking inventories, dividing the patients according to nationality, choosing group spokesmen, scheduling meetings. As in Cueva, Hodann made it clear to these men that their removal from the front lines did not mean they were demobilized. Without guidance many had forgotten that they belonged to an army. Once again it was shown that internationalism, though advocated by each one, had not yet found a common tongue, that it could all too easily sow discord between people from various countries. In the internal disintegration no one had worried about clashes and encroachments. Everything being prepared on a smaller scale in the Cueva camp could already be found here in its ultimate consequences. Not only should Denia have a pedagogical effect, it had to offer a new beginning. Initially the building of order and discipline also meant the preventing of violence, which could suddenly erupt out of lethargy. The ocean air made it easier for Hodann to breathe, he would gaze across the white sand, across the houses in between flower beds, almond trees, fig trees, across the rugged mountains up to the highest, blurring peaks, but when he opened the door to his room, he came upon warped faces. Behind the desk in the administration office a woman stood, her cheek and forehead scratched bloody, two men were stepping away from her, a third stood passive in the corner. In my report I had to log the incident, which was presented distortedly. One of the few women in the hospital center, Marcauer unsettled the imaginations of many of the isolated men, and when Ducourtiaux and Geyrot, tipsy members of a French battalion, burst into her office, they made crude off-color allusions to scuttlebutt about her amorous relations. Forgetting all their Party training, dishonoring their brigades, in which they had proven themselves for many months until they were wounded, they pounced on their female comrade, who wore the same uniform as they did, and the irruption of anarchy was certified by the presence of the mute witness. These facts, set down reluctantly amid grotesque insults and the loss of precious time, belonged to the first day. The features of the soldiers' faces, reddened by alcohol, wet with spit and sweat, were engraved in my memory before the police car's tarpaulin closed over them. And yet one could tell from Hodann's posture, from his eyes, that his constant fear of the next asthma attack had waned, the psychological pressure that increased his suffering had eased. The conquest of Teruel by the Republican troops, the defeat and capture of Falangist regiments aided the emergence of optimism. Here, in this mild climate, while icy cold still prevailed on the northern front, people were becoming more and more certain that a change would come in the war, a conviction that was not frustrated by the wounded and gravely ill, who had been brought here in mud-splattered trucks. As peculiar as this confidence in victory was the sight of the orange trees, which, together with the ripe fruit, also bore blossoms for a coming harvest. Lindbaek and Grieg returned from Teruel in mid-January. She had driven the Norwegian writer in a tank from a snowed-in Valverde, through the hotly contested mountain region, all the way to Plaza Torrija in Teruel. For a year now, she had been a member of the Thälmann Battalion in order to write its history. She talked about working on the foreword to her book and about the difficulties of the overall enterprise. Starting with Jamara, she had taken part in all the battalion's clashes, but as a journalist since women were not permitted in the military formations. However, she was allowed to wear a uniform and carry weapons. Colonel Kahle himself had invited her to tell the story, but how, she now asked, could history be written during an as yet incomplete stage if many connections still had to remain concealed. The beginnings are open, she said, the spatial and temporal developments of battles can also be depicted, and eyewitness testimonies, characterizations of individuals can breathe life into the text. Nevertheless such reporting is unsatisfying because it lacks the perspectives that go beyond the daily need. As political writers, said Grieg, we are steadily confronted with the problem of how research for the sake of knowledge can be harmonized with our consciences, which are submissive to Party axioms. Artistic principles can no longer entirely dissolve into a revolutionary social situation, as was the case during the first few years after October. Back then, every word, whether adhering to immediate facts or to poetic images, was borne by the conviction that it was accelerating a transformation. Prose and poetry, expressing an individual voice here, a collective will there, were clearly recognized as being on the side of tempestuous progress without ever feeling restricted or shepherded. They could certainly be subjected to criticism, often a vehement, biting critique, but they were received and evaluated as a force that was changeable, that was searching for new forms and that could indulge in all eccentricities. Today we continually have to deal with the question of how willing we are to subordinate our discoveries to tactical directives. For this reason, he said to Lindbaek, your account strikes me as meager. No matter what angle you view it from, you stumble upon ambivalent, contestable things. Whatever you may think, not even the beginnings are open, with Beimler's arrival, at the latest, they become obscured. Your book says nothing about Schreiner. And all we learn about Beimler is that he was a front-line soldier, a member of the sailors' council in Cuxhaven, that he was condemned to death at Dachau, but managed to escape on the eve of his scheduled execution, lived in Moscow, and, in early August nineteen thirty-six, made it to Spain, where he died in combat on the first of December, shot in the heart from up close. You could reveal no details of his flight from the fascist prison, either because you yourself know nothing about it or because the enemy must not know what you know, and so the Monument to the Unknown Soldier is erected upon his death. In regard to his escape, said Lindbaek, he supposedly strangled a guard and then fled in his uniform. He distinguished himself, she said, through this deed. When he died in the western park, together with Schuster, the battalion commander, in the fire of Moroccan snipers, a rumor circulated that he, like Durruti, had been killed by our own people. That's nothing new for us. The people who spread such lies are the same who now report that Teruel is back in the hands of the Falangists. They are intent on making the fighters appear suspect, on degrading them, causing agitation, and driving a wedge between the Popular Front and the army. They also claim that the German battalions were deliberately led to their doom. They call the volunteers sheep being sent to the slaughter. I do not mean such distortions, said Grieg, rather I want to ask what radius we can draw around an event, where we can stick purely to the circle in which we live up to the current considerations and fulfill the watchwords of the moment, or whether we dare to forge ahead to an uncomfortable overview that is full of contradictions, yet rescues a more valid picture in those contradictions. We are Communists, he said, we keep silent within the ring that we ourselves have drawn. With our silence we accept the commandments issued by the Party. We do not ask about the reasons for the even deeper silence surrounding Rosenberg and Ovseyenko, who formed the guard of honor at Durruti's coffin. We do not ask why the mysterious General Kléber, a German or Austrian, the hero of countless battles, is never named anymore and is vanishing as if he had never existed. We keep silent on the assumption, or in the conviction that there are important reasons for these events and decrees, but while keeping silent, in the hope, in the certainty that the Party will explain its decisions at some later time, we enter that region of thought in which we feel an urge to write not only for our time but for an era when the need for truth will break through all the present rationales. We know that some day, when the Party feels that the time is right, it will illuminate all the particulars of its often puzzling decisions, for it would not be a Leninist party if it wanted to keep its actions beyond our ken. Once the crisis we are now in is overcome, we will be informed about the quarrels and upheaval that are now occurring within the Party, and yet, precisely because the idea of justice is inseparable from the foundations of the Party, we are getting involved in a moral conflict in which the historian's objective standpoint, demanding nonpartisanship, is clashing with the self-restriction of the Party politician. We are humanists, but we also have to practice inhuman severity against ourselves. For an author, said Hodann, truth is indivisible. For him, truth has to be a criterion that can be grasped by science and scholarship. At times he can keep back certain considerations if his statements might interfere with a greater and more important strategy, but he would no longer be trustworthy if he gave up his overall picture. His quality can always be measured by the degree to which he transcends the limits set by the politics of the day and focuses on the strivings of contemporaries to interpret the world we exist in. Truth is a changeable concept, Lindbaek retorted. For me a thing is true if it best serves our cause at a given moment. And yet you are uneasy, said Grieg, for you are moving on shaky ground. That is not my uncertainty, replied Lindbaek. What I regard as true belongs to our agreement. We are expecting a world war, so no word that I utter can allow doubts about absolute agreement with our strategy. I have seen mass dying. If I want to explain this, I cannot be helped by naming questionable things. At the front lines we all run an equal risk of dying. The decision to resist is tied to the possibility of death. I do not overrate the importance of the Brigades. Émigrés in Paris, in Prague delude themselves into thinking the war will be decided by our battalions. Granted, the Thälmann, André, and Beimler units are constantly under fire, but each has no more than five thousand men. The total number of volunteers is estimated at thirty thousand, thirty-five thousand, a fragment of the people's army with its seven hundred thousand men. The Falangists are intent on magnifying the significance of the International Brigades. They announce that without them Republican Spain would have fallen to pieces long ago. They assess the Soviet troops at tens of thousands. They want to make it appear that foreign forces have inundated Republican Spain in order to import Bolshevism. This impression is taken over by the bourgeois press in Europe and America, together with the justification of the defense alliance between nationalist Spain and Germany and Italy. But it would be as dishonest as the charge of Communist infiltration if we were to minimize the commitment of the International Brigades. Half of them have remained in the earth that they came to defend. The breaches in their ranks have been filled by Spaniards, in some divisions the Spanish comrades are already in the majority. And yet despite its numerical negligibility, the international participation in this war is inestimable from the standpoint of solidarity. The figure of thirty thousand men is infinitesimal compared to a single demonstration of the Popular Front in Paris. But because the hundreds of thousands are not giving their all to smash the fascist assault, the thousands have to be named over and over, for they are the ones who are acting upon their political insights. Their significance is palpable, just as the Soviet arms supplies, viewed by many as inadequate, assure the combat power of the people's army. Given the transport difficulties caused by the blockade, it is a triumph to have a machine gun in every regiment, and at Brunete we actually received antitank guns, the latest models. I can report on the strength of the forty-five-millimeter grenades, I can repeat data, but the trouble begins when I have to depict the personal forces behind each action. In this regard, I have gathered facts on a small formation whose name has a symbolic importance. André has been executed. Thälmann, despite protests from all over the world, remains in prison and is threatened with murder. The choice of these names for our military units serves as guidance. By joining these battalions, a man confirms a political affiliation. But how can I clarify this since I cannot determine the background of the individual fighter, since I am unfamiliar with the impulses, the paths that led the volunteers to the Irún front, to Catalonia. So most of them have to remain anonymous. Only individual names can be emphasized as representatives of the countless men I have met in the various sectors, at the front lines. When Beimler died, other leaders of the Thälmann Battalion also perished, I know of Adler, Wille, Schuster. When Geisen was wounded during the attack on Santa Quiteria, Platoon Leader Preuss also fell, and so did the centuria's standard bearer, his name was Pukallus, and the appointed successors were the three Danish brothers, the Nielsens. That is what I find so agonizing, she said, the fact that I do not know who they were, any of them, whose most outstanding quality was that they laid down their lives for Spain. And now I saw her broad, powerful face suddenly freeze and turn gray. I had asked her about the casualties when the monastery mount was conquered, and she had started calculating, she listed nineteen dead, Gummel, Wagner, Schwindling, Hirsel, Engelmann, Pfordt, Lösch, Mayer, Baumgarten, Heras, Vigier, then faltered, was unable to name the others, then she spoke of fifty-two wounded. When I said I had heard from a different source that forty-three men had been killed and forty-one wounded, she became lost in thought. Perhaps, she said in a toneless voice, only some of the wounded could be saved during the retreat. Nor could she validate the figure of one hundred thirty-four men who had mounted the assault. Every description of an engagement could be refuted, could be tackled from an opposing viewpoint. If the number of soldiers in a regiment, the numbers of dead and wounded could not be ascertained, then how could even a single person be profiled. Grieg said that the three Danish brothers could be drawn forth out of vagueness, they were, he said, characters for a play, perhaps they could serve for pinpointing and exemplifying individual features. Lindbaek produced a letter, from Copenhagen, written in Danish by the father of a fallen soldier named Larsen, likewise in the Thälmann Brigade. He was a good son, wrote the father, I can say nothing but good things about him, and the cause to which he sacrificed himself was good. I have only one favor to ask, let me know where my son is buried. There is no hurry, you are busy day and night freeing the world from barbarity. But when the victory is won I would like to go to my son's grave and see the spot where he last fought. Yet no one, said Lindbaek, knows where Aage Larsen is buried. There are many mass graves near Teruel. His father, who is a worker, residing in Copenhagen North, Mimersgade thirty-five, second floor, may come to Teruel some day. He will see the city rebuilt from ruins, lying between the massifs, Teruel with its high viaduct bridge, its gigantic arena, its steep slopes, and I will now track down the whereabouts of his son's unit before its annihilation, so that once we have beaten the enemy we can place an indication there, distinct enough for the searching eyes of the worker Larsen. But several weeks later, when Lindbaek was en route to Teruel, in rainstorms, the access roads north of Valencia were already cut off by advancing spearheads of the fascist armies. After an incessant bombardment, the exhausted Republican soldiers in Teruel were encircled by the foe, reinforcements could not be brought since a new Falangist offensive was prepared on the Aragón front and on the Ebro, and by the time Lindbaek and Grieg returned to Denia, Teruel was about to fall.

Meanwhile the Villa Candida had become the headquarters of the hospital center. There was no determining whether Hodann had arbitrarily requisitioned the house or personally negotiated with the owner, nor did we ask any questions, we viewed the takeover of the estate as an act of martial law. Patients in need of special care were put up in the terrace rooms, while the rest of the space around the gallery was at the disposal of the physicians and the staff. The dining room downstairs and the salon behind vast French doors were used by the administration, meetings took place in the hall. Settling in and establishing solid communications between the widely scattered buildings, we also changed our attitude toward the previous period, which had struck us as muddled. When each day went by according to a schedule, the earlier time likewise became easy to grasp. We had been thrust, unprepared, into the midst of a state of exhaustion and disintegration, we had to act, and it was from our current position that we saw everything that had been put in motion, we considered ourselves the agents of the events. Only then did the individuals become visible, and during our joint work, shards of the past emerged, slowly clarifying the larger picture. We got to know what had happened before our arrival, and, like everywhere else, that time span had been full of improvisation, with sporadic efforts toward organizational initiatives and setbacks. Every hospital, every military camp, every supply station was subject to this rhythm, every area was paralyzed at least part of the time. The Republic's munitions plants were unable to make up for the shortages caused by the blockade, and production in all other domains was likewise insufficient, they were constantly threatened with the collapse of rations and supplies, if any symptoms of weakness, despondency appeared, they instantly affected everyone who already felt lethargic, hopeless, and they became waves of defeat. And the defense system was always there, with achievements that were barely appreciated, that were lost amid constant demands, arms, clothing arrived here, refugees were fed and housed there, worn-out men needed to rest here, units with new forces marched off there. However, people asked why the workers in France, England, and Scandinavia were not offering enough help, the inflow of money, pinched and scraped from the individual donor's salary, was infinitely small compared with what was needed, where were the militant actions, they asked, where was the powerful general strike, how could it be that France's working class was yielding more and more to its reactionary government and allowing the Popular Front to gradually fall apart. There was something unstable about the snapshot moments around the new year, at Christmas the coast had been bombarded by German naval units, typhus cases had been reported at the same time, side buildings of the hospital were destroyed, roads blown up, a quarantine ward had to be set up, the unsupervised children, wandering around, had to be kept away from the contagion zone. For lack of equipment the infected patients had to be treated in a shed, the first deaths occurred in early January, when the Denia camp was shelled anew, from our tiny, isolated realm we came into this unprotectedness, into these confused efforts, and in our initial assessment of the situation, we fell victim to the same mistake that was repeatedly made in crises, we looked for the culprits responsible for the disorder instead of finding out what had been accomplished, we saw only failures and complained about shortcomings. The labor force, tackling the reconstruction with new impetus, consisted of the same people we had met, exhausted, frazzled, but they had already been on the job earlier, untrained volunteers, their character had not changed, they were still capable of overwhelming fear and irresoluteness, self-reliance and willingness to work. Can we really claim, said Grieg, that we are different from them, do we too not often go through periods of stagnation, hopelessness, which we then overcome with the help of others or sometimes through our own thoughts. And just what are these thoughts, he said, what are these maxims that we write down, compared with the deeds being performed all around us. We pull ourselves together to make a report, we cite the humanistic responsibility, we voice our anger, our despair about the injustice, the suffering that we witness, but here the wounded, the dying are carried in people's arms and put in beds, here the injuries, the illnesses are treated with smidgens of medications, instruments, and with a plethora of devotion, of appreciation. To ease our consciences, because the whole of Europe is not doing enough to assist the Spanish people, who are fighting for us all, to apologize for our inadequacy, we are here, driving around in this devastation and sending out our accounts, which are less valuable than the smallest effort to lend a hand in a trench or at the first-aid station. I was not acquainted with Grieg's work. I studied his face, trying to glean something of what he had written. It was a bright, smooth face, with a straight nose, even lips, attentive eyes, a high, broad forehead, above it dark-blond hair with a part. But under the closed, solid, concentrated features there was another look, which was hard to capture and which sometimes appeared to be disappointment, almost grief. He had a gigantic build. In his long, gray sweater, which hung loosely like a coat of mail, he might have recalled a prehistoric Nordic warrior if not for his constant brooding, which lent a streak of hard-won triumph to his strength. At first he seemed harmonious, self-contained, but then his gaze could take on this touch of melancholy, and his gestures, underscoring his speech, were likewise marked by something timid, fragile. We are humanists, I heard him repeat, but our humanity is covered with shame. All too many people who constantly mouth words like humanism, pacifism, who see injustice but are unwilling to fight for change, are, in their discreetness, nothing but apologists for the ruling classes. I did not understand his self-accusation. Was it not enough that he was here, I wondered, was he not doing his share by contributing his front-line reports and political overviews to the enlightenment of others. Anything we could do was subject to boundaries, we criticized weaknesses in ourselves and others, we fell prey to foregone conclusions, we endeavored to peel rudiments of truth out of the deformations, it was precisely writers like Grieg who were crucial because, by focusing from the outside on the confusion, they could discover some coherence. In the diffusion of news, said Hodann, we now proceed according to the same patterns, which we piece together impatiently, in our confined circumstances. Scapegoats are being sought for the evacuation of Teruel and for the retreat with its heavy losses. First, anarchists were named, straggling followers of Nin, although it had long since been reported that their influence had been broken. Suddenly they popped up again and, in their recalcitrance, in their refusal to follow the army staff's orders, they had let the city fall into the hands of the enemy; then the attacks focused on Prieto, the minister of defense, and they demanded his resignation. We saw the dichotomy in the people's war re-emerge on the soil of daily exertions. At the moment when the nationalist armies threatened to advance northward from Teruel to the sea in order to carve up the Republic, the disharmony in government policies grew into a crisis, the parties turned against one another, while the troops gave their utmost to hold their positions near Caspe. In the field the supreme effort at defense, in the administration factional strife. But this too could be judged differently, said Grieg. Just as there could be no giving in, no unreliability in the military ranks, so too they could tolerate no member of the government who leaned toward defeatism, toward high-handed actions. Prieto no longer believed in the possibility of a Republican victory. Working with the British cabinet, he had been preparing for a negotiated peace. Mewis, who, in early March, had come to Denia for informational talks, cited further reasons why it was necessary to dismiss Prieto. All I knew about Prieto, who belonged to the socialist right wing, was that he was round and chubby and nicknamed the Frog. I had heard only about rivalry between him and Caballero, about friction between him and Negrín, the prime minister. Then, it was said, Prieto, as a protégé of the Communist Party, had risen beyond Caballero. How bewildering was this triviality of the pieces of information, this dependency on the total divorce of jurisdictions. The awareness of this partition had surfaced repeatedly, in all our discussions, and then was submerged again under the brunt of immediate demands. And now we learned that the minister charged with leading the war was betraying his own mission, he, who had to inspire the troops, was watching them march to their doom. Along with his incapability, his pessimism, said Mewis, he was also trying to rip apart the alliance between the Socialist and the Communist Party. The Popular Front had to be protected, its opponents had to be locked out, not only because it now had to prepare a counteroffensive, but because unification efforts had to resume on a large scale. The French government was about to be reshuffled, with a socialist orientation, and though Blum had earlier shown his lack of resoluteness, now, with the intensification of the conflict, they could look forward to a revival of the Popular Front in France. Within a few days German Social Democrats and Communists were scheduled to gather in Valencia, this meeting in the midst of the battle zone was significant for the talks of higher functionaries in Paris. The military front in Spain was part of the big political front that ran straight across Europe. Here common interests of the workers' movement had been demonstrated. The maintenance and consolidation of our sector not only had a direct impact on the partisan negotiations, they also strengthened the Soviet arguments, tirelessly voiced at all conventions, for the necessity of the international antifascist alliance. In London Ribbentrop conferred with Halifax about the German claims to Austria. They discussed a Greater German Reich with two capitals, Berlin and Vienna. Göring demanded the liberation of the Germans in Bohemia and Moravia. The executive committee of the Social Democratic Party, said Mewis, was being pushed to make up its mind. Braun, Garbarini, Martens, and other Social Democratic members of the brigades had already initiated the armed cooperation. But this also revealed all the difficulties, said Grieg, in which the negotiations were caught. Western diplomacy and the Social Democratic heads were intent on delaying the European war, they also wanted to ward off the Communist influence. Under the pretext of noninterference, he said, they were generally ready to recognize a nationalist Spain. Not for nothing had Prieto caused a break. He must have acted with the approval of the Social Democratic leaders when he emphasized his oppositional relationship to the Comintern, the Soviet state. He had used the Communist Party to make his way up, just as the Party had supported him so long as it found him useful. He was already blaming the loss of Teruel on Communist miscalculations and intrigues. The Social Democrats, said Grieg, would explain their rejections by pointing out that Prieto, like Caballero, had merely been employed by the Communists as a tactical ally within their strivings for power. The goal was the same as before, he said, prestige and influence, tugs-of-war and hegemony, and, given the basic differences of opinion, this was unavoidable, he doubted whether even mortal danger could bring the two parties together. The time of voluntary action had slipped through our fingers. Unity could be attained only through coercion, violence. All this is hard, he said, and we would so much like to be tolerant. This dualism has thoroughly changed most of our ideas. In politics, the art of the possible, there is no room for feelings, and by the same token, in the art of the impossible, which comprises our emotions, our sense of form, our poetic sensibility, everything must be seen in terms of necessity. Beauty is action. We find harmony in a generous deed. Our model is Aeschylus, who went to war heavily armed. Poetry is always an overcoming of the self. That is why, he said, laughing, I travel by boat even though I get seasick, I climb the highest building even though I suffer from vertigo, and I head for the most dangerous places even though I fear death. Ever since Dahlem had been summoned to Paris, Mewis had been running the Party's commissariat in Barcelona, and for him the practical problems had to supersede any brooding and theorizing. His half-green, half-blue gaze was focused on Grieg. His narrow mouth seemed to express scorn in the presence of all these VIPs who had come to Spain to translate their thoughts into the power of action. Or else he pressed his lips together, anxious as he was about the expected squabbles with Social Democratic cadres and with Marty, who was blocking the plans of the German antifascists in Spain to now concentrate their activity on the struggle in their own country. Marty, rejecting the notion of a second front as an impediment to his own plans, had asserted his annoyance about the conference in Valencia and tried to order the delegates not to participate. And so, among all the tensions and splinterings in the government, the ruckus between the nations in the brigades again made itself felt, and if that was not enough, as this situation crystallized, the differences in political thinking within each unit forced their way to the surface. Hodann, propping his hands on the rams' heads at the front of the armrests of his chair, Lindbaek sitting next to him, sporting her torrent of black hair, resembling a woman with second sight, a witch, Grieg walking to and fro, contemplating the coats of arms in the floor, Mewis, peering through the window, watching for the car that was supposed to pick him up, Marcauer, at the table, glancing up from the papers, waiting to see if anything else had to be recorded, these few people, brought together in a tiny group for the same tasks, professed opinions that could never overlap in many points. I saw Marcauer's forehead, crisscrossed with small, white scars, Lindbaek's wide mouth blurred in its lines, Grieg's nervous fingers playing some invisible keyboard, and merely the chair Hodann sat in claimed all attention, with its artistic architecture, its ribbed sidepieces undulating into one another, bracing the leather seat. However, Mewis aimed his sortie not at Grieg, but at Hodann, who had been thinking all this time about a statement of Grieg's and then averred that it *was* necessary to hold on to a humanism, a socialist humanism. Here they are again, those paradoxes, those fixed ideas, exclaimed Mewis, suddenly agreeing with Grieg's earlier arguments, that socialism with a human face, that freedom-loving communism, as if socialism did not constitute the most humane form of living together, as if communism were not already synonymous with the freeing of the majority. His swift exit at the orderly's appearance allowed no response, and it was questionable whether Hodann or Grieg even wanted to reply, for behind this subject lay something else that had not been articulated and that weighed more heavily on us than all the Spanish disharmony.

During this period every day could be called historic, each was the product of an achievement of many days that pushed for a decision, chock-full of events on which hung the future of the nations, of the continents, of the whole world. However, the feuding forces could be overpoweringly felt between the second and the fifteenth of March. It was barely possible to distinguish between the various levels of what was happening, the images of the centers where power and violence were concentrated thronged into our steps, our actions. For news we monitored the British, French, Czechoslovakian radio broadcasts, we were instructed by the Scandinavian shortwave transmitters and by the German radio stations, whose sonorous triumph Grieg translated into words hinting at the true facts. What we heard were incoherent signals, dots and dashes, tips that had to be explicated. Right outside the Kremlin, on Marksky Prospekt, in the House of Unions, in the former clubhouse of the aristocracy, amid the marble columns of the banquet hall, between the azure walls, under the gigantic pendants of the chandeliers, Bukharin sat on the dais, together with

Rykov, Krestinsky, Rakovsky, and the other defendants, and admitted to being the leader of the counterrevolution, whose goal had been to restore capitalism in the Soviet state. Grieg pictured him three and a half years earlier, giving his great speech up there, at the lectern, during the first All Unions Congress of the Writers, his speech on the freedom of revolutionary art, on the unconditional openness of forms, his words had been polished hard, there was something crystalline about them, they contained a vision, not in the meditative sense, they were a fiery attack, a skirmish, a parrying, it was a vision resulting from vehement debates, a smashing away at narrow-mindedness and dogmatism, at the handicrafters of heroic idealism, an abjuration of all directives, a call for the development of individuality. There, in the final days of August nineteen thirty-four, they seemed to be laying the foundation for the new culture that had sought expression since the October Revolution, every sentence showed the way, borne by the speaker's great responsibility, behind him stood the Politburo, the Party. Grieg could still hear the utterances of joy, the storm of applause, the embraces of the attendees were captured a thousand times by the facets of the lamps, and these mirror surfaces, which had once sent back the images of dancing nobles glittering with jewels and medals, now reflected the wretched crew of doomed prisoners. Despite knowing that Bukharin had lost all influence one year later and any support within another year, Grieg nevertheless found Bukharin's appearance after the last year of imprisonment unbelievable. Had I still hoped, he wondered, that Bukharin would be able to clear himself of the charges inundating him too during the trials of Sinoviev, Kamenev, Piatakov, Radek, and Tukhachevsky, had I still believed that he was capable of fending off the national panic triggered by fascism, of bringing back socialist law and order. What had induced him, Lenin's closest confidant, to describe himself to the world as the organizer of the anti-Soviet bloc and to deny everything he had fought for all his life. On the opening day of the proceedings, Krestinsky, short, frail, slumping, the steel-rimmed glasses wedged on his nose, did something that, Grieg had felt, could lead to exorcising the terror. He was the only prisoner who had refused to make a confession, he said he had never belonged to the bloc of right-wingers and Trotskyites, he had never even known of its existence, and he had never, as he was accused, maintained communications with the German and Japanese espionage services. Simultaneously with the bulletins on the victories of the Falangists, who were advancing toward Fuendetodos, Goya's birthplace, west of Belchite, the prosecutor zeroed in on the refractory defendant, who had fallen in absentia. Listen, said the state prosecutor, You will not claim you heard nothing, and Krestinsky, the Soviet Union's former envoy to Berlin, replied almost in a whisper that he felt nauseous. Grieg blanched on this Wednesday when the occurrence was reported in multiple languages, and he explained several times that Krestinsky had taken a medicine enabling him to follow the proceedings. The daring with which Krestinsky had broken with all earlier procedural rules must have cost him all his mental energy, he probably reached his decision hoping the others would follow him. The possibility existed on that second of March, the change could have come, the international press was gathered, a collective appeal, in the few moments of dismay, paralysis, could have led to exposing their innocence. But nothing happened, the others abided, broken, awaiting their annihilation, the interrogation juggernaut was already rolling over the incident again, crushing it into meaninglessness, the fellow defendants remained the allies of the court, needling Krestinsky to retract his remark. But until the evening session of March third Grieg still expected Bukharin to stand up, there, in the hall of columns, in the ballroom, to illuminate the situation in terms of his Bolshevist past, in terms of dialectical and historical materialism. But then Krestinsky's confession was transmitted to us through the ether, we wrote it down verbatim in order to run it, framed in black, in the next morning's wall newspaper. We reported nothing about the defeats on the northern front, tactical withdrawals could be noted here and there, Fuendetodos and Caspe, Quinto and Montalban were held by our troops. Grieg repeated Krestinsky's testimony, he stood behind the large table in the hall, aside from me only Hodann, Lindbaek, and Marcauer were present. Grieg tried to project himself into the mind of the confessor. Making Krestinsky's words his own, he strove to get at their meaning. Under the pressure of shame, he said, triggered by this prisoners' dock, exacerbated by my poor health, in the face of world opinion, I was not capable of telling the truth, but now I ask the court to take down my statement that I am fully and completely guilty of the most serious charges, of disloyalty and treason. He stood silent for a while, his hands propped on the table, here too, in Cueva, we had suspended the long red bunting from the glass roof, letting it hang deep over the gallery. And if I now acknowledge that I am a Communist and that I will continue to work for Communism until the end of my life, I hear the judge's voice. You are no Communist, that voice shrieks, you are a miserable fraud, you are a stinking pile of human garbage. I imagine hearing this for more than a year, day and night, till I black out, in my prison cell, in the interrogation rooms, but I feel nothing, everything remains abstract, beyond understanding, we have left them alone, they have become incomprehensible in their abandonment, and if they, who were infinitely more deeply rooted in Communism than I, who demonstrated Communism with their deeds, have let themselves fall, if they are willing to be no more than a shadow of their former selves, then how could I claim that I, so much weaker, so much more irresolute, would be able to preserve my conviction, my inner logic and continuity. What is this, he asked, that has ripped apart the strongest representatives of the Marxist science of society, the toughest and smartest champions of the socialist system, shredded them so thoroughly that they can no longer recognize themselves. That is no longer Krestinsky. That is an anonymous man. Those are no longer Rykov, Rakovsky. That is not Bukharin claiming he prepared a fascist coup d'état. You sank into direct, naked fascism, said the prosecutor, Vyshinsky. Yes, that is correct, replied Bukharin. At the end of his speech in August nineteen thirty-four, said Grieg, Bukharin cried out, We must risk it, which meant that he felt the time was ripe for coalescing cultural, social, industrial, and political life into a unity, literature, art would grow directly from the overall production, with participation by all, this the first time, I understood him to be saying, that the consciousness of a Communist existence had manifested itself. And what happened then, he asked, where did our attention lapse, it could not be possible that what we all felt at that time could be destroyed by a lone man, that this lone man established a position that made any dissent impossible, that let the enormous intellectual energies next to him dry up. Nevertheless, he said, straightening up, nevertheless, for reasons that are not yet evident, we have to agree with the court and turn our backs on people whom we used to trust. Yes, he went on after pausing to reflect, we have left them, the defendants, in the lurch, but even more so, all of them, the entire nation, which is an accuser here. In our attachment, our hopeful expectation, we failed to see the coming of events that would force the leadership to resort to such violence, how could we now dare to take offense, raise objections, criticize measures, that could only be implemented in this manner and no other. Without the development of power there, the country would have shattered under the incredible pressure, and we would not be here. I was acquainted with the circles frequented by Trotsky in France and Norway, all the enemies of Communism were on his side, the reactionary Western press supplied a forum for his articles against the Soviet state. What good did it do for him to picture a different kind of socialist life if all he wanted was to eliminate the man who had once expelled him, what good was it for him to claim he was working for the good of the proletarian state if he was backed by the worldwide organizations, which, intertwining with his slogans, ranged from humanistic liberalism to the profiteering alliance with fascism, and whose sole desire was to topple the Soviet Union. And so will you people, with your need for truth, asked Marcauer, recognize and defend the verdicts. I will say nothing against them, said Grieg. The threats targeting the Soviet state are so huge that every word we publish must first be checked and double-checked over and over in regard to its defensive force. We cannot keep still about the events, said Hodann, that is why we have to interpret them according to principles that are necessary today. We cannot allow any uneasiness to crop up, we have to show the troops that forces exist that are ever on guard, that expose any conspiracy, any undermining, we have to convince them that the Soviet Union will emerge stronger than ever from the dreadful conflict with her domestic opponents. The public presentation of treason should lead to a catharsis that will give people new courage, new perseverance. In the course of baring themselves, the defendants will be given the certainty that their sacrifice, albeit terrible, will provide a final service to their Party and their country. You advocate that sort of distortion, cried Marcauer, because you are still trapped in your male world. Why, she asked, does Grieg refuse to understand the rule by one man, with its consequences. He says that a lone man is incapable of laying claim to such an inviolable authority. Yet he himself did not create the cult that has developed around him, the cult has come to him. The sanctification comes from the people who want to preserve their system. He is nothing but the executor of that system. All those people bowing at the courtroom bar are in bondage to the system, are victims of obedience, respect, discipline. They are being destroyed by the laws that they themselves have written, but if they had not written those laws, then they would not include the right to the authority of command, and it was this right that everyone strove for. A person can be that shattered, that obliterated only if he has fallen from great heights. Having lost their authority, they have plunged into the abyss. They wanted to lead, but now they are dishonored, declared legally incompetent. I can see no tragedy in their situation, only madness. When dealing with the bellwethers, the big shots, the chieftains, they parroted whatever was drummed into them, with alien tongues they pronounced their own death sentences. You spoke about enormous intellectual energies, she said, turning to Grieg, but these energies focused on only one thing, greater influence, amid constant urging one of them was shoved to the top, the principle of climbing put him in his place, where everyone paid homage to him and everyone envied him. They wanted to occupy the throne that disciplined them, for their world consists of vanity and bondage, of arrogance and degradation. The ultimate consequences of your system, she exclaimed, is shown in the hall of columns. How they wallow, she said, in their potency on the judges' chairs, and how terribly they make their expelled rivals debase themselves in their powerlessness. They belong together inseparably, the impotent and the crowing cocks-of-the-walk with their swollen combs, they are fettered to one another, they need one another, the commanders and those they are mauling. Grieg defended himself, saying that Marcauer was talking like an anarchist, she did not understand the rigorous structure of the Party. The positions were occupied not as a result of intrigue-ridden duels but through the elections of the democratic centralism. It was only the bond with this system, he said, that explained why the persons on trial accepted the verdicts handed down by the collective. And you advocate that, said Marcauer, you call such exaltation Communistic, the torture that is part of the executive power of your world is the only thing that can force a person to relinquish his own self so thoroughly that he gratefully accepts his annihilation. She brought up Radek, that bootlicker, who first perjured himself in order to save his skin, in order to continue his climb, then he kept glorifying the great patriarch, the all-knowing, all-seeing, the wisest of the wise, until Radek too was swept away and went under amid self-accusations. What we see here, she said, is merely a selection from the array of superiors, it is they alone who play the game to the bitter end, many who saved face, who let no one force them to deny their own selves, the lower ones, the true Communists, were secretly mowed down, in Krestinsky a spark still glowed, but then he too lost his conviction. Just look at how the defendants were blackmailed. They admit to misdeeds they never committed in order to save their children, their wives. At first this appears noble, but it merely benefits the survival of their system. They tear along their families in order to give themselves a final satisfaction in their disempowerment by deluding themselves, by imagining they are protecting their wives. But their wives are the fellow prisoners in their selfish structure, the women can serve as hostages or be taken over by other men. What is happening here, she said, may seem incomprehensible in its details, but in its essence, in its infinite uniformity, it is all too familiar. The male world, she exclaimed once again, is letting off steam. The most cunning people, those who best know how to flow with the current, are at the helm, the undemanding ones fall by the wayside. Women are merely reckoned as refuse. And if you call me an anarchist, then I am one in the sense that I think that courage needs no directives, I appreciate planning as much as you men do, but I want it to be classless, without privileges,

I favor extreme violence against the enemy, but violence does not have to be drawn by a buffalo, it is most effective when the collective is intact. Grieg was pale, he stood erect at the table, Communism has not yet achieved its objectivity, Marcauer told him, and you are the ones who are holding Communism back in emotion, in irrationality. Whenever you do not know what to do next, you want to believe, you must believe, otherwise your house would collapse. If you were in the prisoners' dock, you too would forgive your judges, you would praise them, for they are identical with your ideal. I agree, said Hodann, with all of your denunciation of the patriarchal world. Even the land of socialism has failed to realize that it must clear away the features of male dominance. With their egotism men built the system of capitalist oppression. Even the proletariat has seldom overcome its discrimination against women, their position as deceived and blackmailed was the same in all classes, it was only in crises that she, the female worker, could get closer to her male comrades. In moments of great distress or great hope, in a strike, a revolt, a revolution, working men transcended the boundary between the sexes, in the struggle against the common foe men forgot their constitutional privilege and gave women equal rights, breaking through the usual constellations of power, women stood next to men, fundamentally and existentially. Those were always temporary phases, women excelled particularly during the Commune and in the October Revolution, we are all familiar with them from the actions at work and on the street. Only in a few cases did we learn that all of us, on all social levels, were marked by capitalist civilization, that the system of exploitation had also passed into the very blood of the exploited man, and that upon reentering so-called normality we would have to continue fighting against the old values, which instantly made themselves felt. After each upswing the repression recommenced. But here, he said, Marcauer is also making the mistake of seeing the position of men as determined by nature. The capitalist male world is still ruled by the struggle of all against all. Male hordes defend their property against one another. But the socialist state has begun dismantling the results of the atavistic and antagonistic relationship between human beings. Throwbacks have occurred, mechanisms of division of labor have spread out again, a true equality has not yet emerged. But it would be wrong to complain from the outside about the things that are still missing, for what have we accomplished in our own countries for the development of a socialist order, what have we ourselves contributed to changing the situation. The Soviet state began with crucial upheavals in many realms, in social, educational, and executive areas the boundaries between planners and implementers, between men and women, boundaries that are still customary here, have shifted and vanished. Marcauer sees the processes as belonging to the world of men, and her view is justified. But these men no longer interest us as personifications of their sex, they now represent the economic factors behind them. What the trials express in such tireless, obsessive precision is the attempt to justify the current policies vis-à-vis the defenders of the school that originated in the Leninist period. When Bukharin admits he wanted to introduce capitalism, he is talking about the actions of the planners during the time of the New Economic Policy, when the economy was to be stepped up by Taylorist measures, when state capitalism was regarded as a temporary expedient, when they promised the peasants advantages in order to egg them on to increase their output, tendencies now fostered by the Communist Party in the Spanish Republic. It is not the obvious thing, the cult worship of the leader personality, that is significant, this we have determined, no, the important thing is the principle of dictatorship from above. At stake is the building of socialism in a single country. Locked out of the rest of Europe, threatened by fascism, the Soviet Union has to collectivize and industrialize virtually out of thin air. For the socialist accumulation, masses numbering in the millions have to be assigned to where they are needed. These violent solutions, attainable purely through extreme centralizing, were opposed by many of the old Bolsheviks. More than a decade later, after the completion of a dynamic development, we see Lenin's final struggle being waged by his companions against red tape, Party hierarchy, the omnipotent state machine, for the demand for access and democratic control, for the participation of workers in politics, for the continuation of the cultural revolution. You people, said Marcauer, are like Brecht, who, for many, embodies the critical conscience, but who, in regard to the arrest of his teacher Tretyakov, clings to the assertion that the trials are just and that a gigantic conspiracy is being exposed and punished. When it is claimed that new generations are coming to the fore in order to ensure that they will go on with what has been started, and that they have to clear away the worn-out and degenerate stuff that is blocking their path, then your silence is concurrence. When you become aware of the terrorism involved, you cite the development of any other revolution. You have witnessed the smashing of one figure after another from among the founders of the Soviet state. You put up with their degradation in the court, which styles itself the people's court but is an arm of the leadership. If Lenin were still alive, he too would be indicted; after all, Krupskaya has been victimized by all kinds of insults. It was not till later that I caught the drift of her remark. She meant that everything now happening could occur only because Lenin was no longer alive, that he was the only person who could have worked against the tendencies now triggering self-destruction, after all, every last one of his letters, writings, jottings from the period before his death spoke about this intention. But now I was faced with the unsettling question of whether I was ready to cause the liquidation of Marcauer, who, during the early months of the war, when men and women had fought side by side, had belonged to the Luxemburg Battalion and been wounded in the Sierra Alcubierre. I refused to acknowledge the thought of reporting her. Yet I had often enough watched comrades letting one of their own be taken away, and instead of protesting they explained that it was necessary for the protection of the Party. The embarrassment after the dispute had an aftereffect several days later, when Mewis arrived, when Bukharin kept entangling himself in a plethora of contradictions from morning till late at night, when Fuendetodos, that village under the steep mountain slope, with its wellspring, which belonged to everyone, with its walls of red stones, its narrow streets and the painter's house, with its surroundings of white sand and scattered tussocks—when Fuendetodos was taken by the enemy, and France announced the closing of the Pyrenees border. I am no longer fighting for my life, said Bukharin after Mewis had set out for Barcelona to make the final preparations for the Valencia Conference of March thirteenth, I have already lost my life, rather I am fighting for my reputation, for my place in history. The impression left in me by Mewis had remained shadowy. Cool, matter-of-fact, completely dedicated to the political tasks, his character appeared to differ from the complexity and versatility of a Hodann, Grieg, or Münzer. He had been close to me for only an instant. He had asked me why I had not applied to join the Party. It was only upon noticing my difficulties in responding that I realized how premeditated and purposeful his words had been. I was again dealing with the problem of how I would behave if Party interests required me to cut myself off from my friends. I had no reservations about the basis and the goals of the Party. For me the Party had always been the immediately accessible instrument of struggle. It was the Party of my class. I saw myself as belonging to the Party even without a membership book. I did not view submitting to majority decision as renouncing the self-reliance and voluntary action involved in joining the Party. But never must rationality take a back seat, never must metaphysical demands be put forward. There had been unclear things that contradicted my demands for absolute integrity. However, the Party was also the party of dialectics. It had taken in worn-out, orthodox ideas, but it also had youth, an ability to change, it had forces that aimed at the future. Hardness, severity, discipline were part of it, as were a keen perception and imagination. The opposites could be brought to a synthesis. My response to Mewis's almost casual question had to be deferred. Events were speeding by too quickly now for us to find peace and calm for a discussion. Other processes had to be watched. In a nonstop sequence there came those dark, impenetrable accusations, there was that restless seeking amid the rubble of shattered arguments, that search for motives from which rehabilitation might still be gained. We were shown the peculiar warpings of the idiom used by the prisoners in the trial, a diction that was in part totally incomprehensible, but then again seemed to hold secret allusions and allegories. Bukharin had touched upon Hegel, You are a criminal, not a philosopher, the prosecutor threw in, to which Bukharin retorted, Fine, a criminal philosopher. That designation, said Hodann, fits him exactly, for a dissident opinion is a criminal opinion. He is turning himself into an Aesop, whom the rulers prohibit, on pain of death, from spreading his knowledge. Some day, he said, when the archives are opened and made accessible to us, we may find the key to this final device of the slave language. His words are targeted at posterity. By admitting he gave sharp, slanderous speeches about the Party leadership, he is trying to shift attention to the alternative that he championed. Stamped a traitor, he calls himself a traitor, and for him this is synonymous with Bolshevik, so he makes Bolshevism the antithesis to the current form of the Party. He keeps labeling his activities as illegal, and his obstinacy in underscoring this illegality highlights the view that his actions can be seen as illegal only from a specific vantage point, but that they *are* legal for him and the opposition. Likewise his emphasized responsibility in preparing, constructing, and leading the treasonable bloc is indicative of his clinging to the need for returning to a different conception. Undeterred by Vyshinsky's vehement dismissals, he has repeatedly compared his plan to a palace revolution. This is an atavistic concept, which can have nothing to do with a socialist state. But that is precisely why he conjures up this image. He is confronting backwardness with the scientific approach, for which he sees himself as the spokesman. Yet what can he gain with such ambiguities, I asked, since he has nothing left to lose, why does he not come right out with what he means, why does he leave the interpreting of his fables to other people, who will be out of patience. He must have realized, said Grieg, that he is in the midst of an apocalypse, so he assumes that we too will switch gears when listening to him, that we too expect nothing conventional, nothing directly recognizable in his utterances, all he can provide is riddles, otherwise he would have to hold his tongue. We were walking then, on that eleventh of May, through the garden, in the heady smell of orange blossoms, which had given their Arabic name, Azahar, to the entire coastline all the way up to the Ebro. As bizarre as the words still resonating in our ears from the trial was Grieg's remark now, about Bukharin's son, born just when the great Congress of Literature had taken place. He had mentioned visiting Bukharin's home, had talked about his young wife, about the affectionate movements and gestures between them, and then about Yuri, the son, and this was a sentence that, in its formulaic manner, kept going through my mind, he idolized that child, said Grieg, and the pre-stamped, completed, unchangeable nature of that verbal arrangement gained an unbearable significance that evening in the garden, the sentence hung in the still air. Grieg had stopped, pulling his head way back, the sky lay on his face, Hodann's features were twisted in a smile. This fragrance, he said, supposedly has an effect that makes us particularly susceptible, all externals recede, and the essential comes closer. That is why, he continued, laughing and coughing, the Ejercicios Espirituales are performed chiefly in an orange grove, during the week, which, after all the priestly blabber about heaven and hell, is spent in utter silence. But our spiritual exercises were interrupted by the news that the Schuschnigg regime had stepped down and German troops were marching along the Austrian border. Swastika flags had been hoisted in Vienna, and the Jewish neighborhoods had been invaded and looted. We did not yet report that Belchite was lost, but we could report on our own successes, on the front northwest of Madrid and in the Guadarrama Mountains, huge letters on the message board conveyed Vyshinsky's demand for a maximum socialist defense, which in this case meant a bullet in the back of the defendant's neck. The subsequent roaring applause had again reminded Grieg of August twenty-eighth, nineteen thirty-four. What did Bukharin mean, he asked, when he spoke about the development of individuality. He wanted to say, Grieg instantly went on, that you can grasp the essence of revolution, the upheaval of the whole of life and can realize them in yourself and in the outer world only if you are fully self-possessed. With a small indelible pencil, Bukharin, whom Lenin had called the favorite of the Party, was still feverishly making notes for his defense speech, when Quinto and Montalban fell, and the Italian brigades of the Black Arrow, the units of the Foreign Legion, the Moorish troops smashed through the Republican lines, the world press, to the detonations of German aircraft bombs, began to speak about the imminent end of the Spanish Civil War. Bukharin's Final Word, at six P.M. of March twelfth, was drowned out by the booming of tanks and by the tramping of the sixty-five thousand troops who marched into Austria. The course of every minute was now made known, at four in the afternoon the native of Braunau had crossed the Inn River and now, having started from his hometown, was en route to Linz, where the throng was waiting for him in the marketplace. Bukharin had spoken for an hour, I am now coming to the conclusion, he said, I bend my knee to the country, to the Party, to the entire nation. The man named Himmler had already appeared on the balcony of the city hall, and we are proud, he cried, that this piece of German earth that brought forth our Führer has now been liberated and is returning to the great Homeland. The hall of the Villa Candida was packed, the windows were open to the black garden, the faces of the listeners had hardened, their mouths were grim, their eyes squinting. Most of them came from Germany, from Austria, from Czechoslovakia, they spoke various dialects of the same language that was gushing out of the radio, years of illegal political activity lay behind them, some had been in the prisons, many had already spent a long time in exile, and all of them felt the demarcation line that the ideological struggle had drawn through this language. We understood every word, and yet it was as if we had to translate it since it came from the enemy's mouth, we had heard these utterances earlier, when we had still been living in our country, we had heard them being shouted and answered in a collective bellowing, we had heard the sob of poignancy in the speaker's voice and seen the faces of the enthusiastic people all around us, we thought about our earlier jobs, about the conversations in the factory canteen, our evenings off, there had still been the sober words adjusted to practical purposes, there were still tools, machines, houses, streets that made up something we had in common, certain activities had bound us together, but then the slogans of the new order likewise pushed their way into our language circle, possibilities of communicating shrank. Distrust emerged, the conversations were monitored and they dwindled into silence, only the most necessary things were said, whatever pertained to us was stated only in the smallest group. Nevertheless, the segmentation of the language had not yet struck us as definitive, we were surrounded by everyday words, we heard the voices of the children, the neighbors, we stepped into the stores, the libraries, the museums, everything was still close, we thought that the deformations of language were external, that the workers would basically not be infected by the terminology of the demagogues. Only now, from the outside, did we comprehend that the distortions, like an epidemic, had penetrated deep into the core of the people. A vacuum had grown into a coma, the mental distress of all those who had been unable to recognize their situation or to interfere on the strength of a political resolve found a surrogate, a comfort, everything now read and stated was testimony to comprehensive self-deception. A lifestyle in passivity and mental paralysis emerged in language, showing the gap between it and the language we had carried along. The reporter spoke about the many lit windows around the marketplace, they indicated the homes of friends, Party comrades, but several windows, he said, were still dark, that was where the enemies of the people lived, the Jews, and everyone should note the addresses. Then he suddenly burst into laughter, which infected the people waiting below, for a few of the designated windows had now also lit up. This laughter, coming to us from a cavity, this infernal laughter, had nothing to do with the self-satisfied, fatalistic yowling that we were familiar with from mass demonstrations, it resembled an intoxicated longing for blood, for murder. At that instant we recognized the fascist might towering up, the gigantic strength that confronted us and that would keep growing, demanding an as yet unimaginable amplitude of resistance. Our small Spanish bastion tightened up, the Republic's survival was not the only thing being fought for on the shrinking defense lines, the troops were already fighting the preliminary battle of the coming great war. The jubilation that began at ten minutes to eight for the commander's arrival had been full of destructive rage, and now the hush when he stepped out on the balcony of the town hall was charged with the expectation of an oracle. The new Austrian governor, Seyss-Inquart, linked the welcoming ceremony to the annulment of Paragraph Seventeen Eighty-eight of the Peace Treaty of Saint-Germain, which, in nineteen nineteen, had guaranteed Austria's independence, and the bellowing of voices was followed by the mustachioed man's declaration, which, slow and manly, at first husky, then, intensifying, hoarse and shrill, was addressed to the entire world. Readiness and commitment, devotion and dedication, providence and fulfillment, commissioned, obligated, faithful and willing to sacrifice, witnesses and guarantors, those were some of the stigmata that his syntax surrounded, and the howling bloated the trivial into an *Übermensch*-ness. Anyone touching the radio's casing perceived the vibrations of lunatic fury, and we thought about the people now keeping silent amid them and clenching their fists, still powerless, in this Reich, which carried death. How careful they would have to be to avoid betraying themselves with words that still existed in their language, cornered they would have to keep to themselves the ideas that gave language its life. Also, anyone who now entered that country for the underground struggle would constantly have to remember that the thoughts brought into his language were always recognizable as a provocation. Would communication still be possible, we wondered, could the people yelling there, conjuring up *Heil*, salvation, and *Sieg*, victory, ever again be brought back to thinking, would they ever be able to realize what had happened to them. That night we began to understand how long the fight would last, so far we had thought about armed violence, now the trench warfare of thoughts would have to be waged with the same intensity, words, statements had to seek the enemy camp unremittingly and cunningly, the advances had to be planned like military actions. Thus we now saw why the political leadership made sure never to break off contact with those who remained from the ranks of the Party, the labor unions, why it made a point of finding them, talking to them in safe hiding-places, speaking to them in the language that contained our views and conceptions. Many who mastered this language had gone abroad, there they continued working on series of sentences that were not gobbled up by hostility, by the decay of morale, by despotic distortion. These works, preserving the traditions of a literature, were outside the raging that spread through the birth country of that language, but given the vacuum they found themselves in, would they, we asked ourselves, manage to bridge the gap and establish a relationship with the people whose receptivity was being destroyed more and more each day. Now we again had to refer to the idea of the everlasting nature of fundamental values, which survive all catastrophes, we had to recall the reasons why consciousness yielded to and followed the changes in the situation, and those values could deal with the far-reaching events and also resolve the mental blockages. In our isolation, we focused sharply on not ruining the consistency of our actions, and likewise, on the inside, in the encirclement, thousands of others, like Coppi, like Heilmann, were intensifying their faculties in order to preserve, albeit only in secret, their image of a further development. However, the enemy was just in the first stage of his offensive, he had taken Austria, his vociferous, threatening slogans were now aimed at Czechoslovakia, at Danzig, and the Western powers refused to let themselves be warned by the tirades, rather it was as if they sympathized with the tone of voice, after all, they were acquainted, from their own histories, with the drive to expand, seize property, exploit colonies. The British and French diplomats were negotiating not with a madman but with a business competitor, who was far superior to them in dodges and surprise tricks, the economic emissaries were not out to stop a regime of torture, robbery, and murder, they were intent on safeguarding their own profits, the ruling classes of the West were ready to give in to anything so long as they could retain their own markets while German rapacity turned to the East, to the Soviet republics with their wealth of natural resources. And so not only did enslavement and exploitation meet with apathy, they also inspired a network of plots and intrigues. Could any voices, we wondered, still penetrate and call for unity. And even if the conference in Valencia were to issue a manifesto tomorrow, what clout would it have since the Social Democratic leaders refused to defend the Spanish Republic and backed the bourgeois condemnation of the Soviet state. With a clear conscience, they, who had fought for years against the coalescence of the working class, could now invoke the alternative, pitting it against the crisis that afflicted the socialist state. At nine-thirty P.M. the Military Council of the Supreme Court of the Soviet Union had withdrawn to deliberate, while Negrín haunted Blum's antechamber, trying to request his help, Blum was negotiating with the Radical Socialists, who would participate in the Popular Front government only if it continued its policy of noninterference in Spanish affairs, and at the Linzer Hotel, whose name, distorted by the roaring, we interpreted as the Wolf's Trap, Austria's conqueror was asleep, gathering strength for coming actions. On Sunday morning, at four A.M. Moscow time, amid the whirring of movie cameras, the verdict was announced to the defendants, who were harshly lit up by the searchlights. This went swiftly, no moaning, no shouting, no fainting, they were already being led out, in single file, each man flanked by two soldiers, Bukharin the last, deathly pale, his gray goatee making him closely resemble Lenin. Through the cold darkness before sunrise they were driven to Lubyanka Square, to the sumptuous building with the immured windows on the lower stories. Then around noon, while Grieg was gazing across the whitish flickering sea, the native of Braunau, a deeply moving unforgettable event, a reverential hush, stood at his parents' graves in the Leonding Cemetery, Blum's newly formed government refused to assist the Spanish Republic in any way, passing Caspe, which our forces still held, spearheads of the nationalist armies pushed toward the coast, and no news from Valencia. It was not until days later, when Caspe had fallen and thousands had been killed by the air raids on Barcelona and the Falangists were outside Tortosa and Vinaroz, that we managed to receive the conference's appeal to keep striving for unity and we learned that Mewis and the other leading cadres of the Party were about to head back to Paris, where they would organize the underground work. We who were staying behind no longer asked about the men shot in the cellars, nobody wanted to think about the justice or injustice of the verdicts, the guilty or innocent road to death, nobody wanted to debate errors, blunders, chimaeras now that the world had unprotestingly accepted Germany's annexation of Austria, for the Soviets would now have to concentrate on their own defense, thereby supplying fewer weapons, for our country was on the brink of being carved up, hacked to pieces, we could focus only on the most urgent tasks, on mobilizing our very last forces, on holding out against impossible odds, thereby playing for time, before the whole of Europe was engulfed in the decisive conflict.

During the summer months, when Grieg was away, Marcauer under arrest, and Hodann again suffering violent fits of his disease, a foundation solidified inside me for a task that I saw as my future work without my being able to name it precisely. The only thing that had set in was a timbre which made it appear that I would be able to express all thoughts and experiences. Words or images, whatever was needed, would be their media. However, the steps that were to take me to carrying out my intentions were impossible as yet, the desired development was so thoroughly obstructed that its mere mention was presumptuous. I did not even know where to go if the volunteers had to leave Spain after the decisions of the Geneva commissions. What commenced in my mind had been transmitted to me by the people who were close to me, albeit constantly changing. Their voices, their facial expressions, sometimes just a glance, a gesture, a brief remark, the endurance of their sufferings, the passage from weakness to confidence, the attitude marking each person, the material within them, often bound, emerging slowly, spreading from one person to the next, all these things wove into a tissue that already seemed to contain its own perfection. Rendering this seemed easy, I was a blank page, all I had to do was wait for signs to line up together, I came close to perceptions that, in my early youth, had prepared me for this moment. The task I set myself was not one I had to accomplish for my own sake, I viewed it as a force that was also operating in many other people, driving us all to a clarification. We possessed this sharpened alertness jointly. We knew we were at the mercy of the enemy, and it was precisely this condition that enabled many people to hold out against the storm of gigantic technological superiority. Blum's pusillanimous government had collapsed, Daladier had wiped out the final attempts at maintaining the French Popular Front, British envoys examined the complex of Czechoslovakian problems in order to prepare their betrayal, Chamberlain concluded a pact with Italy for the protection of the Mediterranean, the entire Western world, backed by the United States, approached Franco, the future victor, negotiating favorable partnership conditions, and the Soviet voices likewise grew conciliatory toward El Caudillo. We accepted everything, we knew how to rationalize everything, Republican Spain was an object pushed around on the chessboard of higher interests, it had to be played off for the benefit of the harried Soviet power so that the latter might continue its efforts toward an alliance with England and France. When we heard that Ehrenburg had penned an article praising the Falangists as patriots, that Litvinov had declared at the League of Nations that the Spanish conflict must be settled by the Spaniards themselves, we saw these things not as demands to lay down our arms but as a further impetus to dig in our heels and ease the Soviet Union's burden. The clearer the determination to defend the Republic, the stronger the pressure we could exert on the bourgeois governments, precisely because we could tell from the press that we had lost our support and that our country was to be sacrificed, we all clung to this soil, and the units of the brigades, having little time left, again saw ahead of them the victory, for the sake of which they had come to Spain. After the launching of our Ebro offensive, it actually looked as if we could still succeed in fending off the enemy until the war engulfed the whole of Europe, requiring the departure of the German and Italian troops. After the breakthrough to Villalbia and Gandesa, the lines had been stabilized, which showed that we still had reserves of energy, and we clung to the notion that the great unified front against fascism would materialize at the very last moment. Viewing this as self-delusion would have been tantamount to betraying our principles. Everything we did focused on cooperation, we saw internationalism rising before us, from country to country. Without the confidence that solidarity would increase all around us, the battalions, reduced by over half, and the Spanish units of the People's Army would not have captured the river and the enemy positions. These actions revealed the indispensable unity, the dogged harmony of thinking and doing. The possession of life was committed unhesitatingly, some of the wounded, dragged back, may have recalled some distant support, but then they were immediately linked again to the soldiers lying on the battlefields. In our hospital, which we were preparing to dismantle, it might happen that some minds, for an instant, wandered, the faces turned flat and empty, until others pulled these men over, and they again became one with the events. Various motives may have led certain people to the brigades, and everyone certainly went through hours of weakness, of discouragement, and indeed a few people might even make themselves guilty of an aberration, a delinquency, or entirely abandon themselves and thereby dissociate themselves from us, yet all of them had to be counted as part of the comprehensive force gathering here. Each person had received his own special impetus and broken away from a milieu that belonged solely to him, each person was subject to vacillating, and yet from the very day of their arrival, they were all of the same origin, involved in a new, joint beginning. This summer, if it had not been shown to them before, they felt how deeply they were rooted in one another and how indissoluble this bond was. If nevertheless, in an abrupt sagging, in a speeding-up of the drive to preserve only oneself, somebody deceived the unity and ousted himself or had to be ousted, this revealed to us mainly that it was hard to be in constant harmony with oneself, and that the individual had to be affected not just by himself but also by everyone else. And since these people were not only our kind, responsible for one another, under steady guidance, and since we were attacked from countless directions, the exhaustions and collapses belonged to us, and we frequently recognized ourselves in them. As I drew arrows and red lines on the map in the Villa Candida and shifted the flag pins, the numbered hills, roads, and villages in the Ebro's bend between Fayón and Tortosa came directly toward me. In early September, when the convalescence home had been cleared in a month's time and the wounded shipped south, I would report to the Valencia recruiting office for service in the armed units. After April the fifteenth, when the Republic had been divided near Vinaroz, I kept spreading the hatching that I drew with a ruler to represent the invading enemy troops on the map until it stopped behind Castellón. Over and over again, each push toward Sagunto, threatening Valencia, had been beaten back, and on the northwestern front, the capital, in a fluctuating semicircle, was likewise held. Viewing the map, we saw the massive, battered, tortured body of our country, the trunk cut off at the chest and, at the top, the neck and head exposed to relentless blows. Like nerve fibers the roads stretched toward Murcia, Almería, Albacete, Cuenca, meanwhile Barcelona, the seat of the government, was now beyond our reach, but the pulse still throbbed in Madrid, we still felt the openness to the sea. And so we focused on the eye of the battle, though things were quiet over Denia, we did hear the booming of the barrage, Liebknecht, Thälmann, André, Beimler were the first to cross the river, they were accompanied by Garibaldi, Gramsci, Lincoln, Dombrowski, Dimitrov, and the Twelfth of February and the Commune de Paris, combat patrols in the ranks of people from all regions of Spain, Mora de Ebro, Miravet, Benisanet, Pinell, Corbera, Fatarella, Mequinenza, the mountains of Pandols, these dots, spots, strokes were in the midst of the glistening light, of the swarms of bullets, the soil spurting up, we were among the soldiers creeping through sand, stones, detritus, storming the hamlets, the rises, we were in the row-boats casting off from the embankments, behind us, looming from the shore, the brick walls with arched windows, arcades, turrets, we waded through the raging water, the enemy had opened the sluices in the north, in our hands we felt the grip on the pontoon planks, on the shovels solidifying the bridgeheads. All the people lying here in Denia, with their injuries, their mental shocks reexperienced what had happened to them in the fighting, and we, changing their bandages, washing their stumps, felt their shudders in ourselves. Our body, the body of the country, was sheer pain, it was bloody, hacked up, yet everywhere this body developed new ways of grabbing, repulsing. We had said we understood everything occurring on higher levels, in the embassies and cabinets, the economic centers and general staffs, but we only pretended that everything made sense, we chalked reports on the board, bulletins from the ministries, from the halls of the League of Nations, we wiped them away, covered them with new dispatches. We had no part in historiography, others wrote history for us, throngs of facts were adduced, material for future books, for libraries or for archives, made inaccessible, notes were feverishly jotted down, the telegraphs and the reporters' voices hummed crisscross, for us there was always something new, something that was not named, that had nothing to do with the things spreading out in seeming lucidity, in huge headlines on the pages of the newspapers. The things surfacing among us were unsystematized or, rather, were ruled by other kinds of consistency, they were not part of the broadly flowing strategies, they came dripping, barely audible, from dry, scurvy lips. The press services named everything by its name, which was significant for us too, the villages under fire, the dates of attacks and retreats, the numbers of dead and wounded, the names of army leaders, and yet those things, printed or broadcast, were alien, they were spoken casually as if basically no one need be bothered, we could see them flash by between coffee and rolls on the breakfast tables or hear them as noise accompanying our evening beer, the people transmitting and the people receiving stayed uninvolved even when literally encircled by mountains of corpses, even when talking about how serious the situation was. Knowing that most people no longer reckoned with us was part of surviving in Spain, anyone who thought about us viewed us at best as something like gladiators playing some deadly game, film strips brought the still unmarred world a few clouds of dust in which fighters perished. But this picture of people outside our realm, going about their peaceful activities and taking such everyday things as natural, touched us only lightly, for us the notion of a distance to be kept no longer existed, the thing that was known on the outside as a theater of war, a piece of geography to which absentminded eyes could turn, was our bared skin, trenches were cut into it, a knife dug all the way to the bones, sand burst forth, the fingers cramped up in the sand, sand crunched between teeth. A blurted reference to troop movements, for us that was an infinite trail from earthwork to earthwork, whereby we fused with the gristly trunk of an olive tree, with a boulder, with grass and bushes growing rankly over our faces. Lindbaek said that many people huddled over the sketches, which, printed at night, no longer corresponded to the day gone by, she said that these dotted lines, these spearheads, on which companies, battalions, divisions depended, likewise merged into their flesh and blood, that they gazed at the small, scrawled hints of shambles and linked them to their own lives. We promptly agreed with her, we promptly were ready to see international unity, we had, after all, emerged from it ourselves, but then we were on our own again, this was our war alone, our mangling, and ours alone was the triumph whenever we wrenched an hour from the foe. Marcauer had received her first warning when she said that no one would care if the German and Italian forces did not leave Spain along with the retreating remnants of our brigades. It was as if, until August, we believed that our land would never say die, we turned a blind eye to all signs to the contrary, not even the mammoth losses made us aware of our agony. We spoke about our victory, and this toughness was indeed a victory. Yes, said Marcauer, we are providing an example for the world, we are doing what has to be done, but what good is it since no one is emulating us, since the wreath with the ribbons of parties and unions is already waiting for us, the funeral orations are already composed. Was it really a victory that we still had not fallen back, that we were still within reach of Villalba, Gandesa, still holding the delta of the Ebro, was it a victory, we wondered at the end of August, that the final members of the International Brigades were throwing themselves at the enemy more vehemently than ever before until the order to retreat would be issued. Was it a victory to hold out with fraying nerves while the military leadership was at loggerheads, many generals wanted to halt operations and end the war. It was a victory. This was also confirmed by the wounded who arrived day and night, remaining briefly before heading south. It was a victory so long as we saw brotherhood persisting. It was a victory so long as internationalism was not entirely ground down. Over and over names were named, in which the lives of all fighters were concentrated, Kahle, Líster, Walter, Flatter, Mirales. Names that stood out against the timid, the people planning betrayal, surrender. There were many reports about Modesto, the twenty-eight-year-old. He was small, indeed frail, but his courage infected the others, or he handed on the strength that had flown to his youthful openness. *Heldenmut*, heroic courage, Hodann talked about this word, which had grown disreputable for being used for the wrong ends. Were the events occurring on the Ebro not heroic, we asked. And if they were heroic, were they heroic only on our side and not on the other side too, could people actually commit their own lives for diverse reasons, didn't the enemy have as much right as we to speak about his heroes. We had usually avoided the notion of heroism. Though inseparable from the achievements of the proletarian struggle, it had false, grandiloquent overtones. But then how could our side's deeds be differentiated from the enemy's actions. Heroic, that was first of all the step beyond the normal, the deliberate break with any security, any prospect of private advancement, it was the integration into a principle imbuing a more-than-personal cause. Heroic were thus the people who, despite fear and dismay, stood up for their resolve and risked losing everything they loved for the sake of the idea that they found valid. Heroic was unselfishly championing the improvement of many lives. The people on the other side were certainly exposed to the same dangers as we were, but their goals did not belong to them, could not bring renewal for them or their near and dear. They had not reported out of conviction, rather they had let themselves be drawn in amid the indifference that matched their lack of judgment. The sole rationale they might have offered for fighting was whatever had been drummed into their heads. But did that give us the right to disparage them, people asked, did they not have to pay the same price, did they not have to endure the same sufferings. And ultimately, was it not almost more heroic to fight for something that was forced on you than to fight voluntarily, with the future of being a class of people before your eyes. Here the only possible answer was that the man sacrificing himself in the fanatical predatory war was making a senseless sacrifice. Our victory, what we called our victory, lay in our demonstrating, albeit briefly, the will to liberation, the idea of justice, lay in our managing to hold back the overwhelming material superiority, indeed, causing it to panic. That is today's balance of strength, said Hodann, between progress and reactionism. All the power that the old wants to achieve is on the nationalist side, while we have only the hope that our present inferiority will some day be atoned for. The whole story boils down to a single irrefutable argument of tanks, artillery, and air squadrons, while the people standing up for the Republic are inwardly torn, and dreadful provocation is needed to turn sympathy into active participation. For

Hodann, the events on the Ebro symbolized the birth of a new culture. Only such actions, which transcend personal limits, he said, could produce intellectual and social development. That was wishful thinking, replied Marcauer. Politics had long since stopped taking our heroism into account. Holding our positions, she said, might provide us with satisfaction, but the only thing of historical significance was that England, France, and the United States had already recognized the generalíssimo since he had promised that his government would remain neutral in the coming war. And then she again outlined what we had rejected earlier, namely that the collapse was inevitable because the fighters had been out of their depth from the very start, because the disavowal of the revolution had paralyzed the strength of the populace. Here Hodann also angrily disagreed. This could not be determined as yet, he said, the interpretation of this period had to be left to future research. We regarded Marcauer as distraught, Lindbaek recommended that she rest, restrain herself during the few weeks until evacuation. But she was obsessed with voicing everything that beset her, with constantly dredging up events that had become trivial in our eyes given all the difficulties lying ahead. She once again brought up that bluntly shot-out name of the small, resistant Marxist Party, whose captured leaders were about to be court-martialed. Why, she asked, at a time when the Republic is facing life or death, are the government and the general staff concentrating so hard on a handful of oppositionals, who are no longer capable of exerting any influence anyway, unless the Republic is redemonstrating the thesis of betrayal over and over in order to explain away failures in its own policies. Her main concern, however, was Nin. His liquidation by police agents last year, she said, was reason enough for indignation, but she felt it was even worse that the acceptance of such an occurrence revealed an attitude that made a mockery of our goals, swindling all those who had come to defend this country. We reminded her of Badajoz, where, in August nineteen thirty-six, the murdering began after every fascist conquest. Thousands of people had been taken to the arena there to be mowed down by machine guns and skewered with swords. Guernica, Bilbao, Gijón, Teruel, what are those names, we said, against a few loners who have to be eliminated because they jeopardize our own front. How can the Spanish people's war, she asked, ever be presented as just by our side if we seal it with hypocrisies. I do not belong to Nin's organization, she said, nor am I a Trotskyite, I have been a member of the Communist Party since my teens. I want to know what method my Party is using to shape the historical image, for which I too share responsibility. Nin, we objected, had escaped to Saragosa, where he had been shot by the fascists. That was what we had heard. In the place where he was, said Marcauer, there was no possibility of flight, and as for the place he was brought to, he could leave it only as a corpse. He had been arrested on June sixteenth, nineteen thirty-seven. Yet his name was missing from the list of prisoners. Still, Spanish comrades knew he had been interrogated by officials of the Soviet security service in a Party building in Madrid. There was nothing wrong with his being apprehended, we retorted. In Barcelona, we said, he had joined the antigovernment uprising. It was also understandable, we went on, that the power protecting us was intent on clarifying the case. It would have been the job of his compatriots, said Marcauer, to deal with him. But he was beyond reach even for Caballero, who demanded his release. The public kept asking, Where is Nin, What have you done with Nin. The stunned members of the Party, of the unions, of the cabinet complained that legality, which they saw as the basis of the Republic, had been repealed. The Ministry of Justice, condemned to powerlessness, could only announce that Nin was in safekeeping, in protective custody. The investigating commission had been set up by Rosenberg and Antonov Ovseyenko. These men, she said, have now themselves become the victims of the despotism that they helped to install. We tried to keep Marcauer quiet, to shield her from her own words. But whenever we talk about our own war, she said, in the presence of the political commissar, we also have to talk about the other war, which is being waged simultaneously in our own ranks against holders of dissident opinions, a war whose weapons I can never approve of. Nin was tortured. He had to be forced to confess. He refused to say anything. People were getting more and more worried, so on August fourth the government responded with a note, saying that nothing further could be ascertained regarding Nin's whereabouts, but by then he had already been transported to Alcala de Henares, outside Madrid. I was there, she said. I saw the sand pit where he was executed. Goya once painted this embankment and the view of the muzzles, and I am haunted by that view. No one could help Marcauer when her arrest was ordered. We wanted to reduce the significance of the interrogations that she could expect. Hodann's medical statement would certainly save her from serious punishment. Her achievements were recognized, her utterances blamed on stress. Yet we already knew that we would repress any thought of this woman who came from an upper-middle-class Jewish family in Hamburg. And soon the hour was blurred, the early morning when she was taken away by the military police, and all we retained was the image of her down in the hall of the Villa Candida, describing the sand, illuminated a pale yellow by the lantern that had been set down, the whites of the gaping eyes, the backs of the execution commando crowded together, and off to the side, behind her, we could see some of the banker Merle's framed engravings showing the ruin of Diana's temple on the castle hill of Denia, the amphitheater of Saguntum, and Hannibal's elephants on the rafts crossing the Ebro.

But what, wrote Heilmann, if Heracles, constantly envisioning the liberation of the underdogs, had not undauntedly acted against monsters and tyrants, what if we had to say that he was plagued by fear and terror and that his deeds served merely to overcome his own weakness and isolation. It had taken two months for Heilmann's letter to reach me in Denia after it had been mailed to Warnsdorf, then forwarded to Prague, then to Paris and Albacete. But perhaps, he wrote, it makes no difference whether Heracles' route was full of fun and exuberance or arduousness and self-denial, since we count only the achievements and ask only who benefited from Heracles' efforts. We had seen him as the man who left hierarchy and irrationality behind, who, without his privileged position, first egotistically shattered the ancient laws, but then learned to intercede for the good of other people. For us he was the earthly man who was intent on controlling nature, who was the first to make it clear that the changes, the improvements had to come about here in this world, that the only things useful to us are the things that are felt immediately, that, when firmly seized, ease the situation. Even if he struck us as smug, as boastful in his nakedness, which was cloaked only in the lion's skin, in his renunciation of any warlike arms, in his being armed solely with a club, he had nevertheless aroused our admiration, for his foolhardiness, his scornful raging always focused purely on helping mortals against the monstrous and the destructive. From his birth, he the son of Zeus, was exposed to malice and perfidy, to deceit and encroachment, and his reactions had shown us that violence was necessary to conquer the hostile hurly-burly. Well, wrote Heilmann, I have studied not only the Dodekathlos again but also other things reporting on the traces of Heracles, and his character has thereby become more varied, but also more questionable. What else were the monsters he fought against but dreams that he had to keep confronting. The kinds of entities that he encountered and had to kill afflict us only in our sleep. I am familiar with those lionlike, birdlike, serpentlike creatures, I flee them, but they catch my scent, then track me down when I lie in the underbrush of night, they bite my hips, I wrestle with them, this is a dreadful compulsion, and I never wake up until I should have been torn from limb to limb, yet there is no wound, no pain. Such beasts harass us when we have discerned some overpowering entity deep inside ourselves, when we tremble at the thought of our own superiority. These gigantic, fire-snorting brutes with their many heads and bodies come upon him, or else he hunts them down in their out-of-the-way ranges, which indicates that he was caught up more in his dreams than in everyday life. The menace is certainly normal, something we are all acquainted with, but when we compare it with its effects, which Heracles has to endure, then there is something bizarre about the threat, something that not everyone is conversant with. We might say that in the sudden blazes of these hallucinations, everything that generally occurs on a small scale is enormously magnified into something exemplary, so that others may comfort themselves by saying, Look, if Heracles can triumph over such obstacles, then we should be able to deal with our own stuff. But that is not the case. If the hungry, if the tenants of slums are so much as capable of fancying anything in the feats that Heracles performed in some foreign land, then these clashes are bound to remain purely conceptual, and I believe that they remain conceptual for him, they seize hold of him when he stares into himself. The multiplicity of his deeds, which made him so famous and which has been handed down to us, is like a book of the hours, like a series of votive pictures noting the individual stations, we, akin to the history tellers before us, have recognized Heracles as a helper in need, a savior, whose courage is repaid with the highest happiness. But what kind of happiness, I wondered, was this. Was he happy because better times had now come and most of the horrors and devastations had been warded off. By no means. Now the wars really began, and the destitution grew in the cities. Unable to content himself with a mundane death, he perished amid incomprehensible agonies and was then taken in once again by the gods and henceforth belonged to Mount Olympus, all of which made him suspect in my eyes. Why did the supreme deities ultimately view him as one of their own if not because he had done nothing to shake their positions, indeed, because he had actually succeeded in spreading the faith in superhuman, that is, divine abilities. I had always felt there was something dubious about his fits of madness and fury, his crying jags whenever things did not go quite as he liked, the way he blindly struck out all around. But I had tried to see these things as signs of an earth dweller's life, he was close to me in his confusion, his jealousy, his ambition, his overestimation of himself, his despair, but all this was eclipsed by the impression that we were dealing with someone who was doomed, incurable, who deployed all his strength and force against evil and yet did not know how to eliminate it. The unclarity he left behind likewise, no doubt, induced those we considered his adversaries to claim him for themselves. He became the patron saint of merchants, bankers, all the people who strove for profit, for success, he became a paragon of gluttony, libertinism, the needy could make little of him. Furthermore, he became the inspirer of colonialism, with him a new era began, in which Greeks and Ionians sailed out across the sea to the ends of the earth, his descriptions of the riches of foreign countries lured the affluent, the entrepreneurs to invest their money in ship building and develop faraway natural resources. I realized, said Heilmann, that the difficult labors supposedly inflicted on him by Hera were triggered by his own unspeakable restlessness, and while most of the things we know about him may overlap with his pipe dreams, there are nevertheless a few aspects that we can utilize, for they supply information about a life ground, on which you are now literally standing. At first Heilmann's letter carried me back to the days before my departure from Berlin, then it was more as if he had come here, to my present. What I am reading about Heracles, he said, no longer derives from a myth, it may still have epic features, but it is marked by the imperfections, the roaming and seeking, the setbacks and constant new beginnings that belong not only to the very essence of poetry, of dream interpretation, but also the urge to validate oneself in the world. I can no longer see him as I did a year ago, at first I was disappointed, our main argument, after all, was that he had cut off his ties to the gods, I then often returned to our frieze and watched the paw of his lion's skin swinging between Zeus and Hera's furiously advancing team of horses, Hera, who had shown him her favor after his existence in the vale of tears, and directly beneath Heracles, or rather beneath the void into which we projected him, sits one of our brothers, impaled by the lightning bolts from the father of the gods, who hurls them at anyone who dares to rise up against him, and perhaps he, of whom we expected so much, is hauling back his club in order to crush the mortal's head. Nonetheless, said Heilmann, I am not yet giving up on Heracles. I do not wish to take him as the rulers have depicted him, demagogically demanding his integration into their class and their art, nor can I now recognize him as the victorious helper of the enslaved, I can see him only as a man who sometimes rose far beyond himself, but then was helplessly trapped in his fantasies. Starting from his death, which nonetheless has stimulated countless analyses in drama and poetry, I now approached him from a different angle. What about Deianeira, I wondered. In any case, when analyzing the duel in which Heracles won Achelous's beloved, we could not possibly claim that he had ever been caught in the dilemma of having to choose between renunciation and virtue. I was captivated by his lust, we had never, after all, demanded chastity from him, it was precisely his drives that convinced us of his strength for action, that tore him out of his brooding. Fine, we had overestimated this side, we had even mistaken him for an anti-intellectual who terminated every argument with crude blows. And here I am recurring to his trauma, in which he confronts the powers in order to cunningly overtrump them. Achelous, styled the god of the river, raised wild buffalo and was himself a bull, we may assume Deianeira preferred life with him to an existence with the fickle, roving Heracles. She never forgave him for abducting her, it was an unhappy marriage from the very outset. Leaving his wife all alone, he promptly went off on his wanderings, which, however, led him to his last and worst insanities. He, who kept wanting to prove his manliness, fell into the hands of Omphale and was not only degraded as a slave, but had to serve as a maid in female clothes, a henpecked spouse, shattered and trodden by his mistress in her male leather gear, derided if he was unable to satisfy her cravings. When he finally managed to escape this dream, sick, depressed, yet not so weakened as not to promptly resume abducting women, he returned to the wasteland, to his spouse Deianeira, but instead of being amicably welcomed and forgiven, he found only dislike, nay, repugnance, hatred. Naturally the abandoned wife had not wasted her time, she, who had loved the bull in the man, had meanwhile fallen prey to Nessos, who lived among horses, a centaur, who was too much for Heracles, and when Deianeira gave herself to Nessus once again, on the riverbank, singing in order to pretend she was doing the wash, the returned husband shot poisoned arrows at his rival, whom he dared not approach with bare hands. Yet it could hardly have been this venom mixed with blood that, in the soaked cloth, caused the death of Heracles. For one thing, his wife, whom he pulled out from under the centaur's belly so as to use her once again, was not interested in employing a magic brew to regain the love of Heracles, who had arrived with a concubine he had found en route. And for another thing, his wife did not even give him a shirt, she infected him in a simpler way, full of sperm, with the epidemic that was to kill him. The shirt of Nessus, he claimed, fused so thoroughly with his skin that when he tore out a piece of the shirt, his flesh came off with it, down to the bone, but that was his final lie, for Deianeira could transmit all Near Eastern venereal diseases, which the rutting horse-man had thrust into her after years of carrying on with herds of animals. However, such an admission was impossible for Heracles, who was concerned about his posthumous reputation. Hence the bellowed myth about the poisoned garment. Before dying, said Heilmann,

Heracles once again panicked dreadfully, as he had in his cradle, a panic for which he had tried to get even all his life, the terror, the repugnance he felt for women. The sensuality imputed to him can correspond to only those notions that confuse erotic intensity with taking possession, one cannot infer from even a single one of his innumerable liaisons that he liked the woman, he had always only wrenched, thrashed, murdered, or was tortured. His driven rovings began when Hera cursed him as inferior, second-rate, he may have found satisfaction in a few homoerotic relations, with Iolaos perhaps, with Philoktetes, his companions, all his bravado concealed a profound psychological deformation. Even as he writhed in the burning of Cupid's itch, Venus's curse, the Trojan chancre, he cared only about covering up the cause of his downfall, and all of them, Hesiod, Sophocles, Ovid, Seneca, helped him to keep his secret, they all called

Deianeira by her name, which means husband killer, but they drew no conclusions, they even did their bit to depict her as innocent, as a faithful wife, purely in order to save Heracles' honor, the honor of the false family. And yet, said Heilmann, in that moment, when the ring of his life comes full circle, he regains grandeur, almost sublimity. He does not throw himself into water to quench the burning of his wound and vanish unwept and unsung, instead he summons the entire populace so it may see that no opponent is strong enough for him, that even his greatest suffering can intensify, and, shrieking in pain, he crawls uphill to the pyre and lies down in the flames. Now that the agony has become immeasurable, his face takes on the enraptured smile, with which, disintegrating, he enters immortality. And so, Heilmann wrote in his letter, I am turning to the journeys that Heracles, after joining the eastern voyage of the Argonauts, took toward the west, the itinerary blending everything that demanded expansion and discovery. He was not the only traveler, there were many others who, because of the land shortage, the overpopulation in the cities, the growing commercial competition, the rising need for raw materials, headed for the Adriatic, hoping to conquer new markets from the coastal strips. But he, known since time immemorial as the person who, for whatever reasons, overcame fear and constriction and sought the unknown, took responsibility for the Hellenic push toward Sicily and southern Italy, toward Cyrenaica, Corsica, and the shores of Gaul, where Massilia, today's Marseilles, soon became an important business station. The saga of Heracles spread out in widening circles, first it was at home in the Peloponnesian Peninsula, then it encompassed Thrace, Crete, and the Black Sea, and then it reached the Balearic Islands and Spania, from the Pyrena mountains all the way down to Gadir. The gateway to the worldenclasping Okeanos offered an appropriate site for the pillars, here the steep cliffs on Iberia's southern nub and on the hot continent's northern tip rose up as natural strongholds. Atlas was able to walk across in a single step. While some men, wanting to outdo Heracles and find the Isles of the Blest, wandered into the ocean, Heracles himself remained in the Hesperides, with gardens in which the citrus fruits hung from the trees like golden apples. And though dangerous serpents coiled around the trunks, this peril was made up for by all the metals that could be unearthed in the mines ready to be exploited and that were of inestimable value for the wars, which required more weapons. Heracles lingered on and on in Avia, the land of serpents. Nor did he accept Atlas's honorable offer to hold up the heavens for him, let Atlas remain standing there with the load on his bent shoulders, Heracles had better things to do, each saw his task as helping to establish trading posts, settlements, towns. Supposedly he founded Zakinthos, Sagunto, which is now being held to protect Valencia, and he reached the great transshipment ports in Phoenicia, southward from the mouth of Guadalquivir, long before the rise of Pergamum, before the seafarers from Phocaea landed in this place, which they then called Hemeroskopeion and there, on the hilltop, they built a temple for Artemis.

We had long wanted to visit the castle hilltop of Denia, but our work schedule would not allow it, we did not head there until early September, when large parts of the hospital had been evacuated, and the physicians and the personnel were on the verge of leaving. Because the disbanding of the International Brigades had been agreed to, we were about to be violently torn from this country. The demobilization was not only to whittle the war down to a domestic conflict, but also to attack, in diplomatic disguise, the solidarity that had focused on Spain. Since autumn of nineteen thirty-six, thirty-five thousand volunteers had reached the fronts. Lindbaek, who handled their papers, counted five thousand Germans and Austrians, ten thousand Frenchmen, six thousand Britons, Americans, and Canadians, three thousand Italians, a thousand Scandinavians, a thousand Yugoslavs, two thousand Poles. All in all, fifty-three countries were represented in the battalions. The participation of all these people had long since shown that this was no civil war in Spain but a worldwide ideological clash. And this Popular Front, said Lindbaek, was now to be demolished. Her face again took on the gray, stony expression. How dreadful were these compilations, always making the individual a mere component in a cluster of a hundred, a thousand. A few more, a few less, it made no difference. Round numbers encompassing ungraspable life. Bodies that were mere digits, adding up to columns, companies, battalions, brigades, divisions, army corps. Quantities from which they subtracted the number of cadavers that had bled to death. Everyone who arrived, everyone who dropped out merged into an anonymous mass. But how else, asked Lindbaek, could we possibly gain an overview. The strength of each unit was reduced by more than half. Of the original thirty-five thousand volunteers, at most ten or twelve thousand were left in the fighting troops. Now only splinters of the international units stayed on in the people's army. The military assistance they managed to provide was minor. Nevertheless, the surviving volunteers felt that by obeying the order to retreat they would be running out on their Spanish comrades. Till the very end they tried to deny the dispersal of the brigades. Only an expansion of the war could have convinced them of the necessity of withdrawal. Thus the aggravated situation on the Czechoslovakian border offered some hope. Waging a pan-European war against fascism struck us as better than continuously side-stepping and looking for compromises. We were a group of medical orderlies who were supposed to set out for Valencia in the next few days and join the armed units. Spain had become our land. We refused to be driven from our own soil. Expulsion would only be followed by a life in exile. The doctors and several remaining patients were waiting for British naval vessels that would carry them to Marseilles. Hodann and Lindbaek could plan to move on to Norway, but most of the others were facing camps. A few Belgians had lost their citizenship by participating in the Spanish war, for the Germans, Austrians, and Czechoslovakians their countries were closed off, they would have to go begging for a visa to anywhere, always mindful of the risk of being deported to enemy territory. So once again an advance made in the class struggle has been beaten back, said Lindbaek, and the scattered forces will have to reform. But it was not the uncertain future that we were speaking about on this morning, en route to Denia and then up on the castle height, we were discussing events that had occurred along this coast two millennia earlier. The sea constantly lay before us, bluish gray, hazily blending with the edge of the sky, the orange groves stretched out between clusters of eucalyptuses, cypresses, almond trees, here and there, lemon shoots were sprouting from a cut in a branch, budding violet, with young, pale-lavender fruits. We talked about inoculated orange trees that produced lemons and we thereby gradually got into history. An orange tree had the life span of a human being, it needed thirty or forty years to achieve its full capacity, each crop yielded seventy or eighty kilograms of fruit.

However, with their thick trunks and twisted branches, the olive trees, lined up on the field, could live for up to six or seven hundred years. The green on the underside of the longish, slightly arching leaves was dark, intense, with a dull, silvery tinge on the surface. There were countless varieties of olive trees, from which the dove had once brought the branch to Noah's Ark, and which surrounded the hill on which Jesus, far beyond the West Asian shore, had been nailed to the cross. Depending on the influence of the weather, the leaves were shorter, wider, harder or suppler, and when the oval fruits, initially whitish green, reached their fat, shiny ripeness, they took on the colors that were named after them, while other, round varieties changed from reddish, bluish violet to deep black. When Columbus sailed across the Atlantic, the wayside trees had already been harvested, and they bore fruits during the rise and fall of Europe's colonial empires. Lindbaek, originally an archaeologist by profession, wanted to know about the Greek temple remnants on the hill above the city, whose name had been linked to the goddess Diana. Brittle steps, narrow paths led up the slope to the ruins, the joined sandstone ashlars of the fortifications were overrun with moss, scrub pines, and the roots of olive trees. However there was no trace of the temple columns, surrounded by Romanesque walls and towers, as shown in the reproduction at the Villa Candida, all we saw were the crumbled arches and casemates of a fortress from the era of the Conquistadors. Standing at the balustrade of the atrium, we gazed across city and harbor. Toward the left, in the vast bay, the stripes of the surge rolled softly, in an even sequence, to the beach, toward the right, on the tongue of land, stood the Mongó, thinly forested at its foot, its ridge bare, with gray strata. The whitewashed houses, with russet tile roofs, crowded against one another over twisting streets, in the basin, at the narrow jetties swerving off toward the outlet, lay fishing boats, painted black or white and blue, the reddish sail reefed on the long, gently curving, slanted yard. They resembled the boats that had brought the catch to the colonizers, who had come from the Aegean in their triremes. The city, which we wanted to imprint on our minds after living on its outskirts for eight months, was now enclosed in flickering light. A series of loud bells was all that broke the hush. We pictured the hustle and bustle at the docks, on the gangways, around the storehouses and workshops. Mules pulled the fully loaded two-wheel carts, the porters hurried up the planks to the ships, bent over under the bursting woven sacks, the heavy crates. Fish were salted on stone benches, packed in tuns or hung up to dry on hemp lines. Camels brayed in the stables, and the bellows and hammers boomed monstrously in the smithies and smelteries. Pewter and copper, delivered by caravans from Andalusia, silver from Sierra Nevada, Sierra Morena, plus the lead-rich ore from Almeria, the iron ore from Murcia, the rock salt from Cardona, all these things were piled up here. The bars of the noble metal, the rare, heavy zinc, the bronze alloys, so desirable to the owners of the Ionian arsenals, filled the bunkers of the round, sturdy freighters, the whips cracked over the sweating bodies, and while here there was an incessant lugging and shoving, a pattering of naked soles, up in the soldiers' holds there was a deep dozing, a slurring on the long-necked wine jugs. If Heracles had not existed, then such a figure would have had to be invented, for the goods pouring together here demanded legendary descriptions, whereby the collectors gained importance and could see themselves as chosen when stories were told that someone of semidivine origin had summoned them to these shores. After all, the Hellenes had always transposed the historical events to a level of symbols in order to make them more difficult to grasp, thereby preserving the gap between the initiates and the lower populace. The concept of Greek civilization had usually been appreciated as the idea of supreme cultural development. But this idea would have been nothing without its stable foundation. At the top the thought of democracy emerged, the doctrine of the unity and equality of human beings. At the bottom the maltreated laborers, kept away from all rights. The artistic sculptures and the buildings with columns, all commissioned by the propertied classes, were carried by hecatombs of chained bodies. The noble proportions could detach themselves from dankness and putrescence. The patriarchs bluntly established the separation, which was the prerequisite for their economic system. The priests and the philosophers validated themselves in this order, making sure that the masses were kept in check by superstitious dread, anyone who so much as dared to articulate a word of enlightenment was expelled. Slaveholders and slaves, the former allied with supernatural powers, glorifying their thievery in poetry, the latter, existing only as beasts, as living tools, jointly they formed the two-part structure that we were still struggling to dismantle today. Greek civilization rested on unspeakable plundering, wars were ceaselessly fought to conquer slaves, and it was supposed to be a great boon for the rounded-up creatures to be allowed to serve such exquisite masters. The Hellenic market economy grew out of arrogance and brutality, racism and cynicism, in the harshest rivalries between the city-states, competing internally for the highest profits. With its four harbors, Miletus, the most populous city in the Near East, controlled the Aegean commerce, in its expansion the metropolis cut the smaller fortified towns off from any access to the sea. Military campaigns had devastated the farmlands, the young men were forced to hire themselves out to the armies, the large landowners in the coastal areas had to look for new lines of production. In Phocaea, on the Bay of Hermos, the constriction provoked a readjustment from agrarian to maritime thinking, the entrepreneurs, who had never before ventured out to sea, who had been content to steal cattle and loot neighboring villages, were now lured by the accounts of foreign sailors to build ships of their own for bringing cargoes from very distant climes. Their distress, transformed into boldness, was reflected in the construction of the vessels, with which they outdid anything created by Phoenician technology. More than a thousand rowers, on three levels, a machinery, directed by the beat of the drum, drove the ship forward, on deck the merchants lay in tents, overcoming their seasickness, by looking forward to all the treasures they would acquire. Down below, an incessant crunching and creaking, up above, at the command post, a gauging, measuring, calculating. Swift as an arrow, its ruddy sail bellying in the wind, the oars striking down, sweeping up, spraying drops, the galley, with its ram bow thrusting far ahead, sliced through the water, the crew raiding every foreign ship that crossed its path. For the shipbuilders of Phocaea, the superior position they had won soon became their hubris, the breakthrough from petty domestic commerce to the capture of wares from new worlds had changed their personalities, the most valuable object, once the monopoly of kings, had come into their hands, metal, and whoever controlled it was able to rule the state. However, the more inexhaustible their sources proved to be, the more intent they were on underscoring their divine grace. They, who gave away nothing, boasted of being gifted by the gods. Initially, perhaps, they were actually encouraged in the belief that they were led by the celestials, but the more tangible, computable their riches became, the more the merchants could coolly evaluate the guiding forces, the sublime was subjected to their practical goal, ultimately they linked up with the deities only in coins, in which their likenesses were engraved. This was a perfect metaphor for the transfer of omnipotence, whoever owned the coins was also the bearer of divine will. The degree of advantage could now be pinpointed exactly, the concept of gods became usable in gold, in silver, was weighed, gathered in pouches, sacks, strongboxes. Knowing that the wares belonged not to demons but to the men who seized them violently, spreading terror, and knowing also about magic, which was still part of the realm of spirits, they combined the ungraspable with the unfathomable. So the emerging money economy retained the faith in holiness, the worship of invisible donors to divert attention from the principle of exploitation and suppression. Capitalism issued from the temples, consecrated by magic spells and sacrificial fires. The most famous effigies of Olympic beings were created only after the founding of banks, after the start of ample speculation, up to the present Athena and Zeus have presided over the boards of directors. The Phocaean seafarers had settled here on the headland, protected by the massif, and this struck Lindbaek as credible, not so much because of the fragments of weathered marble columns that we had stumbled upon in the detritus, but because of the lay of the landscape. She was familiar with that stretch of the Turkish coast from the village of Palatia, where once the palaces of Miletus had stood, all the way up to Bergama. She had been in the earlier Phocaea, almost on the same latitude as Denia, and, as she recalled this poor, deserted hamlet, where bustling life had dominated the huge shipyards and business firms two and a half millennia ago, her memory bonded with the panorama lying before us. Previously there had been scant evidence that Denia had grown from the soil of Hemeroskopeion, but proof positive was offered by the bay with the foothills, which was like a replica of where the colonizers had come from. No other place on Iberia's eastern coast was more consistent with the name of Hemeroskopeion, the lookout toward the burgeoning day, than this hill, which loomed over the natural harbor, and from which the landed sailors, facing their own city beyond the sea, could turn toward the rising sun. The masters of Phocaea may have called it divine providence that they came upon themselves again, and since they had sailed here to fell all sorts of prey, and since a blossoming, a rebirth were within reach, they put up a memorial to the goddess of hunting and fertility. At first they may have engaged in barter with the Phoenicians, who had one of their docking stations here, but then the greater power of the troops decided on the access of goods, fortifications were quickly thrown up, and one or two Ionian slaves who had been rewarded with manumission, might now in turn become overseers, bossing enslaved people from the Iberian countryside. Within a few short decades, colonial predominance was replaced in Spania, under pressure from armed Hellenic caravans the Phoenicians lost one trading post after another until they were ousted from Gadir, the port where they had shipped out the natural resources that had once helped their kingdom achieve prosperity and fame. They left not only roads, barracks, warehouses, and wharves to the new governors, but above all the mines, which the young, capable imperialists now worked on a grand scale. The age of industrialization was actually launched here with the acquisition of strategic matériel, the setting of prices for raw materials, the transactions on the stock market, the high dividends yielded by the invested capital, and the gigantic attrition of manpower in the extracting and processing of goods. For when picturing the activity in the metal works and the foundries during the seventh and sixth centuries, we felt that, given the time that had worn by since then, today's changes were utterly negligible. There were still enough mines in Africa, in Latin America, where the workers were prey to the same wearing down as the subjugated Iberians hammering the silver and the pewter, and for many of us it was no great sign of progress that we had to lie in the tunnels for only eight hours a day and without leg irons, compared with the fettered peons who were there for as much as fourteen hours. The dust in lungs, the wetness, the strong draft, the physical torment were the same, only we endured somewhat longer, formerly life there had been spent within a few years. And though we had won a couple of rights and reforms barely half a century back, we were still despairingly close to the workers of two and a half millennia ago, and like them we hoped for a world of liberation. Then the garrisons developed an upper class, which made the peasants harvest the fruits and the cereals, tread the grapes and guard the livestock. Fountains provided coolness in the interior courts of the country villas, mosaics adorned the floors and polished paintings the walls, unspeakable was the misery in the clay shacks of the serfs, the camps of the mine slaves. The families of the financial aristocracy became domiciled in the land of serpents and golden apples, the Pillars of Heracles were joined by towering lighthouses, where the fires devoured the resin-treated wood, and the fleets of merchant vessels could be spotted far away. The traders may have controlled the sales of their commodities over in the West Asian ports, but in sober foresight they were more preoccupied with expanding their overseas settlements. Phocaea had grown from a market hamlet to a colonizing power and, with all its metals, was on the verge of surpassing Miletus, known for its carpets and ceramics, its woolens, purple dyes, and gold embroideries, its poets, scholars, and philosophers. But enemy assaults perpetually threatened the continent, the armies of an expanding Persia were pushing toward the Aegean coast. The businessmen found their trusts and companies in Spain and Gaul to be safer, it was easier drumming up foot soldiers there to protect their property. The year five hundred forty before our era marked the first time that Phocaea was thoroughly looted and burnt to the ground by Harpagon, who was general under Cyrus the Second and was nicknamed the Magnanimous and the Mild. From now on the skippers, returning with their cargoes, were never certain of finding their city where they had left it, and Phocaea was not the only town that was razed to the ground several times and had to be rebuilt with increasingly depleted energy, Miletus too, with its tremendous detached fort, fell victim to the Great Power that was Persia. The beautiful Miletian statues and buildings sank into the rubble, from which they were to be excavated only by the Prussian archeologists. Phocaea left very few artworks in the earth. The prosaic noblemen had set up more utilitarian monuments, by investing in banks, industries, and shipping companies, they ascended directly into their own glorification. All they had to do was have their ships change course in order to find refuge and a rich income in Corsican Alalia, in Gallic Nikaea, Massalia, and Agathe, or in Spanish Zakynthos, Hemeroskopeion and Maenake. However, the populace remaining in the city had to serve the Persian occupiers and to feed their armies or enlist in them. The Greek dream of the faraway paradise islands, where immortal heroes dwelled in bliss, had gone through its metamorphoses. For the big merchants that dream had become the incarnation of eternal growth, there were no dead people there, just pliant slaves who fulfilled the businessmen's strivings for hefty profit margins. They governed this earthly Eden with profiteering, in them Elysium lived on as a yearning for a constantly soaring added value. It was only among the others, who were still shadows, like the shades in the land of the dead, that the paradise retained features of its original image. Here too the Elysian Fields had shifted to this world, but they did promise justice to the people to whom every justice was otherwise denied, and redemption from poverty, slavery, and war. The powerful kept fighting for the hegemony of the new countries rising from the seas, the disempowered still waited, not yet aware that it was possible to push off the inflicted yoke, to have your own voice smash through the condemnation to silence, first the Phocaecians in Iberia had to yield to the strengthened Carthaginians, who in turn were driven back by the Romans, and Alexander had to defeat the Persians, and Pergamum had to occupy a deteriorated Phocaea and then move toward its own decay before the serfs drew strength from their conception of the Islands of Spring and rose up, as citizens of the sun, as Heliopolites, led by Aristonicus and by Saturninus of Sicily, and then against Rome in the wake of Spartacus. In between the gritty column fragments with the boreholes for the linking rods, our eyes wandered over the sandy coast, over the forests and meadows, the serpentine paths, the hills and mountain chains, and the hush was unreal when we thought of the tremendous clash of forces taking place farther up the Ebro. The Greek settlement below us also vanished, the Carthaginians now guarded the harbor, had the ores mined, the rock salt and the sea salt washed in the salteries, and powerful armies once more geared up to march out. There they came, from Carthagena, the new port on the southern coast, ninety thousand Iberian and North African infantrymen, special troops catapulted from the Balearic Islands, twelve thousand Numidian horsemen and the gray surging mass of elephants, and, under parti-colored insignia, surrounded by the glittering lances of the bodyguards, rode Hannibal. This was the start of the great northward trek that was to restore the border on the Ebrus between the Punic and Roman spheres of interest. The first battle was fought at Saguntum. The Roman cohorts were driven from the city they occupied, but the Carthaginians did not stop at the Ebro. In July of the year two hundred eighteen, Hannibal and his army crossed the river. He installed his brother Hasdrubal as governor, left him fifteen thousand mercenaries to protect the Iberian colony, and went on with his army through Catalonia, through the Pyrenees, through Gaul, through the Alps, no one knew why and no one could foresee where they were headed, and meanwhile the Romans gathered their forces to retaliate, sent a fleet commanded by Scipio to Saguntum, routed Hasdrubal, conquered Carthagena, Malaca, and Gades, seized enormous amounts of weapons and catapults, of gold, silver, and grain as well as eighteen men-of-war and sixty-three freighters. In the year two hundred six, Spania was pacified by the Romans, and thus began the fall of the Punic Empire. What did the utopias of the slaves still have over them, how far was it still to the step that would take them from the world of distress and misery, Scipio prepared for the crossing to Africa, in Pergamum Attalus the First concluded his protective alliance with Rome, Hannibal with his last soldiers fought his way through Italy, after killing his horses and elephants he was evacuated by the remnants of the Punic navy and defeated in his city by Scipio, who added the epithet Africanus to his name. The Romans burned down Carthage, Hannibal fled to Crete, offered Prusias, the king of Bithynia, his service in the war against Pergamum, was captured and drained the cup of poison, and once again the Romans fell upon Carthage and razed it to the ground. What struggles still lay ahead under the changes of dynasties. Passing the olive trees, with their widely sweeping branches, which were suitable for hangings, we walked along the dirt road to the Villa Candida, uprisings, revolts blazed up and were quelled. The peasants rebelled against the Romans, in the vast migrations Vandals, Suebi, and Alani inundated the country, the Visigoths founded a kingdom here, the Berber Moors thronged in from the south, Arabian caliphs instituted their rule and were superseded by Christian kings in Castille, Asturia, León, the rural populace fought for its rights, achieved self-administration, independence for a while, was again subjugated in Aragón, constant insurrections, constant battles, knives, sickles, pickaxes tore into flesh, blood soaked the earth, Castille conquered Córdoba, Aragón conquered Sicily, then, under Ferdinand and Isabella, a powerful unified Spanish kingdom, establishment of the Inquisition, extermination of the Moors and Muslims, expulsion of the Jews, the discovery of the West Indies, Spain as a world power, Spain under the Hapsburgs, major portions of the Netherlands, Belgium, Italy owned by Spain, after England's rise the annihilation of the Spanish Armada, the loss of European vassal states, riots in Catalonia, Napoleon's invasion, guerrilla victory over the enemy troops, the revolts and secessions of the Latin American colonies, the disbanding of the Inquisition after more than three centuries, national popular war for a democratic constitution beaten down with French military assistance in eighteen twenty-three, three decades later the first organization of Spanish workers, the failed bourgeois revolution, the proclamation of the Republic, restoration of the monarchy. Cuba, Puerto Rico, Guam, the Philippines were lost to the new imperium in the Spanish-American War. The final possessions in the Pacific, the Mariana, Caroline, and Marshall Islands, were sold to the German Empire. However, nearby Morocco could be conquered and then held as a protectorate until now. Nineteen seventeen general strike, armed rebellions in several places. Military dictatorship, but a Republican victory in the elections of nineteen thirty-one, dethroning of the king, division of the feudal latifundia, separation of church and state, autonomous administration in Catalonia, in the Basque Country, renewed consolidation of the reactionary forces, nineteen thirty-four, first collective attack by a proletarian front. What efforts, what incalculable sacrifices and victims, and what silence over the gardens that we would soon be leaving.

They had peered down at us, the Empecinado, the Espoz y Mina, and the priest Merino, the pioneer fighters in the heroic era of the eight-year war against Napoleon, gigantic papier-mâché figures held up by scaffolds on wagons full of dried flowers as we crossed the courtyard of the town hall in Valencia, this year they had for once not ridden out to the fallas, the big fiesta that normally took place in the city on the ninth of March, accompanied by drums, fifes, and bagpipes, the hubbub of fizgigs, rockets, and gun salutes. This year, all the grotesque dolls, built up behind the walls of the alleys, could not sway through the streets in the raucous torchlight parades and then go up in flames on Plaza Castelar, while the crowd sang and danced, for the night was dominated by a different kind of fireworks and detonations. So the dolls merely towered, dark and drastic, with huge gaping eyes, raised swords and flags, we found them to be splendid and hollow, and also mocking, we who reemerged from the Baroque hall, disappointed, embarrassed, rejected by the military commission, because it could no longer sign on foreign volunteers, there was no time for training, the brigades had to leave the country within a month. We again realized how inconceivable an end to the war had been without our victory. Now suddenly, on this confusing day in the second week of September, we were no longer needed. We had lost any function, we had to think about new tasks. At the Party Bureau we were ordered to return to Denia that evening in a transport and to try and reach Marseilles on any of the departing ships. As once before, long ago, I wandered aimlessly through town before reporting to the departure point for the truck convoy. And, as so often before in Spain, I stumbled upon an event that was strangely behind the times or timeless. At a side door of the cathedral, next to Plaza de la Virgen, I saw a dense throng of people, going over I found myself in front of the water court, which had its public session here every Thursday. To the left of the entrance, under the stone figures of the saints, behind the semicircle of a green wrought-iron grill, the peasant judges, wearing baggy black shirt-jackets, sat on high chairs. On the back of each chair there was a brass sign with the name of the water district, Mislata could be seen, Favara, Rovella, Pautahar, and Rascania. The court was dealing with disagreements such as might come about in relation to the use of ditches and canals in the low-lying rice paddies around Lake Albufera. The judges could have been sitting like that centuries ago, with tanned faces, some old, creased, bearded, all of them attentive, intelligent, experienced, dignified, often with a sense of humor, evoking laughter from the spectators, responding to the plaintiff, the defendant, and handing down their decision. And yet even though their superiority is so blatant, said a voice at my side, they still have to cope with the ancient property laws. Granted, they have the traditional right to pass judgment, for they alone are familiar with every furrow, every boundary wall in the fields, yet all that the state, whether feudal or republican, allows them to do is make sure of the survival of the systems. It was Ayschmann standing next to me. A bandage ran crisscross over his chest and shoulders. Only a broken collar bone, he said, a couple of fractured ribs, a brain concussion, a tear in my liver. A mine explosion had hurled him sixteen feet through the air into a wall. Under his arm he carried a few books and notebooks. After some reconnoitering he indicated the place where he had purchased them, a second-hand book shop on Calle Castellón, between Plaza de toros and the long brick façade of North Station. He pulled me over, wanted to show me the reproductions. We walked past the alabaster portal of the Palace of the Marqués de Dos Aguas, with its dolphins, lions, and titans, through the city gate between the circular towers with firing slits, and on the Serranos Bridge over the broad dried-up riverbed. Herds of sheep grazed on either bank of the Turia, which was now trickling as if through a mere ditch, on the other side, fields and orange plantations spread out behind the high embankment. Ayschmann walked stiffly in his bandages, he was heading toward the orange forest, there behind the last suburban houses. We went deep into a path between the trees, sat down on a slope. Ayschmann opened the magazine, *Cahiers d'Art*, which contained the reproductions of the preliminary studies and various phases of *Guernica*, until its final form. The insert, which could be folded out, enabled us to visualize the image in its gray and swarthy tones, nor were there any other colors in the painting, which, some eleven by twenty-five feet in size, had been shown one year earlier in the Pavilion of the Spanish Republic at the Paris World's Fair. First the painting, which we held in our outstretched hands, contrasted bizarrely with the shiny, intensely glowing blue-green of the leaves of the orange trees. The painting presented something utterly new, incomparable. Crudely, violently, the sharp shadows and cones of light, the flatly intersecting mastodontic limbs and faces, the hard diagonals and verticals contradicted the deep, motionless density all around. The air was filled with the metallic singing of crickets. No sounds could be heard from the city. After a while, the composition, with its central pyramid of figures, its sideways towering shapes, assumed concreteness. Without fully grasping the manifestation, we saw what was happening in Spain. Hammered into a language of few signs, the picture contained shattering and renewal, despair and hope. The bodies were naked, beaten to a pulp and distorted by the forces breaking in on them. From jagged flames the arms loomed steeply, the overlong neck, the rearing chin, the facial features twisted in horror, the body shrunken into a bolt, charred, hurled aloft by the heat of the fiery oven. At an angle from the bottom right, the bent woman was thrust from the blackness into the cone of light, her feet, her legs, earth-heavy shards, still bore her up, her hands flew back powerlessly as if in a strong draft, but her face was raised high, her eyes fixed on the glow of the candelabra that a knotted fist on a smoldering arm stretched into space. At the left the woman was a crouching bundle, her hand dangled bloated, in her arm the child with the tiny wretched toes, the flattened-out ragged hand was as dead as it could possibly be. Right over her screaming profile, with its tongue sticking sharply out of its mouth, the turned head kept watch, the head of the bull under which she had sought refuge, massive, snorting, it stood there, its tail vehemently lashing upward, its human eyes staring forward. Over the felled statue of the warrior, made of plaster, yet with dreadfully live hands, one hand opening its lines, the other clutching the hilt of the burst sword, the horse, divided into muscle bulges, spread out, with a gigantic gaping wound, bored through by the lance, on one knee, yet still stamping, dangerously, roaring from a nasty mouth. The hand lump on the cloudlike arm stretched toward that undulating mane, carrying the poor kerosene lamp such as could be found in peasant huts, and there was something special about this old-fashioned light, that, with such a sweeping gesture, was shoved through the narrow opening by a Nike, whose other hand, in the shape of a star, rested between her breasts. Her dominating face, emerging from infinity, pushed through, flowing out from inside a building, under roof tiles, past a lime-washed wall fragment, but in this movement the face went back inside, into the spare, elongated room where the apocalyptic event was taking place, brightened by the electric sun of the kitchen lamp, next to whose cold rays the flame of the wretched oil lamp stood mild and intact in its glass shield. These were the first hints of recognizable elements in the painting, yet they could be read differently, every detail was ambiguous, like the building blocks of poetry. Wasn't the gesture of the woman leaning toward the center humble, we wondered, didn't the hands fluttering in their emptiness reveal that she had just laid out a corpse, and didn't the outspread, staccato hands of the body lying in front of her recall the attitude of the man taken off the cross. From the hand cramped on the sword a flower stem grew, thin and blurry, on the dark, merely outlined table in the background a bird fluttered, perhaps a dove, unshapely, with a large upturned beak, and the lines in the hand of the fallen man recurred as a pattern in the hands of the women and the child, and also in the hoof on the horse's sole, everything was interconnected, interrelated, subject to the same fate on the stage of this barn, of this kitchen, of this everyday life that had become the extraordinary. The sketches in the journal, the drawings, the first few versions of the painting made it clear that from the very start the vision was overshadowed by the bull and by the out-thrusting hand with the makeshift light, and since the bull grew more and more human and the horse more and more bestial, we saw the Taurus as representing the endurance of the Spanish people, and the narrow-eyed, stiffly crosshatched horse as representing the hated war inflicted by fascism. A series of engravings, which prepared the theme of the mural, showed the horse as a nauseating monster with facial traits recalling the generalíssimo, and the bull as a superior force, while in pencil drawings the nag kept getting frantically battered and strangled down, and the bull remained in its triumph. However, a closer study of the magazine, a perusal of the few drafts indicated the possibility of a different interpretation. For one thing, a small winged horse was flying from the wound in the nag's body, and that winged horse was to be found again, sitting daintily on the tamed, saddled bull. In the painted version, the winged horse was gone or else transformed into a dove, but the black, rhombic wound was so gigantic, almost disturbing, that it constantly reclaimed your attention. With such a hole in its torso the creature could not really stay erect, its soul must have already slipped away. Thinking about the penetrating drawings of Pegasus, we wondered if the absence, the terrifying hollow, was meant to point out a principal motif of the picture. But if, on the basis of the stream of secondary images, the piling-up of human and animal suffering, we wanted to add a lament for the escape of Pegasus, then we would have to go along with the critics who, demanding agitation, reproached the work for being opaque and broken. Two different notions of realism collided with one another, said Ayschmann. The painful deformation of human beings under the impact of destruction contradicted the Party's view that the fighter had to keep his strength and unity in any situation. There were grotesque features here, virtually childlike scribbles, unfit for championing the proletariat's cause. The painting's antagonistic forces, bonding into a synthesis, unleashed a violent controversy because the lesson given by Picasso became comprehensible to the thinking person. The external stratum of reality had been lifted off. Suppression and violence, partisanship and class consciousness, deathly terror and heroic courage were revealed in their elementary, dynamic functions. With the shredded entities fused into a new totality, the foe encountered a resistance that was unbeatable. In the midst of the attack on all life, the picture, with its horrifying wound, still asked a question about the whereabouts of art, and this did not soften the effect. Each of Picasso's works was to be seen as part of a multiplicity, the sum of which drew in even the most casual notice. In this torture chamber, nothing remained of the genius of the muses, the painter had repressed his original idea, but the event was all the more there, bared and exposed. However, the fact that Pegasus, invisible, belonged in the painting was confirmed when we found a statement of Picasso's that left no doubt about his work method, which regarded no preliminary study as lost, as rejected. His entire life, he had explained at the conception of this painting, was nothing but a never-ending struggle against the backwardness of thinking and against the death of art, and these words meant reactionism's encroachment on the people and on freedom in Spain. He equated the struggle for truth in art with the rebellion against demagoguery, for him artistic labor was inseparable from the social and political reality. The destructiveness descending on Spain was meant to wipe out not only people and cities, but also the ability to express things. In the suite of pictures that he called *Franco's Dream and Lie*, El Caudillo, a mollusk-like proboscidate wielding a pickax, was attacking first the portrait of the Arts and, fenced in by barbed wire, was sacrificing to the idols of money, then the bull furiously gouged him, and the tear-filled faces of the human beings rose toward the stations of the life-and-death duel, until, at the end, only the squatting woman remained, outside the burning ruin of the house, with the corpse of the child in her arms. Much of the message was still hidden, could be researched in the future. The bombing of the Basque town of Guernica, on the afternoon of April the twenty-sixth, nineteen thirty-seven, by German planes of the Condor Legion, was a signal, even greater devastations seemed to be developing from the flat, mobbed kitchen space. The door behind the bull's tail was open, and the space continued way out, even next to the woman perishing in the firestorm. The section of a prophecy was captured here, in harsh illumination, and since the ceiling bulb, with its knotted wire, might soon go out, the other oil lamp, a reliable one, had been brought in, and this was the light of consciousness, of understanding. In the sketches, the toro, after at first broadly overlying all the other figures, kept yielding more and more to the initially felled, then high-rebounding horse, which displayed its mortal injury from the very start. In this way, the Spanish bull, during the continuation of the war, had approached a possible retreat, while the horse, transfixed by a spear and surrounded by flying arrows, raged in the middle. The picture challenged us to use the first impression merely as an impetus to take the givens apart and examine them from different directions, then fit them back together, thereby making them our own. This confirmed the rule I was familiar with from my earliest artistic investigations. As once, in the confrontation with Léger's crystalline painting that he titled *Nudes in the Forest* instead of *Lumberjacks*, these colliding hard-edged components transmitted an energy that forced your vision to build, to combine. The gray and bluish-violet cubes, cones, and cylinders of wood, of stone, of bodies in the forest spoke of being wedged between trunks and stumps, but along with the violent strenuousness of the labor, along with the clublike musculature, a different world was depicted, or rather, the sight of these earth-locked cyclopes awakened our eyes to our own condition in the pipe-work of the machines. Thus the extended vanishing lines of the contours of Feininger's houses opened up an entire city, and, spraying like comets, the shapes on the tower of the blue horses introduced a vitality that could never be reached by conventional methods of representation. Such surprising depictions, based not on a closed aspect but on a multivalence, supplied more details than static arrangement could about the mechanisms we lived among. Characteristic of that ambiguity was its ability to get the imagination to seek links, thereby expanding the realm of receptivity. A Picasso pastel, showing a woman climbing a ladder with a dead child, pointed to the region occupied by the bull, the horse, the outstretched hand with the light, and when Ayschmann opened the reproduction of the minotauromachy, it conjured up the kitchen of the farmhouse near Cueva la Potita and the cellar buried deep in the ground. This drawing was the wellspring from which the Guernica painting had arisen. There the bull-man with the mammoth head was bending protectively over the collapsed horse, which formed a unit with its rider, here a dying female toreador clutching the sword. We saw the darkness of the stone wall, and in the niche the dove reflected a speck of brightness, which, on the bird in the great opus, became the dazzling blade of a knife, and in front of that darkness stood a child, holding a burning candle and a bouquet of flowers, while behind him the countryman, as an ancient wanderer, as Odysseus, clambered up the shaft. Even in this etching, exterior and interior permeated each another, the Minotaur, coming from the open sea and sky, leaned into the deep blackness of the cellar, and I saw the young son, the lamp raised aloft, and the peasant over him on the steep stairs, lugging the carafe on his shoulder. I found it immediately comprehensible that the destruction of Guernica should take place on the square tiles of a kitchen floor. It was in such a room that I had come to understand that there was no distinction between social and political materializations and the essence of art. But, asked Ayschmann, did you not always feel your disadvantage vis-à-vis the people who could pursue their studies unhindered. His words knocked me out of an equilibrium that I had claimed I possessed. My education had no solid underpinnings, it was acquired through sporadic readings. I could not produce a so-called Gymnasium degree. On the other hand, I had legitimized myself by laboring in workshops, warehouses, factories. For an instant I was hostile toward Ayschmann, who had laid claim to an academic formation entirely as a matter of course. I felt rebellious against his world, but then I was ashamed of my reaction, for his question was premised on the idea of solidarity. We did not see ourselves as inferior, I said, with our practical knowledge we often actually felt superior to the university students since the contents of their textbooks were accessible for us too while they knew nothing about our basic training. We had learned to use the concept of the intellectual in a wider sense. At home, when we spoke about the intelligentsia, we meant all people who thought for themselves. And yet Ayschmann was right. For all our equality, there was a gap between us. I was an autodidact. My development would have been different had my family been economically privileged. One could therefore appreciate all the more the accomplishment of my parents, who made literature something that was part of our lives. At school, until I was twelve, I was at the mercy of the system, which raised us to be nothing more than labor cattle. Not a single teacher would have ever so much as tried to stimulate the talents existing in all of us. As children of a proletarian neighborhood we were doomed to nothingness, any word testifying to reflection was beaten down with fists and sticks. When my exhausted father came home, he would always sit down at the table with a book and discuss it with me. It was he who got me to visit the library. He brought works from library sections that were closed to us children. Reading, looking at art reproductions belonged to existence. Literature was a necessity. I gained the impression that one could not live without it. I could not say when my interest in books was aroused. In our kitchen there were always travel books, biographies, accounts of discoveries and historical events. They revealed themselves to me page by page, their contents accompanied me even in sleep. Ayschmann saw this as an exception. But we assumed that dealing with literature, philosophy, art was possible anywhere. Everyone had the faculty for thinking. We had always been indignant if we were viewed as incapable of intellectual activity after a day's labor. We were workers, and we were creating a cultural foundation for ourselves. The very hint that this could be achieved purely through special circumstances was, we felt, condescending and discriminatory. We, no better or smarter than others, were able to study, to do research, and this fact proved that everybody else could succeed in doing so. All that was often lacking was the motivation, this began in school, then continued in the trade unions, which promoted petty bourgeois frugality instead of the impatience of thought. Conditions had forced us to devote our own strength, our unspeakably strenuous efforts to conquer the things that should have been granted to us all. That was what I meant when I said that my father, acting on his own initiative, had taken the step from enslavement to the age of science. Striving for insights into art and literature, he had, often full of rage, rejected the populist stuff that was tailored to our needs, and he had argued against simplified guides, which, focusing on easy, limited ideas, were supposed to help us along. Ayschmann asked whether all this had been programmatic or consistent with our deepest convictions, and all I could reply was that Coppi, I, and several others who were close to us had recognized this route as the correct one, and that we had been assisted, an assistance to be regarded as a privilege, when we had attended a progressive school, if only briefly. However, it was torturous being dependent on such help. Under the kitchen lamp the world lit up for us, the things we imagined took shape, we thought our way to a Finisterre, where encounters took place with mythological phenomena. And so, comparing the sketched horse and its dead or comatose rider with the war steed and its disintegrating clay warrior, we stumbled upon further metamorphoses. Just as toreador and horse fused into one another and jointly collapsed, so too, in the compositional studies, horse and warrior perished initially as a single shattered body, and the female figure with the child's corpse tore itself out of the wound. Maleness and femaleness intermingled, there was a reminiscence of Medusa, from whose body Pegasus sprang. Her dreadful face with the petrifying glance was recognizable both in the horse's head and in the warrior's. Turning away from the Gorgon, catching her grimace only in a mirror, Perseus had killed her, and this evasion was also inherent in Picasso. The attacking violence remained invisible in his picture, only the overwhelming was there, only the victims appeared. Vulnerable, unprotected, they were at the mercy of the unseen enemy, whose strength was immeasurable. Perseus, Dante, Picasso remained unscathed, handing down what their mirror had captured, the head of Medusa, the circles of the Inferno, the blasting of Guernica. Imagination lived so long as human beings who resisted lived. However, the adversary aimed not only at material devastation but also at the snuffing-out of all ethical foundations. We agreed that the assaulter must not remain in a vacuum, he had to be depicted recognizably. But this did not rule out the fact that the artistic media could call attention to the degree of difficulty that determined the understanding of crucial events. The catastrophe descending here on the faces and bodies contained dimensions that we could not grasp. The shapes and gestures flattened by air pressure were stamped into the pictorial wall by a light that no eye could endure. Any attempt at directly explaining the depiction would lead to extinguishing the work. The effectiveness of Guernica's memorial plane, and of the tauromachy, grew stronger the more we confronted it outright. With its crudely sliced components the large composition offered an initial, quickly grasped overview. Nothing could change its standpoint here, all relations were given in powerful simplicity. But in becoming comprehensible and pointing to the forces it evoked, the depiction showed us our own state, in which partisanship supplied the external cohesion, while discord, skepticism, helplessness, and anxiety marked the interior. Even when it was possible to analyze the conditions, we usually were stuck with hypotheses that were soon rejected. The absence of security, that sensation of flowing tipped the scales for a thinking that would go under with late-bourgeois society and that had infected us despite our political alternative. It was with a great expenditure of energy that we had tackled bitterness and lethargy in Spain. But then came the disbanding of the front, which feverishly reminded us that earlier initiatives of the workers' movement had been broken off by setbacks. Once more, the struggle against the profiteers had gone awry, making the exploited even more dependent. There were still not enough people who fought back, and so hundreds of thousands had had to pay with their lives. Nevertheless, Spain continued what the Madrid insurgents had begun in eighteen eight, the French revolutionaries in eighteen thirty, the Communards, and the October fighters. All these things, the mighty rising and the foundering, the sinking and the gathering for a new thrust, were contained in the huge picture of Guernica. Two decades ago the workers in our countries had allowed the power to be wrested from them, the reformists had helped to strengthen the profiteers, whose rule had led to fearful deformities. Picasso's battered, bursting bodies and shifted facial features testified to that era. The picture screamed and recalled all previous stages of suppression. It was close to another visualization, in whose center a black, long-stretching horse flew, ridden by a woman wearing a tattered, fluttering dress and holding a sword and a torch, and underneath lay, smashed, the naked fallen men. That was how the Douanier Rousseau had depicted the zooming leap of War over whitish-gray bodies and earth formations half a century ago, and the woman's face, with her big, hard-edged eyes, her gaping mouth, bore the same horror that petrified the inhabitants of Guernica. Picasso's work harked back to Mantegna's Pietà and that of the Master of Avignon, to the Apocalypse of Beatus of Liebana and the cave drawings of the Stone Age. Even the variations of the weeping woman with the bared teeth had traces of flowing tears, the handkerchief pressed to the eyes, such as had already been depicted by the masters of the fifteenth century, and the plunged man in the foreground of Guernica was similar to the dead man stretched out on his back in the sepulchre of Avignon. The eleventh-century miniature of Beatus showed Picasso's compositional elements in a still unwarped landscape. However, the fallen man, the horse, the woman with the child initiated stylization, abstraction, and the dove, inscribed with the word colomba, hope, light, peace, flew up from the olive tree in order to land in the shade of the kitchen corner. Picasso's painting referred to its origins, but the restraint in the grief of his predecessors had vanished. Here the pain was blatant. The tears were needles and arrows that left cuts in the flesh. The innovativeness become more meaningful by revealing its foundations and preparations. In Ayschmann's books and magazines we saw the history of art as a history of human life, in which we could read the degrees of social decisions. Connections were made with our own development. Much of our thinking was molded by pictures and literary works. Periods of changing consciousness were frequently tied to specific artistic themes. So now, in the time of the crucial

political struggle, we thought about the child in the minotauromaquia. Unswervingly he raised his light toward the shadows, he embodied more than poetry, for all his fragility he represented a fine flair without which the monstrously rampant growth of reality could not be grasped. Such paintings stood as road signs in the tangle of historical lines. We also emphasized a few other works. Like Guernica, Delacroix's *Barricade*, with the figure of freedom, was composed according to the pyramid model that presented the agitation as a tamed unity. The color was reduced to leaden tones, to a dull umbra, even the fiery red of the tricolor was tempered by the billows of smoke. Over cobblestones and planks and the waxen corpses thrown down flat, the leader of the people climbed up, the powerful, half-bared washerwoman sporting a loosely fluttering dress, carrying a flag and a rifle, her face turned aside like Nike, who stretched her immense profile into Picasso's pictorial space. In her fleshy fullness, her fist clenching the sharply drawn firearm, her heavy thigh propped forward, she showed the stage in which the idea becomes a material force. In the trinity of the proletariat she was joined by workers, intellectuals, and adolescents. Ayschmann pointed to the man in the black hat and jacket, with the broad necktie around his shirt collar. That was Delacroix's self-portrait. The biographical detail gave the painting further value, speaking as it did of a decision forced by the circumstances of the time. Rather conservative in his character, the artist nevertheless put himself in the front rank of revolutionaries, he was not yet quite up to his role, he was kneeling, slightly recoiling as if seeking support behind him, gripping the rifle somewhat anxiously, his finger clumsily on the hammer, and this moment expressed the complete situation of his life. What he rendered was an ideal, and yet for that very reason it also had something of the bizarreness of a dream, one could tell from his face that he did not really belong here, puzzled, in the exceedingly real depiction, barely aware of his actions and soon also disavowing them, he, a visionary, took the position of a man of the future. One step past the protective woman, the boy had come furthest forward, storming from the streets, enthusiastically swinging his pistol. While the standard-bearer seemed invulnerable, and the other fighters, in statuary stances, waiting, kept themselves alert, all the sweeping, spontaneous, heroic energies concentrated in this adolescent, and when he raised his foot in order to leap over the fallen, with the mammoth ammunition pouch dangling on his hip, it was as if the revolution were about to triumph. But this was also terrible, for not only was the boy, utterly unshielded and exposed to the enemy, certain to be shot down within a second and fall into the heap of corpses, which seemed ready to receive him, but we also knew what came after July twenty-eighth, eighteen hundred thirty. The populace, gathered under the ideal of freedom, was already cheated, it had carried out the handiwork of rebellion as it had done four decades earlier, its sacrifices had paved the way for the higher classes, now too the people remained in the background, a new money aristocracy, a new monarchy pushed their way to the fore. Following the sequence of revolution and counterrevolution, the Napoleonic throne had replaced the Jacobin dictatorship, royal power had been restored on the ruins of the empire, and now the barricade confronted the unrestricted dominion of high finance, against which the struggle would continue in further revolutionary phases. This picture, which, after all, laid claim to praising a leap of history in its boldness and grandeur, had a frozen quality about it because the painter himself halted before the transition to renewal, remaining in an intermediary stage, laden with the remnants of romantic, allegorical views. In front of the people who collapsed here in the gunfire, who pulled themselves up again, lay the bastions of eighteen thirty-one, thirty-four, forty-eight, and seventy-one, and also the artistic conquests, which found form in Courbet, Millet, Daumier, van Gogh. Delacroix wanted to stand out among the rebels, but now he was afraid. He was closer to the bourgeoisie than to his heroes, he was ready to turn against the upheaval. But it was this very brokenness with which he characterized the situation on the barricade. Pale, tense, taking his place, girded with a red sash, his top hat rakishly askew on his head, he represented the class that watched out for its own interests in the midst of the fray. He had visualized a date, just as Picasso had done with his painting, a second of contradictory hopes, and while the populace bled to death under the goddess of freedom, he, the fellow traveler, gloomy, melancholy, glanced ahead at his awakening, and this awakening was full of betrayal. The same held for that day in Paris. The workers had begun to struggle for their rights, but among them, harassing, hindering, binding, was reactionism, it was infinitely arduous climbing to a higher historical level, it was only beyond the wall of torn-up street stones that scientific socialism would come into being, furiously attacked, libeled, undermined in the coming century by the bourgeoisie, which was armed to the teeth. Twelve years earlier the *Raft of the Méduse* had broken into the academic art rooms. Delacroix's painting was appreciated by the man who called himself the citizen king, for it had become the apotheosis of his road to power, he was now served by the well-paid artist. But Géricault's picture was a dangerous attack on the established society. Its huge format alone, twenty-three by seventeen feet, threatened to wipe out all the other works in the Salon, the notabilities could not bear the theme, which exposed the corruption of the officialdom, the cynicism and selfishness of the government. On July the second, eighteen sixteen, the *Méduse*, the flag ship of a French naval unit, was sailing toward Senegal when, because of the commander's incompetence and the negligence of the naval authorities, she ran aground off Cape Blanc. Of the some three hundred colonial soldiers and settlers on board, scarcely half could be accommodated by the lifeboats. The skipper, the higher officers, and the influential passengers used force to gain control of the boats. The other castaways crowded together on a makeshift raft of planks and mast fragments. The raft was supposed to be towed by the lifeboats, but during a storm the ropes were cut, the raft drifted away, and twelve days later, of the hundred fifty starving, thirsting people, who fought one another, only fifteen were still alive. Though the event had taken place three years earlier, the name Méduse was not allowed to be part of the title, the work was hung as a shipwreck scene, in bad light, high above the other paintings. The moment depicted by the painter, the instant when the mast of the rescuing frigate hove into view on the horizon, was charged with such despair, such rebellion, that the representatives of the Bourbon restoration correctly read it as a first step toward revolt against their regime. The unclear reproduction in the book placed us in the situation of the viewers who, despite distance and bad lighting, made an effort to decipher something of the authenticity of the painting. The survivors on the raft stretched upward in a collective motion, away from the corpses in the foreground, pulling themselves up more and more, toward the dark-skinned back of the raised-up man, with the wind lashing aside the cloth in his hand. The composition followed the principle of the double diagonal, consolidating the structure of the large plane while shifting two perspectives. From bottom left the group, in its agitated, intertwining gestures, stretched out toward top right, aiming at the tiny mast, that would promptly be covered by a wave rolling up, from bottom right the other line arose, yanked by the bellied sail toward the top left, so that the direction described by the mass of figures crossed the direction the raft was moving in. This aroused a feeling of dizziness. The raft was gliding not toward the faraway ship but past her, and this perception was further unnerved by the sight of the billow that, unnoticed by anyone on the vessel, towered in front of the empty bow and was about to crash down on the survivors. Delacroix had turned his figures frontally toward the onlooker, his appeal to join the fight was tempered only by his own half-hesitant, half-coquettish stance. Géricault chose to forgo this direct agitation, the castaways mostly turned toward the background, they were entirely self-absorbed, the seated man facing the front, with his hand twisted around a corpse, was immersed in grief and exhaustion, the raft was viewed as if by a drowning person, and the rescue was so remote that it seemed as if it first had to be invented. That emerging assistance, on which the final, awakening, gradually increasing strength was focusing, could be a mirage, a hallucination, it existed in some future, very far from the world of the spectators. The catastrophe that had been singled out had become the symbol of a life condition. Scornfully turning their backs on the conformists, the castaways on the raft represented the stragglers of a vulnerable and hapless generation that, in its youth, had experienced the fall of the Bastille. They leaned on and clung to one another, all the conflict that might have brought them together on the ship was past, forgotten were the struggle, the hunger, the thirst, the dying on the high seas, the shipwrecked had formed a unity supported by each person's hand, collectively they would now perish or collectively survive, and the fact that the waving man, the strongest among them, was an African, perhaps loaded on the *Méduse* to be sold as a slave, hinted at the thought of the liberation of all underdogs. Ayschmann had suddenly blanched, he sank forward, the book dropped from his hand. I laid him in the grass. He pressed his hands on his temples, I was just feeling faint, he said, it will pass quickly, and he sat up again. The pictures we had been dealing with at this time were marked by the swiftness and intensity with which life could be snuffed out. Just like us, the painted figures rose up from annihilation, lying, kneeling, creeping over mountains of corpses. Death was now incessantly present for him, said Ayschmann. The painters had wrested an instant more of life from overwhelming destruction and transposed that instant into timelessness.

Such a strenuous effort was bound to leave something incredible behind, a silence with bated breath. I asked Ayschmann whether I ought to take him to the convalescent home, but he had already reopened the book to Goya's picture of the shooting of the insurrectionists. And yet, he said, peering at the faces with their lips squeezed tight in hatred, their gaping eyes, I feel no terror at the thought that that which is still quite near us can promptly be irretrievably lost, for the sense of this closeness, which is so exceedingly important, is at hand only so long as we are alive, it vanishes when we die. I mean, he said, that we cling to life only so long as we know about life, and that no pain exists for our extinguished life because we ourselves fade away with what is lost. We can fear death only when alive, and yet we have no reason to do so, for we are still alive, this fear stops with death, that is why the fear of death is absurd. I have learned, he said, only one thing, never to yield in my attentiveness so long as I am here, never to forget that I am alive. On the third of May, eighteen eight, the condemned men had only a tiny time span left. The rifles were lifted. The pools of blood shone in the glow of the big lantern on the ground. The men already slaughtered lay with tattered bodies in front of the kneeling squad. A dense procession of prisoners was being led to the slope. Several clenched their fists or had their hands on their faces. But the men thronging together in the foreground, workers, peasants, a monk, directly facing the rifle muzzles, stared in wild defiance. One man, in an open white shirt, stretched his arms way out to receive death. The suspense of waiting for the salvo was unbearable because the tension would never end. The silhouette of a protruding part of the city was extinguished with the yawning arch of a gate, from which the prisoners were coming. The heavy brownish gray of the nocturnal sky was taken up by the mantle of each grenadier, whose finger was curling on the hammer of the rifle. Into the loamy darkness, in the hour before dawn, the yellowish-pale wedge of the hill pushed in from the left, sliced up by the lines of the rifles elongated by bayonets. There was no help from anywhere, and the immediate barking of shots was certain, yet victory emanated from the troop of insurgents, and the backs of the soldiers, lined up like automatons, were bent by the coming defeat. And why, said Ayschmann, should we be afraid of our perishing, since we are not stunned by our nonbeing prior to being born. Does he not, he said, pointing to the man with the raised arm, express what can be achieved in this term between birth and death, is his gesture not full of pride and superiority, since he is letting go of everything and offering his entire body to the end, in the certainty that he has not lived in vain. They all have the same gaze, said Ayschmann, I have seen these eyes repeatedly, at Teruel and Caspe, at Vinaroz, Benicasim, and Castellón, and I assume that I too was staring like that when I flew through the air before everything went black.

The captured insurgents of Madrid, the castaways of the *Méduse*, the populace on the barricade in Paris, the inhabitants of Guernica, they were directly confronted with reality, and what had happened to them was very remote from the testimonies exhibited by the painters. Hard as the latter strove for material precision, the actual process was not to be encompassed or communicated. The sufferings of others could never be truly felt by anybody else, only one's own ordeals could be rendered. With their imaginations the painters created situations in which they kept projecting their personal experiences on the chosen event until an impression of concordance emerged. This concordance came about when the supreme degree of emotional intensity was reached. Just as Delacroix always looked for themes consistent with his passionate nature, which was disrupted by depressions, so too he conjured up the moment on the barricade from his self-doubt, his disgust. Previously he had transferred his unbridled fantasies to carnages and harrowings of hell, the gruesome crushing of the Greek struggle for freedom was still close to him, now he tried to lend form to this day in July after getting involved in its raging. Driven by idealism and also by arrogance, which was part of the feeling of uselessness that sometimes overshadowed his life, he wanted to participate in the unstoppable force that pressed for change, and, in his diffuse, voluptuous feelings he confused the wishes of the people with the aspirations of the Orléanists and Bonapartists. He would have long since left the side of the progressive power, of which there were only inklings during those hours and which were released in Lyons one year later and carried out to the streets by the workers. Likewise, Géricault's vision arose from a harried, distressed life in which unruliness, the constant fleeing from himself were initially expressed in the military campaigns and the collapse of Napoleon's empire, in broadly and vehemently painted martial scenes, then later in wildly dashing horses. There was a touch of the dandy, of the libertine in this painter, who kept wresting a superior color flow, a breathtaking rhythm from his burnout, his exhaustion. The colonial revolts, the mutinies of sailors, the encroachments by a corrupt state guided him toward the motif that was already prepared in his own outsider status, his fits of insanity. Feverishly he absorbed everything, let it become effective inside him, he was almost shattered by his efforts to turn a painting into an eyewitness account. Goya was deeply rooted in his reflected horror, sometimes intensifying its concretion into unreality. All the lightning-like impressions of the ten-year war against Napoleon's troops were expressed in the brutality of the execution. He projected a picture that seemed to correspond to a set of facts in every detail, yet had never occurred as it was rendered on the canvas. Nevertheless, in transposing an actual event to the range of art, the painters had succeeded in setting up a monument to radical instants. They had shifted experience to their own present, and we, who saw each crystallization, brought it back to life. What was shown was always different than what it had emerged from, a parable was shown, a contemplation on something in the past. Things drifting by had become something lasting, freestanding, and if it possessed any realism, that was because we were suddenly touched by it, moved. Picasso had unequivocally expressed the impossibility of doing justice to other people's experiences, his own perceptions, his subjective associations were all he relied on. His goal was not to list the number of bombs dropped, of houses destroyed, of people wounded or killed. Those figures could be read elsewhere. He waited till the clouds of smoke, of dust had lifted, till the moaning and screaming had faded. Only then, for himself, when he was all alone with the surface of the canvas, did he ask himself what Guernica was, and only when it took shape before his eyes, as an open city, as a city of defenseless inhabitants, did it become the tremendous reminder of afflictions, the kind that could still come. Guernica was at the start of a series whose end was out of sight. Géricault demonstrated a final point. He interviewed the survivors, built a model of the raft, visited the hospital and the morgue, researched the physiognomies of mental patients and dying people and the discolorations in the skins of the dead. In prisons he sketched the heads and torsos of guillotined men, and on the Atlantic coast he painted countless studies of the waves, the surf. In the presence of invalids, lunatics, and outcasts, he sought and learned the details he needed for depicting the victims of the budding French colonial state and of the still operative devouring of human beings. Thus something that was dubious and insufficient in the artist's life could abruptly turn into superiority. The drowsing, the feeble lying on the slippery planks of the raft now produced a still unspent energy, and the gestures of the group about to be shot pointed far beyond the horror in the sand pit near Madrid. This dichotomy between uncertainty and conviction, between ghostliness and overly explicit concreteness was of the very essence of the artistic process. Géricault was twenty-seven when his painting became the scandal of the Salon d'automne of eighteen nineteen. He never participated in another exhibition. Discouragement drove him from Paris to London. The four years remaining for him were filled with senseless frenzy, which finally broke his back after wild financial speculations and steeplechases. He died at thirty-two, less as a result of his passion for horse races than because of the lunacy of his era. In the four horses flying in an identical motion high over the ground at the Epsom Derby, he had painted the dream of his death. Here, everything was caught in a listening against a black sky, in a blustering downhill leap. Delacroix, court painter, chevalier of the Legion of Honor, did not protest when his picture of liberty, which now caused offense because of the newly erected barricades, was moved to the cellar of the Musée du Luxembourg. It was only after the proclamation of the Second Republic, in February of eighteen forty-eight, that the canvas was brought from its rural hiding-place, where Delacroix himself had stored it for the past ten years, but then, after Louis Napoleon's coup d'état it was again put behind bars. He may have been an opportunist, but he left behind a political painting that could ignite opinions. Clear-sightedness and indignation characterized the painters, as did fickleness and infatuation. In their works they rose above their own insecurity and defeated the unreliability of their thinking. And so, before being wiped away, they also found a self-confirmation, and this longing may have been the first impulse leading them to their craft. In measuring their strength against transience, they outlined small standpoints, observation posts, setting up and fortifying a Hemeroskopeion. I recalled that while reading, while looking at paintings, I was sometimes overwhelmed by a feeling of helplessness, the entire distrust of a world that captured hardship and disgust in forms and colors. Opening the book once again to the reproductions of Goya's paintings, I tried to imagine what it must have been like in that sandy hollow into which the painter had put such fiery vitality. Presumably, next to the still twitching, bloody corpses there was not the slightest thought of anger, pride, or victory, only choking, freezing, and unspeakable fear, and no trace existed of a future, by the time the shots cracked out, everything had long since passed into dreadful unreality. What could we do with these signs of uniqueness, what good was the perfectly composed massacre if everything around us was still unresolved. But then, as we stretched out in the grass, under the deep-green foliage, in that eternal humming of the cicadas, I again heard my father's voice. For him, I said, these were things that would have inspired him to investigate. Why, he might ask, did Géricault give in to his disappointment, why not really join the fight when he saw the reaction to his picture. And my father would ask whether Delacroix's painting had lost value because the artist had turned reactionary, and then he would have gone to the library and borrowed everything he could dig up on the painter's life, and my mother would help him by translating passages from French books. I had often heard my father say that he could foresee the time when he, an old man, would not be hired by any workshop, could devote himself entirely to such studies. But he must have been thinking of a future that was still far away, and we would have to get to work furiously in order to create the prerequisites for obtaining what he needed. Just as my father had always laid claim to accessing the cultural goods, so too he had insisted that he owned the things surrounding him at work. Art and literature were means of production, just as the tools and machines were. His life was one long straining to get beyond the demarcation line that had been drawn. At the factory, colleagues could sometimes poke fun at him, even call him an eager beaver, when they found him taking excessive care of the machine, when he thought about technological improvements. The fact that we were abused, he said, should not make us view our labor purely as constraint and drudgery so that we were led by reluctance and recalcitrance. Just as we would be lost if we did not appropriate the contents of books and pictures, so too we would perish if we did not already regard every piece of equipment in the plant, every object we produced as our assets. If someone then said that my father was deluding himself since our labor benefited others and not us, he would pull himself up, first mutely turn his broad, bony face toward the speaker, and then, with his restrained persuasiveness, he would reply that all he saw around him was that we were preparing to seize power. I knew how much strength of mind it took for him to stick to his guns despite all the defeats he had to swallow over the years. Even when he lost his job as foreman and could find only part-time work, he would still perform each task in full awareness of his responsibility. We would never, he said, be able to change our situation so long as we were trapped in our half-measures and alienation. Obviously no one thanked him for his commitment, and, also understandably, many people considered him eccentric, a paid laborer acting as if he were in a socialized factory. His motto was the Marxist proposition that labor constitutes the creative principle, the essence of the human species. Problems of art, of literature were always weighed in terms of work. Some day, said my father, we will discover that there has always existed an underground art depicting the life of the working person. Now remembering his words, I repeated them to Ayschmann. I saw my father sitting at the kitchen table, he had been saying that the worker had become a figure in art only in the late nineteenth century. Previously, in better-known works, he had been utterly absent or else present only as staffage. At the top, while people looked through him, one could hear them say that he never got himself talked about. The subversive actions, the revolutionary changes that should have been credited to his initiative quickly became the property of the bourgeoisie. The populace, without its own reproduction apparatus, could recognize the upheavals only with great difficulty and in a fragmentary manner. My father wished for a field of study aimed at tracking down the harbingers of the proletarian struggles in drawings, woodcuts, paintings, and sculptures. This was again one of the topics that, because of their gigantic ramifications, had to be reserved for his life as a student retiree. Yet, in perusing reproductions of Sumerian, Babylonian, and Egyptian friezes and Asian temples, in the chronicles, breviaries, house-books, and cycles of miniatures, in medieval altar shrines and prayer desks, he had already discovered so many indications of the basic forces of society that he had to speak of a tremendous urge that the painters and sculptors could not escape. Stamped indelibly in what the artists saw, said my father, the workers, peasants, and craftsmen surfaced everywhere from the chiseled stone, the carved wood, the brush and crayon strokes. And yet they always remained in the background of art history. Their faces were thoughtful and self-confident, their tools, which they had produced themselves, had the balance and harmony of the functional, there was nothing random, nothing superfluous about their gestures. They were the active ones, everything that was brought forth passed through their hands, at the sight of all these plowers and fishermen, builders and harvesters, there could be no doubt that the entire structure of the priests and the princes, the army commanders and feudal lords would collapse instantly if these small, industrious, attentive figures were to stop supporting it and cultivating it. Nevertheless, they were ordinary, they melted into the landscape portions, into the views of towns and castles, they were no more than a plant, a grazing animal, while the sovereigns, soft and empty in sumptuous garments, towered above them. That was how it was, those whose profession was seeing could not avoid paying tribute to this incessant effectiveness. After all, they too were craftsmen, of a privileged station, they were close to these laborers in the choice of tools, of material, but they were spellbound by the relative proportions, the heads of the divine kings colossally crowned the buildings, their limbs wound omnipotently about the walls, it was only under their feet that space could be found for a narrow relief hinting at the daily life of the common people. What my father wanted to examine and what he needed to systematize his impressions for were the beginnings that appeared again and again, in which the relations to the workers deepened, in which the dimensions shifted, and the laborers were released from their insignificance, sometimes even dominating in a social constellation. Emphasizing a farmhand, a soldier over the lord, the knight, that was tantamount to heresy, which initially required secrecy, conspiracy. However, said my father, the depicted worker was never seen by himself, he was always seen only by the artist, by members of a different sphere of life. We, he said, expressed ourselves solely in our labor, we very seldom got to view what was captured of us in art. We dealt with our tools, our art was cultivating the soil, grafting the fruits, building the houses, these things called for songs, fables, fairy tales, handed down orally, we never made a fuss about the things we signed with our names. The secret art in temples and cathedrals, in manuscripts and statues said something about our presence, it was certainly allied with us, and it also helped us to gradually appreciate our achievements, but we mean something else when we talk about our culture, it is precisely this activeness that is the basis of everything surrounding us in the country and in the cities. Our culture is lugging, pulling, and lifting, tying together and fastening. This culture comes toward me, he said, whenever I see someone piling the chopped wood, sharpening the scythe, mending the net, joining the beams into the roof frame, polishing the pistons of the machine. He did not wish to idealize this, he added, but he saw no other possibility of arousing something of what links us to the overall talent and knowledge of an era. Oddly enough, he said, it was only the artistic representation of a seamstress, a lacemaker, a mower and thresher, a servant girl picking grapes, or a blacksmith that gave value to our labor. It was only in an artwork that labor had cultural meaning, it was only there that labor had become art, while the workers themselves remained without rank. I recalled this conversation so clearly because it was associated with a painting, Menzel's picture, eight feet wide, of an iron-rolling mill. Using a color reproduction, my father had explained to me that because of the growth of a conscious working class the recognized official art had provided a place for workers, a place for them to make their presence felt, and that the establishment had, at the same time, skillfully reneged on its generosity. Menzel's picture, the original of which we saw later on, at the National Gallery, was ubiquitously hailed as the apotheosis of labor. The atmosphere of heavy industry had been convincingly rendered with great technical expertise. The steam, the booming of hammers, the screeching of cranes and drag chains, the rotating of the flywheels on the machines, the heat of the fires, the white glow of the iron, the bracing of muscles, all these things could be felt in the painting. The group of blacksmiths trudged toward the center of the picture, shoving the glaring metal block, taken from the raised cart, under the roll, at the right, protected by a dented disk of sheet metal, a few men were resting, spooning food from bowls, lifting bottles to their mouths, and at the left edge of the painting, bare-chested workers of the previous shift were washing their necks and hair. Every action, every twisting and bending over the tools, and also the weary, burned-out sitting in the corner were components of the gigantic hall, squeezed into the bars, the daylight shimmering through the haze at several points seemed unreachable. All that was stated by the rendering of this nonstop, sweaty intermeshing was that people were working here, hard and unprotesting. The force in the heaving and swinging, regulated and controlled, the moment of utmost concentration for holding the tongs, the alertness shown by the bearded foreman at the lever as the the rolled part came through, the scrubbing of the soot-caked bodies, the exhaustion in a brief pause, all these things pointed to a single theme, to labor, to the principle of labor, and it was a specific principle, which could be defined only after detailed observation. This was not a matter of work as my father spoke about it, nor was it work as a system of self-realization, it was work done at the lowest possible price and with the highest profit for the work buyer. Since only the workers were visible, committing their entire existence to the activities, the viewer had the impression that they controlled the work. Dynamically sculpted by the glow of the fire, they filled out the space. At first sight, said my father when we were in the art museum, they are presented in the overwhelming dominance over the productive forces. And yet all they are doing is thoroughly confirming the rules of the division of labor. They appear to be acting on their own, but they exist only in their bond with the tools and the machines, which are the property of others. Now these others were nowhere to be seen, yet the workers were in their service. Even the ones crouching in the filthy corner, on their own for a while, almost in possession of their own lives, were merely waiting for the signal that would summon them back. They developed their strength purely in the handiwork, and even there the motions of their arms were not threatening, it was plain that they would use their arms exclusively to produce goods. The praise of labor was a praise of subordination. The men who, surrounded by spraying sparks, rallied about the white-hot mass of iron, who washed themselves at the trough, and the ones who, exhaustedly staring into space, sat at their meal, and in front of whom the young woman with the careworn face and the anxious upward glance packed the empty cups into the basket, they were all powerless. The depth of the factory was indeterminable, the rows of vertical and horizontal iron girders moved as a grid into infinity. The building, losing itself in smoke, was a world from which there was no escape. Although today we had a cafeteria, a washroom, a locker room, and we could count on technological improvements, the production process was still the same as portrayed by Menzel in eighteen seventy-five, four years after the crushing of the Commune. The workers devoted their concentrated energy to manufacturing the iron blocks, which became rails, gun mounts, cannon. They recast their peacefulness into a force that would turn against them, against their interests, from far away. One could tell that the woman in the right foreground, with the circles around her eyes, lived in a cellar hole, that her children were starving. The painter had characterized her poverty, he had depicted the rat race of drudgery, the inhumane conditions in which the laborers washed and ate, and yet the painting sparked no indignation. Instead it recalled something ineluctable. The working man was the bearer of the action, he carried out his tasks with self-assurance, every move, every gesture seemed to lend him self-confident grandeur, but his performance capacity, as my father pointed out, was aimed only at filling invisible safes and vaults. For all the sympathy that the artist may have felt with the social condition of the workers, these men, with their furrowed faces and eyes squinting in the bright heat, their fists clenching their tools, were nevertheless detached from the societal knowledge, documentations, and organizations that already had a real existence by then. Serving as a messenger at Alfa Laval, I saw the man whom Menzel's mastery had placed before the admiring public, the German working man from Bismarck's and Wilhelm's empire, unchallenged by the *Communist Manifesto*, on his own authority to be upright and true. His figures, provided with highlights and flowing shadows, were the stooges of iron. The iron had something elemental about it. With its intense fiery glow it was more than metal, it symbolized the expansion of industrial imperialism. The worker was worth exactly the same as the pay he received. The protagonist of the opus, in which the loyalty to material was the expert's joy, was not the worker, but the white-hot, slag-splashing lump that came under the cylinders for the accumulation of capital. This reading might not have convinced me if the painting had not been flanked by two other Menzel pieces in the museum. One depicted King Wilhelm's departure for the army on July thirty-first, eighteen seventy. Devoutly bowing or stiffly at attention, waving their hats, cheering, moved to sobs, the populace stood on Unter den Linden, and the regent in the coach waved graciously and rode toward the Brandenburg Gate, Sedan, Versailles, his proclamation as Kaiser, and the founding of the German Empire. The other picture, from eighteen seventy-nine, showed a supper ball in the sumptuous rooms of the castle, where, surrounded by shining gold and crystal, the bemedaled gentlemen in tails and gala uniforms balanced their plates and glasses, chatting with ladies in full dress. The smoky iron-rolling mill offered itself between those festive euphorias of colors, rustling with silk, aglitter with jewels, and the swaying of fluttering flags, the huzzahs on the sunny avenue. To the left the event that supposedly expressed the heartbeat of the nation, to the right the court society under the round of angels. On the one side the enthusiastic salute for war, the training in bowing and scraping, in boot-licking, on the other side the glorification of magniloquent splendor. In the middle, the harshest drudgery to create wealth for the people on the right and the left. A triptych about modern German history. The centerpiece, with men wearing leather aprons and swinging heavy poles and tongs, demonstrated the entire deception being perpetrated on the working class. And so, the workers, exploited by the powers that be, were forced to make the campaign against France possible, and so, misled by their own party leaders, they had helped to get the world war going, and so now they were forging the weapons for fascism. The painting of the iron-rolling mill, widely circulated as a color print, was set before them, the producers, as an example, as a means of edification. The reproduction could be found in some workers' kitchens. In a larger format and in a frame, it used to be raffled off at labor-union parties, later it was handed out by National Socialist organizations. The workers, placed by Menzel in a prison from which the class struggle was banished, were often redrawn by my friend Coppi, so that struggling men in tails and top hats or bemedaled uniforms, were caught by the tongs. While examining the reproduction, we had stumbled upon a further informative detail. We retraced the perspective pattern of the composition, following the vanishing lines of all the pipes and girders, of the roll stands and raised tongs, of the work pieces on the carts and shifted weight in the movements of groups. All the vanishing lines converged in the background, at the left-hand point where, under the vertical of a supporting pillar, a gentleman was standing, in a hat and a Prince Albert, his hands on his back, facing away from the factory, his profile dreamily raised toward the ray of light that fell upon him through the steam. No one else was so illuminated and isolated, so idle and content. He stood there, inconspicuous, pausing on his round and musing, perhaps about the picturesque charms of this metal structure, perhaps about stock prices or about decorations to be awarded him by the ministers, and about the fact that everything can presumably go on unchanged. Thus Menzel had concealed his patron in the awe-inspiring picture puzzle. I told Ayschmann about how the factory conditions had been depicted by a painter named Koehler, in the United States in eighteen eighty-six. The painting was titled *The Strike*, and its reproduction, taken from an old edition of the magazine *Harper's Weekly*, had hung in our apartment in Bremen. This work, shown at the Paris World's Fair of eighteen ninety-nine, had nothing of Menzel's lush and piquant treatment of color, it was a straightforward illustration, excluding any question about technique or composition and focusing our attention solely on the content. To the left, the plant owner had stepped out of his mansion with its portico. He stood at the top of the steps, behind the ornamented cast-iron railing, elegantly dressed, in cuffs, a stand-up collar, and a top hat, pale, white-haired, and grim, raising the fingers of his right hand as if holding a cigar, but the hand was empty, this gesture expressed surprise, a powerless staving-off. Though he towered above the people in front of him, and though his attitude was still marked by the self-assurance of a class that could not imagine giving up its privileges, it was nevertheless obvious that he was confronted with a growing power that could effortlessly teach him how ephemeral he was. Protected from behind by the ashlars of his home, yet already half-abandoned by his terrified butler, he stood in pasty-faced dignity before the agitated, rallying workers, and all his courage boiled down to one thing: it was inconceivable to him that the workers could climb up to him and tear him down from his pedestal. Even as a child, I had viewed this picture countless times and discussed it with my parents, and it kept stimulating my imagination to come up with new analyses. The group of workers gathering in the empty area in front of the house seemed to contain all the possible ways in which the conflict could develop. Clenching one hand in a fist, stretching the other toward the factory, whose chimneys, unlike the industrial smokestacks on the hazy skyline, were not smoking, the spokesman faced the boss directly at the steps, while the others, waiting in various degrees of menace, observed the dispute or debated intensely among themselves. A woman was trying to calm one of the workers, whose gestures indicated that he was out of patience, that something had to happen right away, and a man in the right foreground, wearing a cap of folded paper, was bending over to pick up a stone from the dusty soil. They had come out of their brownish-black, castle-like factory, they were unarmed, they had been ground down long enough, they had angrily run down the hill to the stairway, the last members of the work force were hurrying out of the smoked-up building, even the coachman had left his team in the clayey hollow. The grab for the stone, a gesture repeated in the background, was the signal that violence was taken to be the sole possibility. The factory owner stood cold and rigid, as an individual, and the workers possessed devastating superiority. Nevertheless, the gentleman remained unapproachable. The stone would not be hurled. Whatever would result from the given situation, it halted at the threshold of the stairs. The movements of the workers standing farther off were full of indignation, resolution, near the brick mansion they yielded, became more hesitant, preferring to wait and see, yet not without courage. The house would not be stormed because the workers knew about the power that protected the arrogance of the morbid gentleman. Behind the house stood, invisible, the heavily armed national guardsmen. How often, I said to Ayschmann, as we headed back to the riverbank, walking along between the orange trees, had I tried to picture how easily the stairs could have been taken and the old man gotten rid off with one blow, but this image was defective, for we knew that this simple act had not succeeded either in America or among us. Only in Russia had they ventured to take the step up the stairs. The crowd of workers dominated the pictorial space, their power was tangible, the past and present were unbearable, things could not go on in this way, and yet they did not take the leap. Later I understood that, for all its fermenting agitation the depicted event contained only a possibility. The painter was not the victim of a utopia, he unequivocally sided with the workers, he was familiar with their working conditions, he had studied his figures just as Menzel had studied his, but, unlike the Prussian court painter, Koehler had shown the workers, in their heavy physicality, as self-assured and not spellbound by the production of wares. In the fight that had erupted, they confronted the exploiter, who, at the iron-rolling mill, was able to meditate unmolested. Their halting at the stairs was dictated by common sense. An isolated attack would have made no sense, they would have been mown down on the spot. The furious waiting, the shaken fists were harbingers of measures that had to be taken within the framework of an organization. At the mere sight of the bony, black-garbed figure at the top of the stairs, I too always felt rebellious. If we then discussed the picture, we ascertained the painter's intelligence, his understanding of history. Eighteen sixty-eight, that was the year when the mass strikes began in the United States, when workers demonstrated for the eight-hour day, and when, on the first of May, a demonstration of workers was bloodily crushed by the Chicago police. The picture painted by Koehler, born in Hamburg in eighteen fifty, died in poverty in Minneapolis in nineteen seventeen, retained its contemporary quality as undisguised testimony to the antagonism between the classes. The labor union had been founded, but its leaders had been corrupted, had been bought by the enemy, the proletariat was still faced with the urgent task of changing its situation. Slowly crossing the bridge toward the city gates with their squat fortified towers, Ayschmann once again began talking about his father. How easily everything used to come to me, he said, I never dreamed that obtaining a book could be so difficult, in our home the bookcases were filled with literature, with long rows of recorded classical and modern music, we traveled, we looked at art treasures, now we own nothing, my father used to be a wholesale dealer, and now he's a peddler, dragging his satchel of samples through London, from one textile firm to the next, and he can barely earn his livelihood. My parents live in a room in a boardinghouse, they no longer read, they no longer listen to music, they are dying. How can I help them, he asked, what should I say to them if ever I go back to them. Where did your father, your mother get their strength. My mother often succumbed to the stress of daily exertions, I said, she went to work, this morning commute was never questioned, but in the evening she could sit and sit there as if extinguished. When my father spoke encouraging words to her, tears would roll down her face. Nor did I know how my parents would cope with the threats piling up in front of them, their country could be invaded at any moment. Yet such had always been the case. What my father tried to express was that as the great events came upon us, as they attempted to crush us, leach us out, shatter us, everything my father did was rebellion against these forces inundating us, and he knew very well how tiny his possible achievements were compared with the overall proportions of the social and intellectual struggle. A procession of workers in tattered overalls came toward us on the bridge. Now, overwhelming, Munch's painting came to mind, the one titled *Workers Returning Home*. With their heavy shadows they walked at a constant beat down the long, bare road, at early sunrise or at sunset. Next to Koehler's painting this depiction of a path of life had special significance for I had always seen my father in the central figure, the hunched man with a goatee, gazing straight ahead in an almost ghostly stare. Next to the poster of the gray worker smashing through his chains, the two reproductions were the sole adornments on our kitchen walls, and while one image showed a strike, an agitation, the other spoke of steady continuation, of the resumption of work. Old men and young went to their daily grind and back, the sirens called to them and released them again, and it was they who gave the workplace its character. I told Ayschmann about this painting because it contained everything I had personally experienced, the weary morning trudge to the plant, the brain-dead return after the shift, the condition of being fettered to the work, the hatred of these fetters and of being compelled to take any job that was offered, the choked-back rage at having to work for others and the fear of losing this job. It contained the solitude that resulted from the numbling, the eternal reiteration, it contained the dejection, the feeling of unfitness, of wasted energies, of the best but fallow possibilities, but also the search for meaning and solidity, and despite the silence, despite the isolation in monotony, there was also a togetherness, a memory of the unused strength still existing in each man and making the torrent unstoppable on the road, which ran straight as an arrow between high walls. Grazed by the sleeves of blouses, catching a few shreds of words, inhaling the smoke of a cigarette, we walked through this to-and-fro, belonged to the road, which, woven together out of opposite directions, would lead us from work to work. The separation was imminent, the war was continuing, we were no longer needed here, but Spain was large, lay everywhere, Spain's cause accompanied us no matter where we went. There would have been a lot more to ask, but the convoy of trucks was already waiting on Plaza Castelar, we did not know where to address letters to one another, but since the path was the same for us both, since the same force was driving us forward, our bond would hold. I could still feel the squeeze of his hand, in the roar of started engines I could still sense, I vaguely heard, that he would now look for what he had not found in Albacete, then all I could make out was his laughter when I swung myself up on the truck, when I moved away, and he stayed behind amid the gigantic domes and towers of Valencia, his laughter in his bright face, his waving, street ravines, boulevard along the shore, exit roads, low plateau, harvesters in the rice paddies, rifles on backs, glittering sickles, narrow strips of land between sea and bay, sand whirling up, bridges over canals and sluices, pine forests, orange groves, the mouth of the Jucar, chains of hills and mountains, darkness breaking in.

Glossary

Robert Cohen

Many, if not most, of the hundreds of names—as well as events, organizations, and works of art—mentioned in *The Aesthetics of Resistance* may be unfamiliar to the reader in the United States, but they are also unfamiliar even to the best informed German reader. Weiss was keenly aware of this. He hoped that readers would follow in his footsteps and acquire knowledge about the characters and events referred to in the novel. Ten years after Weiss's death—and the publication of all three volumes of the novel—I wrote *Bio-bibliographisches Handbuch zu Peter Weiss' "Ästhetik des Widerstands,"* a handbuch that provided German readers with much of this information. The following glossary provides an English translation of a number of the entries from the handbook, as well as some additional entries. The reader needs to keep in mind, however, that while almost all of the hundreds of figures in *The Aesthetics of Resistance* are based on actual historical figures and their actions, painstakingly researched by Weiss, they are not identical with those whose names they bear. The glossary that follows may serve as a frame of reference for the figures in the text who are transformed by the literary context in which they appear. (The narrator and his parents, the only fictional characters in the novel, also retain some similarities to Weiss and his parents.)

Since the novel uses no first names (except for identification purposes), the first names of the corresponding historical figures are added in parentheses. Cross-references to another entry are indicated by an asterisk.

Ayschmann (Jacques). No independent information available. Appears as a friend of the narrator in Weiss's autobiographical novel *Leavetaking* (*Abschied von den Eltern*) as he is about to embark for Spain to join the *International Brigades.

Antonov Ovseyenko (Vladimir, 1884–1939). During the Russian Revolution of 1917, led the Red Guards that seized the Winter Palace; after the revolution, appointed commissar for military affairs in Petrograd and commissar of war; lost his military command in 1923 because of his support of Trotsky; Soviet ambassador in various countries; Soviet consul general in Barcelona during the Spanish Civil War; after his return to the Soviet Union, arrested and executed during the *Stalinist terror.

Beimler (Hans, 1895–1936). German metal worker; member of the *Spartacus League and the *Communist Party of Germany; 1932–33, member of the Bavarian State parliament; April-May 1933, subjected to torture in Dachau concentration camp, from which he escaped; at the beginning of the Spanish Civil War, helped organize the international volunteers; fell near Madrid on 1 December 1936.

Bolsheviks. From a Russian word loosely translated as "majority." During a meeting of the exiled leaders of the Russian Social Democratic Labor Party in London in 1903, a split occurred; the majority faction, led by Lenin, was henceforth referred to as Bolsheviks.

Bredel (Willi, 1901–64). Trained as a turner; later became a writer; member of the *Communist Party of Germany; 1933–34, in Fuhlsbüttel concentration camp; after his release, escaped to Czechoslovakia; 1936–39, coeditor, with Bertolt Brecht and Lion Feuchtwanger, of the literary journal *Das Wort*, published in Moscow; 1937–39, volunteer in the Spanish Civil War, serving as political commissar of "Ernst Thälmann" battalion of the *International Brigades; 1939–45, in exile in the Soviet Union; 1945, returned to Germany; 1962–64, president of the (East) German Academy of the Arts.

Brigades. See International Brigades

Bukharin (Nikolai, 1888–1938). Joined the *Bolsheviks; close collaborator of Lenin and important Marxist theoretician; 1917, elected member of the Central Committee of the Russian Communist Party; 1924, became member of the politburo; 1926, became secretary-general of the *Comintern; relieved of all his Comintern and politburo duties in 1929; 1934, reinstated in many of his party duties; in 1938, during the third of the *Moscow trials, sentenced to death and executed.

Caballero (Francisco Largo, 1869–1946). Vice president of the Socialist Party (PSOE) and of the Workers' General Union of Spain (UGT); during the Spanish Civil War, prime minister from September 1936 until May 1937.

Caudillo (El Caudillo). Spanish: "leader," "chief"; title that the Spanish dictator *Franco bestowed on himself.

Comintern. Short for Communist International (also referred to as International or the Third International). Founded in Moscow in 1919 as an international association of Communist parties from numerous countries; under Stalin deteriorated into an instrument of Soviet and Stalinist foreign policy; disbanded in 1943.

Communist International. See Comintern

Communist Party of Germany (KPD). Founded on 30 December 1918 by members of the *Spartacus League (Rosa *Luxemburg, Karl *Liebknecht, Klara *Zetkin, and others); joined the *Comintern in 1919.

Coppi (Hans, 1916–42). German worker, trained as a turner; at age 16, as a member of the Communist Youth Organization, spent a year in jail for distributing anti-Nazi leaflets; in 1941, became a radio operator for the resistance group led by Harro Schulze-Boysen, which was associated with the Red Orchestra resistance organization; arrested with other members of the group on 12 September 1942; executed in Berlin on 22 December 1942.

Dahlem (Franz, 1892–1981). In 1927, became a member of the Central Committee of the *Communist Party of Germany; 1928–33, member of the Reichstag; during the Spanish Civil War, representative of the German Communist Party and the *Comintern in the *International Brigades; after the civil war, in France; in 1941, turned over to Germany and held at Mauthausen concentration camp until the end of World War II; held high offices in the German Democratic Republic; member of the Central Committee of the Socialist Unity Party of Germany (SED).

Dimitrov (Georgi Mikhailovich, 1882–1949). Leading figure in the international Communist movement; Bulgarian printer and trade union leader; member of the Bulgarian Communist Party; in 1923, emigrated to Berlin; made the main suspect in the burning of the Reichstag building in 1933; his conduct of his own defense won him world renown and forced the Nazis to release him; secretary-general of the *Comintern in Moscow until its dissolution; 1937–45, member of the Supreme Soviet; in 1944, returned to Bulgaria; 1946–49, prime minister of Bulgaria.

Ebert (Friedrich, 1871–1925). 1912–18, member of the German Parliament; 1913, head of the *Social Democratic Party of Germany; November 1918, first Social Democrat to become president of the Weimar Republic.

Ehrenburg (Ilya, 1891–1967). Soviet writer and journalist (among his works: *The Stormy Life of Lasik Roitschwantz*, 1928; *The Fall of Paris*, 1941; *The Thaw*, 1954; *Memoirs*, 1966–67); 1936–37, correspondent for the Soviet newspaper *Izvestia* in Spain.

Falangists. Members of the Falange, a totalitarian right-wing political organization founded in the 1930s in Spain; during the Spanish Civil War, fought against the legal Republican government.

Franco (Francisco, 1892–1975). Spanish fascist general who led the assault on the Spanish Republic in 1936; dictator of Spain from 1939 until his death; assumed the title El Caudillo.

Gaudí (Antonio, 1852–1926). Catalan architect; highly innovative figure in the Spanish art nouveau movement; created many buildings in Barcelona, including the Sagrada Familia cathedral.

Generalísimo. Spanish: "commander in chief"; title awarded *Franco in 1936.

Grieg (Nordahl, 1902–43). Norwegian writer (his play *The Defeat*, 1935, inspired Bertolt Brecht's play *The Days of the Commune*, 1949); 1933–35, in Moscow; war correspondent in Spain during the civil war; during World War II, served in Norway's government-in-exile; did not return from an Allied bombing mission over Berlin in which he participated as an observer.

Heartfield (John, born Hellmuth Herzfeld, 1891–1968). Central figure in the German and international avant-garde movements of the 1920s and 1930s; during World War I, involved in both the Dada movement and the *Spartacus League; member of the *Communist Party of Germany from the time of its founding; pioneered photomontage; famous for montages that caricatured Nazism and its leaders.

Heilmann (Horst, 1923–42). In 1940, while studying political science in Berlin, met Harro Schulze-Boysen, leading member of the German section of the resistance group Red Orchestra; in August 1941, became a volunteer in the German army, deciphering allied documents and secretly passing them on to Schulze-Boysen; arrested with other members of the group on 9 September 1942; executed in Berlin on 22 December 1942.

Hodann (Max, 1894–1946). Physician, psychiatrist, leading sex reformer of the Weimar Republic, author of sex education books for the working class; member of the board of directors of the Union of Socialist Doctors; incarcerated by the Nazis after the burning of the Reichstag in Berlin in 1933; after his release, in exile in Norway; in 1937–38, during the Spanish Civil War, served as a physician in the *International Brigades; in 1940, in exile in Sweden, where he became a friend and mentor for the struggling young refugee painter and writer Peter Weiss; committed suicide.

Independent Social Democrats (Independent Social Democratic Party of Germany,

USPD). Founded in 1917 by left-wing members of the *Social Democratic Party of Germany; dissolved in 1920, when many of its members joined the *Communist Party of Germany.

International. See Comintern

International Brigades. Formed in the fall of 1936, during the first months of the Spanish Civil War, with volunteers from numerous countries who had come to Spain to defend the legal Republican government against a fascist putsch led by *Franco; officially dissolved in the fall of 1938, when the defeat of the Republic became apparent.

Katz (Otto, a.k.a. André Simone, 1893–1952). Czech journalist and collaborator of *Münzenberg; exiled in Paris, where he continued to work as an editor for Münzenberg's publishing houses; during the Spanish Civil War, worked for the press office of the Republican government; returned to Czechoslovakia after World War II; indicted in the Slansky trials in 1952 and executed.

Krestinsky (Nicolai, 1883–1938). Joined the *Bolsheviks; close collaborator of Lenin; studied law in St. Petersburg; in 1917, member of the Central Committee of the Russian Communist Party; in the 1920s, Soviet ambassador to Weimar Germany, where he befriended *Münzenberg; in 1930, became deputy foreign minister of the Soviet Union; in 1938, during the third of the *Moscow trials, sentenced to death and executed.

Kronstadt (Kronstadt revolt). In February 1921, sailors at the Kronstadt naval base near Leningrad who had originally supported Lenin's *Bolsheviks rebelled against the repressive measures taken by the Soviet government; the rebellion was ruthlessly suppressed on the orders of Red Army chief Trotsky.

Liebknecht (Karl, 1871–1919). Son of Wilhelm Liebknecht (cofounder of the *Social Democratic Party of Germany); studied law; 1912–17, member of the Reichstag; cofounder, with Rosa *Luxemburg and others, of the *Spartacus League and the *Communist Party of Germany; murdered after World War I, together with Rosa Luxemburg, by right-wing military officers.

Luxemburg (Rosa, 1871–1919). Born in Poland; 1898, doctorate in political economics in Zurich; moved to Germany and joined the *Social Democratic Party; during World War I, jailed for opposing the war; a founding member of the *Spartacus League and the *Communist Party of Germany; murdered after World War I, together with Karl *Liebknecht, by right-wing military officers.

Manifesto. Refers to the *Communist Manifesto* by Karl Marx and Friedrich Engels, published in 1848.

Marcauer. No independently verifiable information available.

Marty (André, 1886–1956). French naval engineer; member of the Central Committee of the Communist Party of France; during the Spanish Civil War, commander in chief of the *International Brigades, known for his ruthlessness.

Mewis (Karl, a.k.a. K. Arndt, 1907–87). Trained as a locksmith; in 1924, joined the *Communist Party of Germany; after 1933, leading figure in the Party in exile; during the civil war, represented the German Communist Party in Spain; later exiled in Sweden; after World War II, held high offices in the German Democratic Republic.

Moscow trials. Public trials held in Moscow in the 1930s, at the height of the *Stalinist terror, with extended international press coverage; specifically refers to three trials of the old *Bolsheviks held in August 1936 (among the accused: Zinoviev and

Kamenew), January 1937 (*Piatakov, *Radek, and others), and March 1938 (*Bukharin, Rykov, and others); most defendants sentenced to death and executed.

Münzenberg (Willi, 1889–1940). Proletarian youth; befriended Lenin in 1916; member of the *Spartacus League and the *Communist Party of Germany; directed a Communist publishing empire in Weimar Germany (newspapers, journals, books, films); after 1933, continued his publishing activities in exile in Paris; during the *Stalinist terror of the late 1930s distanced himself from the Soviet Union; expelled from the party; found dead in eastern France under unexplained circumstances.

Münzer. No independently verifiable information available.

Nin (Andrés, 1892–c. 1937). In 1935, founded the Spanish Workers Party of Marxist Unification (POUM), an anti-Stalinist Communist party influenced by Trotsky; under pressure from the Soviet Union and with the help of Soviet agents, Nin and his followers were persecuted during the Spanish Civil War; though his exact fate is not known, was most likely executed.

Noske (Gustav, 1868–1946). Member of the *Social Democratic Party of Germany; in charge of the armed forces after the end of World War I in November 1918; 1919–20, minister of defense; ruthlessly suppressed worker uprisings throughout Germany, notably the insurrection of the *Spartacus League.

October. Refers to the Russian Revolution of October 1917, which brought the *Bolsheviks under Lenin's leadership to power.

Pergamum. Ancient city located 16 miles from the Aegean Sea, 40 miles northeast of Izmir (ancient Smyrna) in northeastern Turkey; in the second and first centuries B.C. under the Attalids, Pergamum became a major power and a principal center of Hellenistic civilization; the Pergamum frieze was constructed under Eumenes II (197–159 B.C.); rediscovered in 1871 by German engineer Carl Humann and shipped to Berlin, where it is still on exhibit at the Museumsinsel (Museum Island).

Piatakov (Georgi, 1890–1937). Member of the *Bolsheviks and close collaborator of Lenin; 1930, member of the Central Committee of the Russian Communist Party; expelled from the party in 1936; sentenced to death during the second of the *Moscow trials and executed.

Piscator (Erwin, 1893–1966). Leftist avant-gardist German theater director close to Bertolt Brecht during the Weimar years; in exile in New York; after World War II, returned to Germany.

Popular Front. Communist-supported mass movements of the Left in France, Spain, and elsewhere during the mid-1930s aimed at resisting fascism; included a wide spectrum of parties, from Communists to antifascist liberals. *See also* United Front.

Prieto (Indalecio, 1883–1962). Spanish politician; during the Spanish Civil War, served as minister of the navy and the air force (September 1936–May 1937) in the government of *Caballero; also served as minister of national defense (May 1937–March 1938) in the government of Juan Negrin.

Radek (Karl, 1885–1939). Polish revolutionary and intellectual; member of the *Bolsheviks and collaborator of Lenin; after World War I, a founding member of the *Communist Party of Germany; after 1921, in the Soviet Union, held high positions in the *Comintern; at times took Trotskyite, anti-Stalinist positions; in 1936, defended the *Moscow trials; sentenced to ten years in prison during the second trial; died in prison.

Renn (Ludwig, born Arnold Friedrich Vieth von Golssenau, 1889–1979). A writer who served as an officer in World War I; joined the *Communist Party of Germany in 1928; in 1933, arrested by the Nazis; after his release in 1935, went into exile; participated in the Spanish Civil War as battalion commander and chief of staff of the eleventh brigade of the *International Brigades; in exile in Mexico; after 1947, returned to (East) Germany.

Social Democratic Party of Germany (SPD). Founded in May 1863 by Ferdinand Lassalle; in 1869, merged with an association led by August Bebel and Wilhelm Liebknecht; generally adhered to the theories of Marx and Engels, who repeatedly intervened in the party's development; toward the end of the nineteenth century, shifted from a revolutionary to an evolutionary position; supported German participation in World War I, which led to a fracturing of the party and the founding of the *Spartacus League and the *Communist Party of Germany.

Spartacist. Member of the *Spartacus League.

Spartacus League. Revolutionary left-wing group that split off from the *Social Democratic Party of Germany over the Social Democrats' support for World War I; founded by Karl *Liebknecht, Rosa *Luxemburg, Klara *Zetkin, and others; on 1 January 1919, transformed itself into the *Communist Party of Germany.

Stalinist terror. Refers to events in the Soviet Union during the second half of the 1930s and especially the years 1936–38, when, on the orders of Stalin, the execution of countless kulaks (land-owning farmers), numerous members of the Communist Party, and others accused of anti-Soviet activity reached its height. *See also* Moscow trials.

Third International. *See* Comintern

Tretyakov (Sergei, 1892–1939). Avant-gardist Soviet writer and journalist (novel: *A Chinese Testament: The Autobiography of Tan Shih-hua*, 1930); befriended Bertolt Brecht and Walter Benjamin; translated several Brecht plays; arrested in Moscow in 1937 during the *Stalinist terror and executed.

United Front. Generally refers to attempts in the 1930s at united action by the left, especially by Communist and Social Democratic parties (during the early as well as the final years of the Weimar Republic, the two German parties had fought each other as much as they had fought the Nazis). *See also* Popular Front.

Ulbricht (Walter, 1893–1973). Trained as a carpenter; joined the *Spartacus League; a founding member of the *Communist Party of Germany, became in 1927 a permanent member of the Central Committee; in 1928, a member of the Reichstag; after 1933, a leading member of the party in exile in France; in Spain during the civil war; after 1938, in exile in Moscow; returned to Germany after World War II; a founding member of the East German Communist Party (SED); 1960–73, president of the German Democratic Republic.

Vyshinsky (Andrey Yanuaryevich, 1883–1953). 1935–39, prosecutor general of the *Moscow trials; 1949–53, Soviet foreign minister; in 1953, became permanent Soviet delegate to the United Nations; died in New York City.

Warnsdorf. Today Varnsdorf, city in northern Bohemia (Czech Republic), where Peter Weiss lived in 1937.

Wehner (Herbert, a.k.a. Kurt Funk, Svensson, 1906–90). Son of a shoemaker; joined the *Communist Party of Germany in 1927; after 1933, engaged in antifascist activities in Germany; after 1935, in exile in the Soviet Union; member of the Central Committee of the exiled party; after 1940, in exile in Sweden; expelled from the party as a "traitor"; after the war, joined the *Social Democratic Party of Germany; in 1949, became a member of the Bundestag (West German parliament); 1966–69, cabinet minister.

Zetkin (Clara, born Clara Eissner, 1857–1933). Prominent in the international workers' movement, notably in the women workers' movement; from 1895 onward, executive member of the *Social Democratic Party of Germany; a founding member of the *Communist Party of Germany; in 1920, became a member of the Reichstag; in 1921, became secretary of the International Women's Secretariat and member of the Executive Committee of the *Comintern; lived in the Soviet Union from 1924 until her death.

Zimmerwald. Small central Swiss town that was the site of a conference held by Lenin and his fellow *Bolsheviks, as well as other left-wing revolutionaries, in September 1915.

Born near Berlin in 1916, Peter Weiss was a dramatist, novelist, and artist who lived from 1939 onward in Sweden; he died in Stockholm in 1982. Although he initially published some of his writings in Swedish, the major body of his literary work is in German. He gained international renown for his play *The Persecution and Assassination of Jean-Paul Marat as Performed by the Inmates of the Asylum of Charenton under the Direction of the Marquis de Sade*, which is commonly referred to as *Marat/Sade* (1964; trans., 1966). Among his other major works are the plays *The Investigation* (1965; trans., 1966), *Song of the Lusitanian Bogey* (1967; trans., 1970), *Discourse on the Progress of the Prolonged War of Liberation in Viet Nam* (1968; trans., 1970), *Trotsky in Exile* (1970; trans., 1971), and *The New Trial* (1982; trans., 2001). His novels include *The Shadow of the Coachman's Body* (1960; trans., 1970), *Leavetaking* (1961; trans., 1966), and *Vanishing Point* (1962; trans., 1966). The trilogy *Die Ästhetik des Widerstands* was published in individual volumes in 1975, 1978, and 1981; the present translation is the first English-language edition of volume 1.

Library of Congress Cataloging-in-Publication Data

Weiss, Peter, 1916–1982
[Aesthetik des Widerstands. Volume 1. English]
The aesthetics of resistance : volume 1 / Peter Weiss ; translated by Joachim Neugroschel ; with a foreword by Fredric Jameson and a glossary by Robert Cohen.
p. cm.
ISBN 0-8223-3534-4 (cloth : alk. paper) —
ISBN 0-8223-3546-8 (pbk. : alk. paper)
I. Neugroschel, Joachim. II. Title.
PT2685.E5A6513 2005
833'.914—dc22 2004028462